HERE
WE
COME

by

Chautona Havig

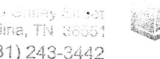

First Edition

ISBN-13: 978-1470019945
ISBN-10: 1470019949

Edited by Barbara Coyle Editing

Many thanks also to Christy for her hours of brainstorming and painful proofreading. She kept me from naming this some pretty stupid stuff.

The brushes used to create the chapter and chapter break images are compliments of ObsidianDawn.com. I thank them for their generosity in sharing with the world.

The events and people in this book are fictional, and any resemblance to actual people is purely coincidental and I'd love to meet them!

Visit me at **http://chautona.com** and **http://fairburytales.com** to meet more of my "imaginary friends," or follow me on Twitter @chautona

All Scripture references are from the NASB. NASB passages are taken from the NEW AMERICAN STANDARD BIBLE (registered), Copyright 1960, 1962, 1963, 1968, 1971, 1972, 1973, 1975, 1977, 1995 by The Lockman Foundation.

~*For Kaylene*~

Maybe now that all of the books are finished, you'll actually read the series. I hope that the end is sufficiently sappy for you. You are a delight as a daughter, and I am so happy that you are not only real in our lives now but also in the eyes of the law. May God's grace continue to shine on you and guide you.

~*For Pat*~

I don't think I've seen you once since *For Keeps* was released that you didn't ask how this one is coming. Hope it was worth the wait. Thanks for being such an encouragement—and not just because you sell my books in your store.

Books by Chautona Havig

The Rockland Chronicles

Noble Pursuits
Argosy Junction
Thirty Days Hath…

The Aggie Series

Ready or Not
For Keeps
Here We Come

The Annals of Wynnewood

Shadows and Secrets
Cloaked in Secrets
Beneath the Cloak

The Not-So-Fairy Tales

Princess Paisley
Everard (Coming 2012)

Chapter 1

A FoUNTAIN NoT FREE...

Monday, November 17th

In Aggie's mind, it was their first true argument. She was furious, and the fact that she couldn't remember what prompted her anger made it even worse. Luke's pain-filled eyes would normally have sparked her compassion, but an uncharacteristic stubbornness had seized her and held her in its grip.

"Mibs..."

"Just go home, Luke. We're obviously not going to agree on this one. I don't want to argue anymore."

"We can't just ignore—"

"We can postpone the inevitable until I'm ready to handle it," she snapped. "I'm tired, I've had a very hard day with five students who did not do well in their studies and three little ones who took advantage of that. The last thing I need is for you to show up and scold me for something that isn't even any of your business. Just go home."

The moment the words were out of her mouth, Aggie regretted them. Before she could try to take them back and apologize, a spider crawled lethargically over her toe, making her jump. Luke's foot came down on the critter before she had a chance to wonder how it had survived so long in the cold.

Aggie glanced up, expecting to meet his eyes but found them downcast. "You know, you're a handy guy to have around."

"I'd be happy to stomp spiders for you for the rest of your life," he whispered before turning to leave.

She would have thought he was joking, but the catch in his voice confused her. "I'd like that."

At the bottom of the step, he glanced back up at her. Seconds, oh how they seemed like hours, passed before he finally spoke. "Would you, Mibs? I thought maybe, but I can't help but wonder…"

He was in his truck and down the driveway before the full import of his words registered in her mind. Aggie hurried down the steps, but Luke was gone. Her hand dug into her skirt pocket for her cell phone, but she hesitated. Messenger.

She hurried inside, flipped open her laptop, and waited for it to boot. Her mind spent the next minute reminding herself that he couldn't possibly get home before she got connected.

A minute later, her cursor hovered over the instant message icon. She dragged it to the left and clicked her email instead.

To: luke.sullivan@letterbox.com
From: aggie.mommie@letterbox.com
Subject: Forgive me?

Luke,
I was wrong. This apology shouldn't surprise you. It seems like I'm always apologizing to someone for something. I want to promise it won't happen again, but I can't. We both know it will. I can promise that I'll be just as disgusted with myself next time as I am this time, and I'll be begging the Lord to be merciful to me—again.
I want to own what I did wrong—be specific. You know? I mean, that's what I was taught to do. The problem is that all I know is that I was rude and hateful to you because I was embarrassed. I just don't know why. I can't even remember why we argued. I think you corrected me as a sister in Christ. I think. Maybe not. Maybe you just should have. My mind is so muddled—probably because I'm writing instead of praying and allowing God to bring my sin to mind, but I wanted this note to be there for you when you got home.
I am so sorry,
Aggie (a.k.a. Mibs)

Not two minutes later, the following email whizzed its way over the information highway and into Luke's email box.

To: luke.sullivan@letterbox.com
From: aggie.mommie@letterbox.com
Subject: Seriously?

Ugh. I just remembered what I got so upset about. Did I really blow up over that? Thank you for not backing down and letting me get away with it. What a terrible example to the kids.
It's kind of cliché too. Really? Spilled milk? Oy, as Laird would say. What is with him and his pet words that change every other day. He never did that before!
Anyway, now that I remember what I was so upset over (and I confess I am now giggling that I was so silly), please forgive me for getting upset about you correcting me for getting upset over spilled milk. Particularly the minuscule amount that dribbles from a toddler's sippy cup. I am mortified.
Prostrate and laughing too hard to be believable when I say I am truly sorry,
Mibs (a.k.a Aggie)

She waited, her eyes rarely leaving the clock at the bottom right of her screen for longer than a few seconds. Mentally, she calculated the distance and time to his duplex, praying he wouldn't go see Libby first. It would be a natural thing to do. The last thing she wanted was to wait any longer than necessary for him to see it.

The phone felt as if it was burning a hole in her pocket. She hesitated and then whipped it out. Her fingers hovered over the letter keys and then she found the right words to send. The wait continued.

One scrubbed stove, two wastepaper baskets emptied, three shoes returned to their proper cubbies, and four thousand glances at her inbox later, a message appeared. With trepidation, she opened it.

To: aggie.mommy@letterbox.com

From: luke.sullivan@letterbox.com
Subject: You're still doing it

Mibs,
You're still crying over spilled milk, only now
you're crying over having cried over spilled milk.
Stop it. ;)
I am just thankful for that spider.
I love you,
Luke (a.k.a. Lucas)

Her brow wrinkled, trying to remember what the spider had to do with anything? Why would he be thankful for—she gave up and opened a new email. She'd intended to go crawl into bed and sort out her spirit with the Lord, but it was impossible to let that one go.

To: luke.sullivan@letterbox.com
From: aggie.mommy@letterbox.com
Subject: Thankful for pests?

And I don't mean me… just why would you be thankful
for a spider?

Glad you still love me,
Migsie (For the record, combining Aggie and Mibs
doesn't work)

Her fingers nearly twitched as she waited for his reply. Apparently, his careful attention to wording was not limited to conversations in person or on messenger. Even letters took him some time to compose. Did he start his occasional notes to her half a dozen times before he got the words just right? She suspected that he did.

To: aggie.mommy@letterbox.com
From: luke.sullivan@letterbox.com
Subject: Aggibs
You're right. It doesn't. Yours is better. I'll

reserve that for when you need to be put in your
place (you know, anytime you dare disagree with my
superior wisdom).
I am grateful to the spider because he inspired my
feeble attempt at gallantry. That attempt was
rewarded with your assurance that you'd like me to
be around to stomp your spiders for the rest of
your life. You see, my gratitude is self-centered
and greedy. I make no apologies for it. I'm afraid
I am not sorry and cannot lie and pretend I intend
to mend my ways.
Now go to sleep. Let's just sort of pretend this
didn't happen. Remember the spider and your words
about him and his kind and forget the milk.
Besides, it'll happen again. That's one thing I
know I can promise.
I love you (tired of hearing that yet?)
Luke the Lucky (It works better with Leif)

Aggie couldn't resist one last quick note back. Although she
preferred the swiftness of the messenger, these emails would
definitely go in the scrapbook of their conversations and his notes.
Already it was very precious to her.

To: luke.sullivan@letterbox.com
From: aggie.mommy@letterbox.com
Subject: No.
I am not(tired of hearing it, that is). Thought you
ought to know.
Aggie de la Mibs

Tuesday, November 18th

Aggie's cell phone blasted Beethoven's fifth symphony, the
latest in a series of ringtones that Laird found hilarious. His changing
them approximately once every other day would drive her to the nut
house or keep her from needing it—she wasn't sure which.

"Aunt Aggie?" Ellie's voice broke through her concentration on

11

Luke's latest text message.

"Hmm?"

"Is it t-o the store or t-o-o the store? I can never remember."

"T-o."

The girl's forehead furrowed as she wrote. "How are you supposed to know which one to use?"

"Well," Aggie's brain raced through her grammar lessons for the clearest explanation. "Ok, t-o-o has an extra o, right? Well, you use t-o-o to mean too much or excessive. You also use it for also. So, too meaning too much or 'in addition' get *more* o's. Does that make sense?"

"Too gets more o's..." her mind seemed to mull it while she scribbled. "So too much, too many, too long all have two o's, but to go, to stay, to eat, don't?"

"Exactly. T-w-o has the w. It's the odd ball. And, since two is also a number, it's also an odd ball—so to speak." She frowned. "Except that it's an even number. I guess that doesn't work well."

"Ok," Ellie said excitedly. "So, t-w-o two girls want to t-o to go t-o to the store t-o-o too."

"Excellent." Her phone played its ominous tones again.

"Aunt Aggie, go talk to Luke. I'll keep the kids going. I am just editing my paper anyway. So far I've found too many sentence fragments to turn it in."

Aggie glanced at the clock. Nine-thirty. They'd hardly been in the classroom for half an hour. Then again, Luke tried not to call during school times...

"Ok, be right back."

Icicles hung from the porch roof, looking beautiful but dangerous. She grabbed Tavish's baseball bat from the empty pot where it rested for these occasions, and swung it while the phone dialed Luke. His "Hello," was drowned out by the crack of the bat against ice.

"Icicles again?"

"Yeah." She whacked another one. There was something very satisfying about beating up ice. The puppies out back howled with each crack. "The pups don't like me to break them off. I think it hurts their ears."

"I bought the cable for the gutters, but I don't think I'll make it today. If we didn't have these unexpected cold fronts followed by warmer days, it wouldn't happen."

Something he said felt "off," but she wasn't sure what. "I don't get weather, ice, and stuff. Never have, don't want to. I can apply to you for your superior wisdom and save myself a lot of headaches." She frowned. "Wait, did you say you *weren't* coming today?"

The line seemed dead for a very long half minute before he grunted, "Sorry, what? I found another puddle."

"Puddle? What are you doing?"

"House on Cygnet. The pipes froze and burst. I missed a whole wall of insulation when I foamed the laundry room. Outside wall of course—the one with the pipes."

"Oh, no!" Her heart sank for him. "How bad is it?" Her teeth tried to chatter, but Aggie rubbed her hands together and set her jaw, listening.

"I'll have to gut the laundry room, replace two walls of the kitchen, and do some repairs on the powder room. The living room has some damage, but nothing too bad. I'm not sure about the kitchen floor though."

"Can I do something?"

"Right now, no. I'm still assessing damage and waiting for the insurance adjuster. I am glad I insured the house *before* I insulated or this wouldn't be covered." His voice sounded strained and weary. "I just wanted you to know I wouldn't make it for lunch. I'm really sorry, Mibs."

"Stop by on your way home if you like." She sounded too eager and she knew it. The last thing he needed was to feel obligated to do anything. "And let me know if I can do something—even if it's just running errands so you don't have to leave. The kids would love to get out of the house."

"I'll call. Got to go."

She stared at the dead phone. "Bye."

As she opened the door to the house, something Luke said clicked. "Lunch. I didn't cut the veggies for lunch." She peeked her head in the library and asked if anyone needed help. Several heads shook, but Aggie saw Cari, Lorna, and Ian getting restless. "You three come with me," she said, scooping up Ian. "I've got to go work on lunch."

"Is Luke coming?" Laird didn't even raise his head from his math book.

13

"He can't. Pipes burst over on Cygnet, and I guess there's a lot of damage."

Laird frowned. "It wasn't my fault, was it? I didn't work on pipes."

"No, he forgot to insulate a wall in the kitchen or something."

"Can I go help?"

Aggie shook her head. "Let's wait until tomorrow to ask. He has a lot to do and take in. The damage sounds extensive."

She shooed the little ones into the kitchen and gave the girls plastic knives and bananas to slice for the Jell-O. Ian enjoyed a snack of banana in the high chair while she chopped vegetables. Into a large bowl went chopped potatoes, carrots, celery, and a couple of cans of stewed diced tomatoes. She covered them with water, put a plate over the bowl, set the timer for an hour, and set it aside. She added the rest of the previous night's chopped chuck steak, garlic powder, and chopped onion into her heavy Dutch oven. The clock was against her.

"All done, Aunt Aggie!" The bananas were definitely sliced in thicknesses ranging from a penny to a thumb.

"Done, Gaggie!" Ian threw his hands into the air, touchdown style, and clapped at the empty tray.

"Good job, guys! Ok, why don't you two go into the bathroom and wash your hands. I'm going to count to one hundred. See if you can get them all clean and be back by a hundred. One, two, three…"

After washing Ian's hands, she sat him on the floor while she browned the meat, covered it with beef broth, and left it to simmer. In another pot, she measured water for Jell-O and put it on the stove to boil. The girls returned on eighty-nine with reasonably clean hands. "Ok, bring me the hand towel now."

The girls exchanged confused glances, but raced back to the bathroom to retrieve it. Aggie arranged the bananas in thirteen by nine pans and tried not to watch for the pot to boil. The towel was damp but clean. "Good job! You got all the banana off with water instead of the towel."

"You said to wash them," Lorna reminded her.

"That I did. You can put that back now." Just as Aggie tried to measure the cold water to add to the Jell-O, she sprayed herself with the faucet. "Ugh!"

"Is that what the water looks like in Luke's house?" Lorna's voice was awestruck.

"Wuke doesn't have fountains in his house!"

"Well, this morning he had fountains of water, that's for sure. It probably looked a lot like that too."

"We should bake him cookies," Lorna suggested. "He likes our cookies."

"Yeah. Wuke wikes cookies."

So much for Cari's improvement with her L's, Aggie thought to herself. *I can't handle that today. Maybe tomorrow.* Even as she thought it, Aggie realized it was the wrong thing even to think. Anything that implied weakness on her part was an open invitation to mischief for Cari.

"Can we play outside?"

There was an L. Relief was a wonderful thing. Aggie didn't need to add speech therapy to her daily list of things to do. The girls stared at her waiting for an answer. "Let's see if anyone is ready for a break."

Thankfully, Laird and Tavish seemed to be ready for a break, as was Kenzie. Vannie didn't want to stop until her paper was finished, and Ellie was now struggling over then and than. She bundled up Ian in warmer clothes, remembering how cold it had been during her brief conversation with Luke, and helped the twins to zip up their coats. "Your coat is too small, Cari. We need new ones."

"It's ok. It covers my bell-bows."

Rolling her eyes at the mental picture of "bell-bows," Aggie shut the door behind them, shivered, and went to clean up her mess in the kitchen, hoping the water was finally boiling. She grew so engrossed in stirring the Jell-O, pouring it into the pans, and scrubbing the cutting board, she didn't even notice the song she sang.

"I am so telling Luke that I caught you singing *There Is a Fountain Free*[1] after hearing about his pipes. You're busted!" Vannie laughed at what Aggie knew must be a comical expression on her face.

"Kind of like his pipes, eh?"

Thursday, November 20th

15

Laird burst through the door at eight-thirty, calling her name. "Luke's outside. He can't stop, but he thought you might—"

She dodged the coffee table, rounded the couch, and stuffed her feet into the mud boots on the porch. It took three steps to realize they were Vannie's and her heel hadn't made it to the sole. Aggie ignored the awkward lumbering movements the boots created and hurried to Luke's truck. She opened the passenger door and crawled in the cab. "Can you circle the drive two or three times while you give me an update?"

She must have said just the right words, because the tension filled expression on his face softened a little. "I like hearing and seeing you happy to see me, Mibs."

"I've been worried all day. Is the damage better than you thought?"

"Worse," he admitted. "But according to Laird, who got it from Vannie, you were blissfully unconcerned about my mess as you hummed about free fountains."

"Oh, I'm so gonna get them! I made Vannie promise not to tell you."

Luke grinned, turning back into her driveway. "That's what Laird said. Actually, I think he said, 'I don't know if Aunt Aggie will ever figure out that she can't leave things open ended. We're too good for that.'"

"What!"

"Yep. I didn't bother to remind him that I've got my resume in for the job of husband slash father, and he is giving away all their secrets to the 'enemy.'"

Short drives in Luke's truck had an advantage over leisurely chats in her living room—he couldn't see her blush. "How long will it take to repair the damage? Do you have to take it off the market?"

"Yes. I called Amber so she could cancel her showings. I won't get it back on the market before the New Year now. Things don't dry in winter like they do in warmer months." He sighed. "They'll deliver a rolling dumpster tomorrow."

"I'm giving the kids Wednesday off next week. You can take Laird that day."

He didn't answer at first, but then Luke nodded. "I think I can have things to where he could be a big help by then. I was hoping to have him on Saturday if you can spare him. That'll give me Monday and Tuesday to fix the pipes."

"Can I help?" She sighed. "I guess not. I'd have to bring the kids. That's not much help."

Luke's hand reached for hers and squeezed before he returned it to the steering wheel. "I'll see about Mom coming to stay for an afternoon the day I have to go shopping. If I have to redo that wall with the backsplash, and I think I do, you might as well come help me pick out the right tile."

The words "might as well" rankled. "I don't want to push myself on you, Luke. I just wanted to help."

"What?"

He slowed, driving past the porch, and Aggie opened the door. "I should go in."

"Wait, Mibs. You're angry."

Aggie pulled the door shut once more. "I—I guess I am. I would have said hurt, but they're the same thing sometimes, aren't they?"

"Why? What—"

Her hand remained on the door handle, and she couldn't bring herself to look at him. "I don't want to be a nuisance, Luke."

"Who said anything about a nuisance?" He braked, throwing the truck in gear much more recklessly than his usual careful treatment of his "tools."

"'Might as well come...' I don't want to be a 'might as well.'"

Though she'd expected a protest, it didn't come. In fact, there was no response at all. He didn't brake; he didn't sigh; he didn't even glance her way, much less speak. Instead, he kept circling the drive, unaware of the confusion he left in Aggie's heart. Just as she was ready to demand that he stop the truck and let her out, realization dawned. He was thinking.

"Mibs—"

A giggle escaped before she could prevent it. "Sorry."

"What—I don't get it."

"I just realized why you were so quiet and right when I realized that, you spoke."

As if unsure what to say, he shook his head. "I just wanted to say I'm sorry." He braked, his truck bed half in the road. Hanging his hands over the steering wheel, he laid his head on them and looked at her. "I didn't mean to make it sound like that. I was thinking more that it wasn't your kitchen and you wouldn't get to enjoy it, but you

17

might as well have fun with it anyway."

Luke yawned. Ready to send him on his way, Aggie pointed to the house. "Let me out and go home. If you can't sleep, ding me. I'll be up for a while yet."

"Can't. No internet at the house."

"On Cygnet? You're sleeping there?"

He pulled up by her front door and put the truck in park. "Yeah. I can work as late or as early as I want. I can also make sure no more pipes burst. I'm going to test all the outside walls for insulation again—make sure I didn't miss any others."

Aggie's heart sank. She'd miss their Internet chat. "Well, come over for breakfast if you like…"

"Can't. I've got food there to eat while I work. I've got to get this done swiftly. Every day lost is money lost. There's a house in Fairbury that I want, but until this sells…"

The temptation to offer him the money was overwhelming. She had it. He'd get it back for her. Soon enough, it would probably be his money too. Her conscience pricked her. It wasn't "her" money; it belonged to the children. She had no business loaning out their money to anyone for any reason. Then again, isn't that what investments were? She had investments—lots of them.

"Luke?"

"No, Aggie. I cannot tell you how much it means that you'd offer, but no."

She blushed. "I hate how people can read me like that. I wish my face was totally deadpan."

"It isn't your face this time, Mibs. It's you. I know you, and I also know just how much of a struggle it was to offer. It means a lot to me, but I can't do it—"

"If things were different…"

His chuckle warmed her heart and sent her stomach flopping in that delightfully peculiar way that was becoming quite predictable. "Even if we were married and I had every penny of yours at my disposal, I wouldn't do it. I have the money in my personal account for a down payment, but I don't mix personal and business accounts. I just don't." He leaned closer, winked and added, "But I do like that your mind went there. I like it a lot."

Aggie struggled to open her heart—share what she'd wanted to say for weeks, but a lump rose in her throat, choking off any hope of coherent speech. Instead, she gave what she hoped was an encouraging smile and stepped from the truck. Just as she started to close the door, she heard him murmur, "I love you, Mibs."

"I love—" she began, but his truck was already pulling away from the house. She pushed it all the way shut before he drove off with it open. "You too."

Quietly, she let herself back into the house and kicked off Vannie's too-small boots by the door. Dishes rattled in the kitchen, telling her that Laird was still awake and hungry. "Need help?"

Startled, Laird dropped his plate into the sink. "Oy! You scared me!"

"Sorry. There's some carrot cake left—not enough for everyone tomorrow."

"Thanks. Do we have any soup left? I'm freezing."

"Doesn't Luke have heat over there?"

"Yeah," Laird explained, "it's just that once you get wet, it's so cold that you never get dry and then you're cold all the time."

"Why don't you go up and take a hot shower and get into warm clothes? I'll fix you some food."

"Thanks, Aunt Aggie." His feet pounded up five stairs before she heard him turn and come back down again. "Hey, Aunt Aggie?"

"Yes?"

"Do we have any space heaters? Luke could use one to help dry stuff out where he's working."

Aggie dumped the soup into the pan and turned to Laird, broth dripping from the edge of the now empty container. "He doesn't have the furnace going?"

"He does, but it's too expensive to heat that big house just for working in one room, so he has it turned down low."

"I'll get him a heater. I can't believe he doesn't have one."

"He does, but they're at some house in Marshfield he was working on and he doesn't have time to go get them."

As she listened to Laird return upstairs and then to the water coming on in the bathroom, Aggie's mind whirled. She wiped up the soup from the floor, pausing to marvel that she thought to do that now when she'd never considered such a thing at the house in Rockland, and then stirred the soup. Cake went onto a plate and half a sandwich did too. She poured milk into a glass and placed it all on the island.

19

When Laird entered the kitchen, she smiled at how boyish he looked when just minutes before he'd seemed old for his age. Aggie grabbed her cell phone and her keys. "I'm going to go grab a couple of heaters from the basement and drive them over. I've got my phone. Eat and go to bed. If you need anything, call me."

He waited until she reached the door before Laird called to her again. "Aunt Aggie?"

"Yes?" It took deliberate self-control not to sound exasperated.

"I have all my work done for this week except for the rewrite of my book report. Can I do that Sunday afternoon; that way I can help him tomorrow too?"

Her natural inclination was to say no, but Aggie remembered Luke's argument that the kind of things he did in his "free time" were educational too. "Ok, this time, but if it isn't on my desk and perfect Monday morning, I won't agree to it again."

"Thanks!"

Melting snow and two heavy space heaters made walking to Luke's house impossible. Every time she ran an errand in the big fifteen passenger van, it felt like overkill, but two cars for one driver seemed even worse. She saw the lights on in the living room and dining room, but there was no sign of Luke when she pulled into the driveway.

At the door, she pounded. Her fists ached as she used them and her toes to try to summon Luke. Cold and ready to give up, she tried the door and found it unlocked. Once the door was open, she knew why he hadn't heard her. The Old Rugged Cross blared from a CD player in the kitchen. The singer was the deepest bass she'd ever heard and then followed by a tenor singing, "I will cling to the old rugged cross…"

"Luke?"

Aggie stood in the kitchen doorway, a space heater in each hand. "I heard that you needed a little heat in here."

Luke swallowed hard. He set down his drill and moved to take them from her. "Not anymore."

Aggie says: Libby? Are you still awake?

Libby says: Sorry, are you still here? I was talking with Luke.

Aggie says: He seemed pretty discouraged tonight.

Libby says: He is. You made his evening bringing by the heaters.

Aggie says: I didn't know what to do—if it was the right thing...

Aggie says: Laird said he needed some but that his were in Marshfield or something. I don't know why he just didn't go to the hardware store here and get one.

Libby says: He is on auto-pilot right now. He'll be kicking himself later.

Aggie says: That makes sense.

Libby says: Aggie, are you ok?

Aggie says: Yeah.

Aggie says: I guess.

Libby says: You don't seem yourself.

Aggie says: I tried to tell Luke...

Libby says: Wrong timing?

Aggie says: Not really—I mean, yes but no, you know?

Libby says: Um, not really. Care to elaborate?

Aggie says: Well, it wasn't anything earth shattering. I didn't have a big speech or anything.

Aggie says: He just said he loved me. He does that now, you know.

Libby says: I didn't know for sure, but I suspected.

Aggie says: Well, I tried to say I loved him too, but he drove off even before I had a chance to shut the door, much less...

Libby says: My Luke is distracted right now. That is very unlike him and dangerous. But you went over to the house. There wasn't a chance there?

Aggie says: *blush* I sort of lost all intelligible thought after he made one of his startling comments.

Libby says: Something tells me I shouldn't ask what it was, so I won't. I won't promise not to wonder, though.

Aggie says: Ask him. I don't care if he doesn't.

Libby says: I just might do that. I just might.

Libby says: You know, Aggie. My Luke is going to love to hear these stories of your attempts to share your heart. They will be very special to him once...

Aggie says: Once we're engaged?

Libby says: It seems so presumptuous to say that, but yes.

Aggie says: Well, I'm a presumptuous kind of gal, I suppose. I fully expect to be his wife someday—if he'll ever ask. Well, ask for real. I suppose technically he already has by informing me that he intends to. Sort of.

Libby says: His sisters are going to be merciless. They're bad enough now.

Aggie says: It'll do him good. Mom says nothing makes a man of a man than enduring good natured teasing regarding his heart.

Libby says: I suspect your father was in earshot.

Aggie says: How did you guess? *giggle*

Libby says: I really would love to chat some more, but I'm developing a nasty headache. I think I should go to bed.

Aggie says: Oh, do! Feel better! Night!

Libby says: Before I go, will you do me a favor?

Aggie says: Anything!

Libby says: Convince Luke to do his tile shopping on Sunday. It'll have been a full week of hard work at that point. He'll need a break, but my Luke won't take one unless forced to. He has a lot riding on this house.

Aggie says: I'll try. Tina isn't going to see her father after all, so maybe she and William will take the kids out for pizza after church.

Libby says: Thank you, Aggie. Goodnight.

Aggie says: G'night.

oVER THE HIGHWAY AND...

Thursday, November 27th

Aggie's heart was heavy as she neared Yorktown. She missed him—much more than she'd expected. Even late night chats had been limited to a couple of text messages. Each day he got up early, ate a cold breakfast, tore out the damaged walls, floors, or cabinetry, cleaned it up, and tried to install it all over again. They went shopping once, she helped with the tiling for a couple of hours, but most of the work was left to Luke and Laird—something Aggie imagined would become a frequent occurrence in their lives. Someday. She'd also received a couple of tender notes, but otherwise, Luke had been noticeably, painfully absent.

The din rose in the van, reminding her to pay attention to the road. "Ok, you guys, that's enough roughhousing back there. Settle down and put your stuff away. We're almost to Grandma Millie's house."

With that chaos tamed, Aggie refocused her attention back on the road. Though she'd looked forward to dinner in her childhood home with family she hadn't seen in months, she already missed what seemed to be the rest of her family. Both Luke and his mother had declined the invitation to join the Milliken-Stuart clan in Yorktown for Thanksgiving dinner.

As Aggie turned onto her parents' street, she saw that Christmas decorations were already making a show in several yards. There was fierce competition amongst the men on Lafayette Drive. For decades, they'd tried to outdo each other's decorative efforts, including one man's miniature city designed out of wire and blue and white lights.

The moment her foot applied the brakes in front of the house, children spilled from the van and tore across the front yard into the house. Anxious to get inside, Aggie crawled between the seats to Ian's spot and stared at the empty seat. Somehow, someone had managed to grab him in the melee. She strolled to the back of the van, opened the door, and pulled the box with Vannie's pies, hard crust and all, from it, shutting the door with her backside. Before she could make it up the walk, Laird and Vannie rushed back out the door to her.

"I'll take that!" Laird reached for the boxes.

"Go see what is out back! Grandma said to." Vannie's eyes sparkled with excitement as she gently shoved Aggie toward the back gate.

Aggie glanced back and saw the children rush into the house again, barely missing a spill that would have created pie goulash in the process. Praying for patience, she pushed open the gate, glancing toward her father's workshop, but she saw nothing. As she rounded the corner of the house, she spied Luke on one knee, his heart in his eyes and a ring box in one hand.

Aggie's heart leapt into her throat simultaneously with the thought, *I hope someone is recording this!* A glance at the family room window assured her that the entire Stuart-Milliken-Winthrop clan was watching the scene with visible relish—truly. Martha held a jar of it in one hand.

She saw through the silly, over-dramatic flourishes he made, sweeping one hand out and clutching the ring to his heart. His eyes told her that no matter how ridiculous he may act to cover his self-consciousness, he loved her. Aggie swallowed a lump—one of many that seemed to reappear as quickly as she thought she dispatched of them.

"Aggie, your father assured me that no one inside that house can hear a thing. So, if I watch the recording of this later and hear myself, I cannot promise I won't be red for eternity."

Still a little stunned to see him, Aggie's first words were the epitome of graciousness that any young woman would hope to express at such a moment. "You said you weren't coming."

"I remembered something you said the other day, combined with something you said after a certain spider dared to live a little too long, and then something Laird —"

"Laird? What did he say?"

"Oh, something about overhearing you mutter that you never get any time alone with me and how can you confess certain delightful things if you never have any time —"

"Ok, ok. I get the picture." She sent an exaggerated angry look in Laird's direction. From the other side of the glass, the boy's eyes widened to immense proportions and he pretended to bite his nails while quaking in fear.

"Um, Aggie?"

"Yeah?"

Luke jerked his head at his outstretched arm. "Mind coming a little closer so I can give my arm something less painful to do?"

Although it wasn't the truly private moment she'd imagined for longer than she cared to admit to herself, Aggie crossed the last of the yard and seated herself on his knee. "Think it can hold me?"

Luke wrapped both of his arms around her and whispered, "If I said I loved you — yet again — what would you say to that?"

Family and window forgotten, Aggie turned to meet Luke's eyes. Her voice cracked with emotion when she answered, "I'd say that it's about time that I told you I love you, too."

Feigning a swoon, Luke collapsed onto the dormant grass, Aggie following right behind him. "Oops. Didn't mean to take you down with me." He helped her to her feet, dropped back to one knee in his previous pose and continued his "scene." "Then, in that case, Aggie, may I ask, in front of God and all of these very nosy people, will you marry me?"

As difficult as it was to hug a man determined to live out the rest of his days on one knee, Aggie squeezed his neck. Behind her back, Luke held up a pre-printed "cue card" that read, "Applause now."

"What — are they —" She glanced at the window where the family cheered and clapped.

"Well," he explained, holding the cue card where she could read it, "I believe they think you have accepted my proposal of marriage, so please don't disappoint them or me and say yes."

The twinkle in Luke's eyes as he spoke was something Aggie knew she'd never forget. She started to agree and then said, "If a yes means I'll disappoint —"

"Mibs…" Luke groaned. "You know—"

"Yes, you silly man! Yes!" She stared at him pointedly. "I said yes! Now will you get off that knee before it grows into the ground?"

In the house, the children jumped up and down, squealing. Her parents hugged each other, and Aggie had no doubt that they fought back tears. However, the scene that tugged at her heartstrings the most was the picture of her twin maiden aunts who looked on with that bittersweet expression only seen in elderly women who watch a new love story begin.

Luke's breath tickled her ear as he murmured, "Should we go inside and be mobbed with congratulations, or," he continued, tugging her away from the window, "do we go sit on that swing under the tree and whisper sweet nothings to each other?"

"And here I thought you'd gotten full disclosure on our family. If we do not get in that house in the next minute or two, we're going to be ambushed." Aggie winked and added, "Besides, you should call your mother. I think she's convinced that I'm going to break your heart."

"That, my dear Mibs, is why I brought the video recorder." He sighed, taking her hand and starting toward the house. "You're right, I suppose. I'll call."

Aggie savored those first few quiet moments of engagement as they crossed the lawn. Just as they reached the patio, however, Luke stopped still. "Oy!" A wicked grin split his face, "And that is for our estimable eldest son."

He produced the ring box once more. Dropping to one knee again, he sighed. "I really blew it, didn't I?"

"You're developing a terrible habit of kneeling. Get up!"

"Thank you. I admit, I don't really know why men do that. It's terribly uncomfortable and puts them at an awkward angle."

Luke watched, seemingly engrossed, while she opened the box and pulled something from inside. There, nestled in her palm, was a ring, one perfectly suited to Aggie's tastes. "It's beautiful! Where—"

"Mom found it and thought of you. She showed it to me months ago—just after your birthday party I think. I didn't know if you'd want to pick out your own or not, but I really wanted to have a ring for you today. The jeweler said we can exchange it."

"How did your mother know just the right thing?"

"Mom knows people. Even if you want to exchange it later, I'd like it if you wore it today for my sake—and mom's. She'll love seeing the picture of it."

That was all it took. She'd managed to keep her composure through dramatic flourishes, eyes that promised a lifetime of love and cherishing, but Luke's fingers slipping the ring over her finger prompted a flood of emotions that spilled into tears. "I wouldn't want any other ring, Luke. It's perfect for many reasons."

As predicted, they were mobbed before they got in the door. Cari promptly promised to love and obey Luke, which brought forth a burst of laughter from everyone but Lorna. "It's not funny! She means it! Cari tries so hard!"

"I do! I do twy!" Her conscience must have been especially sensitive that day because seconds later she added, "Most of the time."

Within minutes, wedding dates were tossed around by the family, until Aggie stood on a chair and called, "Time!!" Once the room quieted, she added, "Can I please enjoy the first *hour* of engagement without being expected to make *wedding* decisions?"

A few "awwwws" escaped, but the peppering with questions ceased. Her aunts sent her a telepathic message that clearly said, "Introduce us, young woman!"

"Luke, come here. Did you meet my aunts?"

"Only briefly—just a nod really—I got delayed and you were right on my tail. Your mom kept me abreast of your position the whole way up here."

Aggie shot a glance at her mother. "Is *that* why you kept asking where we were? I was wondering if there was something wrong with the speedometer or something. You seemed so impatient!"

"Guilty," Martha agreed, trying to escape into the kitchen. Ron shooed her to her chair while he promised to check the turkey.

She swallowed hard and rushed through introductions, hoping he wouldn't connect dots she'd tried to hide. "Well then, Aunt Agatha, Aunt Athena, this is my Luke. Luke Sullivan."

Luke offered his hand and found himself enveloped in hugs, while Aggie escaped into the kitchen, hoping to keep him distracted. However, the moment she opened the fridge, she heard Luke call in an exaggerated fashion, "I guess little *Agathena* is growing up, isn't she? First a mother of eight, now a wife!"

So much for unconnected dots, she grumbled to herself. Aggie

27

closed the fridge and opened the freezer without missing a beat. She grabbed a chip of ice from the ice bowl, closed the freezer, swiped a mug of hot apple cider from a tray on the peninsula, and sauntered back into the family room. Next to Luke, she took a sip and then frowned. "Oh, Luke, I'm sorry. I should have gotten you one. Would you like some?" As she spoke, Aggie reached up to rub Luke's back in an apologetic manner and in the process, pushed the ice cube down his sweatshirt, patting it thoroughly.

Of course, Luke jumped, howled, and dove for her, but Aggie managed to get out of the way just in time to avoid attack and spilled cider. Practical joking on their engagement day—only Aggie and Luke would be that ridiculous. The competition commenced.

Huddled in the corner of the family room with fistfuls of Uno cards, but with very few landing on the table, the Stuart children whispered. The adults in the kitchen were distracted by Ron's recounting of his bungled proposal and oblivious to the conspiracy brewing in the other room. "I don't know how we'd get the stuff we need though," Vannie protested. "I like the idea, I do. But we can't just say, 'Aunt Aggie, can we have a tea party? We need fifty plates, fifty cups, a congratulations sign—'"

"But our birthday is just over a week away," Ellie piped up brightly. "You guys could pretend it's a surprise party for us. We'll ask the Merchamps to let us come play for an hour that day so that Aunt Aggie has to come get us and you can set everything up while she's gone."

"We can't set everything up in ten minutes!" Laird's voice was too loud, but a glance into the kitchen showed that no one in there had noticed.

"No..." Tavish began, "but Mrs. Merchamp would stall Aunt Aggie for a bit, talking. You could say you have to go to the bathroom really bad just as we pass the Pizza Palace. Between everything, we could stall it a good thirty minutes I bet."

Laird shook his head. "We don't need that much time. Aunt Aggie can even help with most of the decorations. We'll just add the engagement stuff after she goes and take down birthday stuff."

"Oh right," Vannie agreed. "Wait, isn't this your golden birthday? We can convince her that we need a gold theme! It'll be more elegant than a regular kid's party."

The kids grew excited, but Cari and Lorna padded downstairs after their early nap, rubbing their eyes. "Oh, great. I forgot about them," Laird muttered. "There's no way we can possibly keep it from them."

"Well," Ellie suggested, "we can try. But if they become suspicious or anything, you can tell Aunt Aggie that they overheard us, and you told them it's a party for her and Luke, so they wouldn't spoil things for Tavish and I."

"Me."

"Spoil what for you, Vannie?"

"The sentence — it's Tavish and me."

Laird's expression was priceless. "Seriously, Vannie? We're plotting the best engagement party ever, and you decide to turn grammarist—"

"Grammarian."

"What?"

Vannie winked at Ellie, who could hardly keep from howling, "The word is grammarian, not grammarist."

Lorna watched as they continued to whisper amongst themselves for the better part of a minute before she wandered over to observe the game. "No one is playing. What are you talking about?"

"Luke and Aunt Aggie," Tavish muttered.

"Will he be Uncle Luke?" The intricacies of familial relationships seemed to confound the child.

"Yes." Vannie swallowed hard and added, "Ian will probably call him 'Daddy.'"

The others looked at her stunned, until they realized that Ian's trademarked 'Gaggie' was already being replaced by Aggie at times. It was only natural that in time he'd call her mama. His wail from upstairs gave Vannie a chance to escape without raising questions. "I'll get him, Aunt Aggie. Where's the diaper bag?"

"On Grandma's bed. You sure?" Aggie's eyes traveled to the group in the corner. "What are you guys playing?"

"They're not," Lorna complained. "They're just talking about how Luke is going to be our Uncle now. I wanted to see Vannie win again. She *always* wins."

"Here, I'll take her place. That way someone else will win this time. I never do."

A more jittery group of card players Aggie had never seen. The usual protests, banter, and shouts of victory with each great move were noticeably absent. If she initiated it, they all jumped in to respond, but immediately settled back into their silent but speedy rounds. At last, Ellie triumphed. "I won?" She stared at her empty hand in shock. "I don't think I've ever said Uno before!"

"If the baby's awake, I'll make the gravy and then we can eat," called Aggie's Aunt Athena. "Maybe the children could wash up?"

Children scattered, leaving cards all over the table. Aggie scooped them up and wrapped the rubber band back around the stack. She turned to lead Cari and Lorna to wash their hands and found Luke already drying Lorna's while Cari soaped up. When her mother went to pull the yams from the oven, Aggie showed off his helpful skills. "See that? I've missed that this past week."

Luke turned and raised an eyebrow. "Huh?"

"Eloquent as ever, Mr. Sullivan."

"Some girls marry men for their money, property, even family. This one," he added, nudging her as she passed, "*Agathena* marries me for my two hands."

The competition continues, Aggie mused. "You can't count using my name more than once," she muttered as she saw Vannie enter the kitchen and took Ian from her. "I'd win this thing with ice that way."

By the time they were seated for dinner, the score was Aggie four, Luke two. Although Aggie had the home court advantage, Luke had a lifetime of practical joking with three sisters. She started to warn him that he couldn't win, when she found herself jumping in the air, clutching her backside in the fashion of Maria von Trapp.

"That'll be three for me."

The temptation to throw a roll at him was huge, but whispering at the end of the table caught her attention. "Would you like to share your conversation with everyone, Laird?"

"She sounds like a schoolteacher anyway."

Aunt Agatha's comment was ignored while Laird stammered something about thinking she was going to lose. Before she could respond to either her aunt or her nephew, Martha asked, "And what is the score?"

30

"Three to four, my favor. After the ice, I got him with the cold water pistol, got the boys to tie his shoelaces together—"

"When did that happen?" Ron sent a questioning look at Luke and got an affirmative answer.

"While you were all playing dominos. Four was when I convinced him that I played Abe Lincoln in the school play."

"I," Luke interjected, "have used her real name half a dozen times, got the flour on her nose without her noticing, and had the pinecone success."

"Aunt Aggie had more failures." Tavish seemed much too eager to remind her of that.

"It just shows I'm not afraid to take a risk."

"Or that you're out of your league."

Martha giggled. "Am I the only one who is imagining their children asking how they spent their first day of engagement and being confused to learn it was playing practical jokes on each other?"

"Anyone who grows up with Aggie won't be surprised."

"I am just *thankful* that he chose *Thanksgiving* to propose. It'll help him remember to be *thankful* that he did when he doesn't feel *thankful* anymore because I beat him—badly."

"*Thank* goodness that is over."

"Oh, any doubt about whether Luke is the right man for Aggie will be over in about ten seconds, won't it, Ron?" Martha beamed.

Aggie bit her lip to bide her time. She was just about to widen the gap between them. Luke had nervously asked how the meal would be served, confessing that he preferred to avoid yams with marshmallow topping. She assured him it would be family style, each dishing up their own portions. She just neglected to mention that there was never room for the turkey or the yams on the table, so her mother served the yams while her father served the turkey onto each person's plate. And there came her piece de resistance.

Ron Milliken prayed; Martha and he stood, and they carried their respective dishes to the table. At each of the children's places, Martha doled out minuscule dollops of sugared yams, larger portions to herself, Aggie, and her sisters, none for her husband, and an enormous portion to Luke. "I'm just pleased that someone else likes yams. Ron..."

She didn't have a chance to finish. Luke realized instantly what had occurred and reached under the table to pinch Aggie's leg. Aggie promptly dumped her milk in his lap. "That cancels out your pinch. I'm still one up." Without a pause, she jumped up, grabbed a kitchen towel, and passed it to Luke.

"Aggie!"

"All's fair in practical jokes, love, and war."

"This seems to be all three," Ron muttered. "Ok, how about we throw out some things we're thankful for before we end up with an all-out food fight."

The suggestion was a good one, allowing Luke and Aggie to enjoy their dinner—at least most of it. Feeling a little guilty, Aggie got up when her Mother mentioned being thankful that most of the family was there, and got Luke a new plate. She removed the old one and winked at him as she sat down after making a show of checking for more conifer seed pods.

The expressions of thankfulness were varied in both type and length. Ron was unusually eloquent and emotional with his, while Vannie's was brief and to the point. Her aunts focused on Luke and the children, while the children did what children do best—amuse and amaze. From gratitude for the new house, to not having to go to Grandmother Stuart's home, to her still being their "mom," some of the comments both perplexed and astounded her.

However, the best comments were spoken by the youngest, and last. Kenzie waited patiently for her turn and then with a very pointed look at Luke said, "I am thankful that Deputy William isn't mad at Aunt Aggie for not marrying him."

Aggie's attempt not to laugh lasted less than a quarter minute. Her shoulders shook, her hands covered her face, and at last, she erupted in uncontrollable laughter. "Only you, Kenzie.

Lorna's gratitude was a little more subtle. "I am thankful that Luke didn't have to eat all *his* yams."

Before the chuckles at Luke's expense ceased, Cari crossed her arms and said, "I think I is thankful that I didn't get in twouble today."

"You think?" Aggie's face was the picture of confusion.

Two blue eyes blinked back at Aggie from across the table. "Well, did I? I don't know what you know."

War with a deck of cards as the weapon was underway. No, they weren't playing the game of War, but there was no doubt in the minds of the other principal players; this was war and Aggie was losing badly. The game: hearts. The players: Luke, Aggie, Ron, and Vannie. While the skirmishes took place at the dining room table, the aunts, Martha, and the other children holed up in the family room and watched a marathon of *I Love Lucy* episodes.

Ron and Vannie may have played cards, dealt cards, and shuffled cards, but they weren't really playing the game; they were filler. Luke was effectively stomping Aggie without mercy. Hand after hand, they watched Luke pass just the right cards to befuddle Aggie — a hilarious sight. It only took two botched runs by Aggie and two shot moons by Luke to ensure that he won and quickly. New score: four to four. Let the tiebreaker commence.

A wicked gleam, or as close to one as she could summon, glinted in Aggie's eye. She pushed back the chair, hurried into the family room where an episode was just finishing, and called for the others to follow. Ron entered the room, shaking his head. "Name that tune?"

"Hey, it's tradition!"

"Tevya, Fiddler on the Roof!" Luke cried. "Oh, we haven't started yet? Ok. Just didn't want to risk losing necessary points."

After years of practice, Ron had a peculiar talent of being able to start and stop an album without scratching it. He perched himself next to the console, blocking the row of albums from view, and readied the first song. Aggie dragged the dining room chairs into the family room with Luke's help and sat them in a long row in front of the couch. Martha, of course, settled into her recliner to enjoy the "show."

"Ok… everyone ready? When you know the tune, stand up. Martha, call out the name when you see the first one stand."

Ron tried to start with easy ones, and the older players held back from songs like "Over the Rainbow" or "What a Wonderful World," but the young children, despite their unique and sometimes hilarious answers, fell out of the competition with their first question. Within minutes, the game was down to Athena, Luke, Aggie, and to everyone's astonishment, Tavish.

Athena finally went down, leaving the other three in a race to the finish. Luke and Aggie were visibly nervous as they each tried to come out the victor. At last, when the children grew restless, they decided that whoever got four in a row or was still standing first, would win. It wasn't a contest. Tavish was not only faster than Aggie or Luke, his answers were impeccable and he often nailed the artist.

"How did you *do* that?"

Her nephew grinned at her. "Radio. I found an old one in the attic and it works great in my cubby. I listen to the Golden Oldies station all day sometimes."

Once he helped Aggie tuck the children into their sleeping bags, air mattresses, or couches, Luke said his goodbyes, thanked the Millikens for having him, and strolled hand in hand with Aggie into the night. "You will take the tape to your mother first thing? I don't want her to have to wait."

"I'm going straight to Mom's, going to sleep for a bit, and then I'm headed over to Chad's for our Black Friday Fest."

"Good." Aggie felt strangely awkward, walking under streetlights, in view of all the neighbors. Most of them had watched her grow up, and now she was out, after dark, with a man, holding hands… It seemed almost risqué for her.

"Mibs? Do you have any idea how happy I am?"

"Took you long enough to ask," she teased.

"I didn't have a clue that you cared until last week, then with the house… I mean, I wondered at times, but…"

"Well, you know it now, Lucas, don't you?" Despite the frosty temperatures, Aggie hardly noticed how chilled her nose was becoming.

"What do I know?"

"You—" she reached to swat his arm, but stopped herself. Standing under the streetlight, with their breath making foggy puffs in the air, Aggie smiled. "I love you." She winked. "Happy now?"

"It'll do… 'til the next time I want to hear it."

Milliken says: Tina? You around?

Milliken says: Oh, Tiiiiiinaaaaaaaa…

Milliken says: Stop flirting with the cops and get on here.

Tina says: Not all… just one…

Milliken says: Well, then. That makes all the difference.

Tina says: So, how did the day go? Was it pretty emotional?

Milliken says: You might say that…

Tina says: ☹ I'm sorry. I should have come.

Milliken says: Got that right. You missed my very public proposal!

Tina says: What? You said Luke wasn't going!!!

Aggie says: There. I don't do well when my name isn't my name on this thing.

Aggie says: Well, he was here!

Tina says: Ok, tell me more!

Aggie says: Well, I showed up and he was in the back yard. You know, right where the family room window shows EVERYONE the whole thing?

Tina says: Back yard? Really?

Aggie says: Yep. I came through the back, because Dad was supposedly working out back on something and I needed to see it, and there he was!

Tina says: Did he get down on one knee and declare his undying love for you? Snort.

Aggie says: Sure did!

Tina says: You're kidding, right? Luke?? LUKE????

Aggie says: Yep, in front of all my kids, both my aunts, and both my parents ogling and salivating at the window.

Tina says: Wait, were your aunts really there? Both of them?

Aggie says: Yep. I bet you know what came next.

Tina says: You're pretty yeppy tonight.

Aggie says: Better yeppy than yappy. Yappy dogs are annoying.

Tina says: You're not a dog.

Tina says: I guess he figured out your name pretty quickly.

Aggie says: Yes (note the use of yes instead of yep???) Then it was war.

Aggie says: It's all on tape too! You should call Mrs. Sullivan. Luke is taking it straight to her house tonight.

Tina says: No, I'll wait. I want to watch it with you.

Aggie says: Because you want to watch my face. Don't bother typing it. I know you started.

Tina says: I want to watc

Tina says: You know me well.

Tina says: So, do you have a ring?

Aggie says: Oh, Tina. It's just perfect. It's ME somehow.

Tina says: Did he pick it out by himself or…

Aggie says: Libby picked it out for me way back at my birthday. Let me send you a picture. Hold on.

Tina says: I don't suppose you set a date…

Tina says: What kind of wedding do you want?

Tina says: I get to wear a pretty dress, right???????

Aggie says: Sorry, couldn't get a decent picture without going into the kitchen.

Aggie says: I'm not sure about the date. They tried to talk about it, but…

Tina says: Not the right day for that, was it?

Aggie says: It felt rushed and Thanksgiving is a family day, not Aggie day.

Tina says: Oh, that ring is perfect for you!

Aggie says: I know, right? I just can't believe she did that!

Tina says: Libby is pretty insightful…

Tina says: What about the wedding? Still want the garden wedding with the tea cakes and string quartet under the archway?

Aggie says: You're going to hate me.

Tina says: If you tell me you're going to elope…

Aggie says: Ok, maybe just utterly despise. I want a little wedding at the house and then a reception somewhere — even after the honeymoon. If we get one.

Tina says: If you get one?

Aggie says: Well, I'm a mom now. I can't just take off for a week.

Tina says: Well, you're going. We'll find a way. I'll be there and maybe Libby can come over or something.

Tina says: We can talk about it later, but you're going. Hey, what about my dress?

Aggie says: You're going to have to have an amazing dress. We have to utilize any chance to knock William's starched socks off.

Tina says: Oh, ugh! Starched socks.

Aggie says: Well, we know he doesn't.

Tina says: But it's not unbelievable — that's the problem!

Tina says: Enough about my love life, I want to know more. Do you know any wedding things other than small? Colors?

Aggie says: That's hard to tell. Every color I come up with makes me think of eighties poof or too contemporary/chic for me. Assuming the color works with white, we're good.

Tina says: White! A dress. Oh, you are going to have a wedding dress.

Aggie says: Mop up the tears.

Tina says: Yes ma'am. Now dress. ANY idea?

Aggie says: I don't want sleeves that are wider than my thighs or enough gathers to hide Luke from the posse.

Tina says: Good. No mermaid dresses either, ok? I think you'd look ridiculous. Takes the right person to pull those off.

Aggie says: Well, since I'm not her, there's no worries.

Tina says: How long of an engagement?

Aggie says: Since elopement was knocked off the table, then whenever we can have time to do it without rushing. December is too busy, January is recuperation from December (and kind of quick)

Aggie says: February is out. Not going there in Valentine's Day month. Maybe March. I don't want to wait too much longer than that.

Tina says: January is sort of quick, but December is just busy.

Aggie says: Doesn't make much sense, does it?

Tina says: Go to bed. You're tired.

Aggie says: You're right. I am. Thank you, Tina.

Tina says: For what?

Aggie says: Just for being you.

Tina says: Love you. Congratulations. Good night. Sleep tight. Bite the bedbugs.

Aggie says: Leave it to you to be revolting and endearing — all in the same breath. Night. Love you too.

Aggie says: Wait! Wait!

Aggie says: Tiiiiiiiiiinnnnnnnnnnnnnnnnnaaaaaaaaaaaaa

Aggie says: Come back! How is Miner's paw? I promised Tavish I'd ask!

Aggie says: Come on, Tina. I know you're researching something instead of sleeping.

Aggie says: I will call you — or worse, I'll call William and have him call you!

Tina says: I was getting a drink! Sheesh! Paw seems better. He limps a little bit, but not too much. I've got both of them in the mudroom with it shut off.

Aggie says: Mudroom!

Tina says: I don't want him to get cold enough that he needs to walk around, but isn't willing to because of the foot.

Aggie says: You are such a pushover.

Tina says: And the dog is healing, so we're good. He'll go back out in the morning.

Aggie says: Ok... thanks.

Tina says: Now SLEEP.

Aggie says: As if I'll be able to.

Tina says: And here note, world, today's the day Aggie became a girl.

Aggie says: Ooooh... I'm telling Luke... he's not gonna like that!

Tina says: Bring it on.

Aggie says: hee hee. Night.

Tina says: *poofs* Again.

Chapter 3

SURPRISE!

Monday, December 1ˢᵗ

Bang! The door slammed shut behind Aggie, but the children hardly noticed. "Ok, guys we have maybe five minutes until she's back and even more obsessed with making up for lost time past and future."

Laird rolled his eyes at Vannie. "Like that little speech wasn't a waste. Let's start planning. Got your sketchbook, Ellie?"

Two long dark braids bobbed as she flipped the pages to a blank sheet between two sketches of snow laden trees. "Got it."

"Ok, first someone has to think of everyone who should come. I think we should ask Mrs. Sullivan to write down everyone she knows. Then maybe Aunt Tina would help us with the other list."

Once more, Laird interrupted. "Why can't we just ask her for everything and leave Aunt Aggie out of it?"

"Aunt Aggie would find out. You know she would. It's better if she thinks she knows what is going on."

"She's right, Laird, and you know it."

"Yeah, I know. Ok. Hmm, do adult parties have games? What kind of games could you play at something like this?"

"Well, we can have games and if the adults don't want to do it, then at least it'd still keep any kids busy—you know, some of the others from church, Luke's nieces and nephews, the—"

"Stuart kids..."

"Ok, Laird. You don't have to be rude." Vannie sounded peevish. "I was just trying to show that it's not a waste—"

Tavish's impatience erupted. "Can we stop the bickering?

We've only got minutes before she's back or the kids wake up!"

"Ok then, games," Vannie said, determined to get back on topic. "What ideas do we have? Something related to weddings?"

"Knot tying? Getting out of a ball and chain?"

"Laird!" The chorus from his siblings stifled him just a little.

"Wait, he gave me an idea." Tavish grinned. "What about 'the two shall become one?'"

"Ok... so how do they become—a three legged race! Great idea!"

The would-be birthday boy beamed. "If it's snowing, it'll be harder too."

"Adults might not want to get all wet..." Vannie suggested regretfully.

"Then they don't have to play. If you don't like my idea, just say so."

"Oh, I like it. I think it's a fun twist on it. I just wondered."

The front door opened before anyone could find fault with Vannie's latest statement.

Aggie jogged down the steps of the basement on her way upstairs to check the little ones. "Did anyone hear anything from upstairs?"

The room froze as if they were all caught stealing. Eyes shifted one to another and then back to Aggie. It was only a couple second delay, but it seemed as if they'd been paralyzed for an hour. Laird found his voice first.

"I don't hear anything." He turned to Vannie. "Do you hear anything upstairs?"

"No."

"I think they're asleep. Want me to check? I'm all done for the day except for reading my chapters. Actually, I just want to finish the book."

Before Aggie could answer, Ellie waved her pencil at her. "I'm having trouble with its and it's with an apostrophe."

Something in Aggie's face prompted Vannie to volunteer to help. "I'll show her, Aunt Aggie." She paused. "Is everything ok?"

"Oh, yes. Good. Never better. If you guys can do that, I'll just see about getting dinner started."

Tavish's head whipped around. "It's two-thirty! I thought you said we were having sloppy Joes."

"We are."

Without another word, Aggie hurried into the ___ obviously distracted. The kids exchanged glances as she disappeared into the living room and around the dining room corner into the kitchen. "Did she really just say she's making dinner—now?" Laird shrugged and left the room, taking his book with him.

Vannie hesitated. It was the perfect time to convince Aggie to agree to a party. However, she had promised Ellie to help with it and it's. "Ok, I'm going to talk to her about the party." She hurried to Ellie's side. "Look, you only use the apostrophe if you are writing a contraction. Otherwise, it doesn't get one. So 'It's a good idea' would have an apostrophe, but 'The cat washed its paw' isn't. See?"

Whether or not Ellie "saw," didn't seem to matter. Vannie dashed from the room and into the kitchen, eager to get the party ball rolling. "Aunt Aggie? Can I talk to you? We've got an idea, but we need your help."

Though apparently a little distracted, Aggie did try to give Vannie her full attention. "What idea and who is we?"

"Laird and me—well, Kenzie eventually, but we wanted to get permission before we got her excited."

"Permission for what?"

"It's Tavish and Ellie's golden birthday next week. We thought it'd be cool to do a surprise party for them. Make it really something special. Mommy made my golden birthday amazing. I was nine too, and she had a big party at Grandma Millie's and everything was about nines. We 'dressed to the nines' and I got a new custom dress because 'a stitch in time saves nine.' I can't remember the rest."

Aggie dumped a tube of defrosted ground beef in the frying pan. "I think I remember that too. She did something with nine yards and that's when you got your charm bracelet, isn't it? The nine days' wonder?"

"Right! Anyway, we thought we'd do a surprise party for them and we figured out how to pull it off without them suspecting or anything; we even want to get them to help!"

Aggie turned to stare at her, the spatula stuck in the frying pan. "You're going to do what?"

"That'll melt again—Aunt Aggie?"

"Wha—Oh."

"See, what we thought we'd do," Vannie continued, "was tell

41

them we're planning a party for you and Luke. That way we can invite people, make plans, and even buy stuff and they won't suspect. They'll just think it's for your party!"

"Wait, I'm not supposed to know about this party that we're having for Luke and me?"

"Right! Well, and we thought we'd tell them that you think the party is really for them."

Aggie chopped the meat swiftly as she thought. "Isn't that a bit convoluted? That's really a lot of lying, Vannie."

"Mommy always said that in the Stuart house, it's not a lie when it comes to surprises or gifts because it's understood that those might not be true."

"How can it not be a lie and not be true?"

The girl giggled. "That's what I asked. She said that for a lie to be a lie that is wrong, the other person isn't supposed to know it might not be true. This isn't a lie, it's a surprise. Or that's what Mommy said." Vannie's planned sniff for effect was unnecessary. She choked at the best place, making her feel like a cheat even though she was truly upset.

"I suppose. Well, if Luke doesn't mind all the double secrets and such, then I suppose..." She dug in the drawer for her favorite strainer. "What about Cari and Lorna?"

"We'll tell them it's your party too. They'll probably be extra good in the days before hand and if they talk freely, it won't ruin things for Ellie and Tavish."

"Just what do I have to do?"

"Make a list of people we should invite?"

Aggie sighed. "Remind me to thank the Lord that none of you were born Christmas week."

It was a dark and stormy night. The living room lights flickered as the power hovered between steady and blackout. Aggie pulled her power cord from the laptop, reached for the surge protector at the side of the couch, jerked the plug from the wall, and plunged the entire room into perfect darkness. *There, at least the TV won't be ruined if we get hit.*

The odd glow of the laptop was the only light in the room, apart from the occasional flash of lightning, but still Aggie pecked away at the keyboard, determined to get the kids' party lists entered into some semblance of order. A pile of scrap paper, notebook paper, envelopes, and of all things, construction paper, had notes of everything from "gold balloons" to "don't forget to invite Deputy Markenson. Kenzie insists. I'm writing this down so she'll quit bugging me."

Lost in confusing food suggestions such as sparkling grape juice and crab cakes, she didn't see the flash of light, hear the booms that rattled the windows, or feel the cool gusts of wind that fought to get into the house. She did feel cold hands cover her eyes and screamed, clutching her laptop before it flew across the room. "Luke!"

"I knocked! I could see you, but you didn't answer. Is the power out?"

"No, I just pulled the plug in case." She sank back to the couch. "My heart is still pounding!" she accused, slapping his arm lightly.

"Well, I have to produce some kind of heart thump in you... it's my duty as your fiancée."

"You like that word, don't you?" Aggie set the laptop on the table and stood, fumbling for the light switch in the dining room. "There. Shed a little light on the subject."

"Yes, I do like that word. I'd like wife better..." he frowned. "Tell me you don't want to serve crab cakes at our wedding."

"Um, no. The kids want to serve crab cakes at Ellie and Tavish's surprise party."

"Ellie—" He paused, then laughed. "You got me."

"No, I'm serious. They want to do a surprise party for Ellie and Tavish's golden birthday."

"What's a golden birthday? Wouldn't that be age fifty?"

"That's the fiftieth wedding anniversary."

Luke winked. "What can I say, I've got weddings on the brain. Now, tell me about golden birthdays."

"It's just when your birth year coincides with the day of the month you were born. They were born on December ninth and are turning nine this year. Vannie did the same thing. Thankfully, everyone else isn't for a long time. Maybe I can get out of doing anything by then."

"They really want crab cakes and sparkling grape juice?"

"I know, right?" Aggie flopped back against the couch, staring at the screen on the coffee table. "I was thinking nine small cakes, nine kinds of ice cream, and nine balloons or something. I planned to invite your nephews and nieces and that's it. They've got a list of everyone we know! They even want to invite Tina's dad!"

"Probably for the great gifts he'd be likely to bring."

Her eyes widened and her chin dropped ever so slightly. "I bet you're right! Oh man, they scare me sometimes."

"Are you going to do it?"

The flashing little cursor on the screen mocked her. It seemed to be an electronic hand, drumming its fingers in impatience. "I think so. It's a lot to do in a week, and it'll cost a fortune, but Allie made a big deal out of Vannie's. I think the kids are trying to tell me that we *need* to do this."

"I take it now isn't a good time to discuss dates and such."

Without hesitation, Aggie closed the laptop, curled up in her corner of the couch, wrapped her hands around her knees and grinned. "It's a great time."

"I suppose," his fingers ticked off days until he was satisfied, "December thirteenth is out."

"Next Saturday?"

"Yeah."

Aggie sighed. "We could just have the Vaughns come—no wait, they're already invited—and have a brief ceremony at the end."

"No dress?"

"Who cares? You get to stay then."

"I could go for that, but I think in twenty years I'd regret not giving you time to have a dress." Luke nudged her foot. "A bride should have the chance to be bridal for a bit."

"Bridal wave, eh?"

"That's better than Bridezilla. The girls are taking votes as to if and or when you will turn into one."

"The girls? Your sisters?"

Luke nodded. "I told Connie you'd get frazzled, but before you could don your lizard skin and bare your fangs, you'd go marching up the stairs singing *It Is Well with My Soul* or something."

His words stung for some reason. "Am I that—that—"

"Encouraging? Endearing? Predictably faithful? Yep."

It only took a second of hesitation before Aggie unwrapped her arms from her knees and scooted next to Luke, laying her head on his shoulder. "Thanks. It just sounded... um..." She swallowed hard. Suddenly, she felt as if it looked like she was making a production out of it to garner attention. "Oh, I don't know. Pietistic or something. Trying to look spiritual or ick... It's just a habit. I usually don't even know I'm doing it."

"That's what is so wonderful about it, Mibs. It's a part of your relationship with the Lord. It's who you are in the deepest part of you. It's a beautiful thing."

"I'd rather talk about dates. Start with months?" she suggested.

"Ok." He hesitated then sighed. "December is out. If we can't do it next weekend, then the following one is too close to Christmas and then there's New Year's at Uncle Christopher's."

"January is out."

"Ok, any particular reason?" Luke sounded disappointed.

"Well, we can do it, but if I can't get married next Saturday, then I'm going to do it 'right,' and that means I need a little more time."

"February then. We can do the cheesy Valentine's Day thing. I can tell everyone it's because—" He stopped mid-sentence as tears splashed onto Aggies cheeks and she shook her head. "What's wrong, Mibs?"

All of her mental preparation failed her at the mention of Valentine's Day. Although she wanted to pretend the day would be salvaged by a happy memory, Aggie had no doubt that the pall of the first anniversary of her sister's death would kill the festive spirit. Trying to explain it, however, proved to be harder than she'd anticipated. "I want people to cry for happiness at my wedding if they must cry—not because it is also a sad day for the Milliken-Stuarts."

"I don't understand."

"Valentine's Day will be the first anniversary—"

"Oh! I forgot!" Luke's jaw slowly tightened as he worked through his thoughts and put them into discussable order. "I—oh, I'm so sorry."

"It's fine. Let's just skip February, ok?"

"Then the date is March. Name the day, but it *is* March."

Aggie dragged the laptop back off the table and flipped it open. Thanks to her good buddy, Google, the calendar appeared. "Seventh, fourteenth, twenty-first, or twenty-eighth."

"Not the fourteenth. I'll take the others, but that's too close to the 'Ides of March.' It feels ominous."

"How about the seventh?"

"Far enough away from Valentine's Day?"

There was no doubt in her mind when Aggie shoved the laptop back onto the table and grinned up at him. "Definitely."

"Can you do the wedding thing that fast?"

"You better believe it." Rain pelted the house even harder than ever, and the thunder rattled more than the windowpanes. "I want hot chocolate. Want some?"

"Are you afraid of storms, Aggie?"

"Afraid is a bit extreme. I just really don't like all the elements at once. One or two at a time, great. All... not so much."

He jumped up to help her, grinning like a kid who just won a new bicycle. "I'm going to love this."

She jumped at a new clap of thunder, shoving the cocoa canister into his hands. "What?"

"Discovering all these little things that we haven't had time to learn yet." For a moment, it seemed as if he'd disappeared into some distant daydream. "I've practically lived my days here for five months. I know you better than I've ever known anyone outside my family, but then it seems like I don't know you at all."

"I felt guilty," she confessed with a sly smile growing as she spoke. "I felt the same way. It seems like you shouldn't feel like you don't know the person you're going to marry, but I kind of liked the feeling. It's like an adventure, and yet that's crazy because I know things about you that no one else does — maybe even you!"

Luke's slow nod told her he understood. While milk heated on the stove, they leaned against the corners of the island, their hands intertwined on the granite. Both Luke and Aggie seemed mesmerized at the sight before them, but at last, their gazes met. The look in Luke's eyes stole her breath and held it for a moment. "March."

"Seventh," she agreed.

"A long time."

"Mmm hmm." Though she tried to drop her eyes, she couldn't. "Too long."

"Sunday after church?"

"Nope. It's Saturday or the seventh of March."

The scent of warm milk jerked her from their conversation. She stirred the pot, readied the mugs, and tried to control the overwhelming temptation to beg him to agree to Saturday or Sunday. It didn't take long for him to say the only words that could assure that she would be Aggie Milliken for at least a couple of more months.

"I suppose preempting the kids' birthday with our hastily arranged wedding isn't exactly something Emily Post would agree with."

"Getting married that quickly probably also gives rise to other, less charitable, gossip."

"Who cares—" Luke sighed. "I suppose we should. The kids would be the ones who got the brunt of it—eventually." He accepted the cup she offered and nudged her back toward the living room. "So, what about houses. Should we live in your house or mine?"

Hot chocolate spewed across the room, landing mostly on the dining table, bench, and chairs. The floor also looked as if the storm had moved indoors. "And I thought you were a gentleman."

"Why would you think that? I was just protecting my back from scalding hot chocolate."

Aggie started to turn back toward the kitchen, but Luke blocked the way. "Go sit down and enjoy your chocolate. I'll clean up your mess."

"Your mess. You know it, too."

From the dining room, Luke peppered her with questions that were at nearly a conversational pace. "Do you know where you want to do this? At the church? Brunswick? Rockland?"

"I know," she admitted, "but you might not like it."

"Tell me anyway."

"On one condition." Aggie waited for him to see how serious she was before she continued. "You'll be honest with me if you don't like it?"

"Of course."

"I'm serious, Luke. I want to tell you my idea without worrying that you'll just feel obligated to do it out of some... some... obligatory sense of... of... obligation."

"Ok then, no feeling obliged to agree. Got it."

She groaned as she sipped her chocolate and wondered if the

idea was such a good one after all. A new thought gave her the perfect way for him to present an objection. "I also need to know if it'll cause any problems with your family. I don't want to start off our marriage by alienating people."

"Just tell me, Mibs." Luke wiped down the last of the chocolate that dripped from the bench to the floor and then strolled back into the living room, sipping his drink.

"I want to have the wedding here."

"It won't work. Not in March. It'll be too cold, windy, rainy... we can't."

"I mean right here. You and me on those steps, Mr. Vaughn at the bottom with his back to the guests, and guests everywhere else. All the furniture out of here, the dining room, and maybe the library—well not the books, but the tables and stuff."

"We couldn't have very many people here..."

Aggie willed her features not to give away her disappointment. "I was afraid it wouldn't work. That's ok. We—"

"Wait. I didn't say it wouldn't work. I just said we couldn't have many guests. Are you sure you're ok with that?"

"I pictured your family, mine, Tina, William, Mrs. Dyke, the Vaughns, Iris... oh, probably Murphy, but that's it for here. Then we do pictures and go somewhere else for the reception. Invite everyone we know to that. The church, my church from home, your and your mother's church and friends, the Rockland church... pack the place for all I care."

"That would work..." He hesitated and then asked, "Do you mind telling me why so few people? Is it because you want the house especially or the small number?"

"Both. I want the house, of course. It's where it all started. You helped make the house become whole again—and now you're helping our family become a whole thing too." A new tear rolled down her cheek and onto her blouse. "I'm sorry."

"That's just about the most incredible thing anyone has ever said to me—except maybe a girl I know who said she loved me."

"Well, that too."

"And numbers?" Luke's voice sounded suspiciously emotional.

"I really wanted to consider having only those people who would take seriously an admonition from our wedding sermon to 'hold us to our vows' in hard times. I wanted everyone to celebrate

48

with us, but only those who understand the sincerity and seriousness of our vows to be there to witness them."

"I see that..." His mind and jaw worked double time until he nodded. "I like it."

"Really? I just want someone to say, 'I was there the day you got married. I witnessed those vows. You said in good times and bad. This is the bad. You vowed. Now let's get back there and I'll help you work it out' if I ever even hint that I'm 'done.'"

"I pray I never make you think that."

She smiled. "You won't. It'll be all me. I know me all too well."

Their eyes locked, enchanting messages flying back and forth between them, until Luke gave himself a little shake of the head and dropped his eyes to the pile of papers on the coffee table. He flipped through them, visibly trying to distract himself, which caused Aggie no little amount of delight. There was no doubt about his feelings toward her, and it seemed as if he understood her heart as well.

One slip of paper, scrawled on yellow legal paper, grabbed his attention. "What? Did you read this?"

"The yellow one? No. What does it say?"

"'There should be a breath holding contest. This will give the little girls a chance to win something. Cari and Kenzie can hold their breaths much longer than I can.'"

"A breath holding contest?"

"It's futile. They'll lose."

Aggie's eyes asked the obvious question, "Why do you say that?"

Luke stood, squeezed her hand, and dragged himself to the door. "No, don't get up."

"But why—"

"Because I'll be holding my breath until March."

Libby says: Have you seen my Luke tonight? He's not home and he's not answering his cell phone. With this weather, I'm a little worried.

Libby says: Oh, and hello! Sorry.

Aggie says: Yes! He just left. When was the last time you tried to call?

Libby says: Oh, about ten minutes ago?

Aggie says: He was right here ten minutes ago. Either his battery is dead, or he left his phone in the truck. I'm sorry.

Libby says: If he's all right, I am too. I've not gotten to chat with you since you returned. I loved the video!

Aggie says: All his doing. I was clueless.

Libby says: Yes, well, you made him very happy. He hasn't quite touched ground yet.

Aggie says: I know exactly how he feels.

Libby says: I know he wanted to talk about dates with you...

Aggie says: Well, we both liked Saturday. What do you think?

Libby says: As in this Saturday, or as in the best day of the week?

Aggie says: This Saturday. We're already planning a birthday party for Tavish and Ellie, so it'd be convenient—everyone here already and everything.

Libby says: Are you teasing me?

Aggie says: Not at all. We both talked about it and that really was the date that suited both of us best.

Libby says: Well, it is a bit sudden, but you do make a good argument about the party.

Aggie says: Yeah. No wait, no fuss, no time to get nervous...

Aggie says: Unfortunately, we also thought maybe it wasn't fair to the children to preempt their day with ours.

Libby says: And then picked another day, right?

Aggie says: Yes.

Libby says: I'm starting to wonder if pushing you two together was such a great idea.

Aggie says: Pushing?

Libby says: You've had at least a dozen matchmakers doing their part to ensure that you and Luke marry. Surely you know this.

Aggie says: Actually, no. I'm relieved that I didn't. I might have resisted.

Libby says: Which is why we were careful not to be too obvious.

Libby says: Aggie? You're very quiet.

Aggie says: Do you think...

Aggie says: Never mind. Oh, and regarding dates, we settled on

March 7th.

Libby says: I'd rather mind it if you please. Are you truly upset that we tried to give you both opportunities to discover each other?

Libby says: My, that sounds so… geographical. You know what I mean.

Aggie says: Not upset, really. I just wondered if maybe it wasn't quite real if it was orchestrated somehow. Then I felt stupid. Making it possible to be together to get to know each other isn't the same as making up stuff to make it fake.

Libby says: Oh, it's Luke. BRB

Aggie says: Have him tell you about my wedding idea. I really want you to be honest if you think it's something that will offend people or not. I don't want to do that.

Libby says: Sorry. I didn't see that. Let me call him. BRB again.

Aggie says: That's ok. I'm just here making party lists

Aggie says: Isn't there some other kind of "fancy" food I can feed people besides crab cakes? I don't know how to make them and I am not paying for a caterer.

Aggie says: And where do I get gold balloons???

Aggie says: Oh, it's not that hard after all. I can get a bag of 100 from a place on Amazon. That'll work.

Aggie says: *theme from Jeopardy plays*

Aggie says: Maybe it was a bad idea to give the job of explaining to the guy who takes a week to say what most can in a minute.

Aggie says: How many Lukes does it take to make my heart flutter?

Aggie says: None! But it doesn't take a Lucas any trouble at all!

Aggie says: A Luke, an Aggie, and a Cari walk into a bar. What does each one say?

Aggie says: Answer—Luke says, "What's a nice girl like you doing in a place like this?" Aggie says, "What's a nice guy like you doing bringing me to a place like this?" Cari says, "Ouch! That huwt!"

Aggie says: Hey, Luke signed on! Where are you? Did you faint? Are you not speaking to me? Come baaaaaaaaaaaaaacccccccckkkk!!!

Libby added Luke to the conversation:

Luke says: Mom was reading me the conversation and cracking up so hard that I couldn't understand her. I thought maybe I could see, but it's not in here.

Aggie says: I'll copy and paste to email. I was amusing myself.

Libby says: I love your wedding/reception idea. It's perfect.

Aggie says: Really? You're not just saying that?

Libby says: Not at all. I like that you're taking the vows part of your day very seriously.

Libby says: Now that I know my son is alive and that my new daughter-to-be is happy, I'm going to scoot off to bed. Goodnight!

Luke says: Goodnight, Mom.

Libby has signed out of the conversation.

Aggie says: Goodnight almost Mom!

Luke says: I forgot to ask what I could do to help with this party.

Aggie says: I don't know what we're doing myself. It's crazy. Why did I agree to this?

Mibs says: There. That's better.

Luke says: That is one of my favorite things to see. The first time you did that was the first time I had any hope at all.

Mibs says: Every time you said, "Aw, Mibs," I think I fell just a little in love with you and didn't even know it.

Luke says: I'll remember to say it often.

Mibs says: I think whenever I need to keep my thoughts to myself, I'm going to have to go upstairs with the laptop and make you stay downstairs to talk to me.

Luke says: I'm starting to be able to "read" your writing too. Resistance is futile.

Mibs says: Then maybe I should say goodnight before I get myself into trouble.

Luke says: Good night, Mibs.

Aggie says: 'Night.

Luke says: I love you.

Aggie says: Love you more.

Aggie has signed out of the conversation.

Chapter 4

GOLDEN MISHAPS

Tuesday, December 9th

"Can't believe that the Merchamps have a birthday on the same day we're throwing the kids a surprise party," Aggie muttered, sliding on a slick patch on the walkway to the guilty family's house. "Also can't believe I let them talk me into a Tuesday. It's not like they knew we'd joked about adding a wedding to it!"

A row of snowmen decorated the front of the house, hinting at a contest. Aggie hoped the one with the saucy grin and cockeyed hat won. Before she reached the door, Ellie and Tavish burst from the house, waving at their friends, and raced for the van. Tara Merchamp shook her head and closed the door behind her, shivering against a blast of wind that swirled around the corner of the house.

"Kids are funny, aren't they?"

Aggie, already turning to follow her charges, nodded her agreement. "Sorry about that. I—"

"Oh, no! I wasn't trying to hint anything. Just a minute ago they were complaining that you'd be here any minute and then when you arrive, they fly out the door as if they can't wait to leave." Tara shrugged. "I just think kids are too funny for words."

"Oh, they're something all right." She tried to shuffle back down the path, but the woman kept talking. "Ellie and Sarah won the snowman contest with that one—" Tara pointed to the one Aggie had liked. "They won hot chocolate kits. I hope that's ok?"

No matter how obvious Aggie was in inching away from the chatterbox masquerading as her children's friend's mother, the woman kept talking. Desperate, she leaned forward and whispered,

53

"There's a surprise party for the kids just waiting at our house. I need to get them there before the people jump out and scream, 'Surprise!' at the mail lady or something."

"Oh, that's great! I was ..."

The rest of Tara's words were lost in a buzz that made her feel as if she had a bee hive nestled in her brain. Waving, she hurried down the sidewalk, slipped on the same icy patch, and clutched at the picket fence for balance. "Thanks!"

"Are you—"

With another wave flung into the air with wild abandon, she rounded the front of the van, opened the door, and climbed inside. "I thought I'd never get away. It's too cold out there to sit around listening to the nuances of snowman competitions—congratulations, by the way. Well done, Ellie."

"I think Tavish had the best idea, but he was paired with Braydon and—"

"When we get home, I need you guys to get your junk put away downstairs. You left a mess down there this morning."

"But Cari—"

Aggie frowned to see Ellie nudge her brother in the rearview mirror. That was odd. "I don't care who, what, when. Just do it."

"Surprise!" Ellie and Tavish whirled and shouted with the rest of the room.

A flash somewhere froze the moment for future enjoyment as aunt and children screamed in unison. Aggie's eyes rose to see the banner hung over the fireplace. "Congratulations Aunt Aggie and Soon-to-be-Uncle Luke."

Her eyes roamed the room, looking for her fiancé to see if he knew anything about the sign—and the wave of well-wishers. Vannie beamed and cried, "It worked! We did it!"

Laird frowned. "Where's Luke?"

Just as he spoke, Luke pushed through the door, carrying a caterer's box from a place in Brunswick. "Aw, I missed it! Surprise..." His eyes absorbed the words in the banner and his forehead scrunched up. "What—"

"We got you to help us pull off your own surprise engagement party," Ellie explained.

Music filled the room as people came forward to congratulate the couple, killing the other questions in Aggie's and Luke's minds. As she glanced around the room, she saw Libby, most of the people from church, and then in the corner of the couch, her mother. "These were some thorough kids," she muttered to Luke.

"Oh, speaking of which, I've got the crab cakes. I better go put them wherever they've spread the food. They have to be put in a chafing dish, but Mom said she'd bring one."

While Luke hurried to find the necessary dish, Aggie smiled to herself and went to hug Vannie. She'd managed to find an incredible man. How had that happened?

A hand beckoned her from near her mother, but it was too masculine to belong to Martha Milliken. She'd recognize that wedding band anywhere. Aggie wove through the guests, smiling and accepting congratulations and arrived, after traversing the whole of eight feet, three minutes later. "I can't believe you're here!"

"We couldn't miss your engagement party!" Ron Milliken hugged his daughter before shifting to one side to allow her to sit and talk to her mother.

No sooner had she seated herself when Vannie rushed to her side. "You've got to come play games!"

"But Grandma just got here."

"Grandma's been here for half an hour. You just got here."

Her protests were futile. Vannie dragged her from the couch to the wall by the library door. "Ok, we're going to pin the bouquet on the bride!"

Hanging on the walls were two long silhouettes of a bride. Luke and Aggie were blindfolded and spun in circles. At the rate and number of spins that Cari gave Luke, he stumbled about like a drunken sailor for several seconds before trying to tape his paper flower bouquet onto Aggie's shoulder. "Not me, the wall!" she cried.

They stood back from the wall and waited to get their blindfolds removed. "Hey, Luke. Wanna take bets on who was closest?"

Luke laughed. "I say you."

"That's not much of a bet. I say me too."

"Ok, how about bets on inches from the mark?" Luke frowned.

"I say six."

"I say twelve."

"You're on."

Ellie giggled as she pulled the blindfold from Luke's eyes. His blue bouquet was perfectly situated on the bride's head—on Aggie's side of the room. Aggie's pink one was nearly perched on the bride's shoulder. "HA! I win!" Doing a victory dance, Aggie grabbed Tina's arm and Tavish's hand and shoved them forward. "Your turn."

By a strange turn of events, only one person managed to pin the bouquet into the silhouette's hands—William. His face flushed, but he accepted the wrapped box prize graciously. Kenzie found him in the corner, toying with the bow.

"It's hot chocolate—lots of flavors."

"That'll be good."

The child wrinkled her nose. "No it won't. You can't stir with a candy cane if the flavors are funny."

"Good point," William agreed, "but since I don't have any candy canes, I think it'll work."

As he watched his little friend, her first teeth missing just in time for singing about them at Christmas, he saw her mouth droop as she leaned her head on his arm. "What's wrong, Kenzie? Aren't you feeling well?"

"Yeah."

"You look like you lost a friend."

Kenzie's lip quivered and she whispered. "I lost the daddy I wanted."

"The daddy you wanted?"

Several seconds passed before Kenzie responded at all. She stood, removed the box from William's hand, and set it on the table behind him. Then, as if something she did every day, she climbed up into his lap, wrapped her arms around his neck, and whispered into his ear, "I love Luke—Uncle Luke, I guess—but I wanted you to be my uncle-daddy."

William's throat constricted as he squeezed the little girl. "I would have been proud to be your uncle-daddy, but I didn't want to marry Aggie, sweetheart. We wouldn't have been happy, and it would have made Aggie and Luke unhappy. You wouldn't like that, would you?"

"You all could have learned to be happy. Luke could have

married Aunt Tina."

"I think," he whispered, trying to word his answer as simply and carefully as possible, "most people don't want to have to try to be happy from the beginning. God knows what He's doing, Kenzie. He knows."

"That's true. I think it's time for the breath contest. I want to win that."

"Breath contest?"

Kenzie grinned. "Yep. Come on. You play too."

Laird called the room to order once more, blissfully ignorant of the frustrated expressions on the partiers faces. "Ok, the bride is supposed to take 'our breath away,' so this game is simple. Hold your breath!"

Luke and Aggie exchanged pained glances before Aggie turned to Libby and mouthed, "What on earth?"

Libby scooted around a couple of guests and whispered, "They really thought everyone would want to play games 'like a shower,' so they worked hard on these. I think everyone understands," into Aggie's ear.

Most of the room made a big show of puffing out their cheeks, holding their breath for about ten seconds, and then exhaling in a gush of air. The prior conversations continued as if uninterrupted, but Aggie and Luke played along with the rest of the children. Twenty-one, twenty-two, Aggie exhaled, gasping for air. "I'm lousy!" Luke only made it a few more seconds before he slowly released the air in his lungs and took a deep breath. "I'm not much better."

Tavish beat all of the children but Cari. The little girl turned a revolting shade of puce as she refused to give in until Tavish did. Aggie tried to insist that she give up, but the girl shook her head, staggering a bit with the movement. Desperate, Aggie whispered for Tavish to stop, and he did, gasping for breath as he leaned his hands on his knees, but Cari didn't give in.

"You won, Cari!"

The little girl's face screwed up in protest and then the child collapsed at their feet. Aggie's eyes went wide, and she reached for Cari. "She fainted! You can really do that? Hold your breath until you pass out?"

"Toddlers have been doing it for centuries," Mrs. Dyke said. "I'm surprised that one hasn't done it before."

Cari stirred, one hand reaching for her head. "My head huwts. Did I win?"

"Yes, you silly girl! You scared me!" Aggie's panicked voice brought a smile to the little girl's face.

"Yay! I won! I get the balloons!"

Sure enough, Vannie arrived and tied a huge bouquet of balloons to Cari's wrist. "I should spank you instead of giving you these."

"The rules said the one who went the longest, Vannie. Next time we'll add a pass out disqualification."

Cari sat up swiftly, swaying, and with one hand to her head. "That's not faiw!"

Libby announced that the food was ready, giving Aggie time to take Cari upstairs to get a little Tylenol and lay down with an ice pack for a few minutes. While the guests munched on crab cakes and bruschetta, Aggie sat beside her youngest niece, brushing wisps of hair off the girl's forehead and trying to get her to relax long enough for the medication to work.

A shadow filled the doorway. "Are you ladies hungry?"

"Did you bring cwab cakes? Vannie said you brought some after all."

"I did." Luke passed the plate to Cari, curious to see what she thought of the food.

"I don't get any cake? I didn't mean to be bad, but I'm vewy good at it. Laiwd said so. He said it's my talent."

"That's not true, Cari. Your talent is in inventing things," Aggie insisted. To Luke, she whispered, "Even if it's just trouble for right now."

"I like that. I want to be an inventor."

Cari's switch from substituting Ws for Ls and Rs told Aggie that the child would be fine. "I think you can come back down to the party if you want."

The girl jumped from her bed, ice pack flying off in the process, and raced for the door. Luke's words stopped her cold. "I thought you wanted crab cakes."

"I do!"

He passed her the golden plastic plate. "That's a crab cake, right there."

"But there's no frosting."

58

"No... most people don't like frosting on crab cakes," Aggie choked.

The little girl took a big bite of her "cake" and spat it onto the plate. "That's awful! I think Luke should ask for his money back. That is a nasty, nasty cake. I don't think we should serve that cake at your wedding. No way. I'm going downstairs for good cake."

Luke and Aggie exchanged amused glances. "Well," Aggie said. "I guess we know what not to serve at her wedding."

"Bet you she loves them by then and wants them on the menu. Can you imagine the toast we could give?"

"I'm terrified at the thought of Cari married."

"Well," Luke said, taking her hand and leading her from the room, "if your mother can be trusted, you weren't very different than Cari at that age—worse she says because of her heart condition. She wasn't very good at discipline she tells me. Something about throwing a handful of Jell-O at your Aunt Agatha because she didn't serve you enough..."

"You are not allowed to talk to my mother until after the wedding."

"Why's that?"

"I don't want her giving you any ideas about revoking your proposal."

"Aw, Mibs. Not possible."

Since she'd never seen them kiss, Vannie concocted the perfect game to ensure the whole party could enjoy it. Much to the boys' disgust, while the guests enjoyed their food, she hung mistletoe on about thirty hooks she'd prepped all around the living room. Aggie watched, nervous, but decided to wait before protesting. Once most of the guests no longer held plates, Vannie went into action.

"Ok, can the men help me push the furniture back?"

The improvisation of Mother May I under the mistletoe made no sense until the group saw how Vannie ordered couples to navigate the floor until they were beneath the mistletoe. Aggie's mouth went dry at the thought of it, and Luke excused himself to speak to Ron. Seconds later, he hurried back to his place in line and challenged Vannie with a gleam in his eye.

Sure enough, Vannie called for him to take four giant side steps which put him directly under mistletoe. Three more people went, Mr. Vaughn kissing his wife and they were excused from the game. A fumble nearly sent William kissing Aggie, but he adjusted his steps to be one step behind her and to her right.

Luke's turn. Vannie called out his orders, and giggled as he bumped William from his spot. "Sorry, man."

"Sure, you are."

Standing next to Aggie and beneath the mistletoe, he turned and called out to Martha, "Mother, may I?"

"Yes you may!"

Aggie's eyes grew wider as Luke bent to kiss her. Panicked, she was ready to cry and run, but couldn't. Why would he do— His lips touched her cheek. "Gotta trust me, Mibs."

The room cheered, but Vannie's face fell. Eager to get out of the game, Aggie missed it but led Luke to the window where they watched the rest of the game, giggling when Laird had to kiss Ellie and William kissed Kenzie. The little girl walked around, hand on her cheek for the duration of the game, but Vannie seemed unwilling to send Tina and Tavish to the same mistletoe.

After a couple of awkward steps, Aggie realized the problem. She tiptoed to Vannie's side and whispered something. The girl, visible relief on her face, giggled and nodded. Aggie stopped next to Ellie, whispered something, and then moved to William's side. He seemed to hesitate until his eyes caught Tina's over the heads in the room.

With two more players on the board, the game ended swiftly. Tavish, already beneath a sprig of mistletoe, was ordered to take one step forward and one back. Tina was ordered to take two steps to her left and one step back. William gave Vannie the romance she'd tried to create—but a little more chaste than she'd imagined. His lips met Tina's for a second—and maybe a half, before he spun her and led her from the floor. Tavish's face was beet red when Ellie stepped one to the right, kissed her brother's forehead, and sent him from the room.

The room erupted in applause. Luke and William, along with a couple of the other men, moved furniture back in place, while Aggie pulled Vannie into the mudroom. "Is something wrong, Vannie?"

"I thought it'd be fun, but—"

"But you forgot that you were forcing people to be publicly affectionate?"

"I just thought engaged couples should kiss at their party, and I knew without something to encourage you—"

"We'll talk about it later, but if you have any more of these kinds of games planned, you need to plan for something else."

"Did you see Deputy William kiss Aunt Tina—really kiss her—sorta?"

"Yep."

"Did you know he'd do that?"

"I suspected he might, but I told him her cheek or hand was sufficient."

Aggie was halfway down the hall before Vannie's voice reached her. "I'm sorry, Aunt Aggie."

She turned, smiling at her niece. "I didn't thank you for a wonderful surprise and a beautiful party. It was thoughtful—special. I'll cherish the memory of every minute of it for the rest of my life."

"Even the mistletoe game?"

Unaware that Luke stood behind her, grinning—eager for her reply—Aggie sighed and gave Vannie the most satisfactory mush factor possible. "Especially the mistletoe game—now."

"Glad to hear that." Luke's voice almost tickled her ear it was so close. "Very glad to hear it."

Vannie crept toward the kitchen, avoiding the hallway where Luke and Aggie stood whispering things that the girl could not hear but knew were delightfully mushy—just enough to satisfy the budding romantic.

The toddler in the pack 'n' play was much too large to be the baby she'd hyped up on caffeine a mere ten months ago. When he'd curled up against the corner, he'd looked properly sweet and infantile, but once he'd relaxed, his limbs spread out over the little playpen, making Aggie wonder if it was a little too small now. Regardless, with arms flung wide and legs in strangely contorted shapes, he looked much too old to be her tiny little man.

She twisted, trying to pop her back after a grueling hour of trying to settle Ian down. He'd fought sleep harder than ever before—a testament to his exhaustion if Libby and her mother were to be believed. How an exhausted child could be so wound up was beyond her. Those words had earned her an ineffectively stifled giggle—from nearly everyone in earshot.

Determined not to make Luke wait any longer, Aggie hurried from her room and down the stairs. She'd have to remember to be quiet when she went to bed or she'd have a bed hog for the night. As she neared Vannie's door, she overheard her niece talking to someone.

"—don't understand why it's wrong to kiss your fiancé."

"It isn't—usually. It's just that your aunt made a vow that she wouldn't, and vows are serious things. You can't break them."

"Why did she do that?"

"You'd have to ask her about it."

"Don't you wish she hadn't?"

Luke's confident, "No," was reassuring. "I have a privilege not many men get. I will know that my wife has only shown that kind of affection for me. No one else."

"Hmm... I wonder..."

A small smile began and grew into a grin as Aggie listened to one of Luke's familiar silences. "I believe that your grandpa made the right decision for Aggie, but I see the gears turning in your mind, Vannie. Just know that if you try to make some kind of similar vow, the day I know of it and have the authority to do it, I'll revoke it. The Bible gives fathers and husbands that right."

"We studied about that in Sunday School." The bed creaked when Vannie sat up in it. The sound was so familiar to Aggie that it shot an ache into her heart. She'd sat up just the same way when talking to her father in that same bed years ago. If she knew Luke, he'd be leaning over the end, his forearms resting on the wrought iron. Her head barely peeked around the corner long enough to verify her suspicion. Yep. Standing there just as she expected.

"Save your vows for your wedding day. Plan to save your affection for your husband if you like, but don't make vows like that. It isn't right, Vannie. We need to do what Jesus said and not vow or swear anything—just say yes or no as the occasion warrants. We don't know what life brings."

"Did Grandpa say you could kiss Aunt Aggie's cheek like that?" Vannie giggled. "I know Grandma did, but..."

"He said it was ok. Any kiss I'd give my mother or sisters—if it didn't involve her lips—was ok. He was sticking to what Aggie meant—no lip lock before the preacher says she's a wife."

"Lip lock." She giggled again. "Older people have the silliest terms for things."

Silence again. At last, Luke said, "Are you ok with it all now, Vannie? Do you understand?"

"Yeah... I think so. I just think it'd be cool to make a vow like that. It'd protect me from being stupid someday and—"

"It'd make you feel good to do something self-sacrificing for the Lord," Luke interjected uncharacteristically.

"Well, yeah. I mean, He died for me, the least—"

"—you could do is worry less about the glory of being so spiritual as to make such a self-sacrificing vow and simply obey His Word to put aside vows and swearing like that. This is about getting glory for Vannie, not honoring the Lord."

Behind the wall, Aggie swallowed hard. Luke's words struck at the heart of the lesson her father had tried to teach her. Even knowing that she'd been foolish, there had always been a little bit of pride in her choice. She had made the ultimate teenage sacrifice to bring honor to... herself. It was such a letdown.

Vannie finally spoke once more. "You're right. I didn't want to admit it, but you're right. I wanted to be able to tell some guy that I had made a vow never to kiss anyone but my husband. It sounded spiritual in my mind. It sounds so silly now."

Luke's answer was swifter than anything Aggie had ever heard. "Vannie, don't let your lack of vow cloud your judgment. You are right to save your affection for the man who will be your husband. Not kissing every boy you think is the one is a good decision—it just doesn't need to be a vow for you to make a good decision, understand?"

"Self-control and discernment again."

Luke's chuckle sent flip-flops into Aggie's stomach. "Aggie has been making you think about things lately, eh? I remember my mother doing the same thing."

"Luke?"

"Hmm?"

The bed squeaked again. Knowing she'd see her not-so-little niece flinging her arms around her soon-to-be uncle's neck, Aggie peeked around the corner again. Her eyes caught the picture just as Vannie said, "I am so glad you're going to be our uncle."

Aggie hurried downstairs and into the kitchen. She heard Luke follow a minute later but was surprised to hear the front door open and close behind him. He wasn't going to say goodbye? Had she said or done something? When the engine didn't start, she stopped the unnecessary introspection and went back to unloading the dishwasher.

Luke opened the door, shutting it quietly behind him. He shivered and rushed back upstairs two at a time. In Tavish's room, he paused and sighed. His shoulders slumped as he placed the present on the nightstand and adjusted the covers. He was too late. Tavish, exhausted by the evening's festivities, was in deep slumber.

In Ellie and Kenzie's room, Luke listened for the rhythmic sounds of little girls sleeping in unison. Kenzie had been brought up by William long before the party ended. The memory brought a smile to his face. Their deputy friend had a decided soft spot for their little gap-toothed Kenzie.

Ellie, on the other hand, was stiff, her breathing coming in ragged bursts. "Ellie?"

The child's head whipped around. "Luke?" Before he could answer, Ellie flung herself from the bed into his arms, soaking the front of his shirt with silent tears.

"Shh… what's wrong, sweetheart?"

"I—" Ellie choked back a sob, her head turning to see that she hadn't woken Kenzie, and then buried her head into his chest again. "It's silly. I—"

"How about you open your birthday present and then tell me about it. I've been waiting to see you open this for days now."

As she pulled the paper from it, Ellie confessed, "I thought everyone forgot us." Her voice dropped to a whisper. "Is that selfish?"

"I think it's reasonable to be disappointed if a special birthday seems to be forgotten by people who usually remember it."

Her face brightened visibly—even in the dim light from the hallway and the moon. "I don't feel bad anymore. Why is that?"

"I think you were feeling guilty for being disappointed. That guilt is gone, and relief from guilt is a wonderful thing." Luke nodded at the present. "Come on, get it out of the box." His eagerness was contagious.

Ellie flipped the lid and her smile was all that he'd hoped it would be. "Oh, I've wanted to try pastels! This is on how to draw from photographs. Look at the brushes and..."

With each exclamation, her voice rose until Luke stifled a laugh and put his finger to his lips. "Shh! You'll wake up, Kenzie."

He gave her a hug, whispered, "Happy Birthday, Elspeth," and turned to leave.

"Luke?" The whisper belonged on a stage.

"Hmm?"

"This was my best birthday ever."

Luke says: Ok, I'm home.

Mibs says: Took you long enough.

Luke says: I knew you were trying to get rid of me.

Mibs says: Yeah, right. Um, we forgot to open our presents.

Luke says: We can open them later. I was a bit preoccupied with something else.

Mibs says: Would that be me or my children?

Luke says: She flirts!

Mibs says: Goodnight.

Luke says: Aw, come on, Mibs.

Mibs says: No fair.

Luke says: No fair what?

Mibs says: Saying, "Aw..." I can hear it. You kill me.

Luke says: I'll remember that for later.

Mibs says: Oops.

Luke says: Oh, before I forget, you might want to talk to Vannie about your venture into the world of vows.

Mibs says: I heard.

Luke says: She was still bothered, huh? I'm sorry. I thought she was ok with it after our discussion.

Mibs says: No, I mean, I actually heard. I was in the hall. You did great.

Luke says: You heard.

Mibs says: You're silent. Are you upset that I listened?

Mibs says: Oh, Luuukkkeeey. Lucas!

Luke says: Sorry. I just tried to remember everything I said. I knew I had to try to prevent her from romanticizing the idea of vows.

Mibs says: I wish someone had been around to explain all that when I was younger. Dad tried, but he didn't make it as clear as you did.

Luke says: I wasn't criticizing you—just trying to prevent something I sensed in Vannie.

Mibs says: But you nailed me. I think that's why Dad didn't let me out of it. He knew all that but didn't know how to get it through to me.

Luke says: Well, I didn't mean for you to feel rebuked. Besides, we have a bigger problem.

Mibs says: What?

Luke says: I didn't say anything when I was there because I didn't want you to feel like you had to try to make up for it yet, but Ellie and Tavish had a special birthday today—one that none of us remembered.

Mibs says: None but you. I knew it was a bad idea to do this ON their birthday instead of Saturday like we'd planned.

Luke says: The kids went all out, didn't they? I mean, they really had us going.

Mibs says: Sure did. I almost didn't agree to the mid-week party. Seemed like a crazy thing to do.

Mibs says: So, what about tomorrow?

Luke says: I was thinking maybe a birthday breakfast tomorrow? Have all the awful things that are not good for you? Turn the tree decorating party into a birthday bash?

Mibs says: My children are blessed in ways they have no idea. Let's do it.

Luke says: Goodnight then. I'll be there in about four hours.

Mibs says: Four hours!

Luke says: Um, yeah! It's almost one o'clock and you know as well as I do that Tavish'll be up by six or six-thirty.

Mibs says: Since when does he get up at six?

Luke says: Nearly every day…
Mibs says: Why?
Luke says: My guess: he likes the quiet.
Mibs says: Yeah… I know how he feels. I just prefer to enjoy mine in bed.
Luke says: Speaking of which, we both need to be there. I'll bring… something.
Luke says: G'night, Mibs.
Mibs says: Before you go…
Luke says: Yeah?
Mibs says: I know I'm feeling sorry for myself, but I can't help wondering…
Luke says: Wondering what?
Mibs says: Will I ever quit forgetting the kids' birthdays?
Luke says: LOL. Yep… my guess is anytime in the next year or two, they'll learn that they have to be your memory in that department.
Mibs says: I'm yawning. I think you're right. Night, Luke.
Luke says: Hey, Mibs
Mibs says: Yeah?
Luke says: Thought you should know, I love you.
Luke has left the conversation

Aggie stared at the screen. "That stinker."

Chapter 5

MERRY BIRTHDAY

Wednesday, December 10th

A pair of blue eyes opened and then blinked as the sun blinded them. His head rose, and he smelled something. A smile. Flopping his head back on his pillow, Tavish inhaled deeply. Cinnamon.

He rolled to climb out of bed and saw a box wrapped in blue paper with gold balloon stickers all over it. Had Aunt Aggie— Without waiting to see, Tavish grabbed the box and tore open the wrappings. He was just about to cry out in excitement when his eyes slid toward Ian's crib. Guilty.

The little bump of blankets in the crib didn't move; there wasn't even a hint of a rise and fall of breathing. Just when Tavish grew nervous, he grinned again and turned his attention back to the telegraph kit. Ian was sleeping in Aunt Aggie's room. They'd wanted him to sleep as long as possible.

A quiet knock startled him. The lid of the box skittered off his knees and onto the floor, but Tavish hardly noticed. "Luke!"

"Happy Birthday, man!"

"That was yesterday!"

"We're celebrating as if it's next year already and your birthday falls on a Wednesday. Now, are you going to stay in bed all day, or do you want some amazing cinnamon rolls."

Tavish snickered. "Amazing? Have you had Aunt Aggie's rolls?"

"No..."

"Well... they're not rocks, exactly, but..."

"Good thing my mom sent these over then, eh?"

Before Luke finished speaking, Tavish jumped from the bed and dashed out the door, the kit abandoned. Downstairs, the decorations were all gone. In their place, balloons were clustered anywhere they'd work—as a centerpiece on the table, a "bouquet" in the corner, and tied to Ellie and Tavish's chairs at the table.

The big bay window in the dining room had been emptied and now looked odd. "Where are the pillows and the table and stuff?"

"We're going to put the Christmas tree there."

Luke's voice at his shoulder made Tavish jump. "How do you do that?"

"Do what?"

"Sneak up on people like that. I try, but they always know I'm coming."

A shrug was Luke's initial reply. After several seconds he added, "Perhaps the difference is that I don't try to do it."

"Stop!"

Luke slammed on the brakes as Aggie glared at Tavish in the rearview mirror. "This had better be good..."

"Sammie's out!"

Luke and Aggie exchanged frustrated glances before he threw the van into reverse and backed it into the drive again. "Ok, everyone out. Try not to get filthy—aaand they're gone."

"Never say out until after the instructions are complete. Trust me on this."

"Now he tells me," she muttered as Luke jumped out of the van, calling for the children to stop chasing the dogs.

Ian babbled happily in his seat while Aggie watched the melee with a mixture of irritation and amusement. The kids were going to be frozen and likely a mess. Miner dashed into the street and spun around in a frenzy, chasing his tail. Three children raced into the street without even a glance to see if anyone might have decided to use it as a thoroughfare to their homes.

"Ian, that dog will—wait! Is that Kenzie's snow boot?" Aggie rolled down the window and shouted, "Drop it, Sammie!"

The dog obediently dropped the half-chewed boot and bounded

to join her brother. Luke strolled past with an apologetic expression on his face. Children flew past him on their way to capture their escape artist pooches. She didn't hear what he said, but disappointed faces turned toward the van and soon it filled with chattering Stuarts. Without half a dozen playmates making the chase into a game, Sammie and Miner followed Luke into the back yard.

"Was that your snow boot, Kenzie?"

"Yeah, I wondered where it went."

"How did the dog get it in the first place? I can't imagine that you took it off while you were playing outside."

The answer was written across the child's guilty face. "Well, it was cold, but I wanted to pet the dogs, so I closed the door to the house and let them come in the mudroom. One of them must have taken it with them when they went back to their pen."

"And you didn't happen to mention that you couldn't find your snow boot, why?"

The girl's face nearly glowed red. "Well, I kind of wondered and thought I'd get in trouble. I hoped the other one would get too small first."

"Kenzie…"

Luke pulled himself into the van again and put the vehicle in gear. "Well, we're going to need a new section of fence. Sammie has managed to dig under the buried wire."

"She's smart," Tavish observed with pride that is usually shown by doting fathers.

"She's a nuisance." At the crestfallen look on the boy's face, Aggie added begrudgingly, "But she's a smart nuisance."

"Can we get a tree now?"

"Yes, Lorna. I think getting a tree now would be a great way to forget this mess."

"Happy birthday to EllieandTavish, happy birthday to—" Lorna glanced around her. "Come on! We should sing! Happy birthday to…"

Once they turned onto the highway, Aggie glanced back at the forlorn looking puppies sitting alone in their pen. Somehow, the affection she'd once felt for the animals was gone. Then, in a move that seemed designed to garner all the sympathy possible, Sammie laid her head on Miner's as if to comfort him. "Dratted dogs."

"Did you say something, Mibs?"

71

"Nothing worth repeating," she muttered.

Squeals pierced the air as the family traipsed indoors with the first live tree of the Stuart-Milliken household. Vannie and Laird thundered down the basement steps without even removing their coats, eager to find the lights and ornaments. By the time Aggie hung up her own coat and disentangled Ian from his bundles, the floor was littered with parkas, mittens, and scarves.

"Hey, get over here and hang these things up. What's with you? Were you born in a barn?"

The joke usually caused good-natured protests, but this time Tavish turned and said, "What's wrong with that? Jesus was."

"Very funny, young man. Get it all put away. I'll make hot chocolate. Where's Tina?"

The answer was on the whiteboard on the fridge. Tina was out with William. "Well," she muttered to herself, "at least one of us can enjoy some time alone with a good guy."

"What?" Luke stood in the doorway.

"You heard me."

"Yep. I like it too. Thought you should know." With that, he disappeared again while Aggie continued to dump hot chocolate powder into mugs.

"The lights! They found the lights and the garland!"

"Yippie doodle," she muttered under her breath.

Aggie gripped the counter and took a deep breath. Whatever was causing the sarcasm and irritation had to end. There was no reason to ruin the day for everyone else. The tea kettle whistled and she poured the water, singing, *"Silent night... holy night... all is calm... all is bright..."*

Wrapping the tree became a comedy of errors. While Luke struggled to attach enough lights to satisfy the children, Aggie attempted to knock it over half a dozen times but succeeded only once. "What is wrong with this thing? It won't stay standing! I think we bought a bum stand."

"It is a bit wobb—oh, look." Luke pointed. "We've got the legs upside down."

"If we ever use another real tree again," she muttered as her face received a pine needle exfoliation process, "I suggest we buy that big round one that doesn't need assembly."

"Deal."

The lights shone beautifully even in the full sunlight. At night it would light the room! Aggie pointed to the boxes. "Those are the ornaments, right?"

"Yes, but we always put the new ones on first," Vannie explained.

"New ones?"

"The new ones we get each Christmas. Mommy always—never mind. Laird," she said turning to her brother, "why don't you pull out Ian—I mean Cari and Lorna's."

"Why not Ian?"

"Because he only has one," the girl hissed.

"But aren't we going to put the new ones up—"

"She didn't get them. That was Mommy's tradition. Just get the boxes," Vannie insisted, tears beginning to choke her.

"What did I miss?" Aggie stared at the group waiting for information, but no one seemed willing to speak. "Come on, something is wrong. What is it?"

"It's just something Mommy always did. We're so used to it that we forgot you might not know." Vannie handed an ornament to Cari. "Here, you put the first one on."

"What don't I know?"

Ellie stepped close and pulled Aggie close enough to whisper, "Mommy always bought us a new ornament to put on the tree every Christmas. We always did that first so…"

"I'll be right back." Seven faces stared back at her, Ian too absorbed in destroying ornament boxes to care. "Our tradition will just be to put the new ones on last. That'll save your mom's tradition for her while still continuing it. Meanwhile, rescue those boxes or the ornaments won't make it until next year."

Luke tried to stop her, but Aggie waved him off. She climbed into the van and took off down the road, unsure where to go first. Her fingers punched the button to call her mom and then she switched it to speaker. "Mom?"

"She's taking a nap. What's up?"

"Dad, I blew it. The kids expected new ornaments for the tree

73

today and I just didn't know so there they were all waiting and I had nothing. I don't even know what kind of ornaments to get or where to look. I am guessing balls in a box of twelve aren't going to cut it. I left without looking. How did Vannie get to be twelve years old without me ever going to their house for Christmas?"

"You did go—just before they moved into the mausoleum, remember? When they still lived in the nice little ranch in Westbury. You know, the one they lived in while she restored the Rockland house?"

"Vaguely. Why didn't she invite us to the big house?"

"Because of Geraldine. The woman was a nightmare and away from there was safer."

That felt familiar anyway. Aggie sighed. "That doesn't tell me about ornaments."

"Sorry. Can't help you and I bet Mom can't either. Well, maybe that's not true," he amended. "I think we might have Christmas cards or pictures here. Want me to look?"

The mental picture of her father weeping over memories of Christmases past was too much for her. "Oh, I'll just call Luke and see what he's finding in the boxes. That'll help. I should go."

"You're doing great, Aggie. That you even try is important to those kids."

It didn't feel as though she was doing adequately much less "great." However, there was no time for pity parties. Bedtime was soon enough to allow herself to dissolve into a fit or two of tears. Perhaps a nice shower before bed. It was a safe place to cry with the noise drowning out her sobs and the water hiding all traces of them.

"Luke, have you seen the ornaments yet?"

"The ones you're getting?"

"Of course not. Come on, this isn't funny. I've got kids who expect a lousy Christmas as it is. Get me some help here."

"What kind of help?"

"What do the ornaments look like?"

His confusion seemed to have culminated in an echo. "Look like?"

"Yes! Are they plastic? Metal? Glass? What about themes? Elegant? Cute? Country? Traditional? Can you zip me some pictures? Get someone to tell you about theirs."

A few pictures arrived while Luke talked to Ellie and Vannie about theirs and what made them special. She heard the door shut and the wind outside and realized this had to be serious. "Um, Mibs?"

"Just tell me."

"They're special to the year. There's the baby's first Christmas ones. Those are pretty self-explanatory. There are ones that look like a favorite book that year or a hobby. From the way they describe it, Allie found things that fit an interest of each year and then scoured places for the right one until she found it."

The moment he spoke, she remembered one shopping trip where Allie had found a miniature Mother Goose book of nursery rhymes and decided to make it into Kenzie's Christmas ornament that year. "Oh yeah. I remember. This is not going to be easy."

"Come back. They understand. Really."

"They do, but I don't. I've got to try."

Aggie dragged herself up the steps, dreading the onslaught of excited children. She'd disappoint them. Again. When the door didn't burst open, she frowned. Did they know she wouldn't find the right ones? Surely not.

It's not like I didn't try, she defended inwardly. *I did. I went to every store in Brunswick—practically.* It was no use. Despite her best efforts she'd failed. Maybe she could make it to Rockland the next day and try the Christmas store in the mall.

The soft sounds of violins playing *Away in a Manger* greeted her—but seconds later, she heard Luke's quiet voice reading Luke chapter two. "…but Mary treasured all these things, pondering them in her heart…"

A lump swelled in her throat. She was not like another Mary that day—no, Martha had somehow possessed her until all she could do was run to and fro, busy with things that did not truly matter. Luke had the right emphasis. He knew what was important and what wasn't.

The picture was almost surreal, as if out of a movie set. The music could not have played a more perfect song, and the children seated around his chair, hanging over the back, starry-eyed and looking particularly innocent and charming in their pajamas—it was almost as if Christmas Eve had arrived two weeks early.

"Aunt Aggie!" Kenzie rushed her, flinging arms around her. "Did you find them? Where are the ornaments?"

"I'm sorry, I didn't. I'll have to try tomorrow. I'm so sorry."

The children all said the right things. It didn't matter; they were happy; it was a great birthday for Ellie and Tavish and that's what mattered. However, their faces told the true story. They were disappointed. She'd have to try again.

Tina breezed in the door and surveyed the family. "What is everyone doing up this late. Scurry off to bed. Go. I'll be up to tuck you in—"

She never had the chance to finish. Vannie fled upstairs, tears flooding her eyes and cheeks. Ellie followed. Laird, shook his head and choked out, "Girls," before he too pounded up the stairs. Tavish shrugged and grabbed Kenzie's hand as the girl picked up on the wave of emotion that seemed to flow over everyone. Cari and Lorna exchanged glances and their subsequent wails were loud enough to stir Ian who had been sleeping on Luke's chest.

Aggie sat on the arm of the couch and closed her eyes, begging the Lord for patience and wisdom—not to mention a healthy dose of self-control. Her own emotions were nearly ready to choke her to death. Tina glanced around once more and went into action. "I've got this."

As Luke soothed the baby back to sleep, he stood. His hand squeezed her shoulder in passing. "It'll be ok," he whispered.

His feet disappeared up the stairs at precisely the moment she realized that she hated that phrase. People said everything would be ok, but it never was. Never. Every time some old problem was resolved, a new one arose. Her life was one series of crises and solutions to slide her into a new crisis.

She hadn't moved by the time Luke crept back down the stairs. From the look on his face she was certain that he'd soothed a few wounded hearts as well. *Epic fail, Aggie.*

"Are they going to forgive me—really?"

Luke gathered her into his arms and held her, his cheek resting atop her head. "This isn't about the ornaments. You know that, don't you?"

"What is it about then?" She didn't believe him, but anything

76

sounded better than another failure on her part.

"It's about missing their parents. It was a familiar memory — one they really remember well, and so it all blew out of proportion."

"Great, and I took off to take care of the thing that wasn't the thing instead of being here for them."

His arms tightened around her. "You're determined to be the bad, bad Aunt Aggie. Is it possible that you're hurting today?"

"Of course, I'm hurting! I failed my kids!"

"No, you didn't. You gave them a wonderful day. Had you remembered the ornaments, the tears still would have been there, but instead you would be hurt because they lashed out at you for trying to step into their mother's traditions. You could have done no right today."

"But I could have tried!" The first sob nearly undid her. "You'd better go before I lose it."

"I won't go until after you do. C'mon. Come sit with me. You need a good sob-fest."

A thought produced a snicker and then a sigh. At Luke's urging she finally said, "I was thinking that marrying a man who has four sisters is going to mean that he has an unfair insight into females."

"Some women would consider that an advantage."

She snickered. "You'd think, right? You forgot you were dealing with an inept mother of eight — at twenty-three years old."

"Stop, Mibs." He waited until she looked at him and whispered, "Don't do it. You are beating yourself up for things that aren't true."

"They feel true."

"That I can't argue, but feelings, no matter how real —"

"Lie, I know. I tell myself that," Aggie said, "but I don't always believe me."

Tina skipped downstairs and collapsed on the couch. "Oy. It's been so long since we've had an eruption, I forgot how draining they are." She frowned. "And now I'm doing the oy thing. How about ugh? Yeah. Ugh." Her eyes caught Aggie's and she sighed. "Sorry. I didn't mean —"

"Don't worry about it. Right now I've got to figure out how to find ornaments that will have meaning to them."

Head cocked, Tina gazed at Luke and Aggie. "You guys are so cute. These kids are lucky — ok blessed, Miss Gotta-give-credit-to-the-Almighty — to have both of you."

"Great. They're blessed. Ornaments. Focus."

"Yes, Miss Terse."

Luke snickered. "I thought she was Miss Gotta-give—"

"Very funny. Why—" Tina's phone rang. "Weird. It's my mom. Since when does she call? I'll be back." She clicked the phone on and answered it. "Hey, Mom, what—"

"Well, so much for her help. What are your ideas?"

"Um, I have a feeling you are going to get sick of this, but my first instinct is to call my mom."

Without hesitation, Aggie pulled her phone from her pocket and dialed. "I think the truth of it," she said while the phone rang, "is that you will get sick of me calling her—or she will." Aggie snickered. "Your mom says she will not."

Several minutes later, Aggie stowed her phone back in her pocket. "Ok, we're making them. It'll be special, they'll draw names and voila."

"Once you started talking, that was my guess. Mom is into making memories together. Corinne's husband is always saying, 'It's still a memory if you just buy the piñata or have the party at the pizza place rather than making them or creating it all.'"

"I think there's a time for both." Aggie's mind swirled with the idea of doing everything with eight children. It made her dizzy and nauseas. "If I tried to do it all with them, I'd go crazy. That's probably why Allie didn't. But, I bet her perfectionism probably meant that she didn't do it as much as she could have."

"Perfectionist, eh?"

"Yeah. Just a bit. She'd go nuts in this house."

Luke nodded slowly, as if understanding something for the first time. "I think the kids like the more relaxed atmosphere."

"Relaxed? You can't be more opposite than we were. She is elastic that cuts off your circulation. I'm elastic that drops your unders around your ankles."

"I haven't seen anyone tripping over anything, so you're good."

Aggie buried her head into Luke's shoulder. "Allie wouldn't think so. She'd think I was lazy."

"She knew what she was choosing when she chose you."

Tina's door banged open and a suitcase rolled behind her. With her purse slung over one shoulder, she grabbed for her coat and stumbled toward the door. Aggie hurried to her side. "What's wrong?"

"My dad had a heart attack. Mom's flipping out and—"

"Do you want me to drive you?"

Both women looked at Luke as if he'd lost his senses. Tina found her voice first. "Why?"

"Sorry, you just seemed upset and…"

"I'm good. Gotta go. I'll call when I get there. I don't know when I'll be back."

That was it. The door closed behind her with Aggie and Luke staring at it.

Tina says: I made it. Dad is in surgery. They had to do an emergency bypass. I'm scared.

Aggie says: We've been praying. How is your mom?

Tina says: A mess. His office manager is here—you know, the one who refuses to be called anything but a "secretary."

Aggie says: Bombshell Babs?

Tina says: Yep.

Tina says: Aggie, I'm scared. He's not saved and he's in there with his heart in the hands of someone else who probably isn't saved.

Aggie says: And that man's hands are in the hands of the One who created him.

Tina says: Why isn't that comforting?

Aggie says: Because you're scared and fear messes up everything.

Tina says: From my internet research, I don't think I'll be home before New Year's or even Valentine's Day. You know how my dad is about illness. He takes it as a personal affront. He'll be depressed for months and when he's depressed, he won't try.

Aggie says: Well, with you there, he'll try harder. He responds to your bullying.

Tina says: Talk to me about something else. Anything. What are you doing about the ornaments?

Aggie says: We're going to make them. I drew names and they'll each do one for another.

Tina says: That sounds good.

Aggie says: You should rest, Tina. Talking to me about this stuff is

79

a certain way to kill time, but he's going to need you alert when he comes out of it.

Tina says: You're right. I'll research kid ornament crafts and email them if I can't sleep.

Aggie says: Night, Tina. Praying for you. I love you.

Tina says: I love you too.

Chapter 6

PROJECTS

Monday, December 15th

The children chattered eagerly as they turned into Willow's driveway. A dog stood guard at the corner of the house but did not bark. She hoped that meant that it was friendly. Her children poured out of the van, some stumbling, others racing to greet the dog. Aggie had to move fast before they disappeared into who knew what strange places.

"Whoa! Stop! Line up and don't move." She greeted Willow with a reassuring smile. If the look on the young woman's face was to be believed, Willow Finley was ready to run screaming from her own home. "Can you give them the boundaries? Cans and can'ts and all that?"

Willow led the children to the barn. "You can come in and visit the animals, but you cannot go in the loft if you can't touch the eighth rung without standing on something."

Tavish immediately reached and stretched just barely to the eighth. "Ok, so me and up can go, but anyone shorter than me is out."

"Right," Willow agreed. "Now, out here," she began as she led the children to the yard. "Don't go in the chicken yard. Period. I don't care if a chicken hawk eats every chicken in sight, do not open the gate."

Aggie looked sharply at the twins. "Did you hear that? What did she say?"

"No chickies. Not at all," Lorna echoed wisely, but a glimmer in Cari's eye caught Aggie's attention.

81

"And if I see you even touch the fence, you'll come inside and sit on the floor with your hands in your lap."

"Yes, Aunt Aggie," Cari whined.

"Other than that, if you can't see the house, you've gone too far. Turn around. If you see water, come back."

Inside, Willow handed Aggie a cup of hot tea and a cherry-almond bar. "What about the dresses? What did you have in mind?"

Aggie hurried to the van, returning with two large plastic shopping bags. From within, she pulled chiffon and peach skin in several shades of pink—nearly to red. "I bought both the white chiffon to go over the pastel and the pastel chiffon. I didn't know which looked best."

"And a style?"

"I was thinking something like the shipoopie outfits at the end of Music Man. Well, actually, it was Vannie's idea, but I like it."

Willow's blank expression sent Aggie into a frenzy of explanation, but Willow still clearly did not understand. "It's a movie right?"

"Yeah—"

"I'll get Chad to bring it to me. I'll watch it. Meanwhile, why don't you bring the oldest inside and keep the boys out until we get her bodice constructed. I'll make the dress to fit the bodices once I know what it should look like. You'll see."

As they worked, Willow and Aggie forged a new, if somewhat tentative, friendship. Willow told hilarious stories of her childhood on the farm and Aggie told even funnier ones of her children and their escapades. By the time they were finished with the dress mock-ups, the awkwardness was all gone.

However, Willow asked a perfectly normal question in such a way that made Aggie wonder what she meant. "How long have you known Luke?"

"Since the end of May or first of June—somewhere in there."

"Wow, that's fast. Do you mind me asking why you decided to marry?"

Aggie sat in Willow's kitchen rocking chair, held her tea warming her hands, and observed as Willow added wood to the stove, put a chicken in the oven, and all while she talked. "It was fast, I guess, but it didn't feel fast. When you see someone almost all day every day for months, it makes you feel like you've known them all your life somehow."

"I know what you mean, and I haven't seen Chad nearly that much. I thought it was because we'd worked together so much. It's like I woke up one day and found Mother dead, but she gave me a brother that I never knew and have always known at the same time."

Smiling, Aggie handed Willow her empty cup. "Maybe it's just the Sullivan men."

"Sullivan, Tesdall... not sure what, but there are similarities to them aren't there?"

There seemed something not quite answered in Willow's question, but Aggie didn't know what it was. "So did you mean you wanted to know why I want to get married or why I want to marry Luke?"

"Well, I think why you'd want to marry Luke is obvious. He's a good man and if you want to marry, a good man is a wise choice. I just see someone my age—almost to the day Chad says—and I wonder why you want to marry at all. What about marriage appeals to you?"

"Well, I don't know. Don't most women desire to be a wife? Most of my friends dreamed about husbands and our weddings— most of our lives."

"Are men like that too? Do they dream of marriage and wives and their wedding days?" Willow asked very quietly.

The whole conversation seemed strange, but Willow was obviously bothered by something. "Why do you ask? I mean, I don't know about guys—I've never been a guy, but I'm pretty sure most don't dream of their wedding day—wedding *night*, maybe, not their wedding," Aggie teased trying to lighten the somber mood that suddenly filled the room. "I think most guys probably grow up expecting it, but I don't know that they spend as much time dreaming of it that women do."

"I just don't understand. At first, I thought Mother's experience warped her perceptions, but she had nineteen years or so with her parents. You'd think—"

"I've never been through what your mother went through, and maybe I'm being a bit naïve, but I think there was more to her rejection of men than marriage. Luke mentioned something about her giving birth here all alone."

"She was," Willow agreed, whispering. "It was raining and she was afraid to walk to town for help, so she stayed alone. She was terrified."

As delicately as possible, Aggie tried to explain that Kari's experiences probably magnified the horror in Kari's mind until it was blown out of proportion. "I'm not sure that your mother was anti-marriage, but rather that she'd been so deeply scarred by a man. Physically she endured the attack and then a horrific labor after it. She had no support—no one to tell her she wasn't crazy when she wanted to kill or maim and no one to encourage her. Labor alone is so intense— my sister used to say she couldn't make it through labor without her husband. She said once that if he even left to use the bathroom she felt like she was going crazy."

Willow stood and stoked the fire, her cheeks pink. "I like watching Chad's parents. They remind me of this couple I saw in a restaurant right after Mother died. They didn't talk much, but the way they interacted—it was... harmonious. The Tesdalls are like that."

Aggie smiled. She thought she knew where the conversation was going and she was excited. "I know the whole family is hoping you guys will get married."

A visible shudder washed over Willow. "I hope they keep those opinions to themselves. Chad and I have a wonderful friendship and I don't want to lose it because all the pressure makes him think he's giving people the wrong idea."

Tuesday, December 16ᵗʰ

Aggie worked with Vannie on a Steampunk styled ornament for Tavish. It was the most pathetic thing she'd ever seen, but Vannie seemed content. That was what mattered, wasn't it? "What if we wrap it in tinfoil first and spray with black spray paint? That might make it look less—"

"Stupid? It looks stupid. I wasn't going to say anything, but since you said it..."

"I'm sorry. I am not very good at this stuff."

"Hey, you're letting me do it myself instead of doing it for me. That counts. I'll get the aluminum foil."

Against her better judgment, Aggie ignored the sounds of

demolition and chaos around her. The twins tattled on each other and everyone else at least two dozen times. Her only response was to holler, "Keep it down to a dull roar," or "Behave yourselves!" They ignored her, and though she knew better, she did nothing about it. Aggie knew instinctively that she'd regret turning a blind eye to the bedlam; unfortunately, she had no idea of just how much.

What she'd expected to be a forty-five minute project took nearly three hours, two trips to the hardware store, and one absolutely demolished house to complete. They called Tavish in to see the results and the delight on his face was worth the hassle. Well, worth it until she saw ribbons shredded all over the living room, heard the running water upstairs, and discovered a trail of jelly along the hallway.

Had it been the first time, she might have had a more reasonable reaction, but everything seemed to converge on her at once—the work, the failures, the loss. She had gotten used to having Tina's eyes—and so had the children. Shaking with repressed anger and burgeoning despair, she turned and climbed the stairs, a wavering rendition of "Haven of Rest" faltering on her lips with every other step. Vannie called after her, or so she thought. She wasn't sure, but Aggie didn't bother to find out. It felt like the clock had turned backward and she was now back in her sister's house in those first days when nothing she did was right.

The door to Aggie's bedroom stood ajar just as it had in the old house in Rockland. Unlike that room, it was clean, the bed was made, and the style suited her rather than her sister or her house. Something about that seemed to buoy her spirits. She closed her eyes, took a deep breath, and then opened them slowly, taking in every detail that Luke had put into it for her. It was beautiful. As was the rest of her home. And now was the time to go back and face the ugly rather than run away from it.

At the bottom of the stairs, it just looked worse from all angles. Toys were scattered from the front door, down the hall, and across the living and dining rooms. The washing machine was thumping madly, a signal that someone had tried to help—again. Just as she reached it, and managed to shift the sheets equally around the agitator, a crash sounded in the kitchen followed by the utterly delightful tinkling of breaking glass.

The scratched record of her life reverberated in her mind.

"Delightful sound my eye," she muttered, racing to make sure that there would be no geysers of blood adding to the day's nightmare.

"Aunt Aggie, we—" Vannie lowered her voice at Aggie's appearance in the kitchen. "—have a problem."

"I see that. Get out."

"I'm sorry—"

"Get. Out." A vague sense of self-recrimination told her she'd regret something later, but Aggie couldn't concentrate. She had one thing to do—clean up four destroyed baking dishes before it became Aggigeddon in the kitchen.

"Can I help—"

"No. Just get out, Laird. Go. I do not want to see a single child's face until I am done with this. Got that?"

"Yeah."

Shattered glass seemed to multiply with contact to the floor. How Vannie had managed to break all four at once made no sense. The last time she had dropped a dish, it just bounced off the wood floor without even a single chip of glass, but this...

Box. She needed a box. Glass would slice through plastic trash bags, right? Of course it would. Box. Where—basement. Cleanup took twice as long as necessary; Aggie's brain refused to cooperate. Every move she made had to be considered and decided. Four times she swept every inch of the kitchen, and each one revealed a new chunk or shard just waiting to slice open a foot in the dead of night, necessitating a trip to the clinic. Now there was no one to stay behind with the kids; there could be no glass left behind.

She grabbed the mop. It took an hour to sweep and mop without any evidence of another piece of the glass. The children were ominously silent, but Aggie didn't have the emotional strength to search them out and discover why. She finished cleaning the kitchen—desperate for one spotless room before she headed into the living room. Ribbons, wrapping paper, and tape seemed attached to every surface. Starting at one corner, she began wadding and rolling, trying to get every bit up off the floor and furniture, hoping that the result would give her some confidence that the kids could finish by picking up the toys.

Kids. She should look for them. A glance out the dining room window answered that question quickly. They stood on each side of the fence that separated her house from Murphy's and listlessly

86

threw snowballs back and forth. What might have pricked her heart only hours earlier, infuriated her. Did they really think they had the right to feel put out? They destroyed the house — knew better and did it anyway — and then had the audacity to get their little feelings hurt because she wanted them out of the way while she cleaned up a dangerous mess?

She grabbed another wad of wrapping paper and stuffed it into the already overflowing trash bag. A sponge scrubbed off the jelly from the walls, and two laundry baskets contained the floor mess within the space of about fifteen minutes. Work seemed to dissipate her anger. Aggie stared at the baskets, debating whether it would be a kindness to put away the toys or a bad precedent.

On her way down the stairs after putting away the first basket, the children traipsed into the house — through the front door. A mud trail led from the door to the mudroom, along with mittens, scarves, and both of the twins' jackets. She blinked. The freshly restored room looked like a mud tornado had left a swath of destruction in its path. The walls were decorated in finger painted mud streaks — likely compliments of Ian and the twins. What had been a sticky mess less than half an hour earlier was now a dirty nightmare.

The little composure she'd managed to achieve dissolved on the floor along with the snow that had coated the children's outerwear. She turned, without saying a word to them, and sang repeatedly under her breath, "*...careful little mouth what you say. Be careful little mouth what you say. For the Father up above is looking down in tender love so be careful little mouth what you say.*"

Laird burst into the house on Cygnet gasping for air. "Luke!"

A voice called from the garage. He started to run across the room, but hesitated and then removed his boots at the door. His socks slid on the floor, but he managed to make it into the garage without falling. Flinging open the garage door, he stopped at the sight of the water heater dismantled on the garage floor.

"What's wrong?" Luke hardly glanced up from his work.

"It's Aunt Aggie. I don't know what happened, but she's not right. She's crying and won't talk to any of us. Vannie broke some

87

dishes and she wouldn't even let us help clean it up."

Indecision tumbled through Luke's mind. He had to go. There was no doubt about that, but the inspector was due the next morning. If he went now, he might not be ready. Luke set down his tools and stood. "Come on."

They climbed into Luke's truck while Luke called the inspector's office. "Hello, Mr. Farley. This is Luke Sullivan at the house on Cygnet. There's been a potential emergency here and it means I might not have everything ready tomorrow as planned. If you think we should reschedule, that's fine. Just give me a call. I apologize for the inconvenience."

"I thought you said you couldn't reschedule that appointment."

"I can't for this year. The inspector goes on vacation on Friday until after the first."

"That'll set you back another two weeks!"

"Yes."

Laird waved his hand. "Just let me out and go back. I'll figure out a way to calm her down. I can call Aunt Tina or —"

"No. Thank you, but I've got to do this. You know that."

"It's not your job yet. Not really. Even if it was, you can't just come home every time Aunt Aggie has a bad day."

Luke allowed the truck to idle at the corner while he spoke. His eyes sought understanding in Laird's face, but it wasn't there. "Listen. Family always has to come first. Now, sometimes that means that I can't come home when someone needs me because I've got to provide for that family. Other times it means that I have to choose people over money. Today, I need to choose people." He flipped on the blinker and turned the corner. "Now, tell me more. What happened from the time you got up this morning?"

Laird's story didn't seem to help much. Aggie had managed an entire house renovation, multiple injuries, and an epidemic of chicken pox. Additionally, she had endured the negativity of the sheriff's deputy and a mother-in-law as a single woman. She could handle a bit of glass, paper, jelly, and mud.

The house did look worse than he'd expected, but it was still nothing to compare to the days of wallpaper removal and footprints in the polyurethane. He assigned jobs to each child, including babysitting the three youngest, and hurried upstairs. Aggie's sobs reached him long before he reached the door to her room. Luke knocked.

"So help me if you do not go away…"

"Mibs?"

"I mean it. Just go."

The sounds of her weeping nearly tore his heart out. Luke stood there, unsure what to do, but unwilling to leave. He pulled out his phone, his fingers hovering over the screen ready to call her parents if necessary. No, it wasn't right. They'd have these kinds of problems for the next fifty years if God was that good to them. He couldn't be calling either of their parents for every little thing.

Discouraged, he turned away and went back downstairs. The cleanup progress was impressive for such a short amount of time. *Sleigh Ride* tinkled from his phone and he clicked it on. "Mr. Farley? Hey, thanks for calling me back. Yeah, I've still got problems with the water heater. Might have to put in a new one. Right. I don't know if I'll be done or not. I feel like I've wasted your time, but I had no choice. Yeah. Thanks."

After pocketing the phone, he glanced around him. "Are there dinner plans in the works yet?"

Vannie shrugged. "I don't know. I don't think so."

The refrigerator didn't seem to have anything thawing in it and the counters were bare. He flipped through the leftovers on the shelves and decided there was enough for a smorgasbord. Dinner would be easy even if the resulting dishes drove whomever had to load the dishwasher a bit nutty.

"How about schoolwork? Who got theirs done today?"

No hands raised. Ten eyes avoided him while six others didn't bother to look. One finger pointed to the school room. "Go. Don't come out until you're done. I'll take the baby." He crooked his finger at Cari and Lorna. "Come with me."

"I don't want to!"

"I didn't ask if you wanted to. Let's go." He waited for the continued protest. It usually would come, but for some inexplicable reason, Cari grinned and said, "Okay!"

"Hey, Luke?"

"Hmm?"

"I only have about ten minutes worth of math and then I can stop for the day. I worked ahead." Laird's eyes looked upward. "If you wanted to go upstairs…"

"Why didn't you say that earlier?"

"You asked who got theirs done. Mine isn't."

With a tongue full of bite marks, Luke nodded and said, "Ok, just get it done."

Lorna piped up and asked, "Can we play with Play-doh?"

"Great idea. Why don't you get it out?"

Juggling Ian while tearing apart salad greens was not as easy as he'd anticipated. Relief washed over him when Laird arrived to take over. "Can I take them downstairs?"

"Sure. I'm going to get some of these dishes in the oven and then go talk to Aggie."

By the time he'd gotten the salad assembled, Play-doh was hardening, abandoned on the counter. Luke impatiently stuffed the lumps into the little plastic containers and snapped the lids on tight. A glance at the clock told him it had been a good half hour. Maybe she'd be ready to talk now.

No sound came from her room when Luke reached Aggie's door. He started to knock, but hesitated. "Aggie?" He knocked at last. No response came. Again he knocked and again the response was lacking.

It occurred to him that she might be sleeping—that she couldn't hear his quiet knock. He turned the knob, opening the door just a crack, hoping to see if she lay asleep on the bed. She was on the bed it seemed, but her sniffles told him she wasn't asleep.

"Aggie?"

"What!"

"Can I come in?"

"No! Leave me alone." There was an extended pause before she added, "Please."

Hesitation overtook him again, but this time he did not yield. "All right. I'll go if you tell me you're okay."

"Fine. I'm fine."

It was a lie, but he heard in it what he needed. She didn't want to discuss it—whatever "it" was. It hardly seemed likely that some mud on the floor and toys strewn over the house could possibly be the real trouble.

"Okay then, I'll go." Luke said, "I love you," before shutting the door behind him.

Seconds later, the door flung open and he found himself soaked in tears and shaken — as well as stirred — by her uncontrolled sobbing. A head peeked up the stairwell, but Luke glared at Laird and shook his head. He led her into her room and to the little loveseat by the window.

"What's wrong? Not what happened," he amended quickly. "I want to know what's really wrong."

"I'm tired."

Though it wasn't the true problem, it was a start. "Nap?"

"Are you nuts? I'd wake up and find the house destroyed."

"Then, tired is really a symptom. What's the real problem?"

A poorly suppressed sigh escaped as she said, "I'm a failure."

"That's a lie. Next?"

"Don't call me a liar." The faintest hint of her usual spunk managed to infuse itself into her words.

"Then don't lie. You are not a failure, so why don't you tell me why you feel like one."

"Did you see the mess?"

"Yeah. They got it cleaned up and are doing their schoolwork right now. Laird said something about a messy living room and broken glass."

"I got it all cleaned up — for all the good it did me." This time there was something new in her tone — something he didn't like to hear. Bitterness.

"Mibs..."

"You wanted truth. You got it. It took us three hours to make a simple ornament for Tavish. Three hours. I don't have three hours a day for a week to put into making stupid ornaments because my sister was an over-achieving lunatic."

"Then don't do them."

Aggie's head whipped up, glaring at him. "Right. Just take the worst year of their lives and make it even worse by ignoring beloved traditions. Because that's not qualifying myself for Worst Sorta-Mother of the Year Award."

"Quit trying to replace your sister. Besides, you're actually one-upping her by making them. She took the easy route."

"Yeah, well it was your idea — sort of."

There it was. She sounded semi-normal. "Go buy them, Mibs. Buy a cheap frame and we'll put a tiny picture of you with each one of them in it. Done. Meaningful, simple, and no-stress."

"And making me into a liar since I said I'd make them with them. Forget it."

A new idea occurred to him, and desperate, Luke switched tactics. "All right, you want to be miserable. I can deal with that. C'mere." With arms wrapped around her, he held her, not saying a word.

Aggie squirmed. "That's not fair."

"Not fair?" he murmured. "How so?"

"You know that I can't be miserable with you here."

Luke listened as the story slowly unfolded. She was tired and already felt the loss of her friend's help. His mind rewound to the stories she'd told of the first days as "mother" to the children and to how things were when they'd first begun work on the house. It was constant chaos back then, but then Tina had come, his mother had visited often, and that seemed to make a decided difference in how the household ran. She needed help, but how to provide it?

"Well," he said, pulling her up and leading her downstairs hand-in-hand, "then I'll just have to be here more."

Luke says: Mibs? You there?

Aggie says: Yeah.

Luke says: Still okay?

Aggie says: Until morning, sure.

Luke says: You still sound a little down.

Aggie says: I think after a good night's sleep, I'll be fine.

Luke says: You'll call me if you have trouble tomorrow?

Aggie says: I will.

Luke says: Then I think I will go to bed so that you'll sleep.

Aggie says: I love you, Mr. Sullivan.

Luke says: And there she says the one thing that will tempt me to stay. Goodnight, Mibs. Sleep well.

Chapter 7

ELF WANTED

Saturday, December 20

The crackling of the paper barely registered in Aggie's consciousness. It crumpled as the words slowly imprinted themselves in her mind. By the time she fully grasped the content of the letter, it was a ball in her hand.

"Aunt Aggie? Is something wrong?" Vannie seemed concerned.

"No… Actually, I think something is right." With that cryptic answer, Aggie climbed the stairs to check on napping children and call Luke. The news was good but with good came complications.

Her fingers flew over her laptop keys as she tried to contact her mother about it.

Aggie says: Mom? Help!

Milliken says: What's up?

Aggie says: I got a letter from Mrs. Stuart's lawyer.

Milliken says: Oh, great. Now what?

Aggie says: That's the problem—it was just a note that said that due to the restraining order, she would not be sending Christmas presents.

Milliken says: What? Really? Allie is rolling in her grave—cartwheels I'm guessing. Aaak.

Milliken says: Sorry, had to do it. Giving it back to your mother, but that's the best news I've had in ages.

Aggie says: Mom! I can't believe you said that. Wait. That's Dad.

Aggie says: I think it creates a bit of a problem

Milliken says: What kind of problem?

Aggie says: Christmas presents. I bought them each one and then toothbrush, favorite candy bar, and something silly for their stocking. You know, spray string, whoopee cushion, bubbles—stuff I usually would ban from the house.

Milliken says: I don't understand the problem.

Aggie says: These kids are used to an overloaded Christmas. From the way you've described it, they spent all day opening presents, practically crying because they just wanted to be done. I don't want that, obviously, but one present and three things in a mostly empty stocking is going to be just one more thing in a long line of disappointing things this year.

Milliken says: You've got a point...

Aggie says: I have four and a half... well, and a quarter days to shop. I can't even shop online because I can't risk it not getting here in time. I need to go to the stores and I can't. Tina's gone.

Milliken says: I'll have Dad bring me down early...

Aggie says: No. We both know that's not a good idea.

Milliken says: Well, I want it to be a good idea.

Aggie says: Gimme another one, Mom.

Milliken says: Start calling everyone you know. Call Libby, the gal who helped when you were still in Rockland, Mrs. Dyke—anyone. Call them all. Set up times to shop with them and do it. Just spend the next three days shopping like crazy.

Aggie says: I don't even know what to buy!

Milliken says: If you see it and like it, buy it. You can return stuff later if you find something better. You're going to spend a ton of money. It's ok. Half will probably go back so don't panic. Go. Make those calls.

Aggie says: Hey, Mom? I love you.

Milliken says: You're doing great and I love you for it.

Finding people available to watch her children just days before Christmas was next to impossible. Iris Landry managed to offer three hours on Tuesday night after dinner. Libby didn't know when she'd make it, but she assured Aggie that she'd come and take over the moment she could. Luke, seeing the distress in her, locked up the house on Cygnet and promised he'd be at her disposal until the day after Christmas.

Sunday, December 21

William pulled Aggie aside on Sunday after church. "How is Tina's father? She hasn't called in a few days and I was wondering..."

"They had to go back in for something—I don't quite know what. She starts speaking medicalese and I have no idea what it all means. I think he's ok now though. Or," she added, "at least he will be."

"Bet you miss having her around."

"Never more than now. Luke has to stop work on his house just so I can do Christmas shopping."

A quick shake of the head told her what he'd say before he spoke. "Waiting until the last minute will mess you up every time." Yep. Exactly what she had expected.

"Well, if I had known that the grandmotherly leopard would change her spots and not overload the kids with gifts, I would have been more prepared. I was—but not for nothing from her."

"That's good though, right?"

"Good except that she told me with only four days of shopping to go for eight kids."

"Ouch. Luke's getting an introduction into big family life quickly, isn't he? At least shopping will give you guys some time together."

She shook her head. "No, his being available lets me go, but he can't exactly accompany me. Someone has to keep the kids from burning down the house and calling 9-1-1 every other minute."

A cry from the van told her she'd better go. "That's my cue. Time to go. Call Tina. It'll mean a lot to her."

The midnight corvette turned onto Last Street just as she flipped on her blinker for her driveway. Aggie frowned. What did William want now? The kids thundered into the house with such abandon that she knew the entrance would be carpeted in all forms of outerwear.

Aggie carried Ian to William's side. "Is there a problem? Do I have a taillight out or did I creep up to twenty-seven miles per hour on the way?"

"No," he laughed. "I just thought maybe I could stay here while you and Luke went out shopping."

"Oh, man that'd be great, but I can't ask you to do that."

"You didn't. I offered, remember?"

Luke's truck pulled up behind William's car. Aggie waved and smiled. "I'll ask Luke about it."

"I love seeing you like this."

She frowned, cocking her head. "Like what?"

"You light up when he's around."

"Do I?" She glanced up at Luke as he arrived at her side and reached for the baby.

"Definitely." William nodded at Luke. "I was just suggesting that you and Aggie go get lunch and then do some shopping."

The remnants of dinner at Luke's favorite steakhouse cluttered the table between them. They were supposed to be discussing where to go first, but instead, hands locked under the table, they gazed wordlessly at one another. Luke smiled.

"You know, I dreamed of this."

Aggie squeezed his hands. "Of what?"

"Just being together—no fear of interruption—"

"Can I get you anything else?" The impatience in the server's tone said that she wanted the table.

"Just the check."

A folder was dropped on the table, without giving much attention to them, and the woman hurried to the next table. Aggie giggled. "Nope. No interruptions—even by rude waitresses."

"It's almost Christmas, and they're bustling with business; you really can't blame her."

"You're going to leave a big tip, aren't you?"

"Yep."

On their way out the door, the server stared at them strangely when Aggie said, "We should have gotten engaged earlier. Maybe I would have learned these little things about you a lot sooner."

At his truck, Luke couldn't restrain his laughter any longer. "Did you see her face? Priceless. Where to?"

"Well, I was thinking we'd start with toy stores. It might not be the most well-thought out Christmas, but we can at least have it be a memorable one."

The aisles of toys that had always delighted her when shopping for her nieces and nephews daunted her now. She stared at things she'd never heard of and read the backs carefully. Luke was in charge of a few family games—things that they could play together and for as many ages as possible.

By the time he returned with an overloaded cart full, Aggie had managed to put two funky looking dolls in her cart—clearly meant for the twins. "Luke..."

"No, not all of them. These were the ones that looked interesting. I got to thinking and I think you need three age groups: younger, older, and everyone." He pulled out a few simple games and said, "Which one? I think this one has the broadest appeal, but it might be a bit much for Lorna and Cari. Then again, they're almost four, aren't they?"

"Yeah... and we could set them aside for a while. Take that one and maybe that—memory and detail games are good for them."

While she debated whether Ellie would enjoy a pottery wheel or not, Luke hurried back to the game shelves with an armload of rejects from the youngest recommended age levels. The process repeated itself until half a dozen games took up a large amount of space in the bottom of the cart.

Luke shook his head as she started to add the pottery wheel to the load. "I think you should talk to Mom about that. Olivia hasn't stopped ranting about what a piece of junk those are and Mom always says that toy tools are a waste of good money."

"Great. It was the one artsy thing I saw that didn't look cheap."

"We'll find something for her. Maybe an art store?"

"Don't have time to shop at individual specialty stores for every kid!"

"You don't need to for all of them, but Ellie would appreciate good tools—even if from a hobby store."

Aggie spied a child's toy oven and grabbed it. "Think this might be fun for her?"

"Why? She uses the regular oven all the time."

"Because I'm desperate?"

With his arm around her shoulder, he nudged her toward the fairyland for boys—that world of boxes and tiny pieces that are designed to delight burgeoning builders and terrify their mothers—or mothering aunts as the case may be—with choking hazards and sore toes. "Legos, K'nex, Erector, and even Duplo for Ian. You could buy nothing but this stuff and they'd love you forever, but look! There's more! Act now and you can buy chemistry sets, forensic sets, biology sets, microscopes, telescopes, and much, much, more!"

"I'll make you a deal," Aggie said. "You pick out a few things for each boy and I'll go look for the twins and Kenzie. I doubt there'll be anything in here that Vannie would like, but maybe Ellie…"

An hour later, the shopping cart was full to overflowing and still they had nothing for Vannie or Ellie. Luke maneuvered through traffic to the hobby store, but they found more bare shelves than stocked ones. "I'll call Mom. Maybe there is a better place," Luke offered.

"Or maybe it's four days before Christmas and stores are getting depleted." She stared at her phone, hesitating. "It's almost dinner. William can't be expected to cook for them too. I've got to go home."

"I could see if Mom—"

"She's got her hands full with your sisters and their kids. I'll figure something out. I have to."

Luke drove toward home and then pulled into a gas station. "Need to fill up. Why don't you go get us some coffee?"

By the time she returned, he looked more chipper. "William said that he can con Shay into delivering pizza. He is back on the clock in an hour and a half. Let's stop at one more store and then go for a walk around Lake Danube before we go home."

Stars twinkled overhead as Aggie and Luke walked hand in hand along the shore of the lake. On the other side, Christmas lights twinkled on houses and reflected in the water. It seemed almost magical. "I should bring the kids to see this."

"We should."

Aggie looked up at him, smiling. "That's right. We should. I have to get used to the idea that I'm not in this alone anymore."

"You never were," he reminded her. "Even in Rockland you had church family, your parents, friends, Jesus. You've never been alone."

"It felt alone—still does more of the time than I'd like to admit."

He didn't respond for some time, making Aggie wonder if she'd hurt him with her honesty. Before she could ask, he stopped and pulled her into a gentle hug. "I forget that a lot happens that I never see—never know about. The girls say a lot of that happens even though they've been married for years. They're home with the kids and it can still be overwhelming."

"True…"

"Call me home, Mibs. Even now, if you need someone for support or to back you up with the kids—whatever. Call me home. If I can possibly do it, I'll come."

"I can't get into the habit of using you to bail me out of hard days."

"Is that what your mom is doing when she needs someone to take her to the doctor or to do something that she physically can't handle? You are young," he said, his hand reaching up to touch her cheek with a gentleness that stole her breath. "But you are not invincible. Let me help."

"You may regret that."

He pressed his cheek to the top of her head, holding her close for just a moment longer. "I doubt it."

"Regrets come in all shapes and sizes—even for things you were sure you wanted."

Luke winked. "Is that a hint?"

"It's a fact. I'm glad you put a stop to it with Vannie."

"I am too," he agreed, "but I think God knew what He was doing when He gave your father to you. Some temptations are best avoided."

"Easy for you to say," she muttered.

"That's what you think."

"Laird! Get back in here!"

The boy shuffled in and picked up the book. "I'll put it away," he grumbled.

"Um, you might not want to do that yet." Aggie passed him his "book report" with a huge red F marked across the single sentence on the page.

"What? Why!"

"A single sentence, Laird? Really? You thought I'd let you get away with a single sentence for an entire book report?"

"You told me it had to be a report about what I liked about the book. That's what it is."

Aggie frowned. "And you think, 'I liked the book *Bad, Bad Beginning* because it was short' is a sufficient book report?"

He started to argue—the angst and frustration written on his face—and then he shook his head. "Ok, how many words or pages do I need?"

"Fill the page." He made it to the door before she added, "In normal sized handwriting."

The genuinely confused expression on his face made her want to kick herself. "Don't get any ideas, boy. Just do your assignment."

An hour later, the finished report was placed in front of her and her red pencil offered with relish. A giggle near the staircase warned Aggie that this was going to be good. She flipped over the paper and began reading.

In my personal opinion, the book The Bad, Bad Beginning by Lemony Snickett was a good choice for this book report. The size of the book, as well as the number of pages and words, make it optimal for a person like me to choose for a book report. Additionally, the frequent use of illustrations to break up the pages also contributes to the things I like about this book.

The size of the book is approximately five by seven

inches—much like a portrait photograph. It is hardbound with an illustrated front and a letter from the author, Mr. Snickett, on back. It fits well in your hand and isn't very thick.

There are only one hundred sixty-two pages in the book. They're cool pages that look like they're from an old book or handmade or something. The margins are wide, which contributes nicely to keeping the story short.

The illustrations are interesting and occur at reasonably frequent integrals. This helps to keep the reader from feeling as if the book is too long. I particularly liked this part of why I like the shortness of this book.

In conclusion, the thing I liked most about the book The Bad, Bad Beginning, by Lemony Snickett is that it was a short book. It was not too long. It could have been shorter, of course. However, it was short, and that is what I liked about it. That is all I liked about it.

One eyebrow rose as she handed him back the report. "Turn it into Luke. Whatever grade he gives it stands."

"What! That's—"

"Turn it into Luke for your final grade, or I mark it as an F and you get to read the entire series with five page book reports on each." She waited until he was just outside the door before adding, "Oh, and by the way. The word is intervals, not integrals. This is English, not math." Laird's chin dropped when she added, "And if you use your sister as a thesaurus and advisor, it might also be wise to have her look it over as an editor."

Luke jogged up the steps, eager to get Aggie out of the house and onto her shopping journey. The whole thing seemed ridiculous, but if it made her happy, it was worth it. Why she needed more gifts was beyond him, but as he mentally calculated what they'd procured for each child the previous day, he realized that it wasn't that much after all. The sheer volume—

"Here. I've got this for you. Gotta run."

The red brake lights signaled that she was gone before he stepped into the house, the paper she'd handed him still clutched in his fist. He glanced down and began reading. What kind of book report was this?

Tavish strolled toward his cubbyhole, but Luke stopped him. "Where is Laird?"

"Waiting in the schoolroom I think."

The boy was right. Laird sat at the table, working on some assignment or another, trying desperately to look uninterested in what was about to take place.

"What is this?" Luke shook the paper. "Interesting report."

"Good. Aunt Aggie said you have to grade it."

"What was the criteria for writing the paper?"

Laird set down his pencil and leaned back in the chair, again with a ridiculous air of nonchalance. "At first, she said to write what I liked about the book. So I did."

"Well, you did a thorough job of it," Luke conceded.

"I had to. My original report got an F for being too short."

"Too short?" This was going to be good. "How long was it?"

"It was one sentence, not a fragment even. I specifically named the book and what I liked."

Luke sat down and laid the paper between them. "Then what?"

"She said it had to be a full page report. So, I expanded on what I liked about the book—in short, its shortness."

"Brevity."

"What?"

Luke glanced around and then retrieved a dictionary from a nearby bookshelf. "Look it up."

"It's not vocabulary, Luke. I did what she said I had to do— twice. I didn't deserve the F—"

"Look it up, Laird."

After a few seconds in the dictionary, Laird retrieved the paper and erased something. When Luke got it back, he saw one sentence changed from "why I like the shortness of this book" to "why I like the brevity of this book." Brevity was written out in a sprawling manner to help it fit into the larger space needed by shortness.

Now Luke saw the real problem. Aggie wasn't concerned about the book report—it was actually quite ingenious considering the requirements given. No, she was upset by the attitude that prompted it. Even now, a smugness hovered about Laird's features. He knew he'd written exactly what was required and had done a good job of it.

After rooting around in the drawer, Luke found the red pencil Aggie used for grading and marked an A on the top of the page. Self-satisfied, Laird stood and nodded before turning to leave. Luke stopped him. "I am not finished with you."

"But—"

"I consider that you did the assignment as requested and within the parameters you were given. The first was a mockery of the assignment and you knew it. You didn't even attempt to hide your disrespect. I'm going to tell her to keep that F on the record. You earned it. You also earned this A."

"That's not fair!"

"Tell me," Luke added, nudging the chair toward the boy, "what would your teacher have given you last year if you had brought one sentence in as a book report."

"But I wouldn't—" He stopped short.

"Exactly. You wouldn't have been that snotty to another teacher, but you will to the woman who loves you and is doing her best to give you everything you need for a good life. Your teacher last year might not have given you the opportunity to make up a failed report. Be thankful Aggie did. I wouldn't have and once we are married, that kind of second chance for insolence won't be permitted."

"You're not our dad, you know..." Laird said.

"No, but I will be the only father you have until you marry, so you'll show me the respect that God requires of you."

Laird's head dropped, making Luke wonder if repentance was at hand. Instead, he heard, "I hate this."

"What? What is it? What do you hate? What has you acting so out of character? This isn't like you..."

"Everything."

The catch in the boy's voice told Luke that it was only a matter of time before he broke down. In an effort to protect Laird's pride, Luke went to shut the doors, locking them behind him. He sat on the couch and gestured for Laird to follow. "C'mon. Let's hear it."

"It's almost Christmas and it's going to be horrible. Mommy — Daddy — they made Christmas amazing. Aunt Aggie tries, but she's no good at this mom thing. You know she isn't. We can't see Grandmother Stuart. It's not always bad that we can't, but the fact that we can't is bad. I want to talk to Dad. I want him to take me on a walk across the field and talk to me — tell me what a jerk I'm being."

"I doubt he said you were a jerk."

"No, but he knew how to make you see that you were. I want him to tell me it's ok to cry."

"But it is ok, Laird. You know it is. I still cry when I think of my father sometimes. Rodney gets me all the time. That kid will turn just at the right angle and it's like looking right at Dad. Cuts me. And I cry. It's ok to cry." He pointed out the window. "And, if it helps to know it, crying it out to a dog is a great way to have comfort when you're not ready to talk with a person."

"That's just the thing," Laird said, obviously fighting back those tears. "It's not. If I cry, and you know even if it was just me and the dog someone would see it, the girls start crying. Then Tavish loses it. Pretty soon, I've just made everything a million times worse."

"Or better. Missing your parents isn't something you want to get over. They sound like they were amazing people. Who would want to stop missing that?"

"Me! It doesn't hurt if I don't miss it. I want it to stop! I want it all to stop. I want to go to school where everything is so busy that I can't remember. I want to go where I'm not surrounded by things that remind me of how everything has been taken away. I want to look at Aunt Aggie and not feel guilty because I've ruined her life."

"You didn't ruin her life!" Luke pulled the boy into a rough hug. "She chose this, remember? She had a choice and she took it. No one forced her. No one — not even herself. She cried at the idea of giving you guys up. In a way, having you helps her keep a piece of her sister."

"But Vannie said—"

"I love your sister to bits, but she reads a few too many old novels that show the world in a very romanticized self-sacrificing way. She's wrong."

"How do you know?"

"I know because I've lived this, Laird. No, I didn't lose my mom too, but I lost my dad, and if it came down to it, Aggie would pick you guys over me without blinking."

"I don't think so."

Luke sighed, stuffing back his own ragged emotions. "I know so. She did back when she thought she had to make that choice. She didn't hesitate—even for a second." He stared at Laird for several seconds before he added, "I'm going to be very frank with you."

"Ok."

"You have to promise me that this stays between us."

Laird sat upright, already looking less like a lost boy and more like a young man. "I promise."

"You're right. Aggie chose a hard path. It was a choice and I know she doesn't regret it, but it was a hard path. Your mother chose that same path, Laird. No one forced her to have eight children. No one forced her to marry a man with a difficult mother. No one forced this on anyone, but it is still hard sometimes—a lot of the time probably."

"See—"

"But with it, comes a lot of blessings. You know that. You have brothers and sisters. You know that sometimes they drive you nuts and you just want them all to go away, but then when you do have time alone, you remember what you love about having them, don't you?"

The boy nodded. "Yeah. I get frustrated sometimes, I guess—but not like Vannie."

"Right. This conversation fits her personality better, but it is still true. I think sometimes Aggie doesn't know how hard it is. We see her struggling, but to her it's just life and that's good." Luke reached over the back of the couch and stretching, managed to snag the paper. "But stuff like this? It'll break her. You might enjoy feeling powerful enough to bring her to tears or knowing that you beat her at a game of wits she didn't even try to enter, but let me tell you something." Again, Luke's eyes bored into Laird's. "You'll hate yourself for it someday. It's cruel. It's disrespectful, and that isn't the Laird Stuart I know."

105

"I'm sorry."

"No, you tell her that. You tell her and you mean it."

"I will."

Luke stood and went to the door. Before unlocking it, he turned. "Next time you feel like you're spinning out of control—as if you want to prove something to someone, you come tell me. I'll help. I know that feeling much better than you can imagine."

"Thanks." Laird stared at his hands, unwilling to meet Luke's eyes.

"Oh, and one more thing."

With evident difficulty, the two green eyes darted around the room before resting on Luke. "Yeah?"

"If you ever show that kind of disrespect for my Aggie again, you will sorely wish you had not. Do you understand me? This is the woman who will be my wife. No one, man, woman, or child will get away with that. Am I clear?"

There it was—the penitence Luke was looking for—in Laird's entire demeanor. "Yes. I understand. I didn't mean—"

"Don't do it. Don't try to defend yourself. Just don't do it again."

Unsure if he made the right decision, Luke walked from the room without a second glance. Laird's eyes followed. He stared down at the paper beside him and frowned at the red A on the top. With a sigh, he picked it up and set it on top of the pile of work to be graded and left the room. Smiling.

Aggie says: What'd you say to Laird today? The boy is almost obsequious in his attitude.

Luke says: He's probably going a little over-board with showing his remorse, but I think he gets how disrespectful those papers were.

Aggie says: Something's not right, Luke.

Luke says: How so?

Aggie says: I can't say. I can just feel it.

Luke says: I'll talk to him again if necessary.

Aggie says: Well, we should probably give him time to process it.

Luke says: I don't know. With kids like Laird, they seem ok, but if the behavior is still off...

Aggie says: That's just it. His behavior is too "on" if anything. It feels almost as if he's mocking me.

Luke says: I thought he understood. He seemed genuinely sorry for it once he saw it.

Aggie says: I'm probably just being overly sensitive. I'm tired and frustrated.

Luke says: Why? What's wrong?

Aggie says: I have a stack of presents a mile high for the three littlest kids, Tavish, and Laird. I have nearly nothing for Kenzie, Ellie, or Vannie.

Luke says: Oh, Mom had an idea for Vannie. Actually, she had a few. She suggested getting some kind of jewelry. She said something about the owl skirt and the chocolate dress if those make any sense to you.

Aggie says: Oh, good idea. What other ideas? You said plural. I need plural.

Luke says: Um, she said maybe go to Boho and get a gift certificate and wrap it. You could both go into the city to pick out her things and have lunch while you're there. Vannie would love that. She also said maybe consider nail polish and a manicure set.

Aggie says: Those'll work. I wondered about one of those e-readers. I mean, with all the literature she's going to be doing, she'd get most of the books free; that'd pay for the cost of the thing over the life of it, and it'd save her eyes not reading the computer all the time.

Luke says: Those should be good. There. Vannie covered. What next?

Aggie says: Ellie.

Aggie says: Nope, Ian.

Luke says: You said you had a mile-high pile!

Aggie says: And he's crying for them now. Gotta go.

Luke says: Love you.

Aggie says: Yeah.. that's really nice to know right now. Love you too. Goodnight.

Luke stared at the screen, wondering what had bothered him during the conversation. Eventually it hit him, his heart sinking into his stomach. She hadn't changed Aggie to Mibs. Something that silly shouldn't bother him like it did, but he couldn't help it. It felt like he'd lost something he didn't know he valued until it was gone. Laird's name stared back at him from the screen. What had he missed? Something was still wrong. Very wrong.

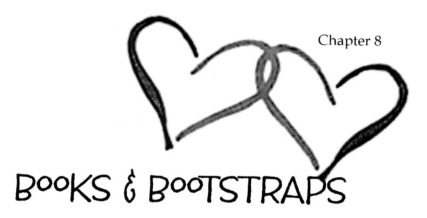

Chapter 8

BOOKS & BOOTSTRAPS

Tuesday, December 23

Kenzie's math book was a mess of red marks. "You didn't try, Kenzie. I know you know these. This is all review."

"Here, Kenzie. I'll help you," Laird said. "C'mere."

"Thanks, Laird. Ok, who's next?"

Ellie pushed her grammar across the table. "I think I understand now."

A shriek from the kitchen sent Aggie rushing from the room. "Check the first three sentences," she called out behind her. "If they're all right, correct the rest. If not, leave them."

A strange sight greeted her as she entered the kitchen. Lorna sat straddling Cari, holding back the other girl's feeble attempts to fight her off. "Not true! Say it's not true! You are a liar, Cari. Liar!"

"Lorna! What's wrong with you? Get off her."

"Not until she says it's not true!"

"What's not true?"

"That you," the little girl sniffed, "told Grandma Stuart that you didn't want us to have any presents!"

"She did! I heard her tell Luke! Grandma isn't sending presents!"

"Lorna," Aggie ordered, fighting back the temptation to laugh, "stand up right now."

"I—"

"Now!"

The little girl gave one last shove and stood up, her fists ready to attack if Cari came at her, but the younger twin seemed a bit subdued by such uncharacteristic aggression. "She started it," Lorna interjected, as if it would make any difference.

Cari flung herself at Aggie. "We are having presents, right? You went shopping and everything."

"Yes, we're having presents."

"See. Told you," Cari gloated with a smugness that would have been hilarious if the situation hadn't been so serious.

"But I heard you! I heard you tell Luke that Grandma isn't sending presents!"

"She's not, but I am. The law won't let her send them, but that doesn't mean there aren't going to be any presents." Aggie led them to the school room where Kenzie wept over her math problems. "You guys sit there—what's wrong with Kenzie?"

"Her brain is fried. I think that's why teachers usually have parties the last day of school. It's hard for kids to concentrate with all the coming excitement." He hardly gave Aggie a glance as he turned back to the math book and tried reminding her how to carry.

Aggie began to reply, but her phone rang, distracting her. "Just finish your assignments. I'll be back." Seconds later she burst through the doors. "Put your books away, Grandma and Grandpa are almost here! They came early!"

"Praise God for salvation."

Her head spun sharply. "What?"

"Isn't that how the song goes? 'Praise God for salvation for whosoever will..'"

"No, it's 'praise God for *full* salvation for whosoever will,²' why?"

"Just seemed like a good song for Grandma's arrival. I'll go make sure their room is ready."

Aggie was just out of earshot when Laird muttered, "If it's relaxing, maybe they'll stay a while this time."

"What, Laird?"

He turned and shrugged, pushing past Vannie with unnecessary force. "Laird!"

"Laird!" he echoed, mocking her as he entered the room. It was cold. He checked the vents and pushed them open. Aunt Tina had only been gone for less than two weeks and already her room was closed off as if she'd been banished from the house.

"What's wrong with you?"

110

He ignored Vannie's accusatory tone and shook his head. "Just trying to get the room warm for Grandma. Is Kenzie ok?"

"Sure. She was just trying to work too fast to get done."

"Most kids don't do schoolwork two days before Christmas."

"Most kids," Vannie countered with hands on her hips, "don't *start* school a month late. What's gotten into you?"

"Did you know she has the vents shut off to this room? Are we so broke that heating one little room is going to make a difference? Why is she buying all those gifts if we can't afford to heat a room?"

Vannie backed from the room, her head shaking. "That's ridiculous."

"That's me. Ridiculous Laird. Go away, Vannie. I've got to make sure the sheets are clean."

"Since when do you care about clean sheets?"

He threw her a nasty look and then stormed to the door, slamming it in her face. "Since now," he muttered between clenched teeth.

William burst through the door seconds after Ron and Martha arrived. "What happened? Who — what?"

A room full of excited people stopped chattering and stared at him. Ron stepped forward, "Glad to see you, deputy. You didn't have to rush over to welcome us."

"You didn't call?" His eyes sought Aggie's. "Dispatch said we got another 9-1-1 call."

"What?" Aggie's eyes darted around the room, illogically landing on Laird, but the confusion on his face was genuine; she was sure of it. "I don't know, William. Ian's asleep —" At that thought, she dashed upstairs, expecting to find the baby playing with the phone in his crib, but Ian was sound asleep, crammed into his favorite corner of the crib.

She arrived at the bottom of the stairs in time to hear Kenzie insist William come see the presents under the tree. "I have a present for you. Look!"

"Sweetheart, I have to find out what happened with the phone, but thank you."

The child was visibly crushed by her hero's dismissal of her surprise, and Aggie saw something else there—something strange. "Kenzie, come here."

Eyes wide, the little girl bolted from the room, through the kitchen, and out the back door. Confused, Aggie started to go after her, but William stopped her. "Let me. I think I understand quite a few things now. Where's her coat?"

Laird followed him to the mudroom and handed him her coat saying, "Thanks. It's good to see that someone cares."

In the living room, he sat next to Martha and asked about their trip. Aggie watched him, curious, until a call from Tina distracted her. By the time she slid her phone shut again, William led a tearful Kenzie into the room and beckoned her to follow them into the mudroom.

"Wha—"

"Kenzie has something to tell you."

"Kenzie?"

The little girl's tears were half-frozen on her cheeks. She stared miserably at Aggie and said, "I called the number."

"How many times, Kenzie?" William pressed.

"Almost all of them."

"And why did you do it?"

Aggie began to protest. Why wasn't really the issue. That she did it at all was sufficient. "She knows better. I don't think—"

"I think she should tell you why."

"I wanted him to come." The girl's sniffles made the next words difficult to understand, but the meaning was clear. "I wanted him to come, so he would like you." She frowned. "But it didn't work. You said no and now you're going to marry *Luke* instead."

The disappointed sniff in Kenzie's voice as she emphasized Luke's name was nearly Aggie's undoing. She stifled a snicker and sent the girl to her room. "I'll be up there in a few minutes."

Just at the door, Kenzie turned and gave them a weak smile. "I'm sorry. I won't do it again."

"Darn tootin' she won't," Aggie said as the door shut. She covered her mouth, trying not to laugh loudly enough for others to hear. "Can you believe that? Poor Luke."

"I knew she wanted me to marry you, but I never realized how much or for how long she's wanted it. She said she got the idea from

112

the first call. I don't know if any others were Ian's doing, but most were hers."

"All this time, I've thought that baby was a Houdini and it was Kenzie playing matchmaker?"

"Yeah." William's eyes seemed to be laughing. "Can you imagine what Sullivan will have to say about that."

"I think you should be the one to tell him. I've got to get to Rockland. I have a guitar on hold at a music store. If I'm late, they'll let it go."

"For who?"

"Laird. I overheard him mention it a few weeks ago and forgot all about it."

"Speaking of Laird, I think something's wrong with him."

Her eyes flew to search his. "Do you think so? I keep noticing little things that make me wonder, but then it's gone and he's normal again. I can't decide what to think!"

"Watch him. If you need help, let me know, but I'm sure you and Luke can handle it."

Aggie gave one last sorrowful glance back at William before she left the room. "I'm not sure of that anymore."

Wednesday, December 24

Aggie's bedroom looked like a wrapping center at a department store. Stacks of presents stood about her and rolls of wrapping paper littered the floor. Bows and ribbons seemed flung everywhere, in an apparent attempt to make everything be as festive as humanly possible.

A knock at her door sent a wave of panic over her. "Who—"

"It's me," Luke's head peeked in the door. "Am I safe or are you still wrapping mine?"

"Very funny. I'm swallowed up by kids right now, thank-you-very-much."

He whistled. "Santa's workshop never looked this full!"

"I have so many—too many. I kept buying like Mom said, but now I can't decide what to do. I evened out the gifts so that there aren't ten for one and two for another, but now we have a pile for each one and a pile to go back. The whole back of the van is full of returns, assuming I ever have the time to go back to all those places."

"I never thought I'd see the day when you spent this much money on anything without circumstance forcing it."

Her eyes roved over the mountains of gifts and her face fell as she realized he was right. She'd overdone it. "What do I do? I couldn't tell—"

"Give me a number. Let's start there. Just give me a number, one, three, ten, fifty. I don't care, but pick a number."

"Five. Seems like I usually had about five gifts at Christmas."

"That works."

From time to time, Luke held out two options, waiting for her to choose, and then put the reject in a plastic bag. It took longer than expected, but after much effort, the piles were cut in half. "There."

Aggie looked up from the audio books she was wrapping for her mother and frowned. "Still looks like a lot."

"It is. You have before you forty gifts—not including the ones you've been working on. We might have to pull a few more out."

"Nope. I've been working on my parents, Tina, your mother, Mrs. Dyke…"

Strong hands kneaded the knots in her shoulders as she surveyed the room once more. "I know this isn't half what they're used to, but I don't think I can pull out more. I'm getting hives just looking at that."

"Then let's get the other stuff out of here anyway."

Luke lifted the closest bag, but Aggie stopped him. "Wait. How can I give them what must seem like a cheap Christmas on the first year they lose their parents?"

"Do you plan to make it huge every year?"

"No…"

"Then they need a new normal. The important thing was to make this Christmas special—not recreate the past ones."

Tears filled Aggie's eyes. "And how did I do that? By disappearing every day, running myself crazy trying to find stuff, and being snappish because I was totally stressed out."

"Then do the twelve days of Christmas to Epiphany with them. One fun thing a day. Cookies one day, caroling another—whatever. Make it a tradition that you do the fun stuff after the holiday. It'll help with the whole letdown thing too."

The idea was beginning to grow on her. "We could watch

movies one day too. Maybe... oh, I've got a couple of days and maybe they can think of something!"

Once more, Luke tried to leave the room carrying the bags of rejected gifts, and Aggie stopped him. "Wait until they're in bed. The last thing we want to do is give them the idea that they are being cheated."

"That's a depressing thought. I don't think they're that greedy, do you?"

"I don't know anything right now," Aggie confessed. "I just know that I'm not going to risk ruining this for them or my parents. Not this year." She stacked another package on her hearth before asking, "Do you think I should give them next week off school? I wasn't going to. I mean, they got part of yesterday off and today. Monday; that means five and a half days. Is that enough of a break or should I give them the week?"

"Why wouldn't you? Don't most kids get at least two weeks?"

"Yeah, well, but we started so late..."

"And didn't you add extra work every day to help make up for that?"

Aggie frowned, thinking. "Yes, but I don't know that it has made enough of a difference. I'd have to look where they are compared to where they should be."

As she reached for the tape, Luke snatched it from the table. "Did you or did you not schedule that extra work so that they'd be caught up by the end of the year?"

"Yes..."

"Then why are you trying to catch them up on top of catching them up?"

The answer unnerved her even more than the question. "I already feel like I'm failing them, Luke. I need proof that they aren't going to be so far behind at the end of the year that I have to put them in school—and back where they should have been this year."

The emotion choking her seemed to change Luke's mind about continuing the conversation. He shook his head and passed the tape back to her. "Why don't we do this? Give the kids the week off. Their brains need the rest. Then, we'll talk about this after the first week that they're back, ok?"

A knock interrupted before Aggie could reply. "Can I come in?"

"Sure!" She beamed at her father. "Just in time to be put to work."

"What on earth is all this?"

"I took Mom a little too literally when she said buy whatever looks remotely interesting. The stuff in bags is going back—unless you think five presents each isn't enough."

"Five is plenty. It's a fraction of their usual, sure, but that'll be a relief. You can't imagine how horrible Christmas mornings were with Geraldine. We tried a couple of times, but Martha couldn't take it. You saw her at the twins' birthday!" He grinned at Aggie's relieved expression. "Between this and stockings, they'll have a Christmas any kid could hope for!"

"Stockings!" Her wail was likely heard at the North Pole, but Aggie didn't care. "I forgot. I got the few little things back when I expected a U-haul truck from the GIL and then promptly forgot about them."

"We'll pull from the bags. Where are the stockings? I'll see what fits." Luke seemed to hover in the doorway, waiting for direction to find Aggie's new nemesis.

"They're in my closet. Top shelf to the right."

She hadn't exaggerated. The limp stockings held the toothbrush, candy bar, and small silly item she'd described to her mother—those things not even filling the toes. "If I had been thinking, I could have bought gloves, scarves, socks—anything to fill them up."

"I'm on my way. You and your dad figure out what you have in those bags that can fit—even if you have to take it out of packaging— and by the time I get to the store we can fill them up over the phone."

Luke's feet thundered down the stairs and moments later, the front door banged shut. Aggie stared at her father. "Oh, I've really blown it this time."

"You know, you've been saying that a lot lately. Ever since Thanksgiving actually. I can't decide if you are regretting your engagement or regretting agreeing to keep the kids."

"Dad! I'm not regretting either."

"Well, it sounds like you are to me, and if I hear it just the little I get to talk to you, what do you think the kids or Luke think of it?"

He had a point. Although Aggie didn't want to admit it to herself or to him, her father made an excellent point. "Maybe that's why Vannie seems to bend over backwards to help and Laird is so

116

strange lately. Maybe that's why Luke seems hesitant to step in or out of things. Maybe I just really am not cut out for this." She sank to the floor and covered her head with her hands, her knees pulled up to her chest. "I won't give up, but right now I want to."

"Why?"

"Because it's hard, Daddy. It's just really hard. I had a mental idea of what difficult meant when I stepped into this mom thing. My head knew it; hey, even my heart knew it, but knowing and *knowing* are two different things. I never know if I've made the right decision. I never know if I'm doing a good job unless someone says so, and even then I wonder if they say it because they mean it or if they think it'll keep me from cracking."

Her eyes flew up over the table and met the tear-filled ones of her father. "Did I just say all that out loud?" she whispered, her voice sounding like someone else.

"Yes."

"I can't believe I said it."

"Did you mean it?"

The pathetic little nod she gave cut her to the heart, but not nearly as deeply as her next words. "I didn't say the half of it."

She found herself pulled from the floor and engulfed in her father's famous bear hug. "Aggs, I want to tell you something that you're not going to like to hear."

"What?"

"I am relieved to hear you say that."

"Relieved?"

Ron squeezed her tightly before stepping back and leaning against the table she'd erected for her wrapping station. "You've been brave—too brave. You have broken down about your loss—about Allie. You've broken down about your concerns about your abilities as a mother. You've broken down when you thought you hurt a friend or something like that, but you've taken the job itself in stride. If you failed, you picked up and made it a success."

"Isn't that good?"

"Aggie, if you walk around holding yourself up by your bootstraps, you'll find that you walk funny and soon the straps break."

"Can I be Scarlett O'Hara and think about that tomorrow? I'm going to have an epic fail if I don't get this Christmas going." She pointed to the stack of wrapped presents. "Can you take those down and put them in the school room?"

Mibs says: Luke?
Luke says: It's almost Christmas!
Mibs says: Four and a half minutes.
Luke says: Bet I say it first.
Mibs says: You'll just type it and wait until the clock turns and then hit enter. I know you of old.
Luke says: Who are you callin' old?
Mibs says: Hey, if the age fits...
Luke says: You seem a bit more yourself. I was worried about you.
Mibs says: Well, I wanted to talk to you, but I knew you needed sleep. Then I saw you online and thought I'd see if you were headed to bed or not.
Luke says: I'm good.
Mibs says: Dad and I got to talk today after you left.
Luke says: Yeah?
Mibs says: I kind of broke down.
Luke says: I'm sorry. I wish I had been there. Are you ok?
Mibs says: I don't know. That looks horrible, but it is true. I just don't know.
Luke says: I'm glad you're honest about it though.
Mibs says: Did you just get a maintenance message?
Luke says: Oh, great now there's a maintenance message.
Luke says: Yes.
Mibs says: I'll talk to you about this later then. Probably not tomorrow. No reason to ruin Christmas.
Luke says: Are we ok, Aggie?
Mibs says: As ok as we with me in "we" can be, yes.
Luke says: That sounds ominous.
Mibs says: I'm sorry. It's just all I can come up with right now that is both honest and reasonable.
This service is temporarily unavailable.

Tears of frustration filled Aggie's eyes. She needed to talk to him—desperately. Her eyes slid across the couch to the phone. She hated talking for long periods of time on the phone, but surely this was important enough. The clock on her laptop said it was ten minutes past midnight. She hadn't even gotten to say Merry Christmas. Her fingers flew over the phone keys. She could at least text him that much.

All the way up the drive, Luke kicked himself for not calling. What if she'd given up and gone to bed? The house was dark, but the Christmas lights were still lit on the tree and outside. Then again, perhaps she'd left them on for the children if they woke up when it was still dark.

The door was unlocked, assuring him she hadn't gone to bed yet. Aggie wouldn't go to bed without locking the door. The couch was empty, the kitchen dark. He stood in the entryway, trying to guess where she might be. The light had been off in her room— maybe the basement.

Just as his hand reached for the doorknob, he jumped, the sound of her voice nearly separating him from his skin. "I didn't see you."

"I just thought it'd be nice to look at the lights. I've always loved lying on the floor and gazing up at the tree on Christmas Eve."

"Well, we have something else in common. I actually did that at mom's last night."

"You don't have a tree?"

He lowered himself to the floor beside her and grabbed a pillow from the chair in the process. "Not this year."

"I'm sorry."

"I'm not." Luke tucked Aggie's hair behind her ear in order to see her face. "I had another tree that I preferred to visit."

"I didn't expect you to come."

"I didn't expect that you would expect me to come. I just thought you sounded as if you wanted to talk."

"I said something awful today."

The idea was so ludicrous to him that Luke had a hard time not laughing. "What did you say?"

"That I want to give up."

119

Dread filled his heart. "Give what up?"

"This pretense that I can do what Allie asked me to do. I'm failing in everything."

"That's not true. It probably feels true, but it's not."

"Well, then I'm also a failure at recognizing my own weaknesses."

"Do you really," Luke began, the despair that had been planted now taking root in his heart, "want to give up on the pretense or is it the reality?"

"What do you mean?"

"Do you regret telling the kids you'll keep them?"

"No!"

Despite the doubts she'd implanted in his heart, the vehemence with which she rejected that notion left little question of her sincerity. "I'm relieved," he whispered when he noticed her impatience at the delay in his response.

"I couldn't do that to them."

Fear crept back into his heart. "Mibs, that's not what I asked you. I asked if you regretted it, not if you'd changed your mind."

Again she shook her head as her fingers played with the tassel on his pillow. "I don't regret telling them what I did. I do regret not thinking about it more fully before I jumped in like I did."

"You would make a different decision today?"

It took some time for her to answer, but at last she said, "No, but at least I might have been prepared for the worst rather than assuming that if Allie thought I could do it then I must be able to manage it. She didn't think I could do much of anything practical."

"I doubt that."

"It's true. I can't tell you how many times I heard her tell Doug, 'Oh well, Aggie is the dreamer in the family, you know.'"

"And how does that translate to not being able to do anything?"

She shrugged. "It's hard to explain unless you've seen it."

"Ok," he began, trying another tactic, "you're failing at everything. What everything?"

"Um, I think the word is pretty self-explanatory. Everything. As a daughter, I barely think to call my parents. If they aren't online late at night, I never get to talk to them anymore. As a friend, I am basically a user now. What can you do to keep my head above water? That's all that matters now. As a sister, well that's irrelevant now—"

120

she choked back a sniffle.

"But hardly something you can consider a failure."

"Ok, how about the fact that I haven't visited the graves once? What about the fact that I have hardly talked to the kids about her at all because every time I do it rips me apart?"

"Mibs..."

"No, you listen to me," she said, sitting up and leaning against the couch. He watched her cross her arms and felt as if they were the first bricks in a wall she was determined to construct between them. "I'm trying to be honest here. This is so hard. I'm exhausted. I can't seem to do anything right. The kids are behind in school, they are bickering almost non-stop at times, and Laird... I think I've totally lost him."

"Remember when Uncle Zeke and I told you that things were too perfect — that you all weren't grieving right?"

"Yeah."

"Well, I think the kids got on with the process pretty well, but you were still holding up the fort. Helping them grieve was just one more to-do thing on that unending list of yours."

"See? I can't even grieve without blowing it!" Her eyes widened and she whispered behind a strangled giggle, "Did I really just say that?"

Without that giggle, his chuckle might have offended her, but thankfully she'd cracked first. "Well, it did sound a bit amusing."

"What am I going to do?"

Truthfully, he didn't know what she meant by the question, but something about it made him hesitant to ask. Instead, he turned the question into another direction. "What were Allie's weaknesses?"

"What?"

"Just what I asked. What were Allie's weaknesses?"

"She didn't have any — I mean she was a bit of a perfectionist, but that's one of those really annoying weaknesses that at least look like a virtue."

"I think you should ask your parents. There were enough years between you that I bet you never got to see the flaws that made Allie an interesting person."

"Flaws."

"Look, Mibs," he insisted, "we all have an arsenal of weaknesses at our disposal. They're there to keep us humble and to remind others that they aren't alone in this walk we call life."

"That sounds too profound for my brain."

"You're tired. Go to bed. We'll go have a coffee and talk about it more tomorrow."

"We can't get coffee anywhere tomorrow."

Luke pushed himself off the floor and tossed the pillow aside. "No, we can't get coffee today, but tomorrow is another story."

As she walked him to the door, Aggie leaned her head on his shoulder, her hand wrapped in his. "Thanks for coming, Luke."

"Do you feel any better?"

"Not really, but I probably will when I'm not as tired."

A sprig of mistletoe, put up by the children just that evening, hovered over their heads. Luke rolled his eyes and jerked it from the tack, stuffing it in his jacket. "I'm just helping them to not make me stumble... or something like that. Call me when you hear the first screech or feel the first bounce on your bed. I'll be right over."

"Are you sure your sisters—"

"They expect me by ten, so we'll have a few hours. They understand."

At home, he stared at his laptop, still sitting where he'd left it, the messenger box open and the cursor flashing. He didn't know when she'd see it, but he had to send one quick message.

Luke says: And she heard him exclaim as he closed the website, "Happy Christmas to all and to all a good night." Love you.

122

Chapter 9

CHRISTMAS CHEER

Thursday, December 25th

Despite her predictions, Aggie awoke Christmas morning with a fresh confidence in her ability to do whatever the Lord gave her to do — including raising eight children. However, by the third tantrum of the morning, her confidence had waned. The enormous pile of presents under the tree had seemed enough for a small army, but an innocent comment by Vannie regarding her relief in not having such a daunting pile of gifts sparked a chain of events, some real, even more imagined, that tore at Aggie all morning.

By the time Luke left, she'd given up her rosy idyllic dreams for the day and decided that she simply had to get through it. The mess swallowed the room, but only Aggie seemed to notice. She ignored her father's urging to relax and made the rounds of the room with a trash bag, stuffing wrapping paper, ribbons, and packaging in it.

"Aunt Aggie, here's one from Luke."

Her heart sank. She'd forgotten to insist he opened his before he left. "Just set it in the window. I'll open it later."

"Come on, open it!" several voices urged, but Aggie refused.

"Who is next then?" her father asked.

"Laird. He has only opened two."

Eager to see which one he'd open, Aggie watched closely, but what she saw disturbed her. Laird's expression was fleeting but telling. He was clearly upset and yet also seemed — smug. Though tempted to call him on it, she decided that it wasn't the time.

Several jokes about the size of the present erupted from the room. However, Vannie's quip about how it should count for all of his gifts just by its size earned her a snarky response. Aggie was appalled. "Laird!"

"Maybe you agree with her? I can go dump it in the van with all the other stuff you decided we didn't deserve."

Ron pounced on that quickly. "That's enough, Laird."

"What—"

"I'm sorry, Laird. It was a bad joke. I want to see what it is. Open it."

She hated the relief that washed over her as he complied, giving Vannie a half smile. As he pulled the guitar from its case, she saw joy on his face for the first time that day. Maybe he was just tired. They'd all had a rough few weeks, and it *was* the first Christmas without Allie and Doug. The kids would feel that—particularly Laird and Vannie—wouldn't they?

The horrible sounds he tortured from the instrument made her wonder if she'd regret the decision. Lessons—she'd have to find a teacher and soon. There went the idea of not having any activities this semester. One glance back at him, and Aggie didn't care anymore. Laird was laughing at something Cari said and showing her how to strum the strings gently. There was the boy she knew and loved.

A text message chimed on her phone. She opened it to see a picture of Luke wearing a T-shirt with handprints all around the words, "The World's BEST Uncle-daddy." A second message followed that read, "Mom did it with the kids a couple of weeks ago. Apparently it was their idea. Thought you'd like it."

Aggie passed her phone around the room so the children and her parents could see Luke wearing his shirt. As she typed out a response, she reminded him that she hadn't given him his gift and told him she was saving the one he'd left under the tree for when he came over again. HUG YOUR MOM FOR ME, she added as an afterthought.

Tavish squeezed her excitedly once he unwrapped the snowshoes she'd thought were a dumb idea but had risked anyway. Out the backdoor he ran, eager to see if they worked. Lorna and Cari stood at the dining room window, watching with evident glee. "He looks like a penguin! Hey! He fell down. I thought they were supposed to make it easy!"

"I think they do if you know how to use them," Kenzie chimed, following them to watch. "He's still a novel at them."

"Novice, Kenzie."

"Right. Novice. Because novels are for novelties?" The girl's eyes brightened as the cogs clicked into what she considered perfect places. "And novelties are short novels, right?"

Aggie giggled. "Not quite. Short novels are novellas now. All novels were once novellas. It all comes from the same thing, but one kind of novel is now a book—" She could see the child's eyes glazing over and chose to stop it. "Well, anyway. It's close, but not quite. Look, he's doing great now!"

Just then, Sammie dashed around the corner of the house, obviously having escaped their latest attempt to keep the dogs penned where they belong, and jumped on Tavish, knocking him over. "Well, he was doing great anyway."

"How come the dogs don't need snowshoes?" Cari asked.

Kenzie snorted. "Because they'd just eat them."

Her door pushed open slightly as Vannie knocked gently on it. "Aunt Aggie?"

"Come in. It's safe now."

She shoved her laptop aside, closing the lid. With pillows to support them and blankets up to their chins, aunt and niece began a difficult but important conversation. "I think something is wrong with Laird," Vannie blurted out without ceremony.

"I've wondered the same thing. Why do you think so?"

Nervous fingers picked at the bedspread while Vannie worked to articulate the troubles in her heart. "He said something about the heating vents being shut off in the spare room and then something about too much school. It wasn't what he said really, but the way he said it was weird. Laird doesn't even care about that stuff! I don't understand what is going on."

The girl was right. It didn't sound like what he'd said was too terrible, but Vannie wasn't likely to overreact over a few words. No, something else had to be bothering her. One look at those hands— nearly shaking with the weight of whatever was pressing on her— told Aggie she had to ask. "There's something more, isn't there?"

"He scared me."

"How?"

"It was the way he shoved me when he went past and how he almost charged me when he wanted me out of the room. Honestly," she ducked her head and dropped her voice to a whisper, "that's the kind of thing I might do if I was upset—not Laird. He just ignores everything and then if he can't take it anymore, he walks away. He doesn't...um..."

"Engage?"

"Yeah! Engage. It's just not his personality. It's hard enough to get him to get worked up over anything in the first place. Usually it's when he can't do anything right, but I don't think that's it this time."

"What do you mean?"

Vannie sat up, her hands pulling the pillow behind her into her lap and clutching it to her chest as if for support. "Laird has always been really laid back. You can make him do everything all the time, push him hard, or totally ignore him and he doesn't say anything. The only time he fights back is if you do all that and you're still not satisfied with him."

"Right..."

"Well, this isn't that. The way he's reacting is different. Laird gets in your face and says that. 'What do you want from me? I can't do anything right so maybe I should quit.' Stuff like that. This is sneaky. Little things under his breath and nasty looks." The girl buried her head into her pillow as she said, "And it's mostly at you when you're not looking or can't hear."

All of Aggie's hidden fears were confirmed in that one half-muffled confession. "Thank you for telling me. I've wondered if I've seen things lately, but then everything seems fine, and I allowed myself to be convinced that it was my imagination." She hesitated— unsure if her next idea was a good one or not, but Aggie was desperate. "If you hear or see anything that you think I need to know, I want you to tell me. You have to do it for Laird's sake."

Vannie dragged herself from the bed a little while later and started to leave the room. At the door she hesitated. "You know, I used to try so hard to tattle to Mommy about everything. I wanted her to see how grown up I was—that I could be a good helper. She never let me and I kind of grew out of it—mostly. I don't think I like it anymore. I hope he just quits. I feel sick."

"I'm sorry. Maybe you shouldn't worry about telling me," Aggie said, doubt creeping into her voice.

"No! That's not even what I was talking about. I was talking about coming up here. I just thought Mommy was trying to punish me or something for being too bossy and stuff, but I think she was trying to save me from feeling bad now. I used to get a kind of satisfaction out of telling Grandma Millie that one of the kids did something wrong and see them get in trouble because of it. This is just icky though."

"Well, if you decide it's too much, you tell me. If I'd known that Allie didn't allow it…"

"Mommy didn't allow tattling. You asked me to report. I think it's different."

"What do you think she meant?" Aggie's hands cupped her coffee, savoring the warmth as she inhaled the comforting aroma.

"I think she meant that tattling is telling with an attitude— either a desire to feel superior or to make someone else pay for something. Reporting is simply relaying facts that might ultimately help the person being reported."

His words made sense; she could see the difference clearly, but Aggie wasn't certain. "I just wish I knew. I wish there was a flow chart for parents. "If the kid does this, answer this question and follow until you reach the final answer."

Luke reached for the gifts they'd brought and pushed hers across the island. "Mom'll be back soon. We can talk to her. Better open that."

The box was long and slim, almost like a jeweler's necklace box. Aggie pulled off the bow and stuck it to the top of her head as she unwrapped the paper. "Do you think we're overreacting?"

"No. I thought he looked penitent that day, but I think I've seen signs of that same arrogance I saw when he handed me the paper with shortness erased and brevity inserted. It's not right."

She lifted the lid and smiled at the carved wood nestled in cotton. "It's perfect."

"I thought we'd be needing a name change, so while I helped

Chad with something, I did that."

Without hesitation or even a jacket, she hurried outside to lay the piece over the names on her plaque. Milliken-Stuart now read Sullivan-Stuart. Luke handed her the box as he stepped onto the porch after her. "You didn't get it all."

Under one layer of cotton, another small piece lay. "I thought we'd put it there at the bottom. There's just enough room there and it seemed like it'd look more balanced if there was more than one raised portion."

His words registered in some part of her brain, but her concentration was on the words of the verse. "…makes her the joyful mother of children…"

"That verse personifies you," Luke murmured between teeth inclined to chatter.

"Let's go in."

She planted herself back on the stool she had been using and played with the little wooden pieces. "Will you use black screws?"

"Not brass?"

Her nose wrinkled. "Ew, no. Too shiny." As she spoke, she looked up at him apologetically and then frowned. "That wasn't nice."

"What's wrong?"

"That verse. It's not like me at all. I'm not joyful."

"You're having a bad week, but that doesn't mean that usually you don't enjoy this life you have."

"Then I'm a really good actress I guess." She dropped her head in her hands. "I'm also a failure it seems."

"Laird?"

"Yes. I took the world's most easy-going boy and turned him into a nasty rebel. Allie is probably crushed."

"You know, a couple of weeks of bad attitudes doesn't mean the kid is a hopeless case—ruined for life. It just means we have to find the root of the attitude and fix it."

"Have any ideas?" Aggie shoved Luke's present across the counter. "Your turn."

"I do, but I don't like it."

"Why?"

"Why what?"

That didn't bode well. He was stalling. She opted for what was likely the less painful answer. "What don't you like?"

"I think he's lost respect for you."

"Or never had it is more like it."

Luke rested his chin on the box in front of him. "You're determined to be miserable, aren't you?"

"That's not fair..." She sighed. "Yeah, I guess it is." She shook her head and eyed the box. "Just open it."

Nestled in a square box were half a dozen hand-tied fishing flies. "Where—Willow. Chad said she made them. You bought them when you went to do the dresses, didn't you?"

"Yep. I hope Chad forgives me. They were supposed to be part of his gift."

Luke grinned as he fingered each one, commenting on their uniqueness and beauty. "We won't tell him then, eh?"

Another package sat between them, but neither wanted to acknowledge it. Once open, Luke would feel obligated to leave. "Oh, I decided not to do school all week. I think a break is going to be good."

"Well, I think I know the answer to my dilemma then. I've been deciding if I should invest the time in a set of built-ins around the fireplace on Cygnet. What if I do it and see if Laird wants to help? Maybe he'll open up to me if we're just working together."

"If he doesn't respect me, will that make it worse?"

"I don't see how it can. We'll see. It can't hurt to try." Luke pushed the gift toward her. "I had to do it when I saw it."

Aggie considered the decision made and the subject changed as she pulled the wrapping paper from the box. "Oh, Luke! It's too much!"

"Now you can have your favorite coffee in half a minute if the reviews I read are true."

She walked him to his truck, her arm wrapped around his and leaning on him. "Thank you. I didn't expect you to have time to come tonight."

"Mom says she's got plans to give us some time to go out and do couple things like registering at stores and all that stuff. I say we spend it kicking back and doing something fun."

"I need it," she whispered. "Besides, it's not like we need to register anyway. We've got everything we need and then some."

Luke pulled her into a hug. "We'll get through this, Mibs. Every mother has bad day—sometimes weeks. We'll start with a few days off from Laird and then a few days away from everyone so you can recharge. I think you just need a break."

Friday, December 26th

"He just loved the flies. It was perfect. I can't thank you enough."

Willow smiled her acknowledgement and pinched at the bodice. "I think this fabric stretches—which is weird. It shouldn't. Anyway, I'll have to take it in a bit, but even if I don't, it'll work."

Aggie smiled at Vannie's pleased face. The dress was perfect. She looked like a red-headed Zenita Shinn. "How does that pink look good with her hair? It should look terrible. We were going to go with blue at first, but this worked and it looks even better now."

"No green?"

"On St. Patrick's month? You're kidd—oh, you are kidding."

"Well, I don't think it would really matter. Not really but this pink and red... I never knew it would look this nice together."

"Ok, this one is ready to go. Ellie's is next."

Neither Ellie nor Kenzie needed any changes to their dresses, but the twins' were several inches shorter than Willow expected. "I'm not going to hem these until the last minute. I don't want to cut them off now and find out that they grew more."

"Children are a'pposed to grow," Cari informed their hostess. "Mrs. Sullivan said so."

"Yes you are! I remember my mother embroidering me a very special dress for spring one winter. By the time she finished it and spring was here, she had to add an underskirt so it wouldn't be too short. I think I got two sets of clothes that spring and summer. About the time we'd finish something and I'd wear it for a month or two, it'd be looking like time to start making more."

"Did your sister get your old clothes? We get Kenzie's old clothes sometimes."

"I didn't have a sister. Just my mother."

Lorna's eyes welled up with huge tears. "That's terrible! You're like—like an orphan!"

"Lorna!" Aggie sighed, apologizing quickly. "I think they were

130

too young to see even our highly-edited version of Annie..."

Willow caught Aggie's eyes over the heads of the children and shook her head slightly. "Yes I am. I don't have a mom or a dad."

"We don't either," Cari said. "Does that make us orphans?"

"Well, yes," Willow said, "but you have other family like your aunt and your grandparents. I don't have anyone—not really."

"Your mommy should have had more children."

"Cari!"

Willow's attempt to stifle a snicker failed. "I remember Mother saying, 'Children say the darndest things,' but I never knew what that meant. I understand it now."

The children were sent to play while Aggie and Willow sat on the couch, chatting. "Are you all set for the wedding?"

At first, Aggie assumed the question was a joke, but the confident expression on Willow's face assured her that the question was spoken in earnest. "I've hardly done anything and now my organizing friend has had to go home just as I'll have time to do something."

"Well, it can't be that much trouble, can it? I thought Chad said you were doing it at home."

"We are, but there's the reception, and I have to find someone to cater the thing. Mom can't do a lot of the things that we'd want to if she was in better health and I wasn't busy with a brood."

"Books always make weddings sound like such a hassle, but when they describe what is causing the trouble, it never seems like a very serious problem. I suppose that's fiction for you." Willow didn't sound as though she thought the problem lay with stories, but with people.

"I don't know. I'll tell you once it's all over. It sounds daunting, but it's probably not that bad. We do have to get going on things. I'm so glad I had you take care of the dresses early enough."

"Do you have yours finished?"

"I haven't even looked. There's a huge sale at one of the chain stores next week though. I'm hoping to find one there—cheap."

"Smart girl. Chad said that some people spend several hundred or even thousands of dollars just on the one dress that they only wear for a few hours!"

"Yes, they aren't cheap."

"I don't suppose you have anything white at home..."

Aggie stifled a snort. "Not that would work for a festive occasion like this, no."

Before she could continue, Aggie's phone rang. She excused herself and answered, telling Luke that all was well, but his words sent her rushing to the window and nodding as she listened. "You're right. We've got to get out of here. Thanks for calling."

Just then, Tavish burst into the house. "It's coming down pretty hard, Aunt Aggie. I can't get Cari and Lorna to come in and Kenzie won't leave them. She's afraid she'll get in trouble."

"We're going. Tell everyone to get in the van."

Ellie crept from her place on the stair landing and replaced a book in the library. "Do you want me to carry Ian out to his seat?" The girl looked pointedly at the sleeping baby on the couch.

"I'll do it. It might be slippery."

"That one listens," Willow said. "She's an intelligent girl."

"She scares me sometimes. She's too adult for a child her age."

"I think," Willow said, retrieving the baby's coat for Aggie, "I would have been like her as a child. If there had been others talking, I would have found a way to be near. You would learn more about people and life that way."

"That's why I said she scares me sometimes. I can't be on my guard as much I probably should be."

Willow's next words sounded terrifyingly odd to Aggie—and true. "I wouldn't worry about it. She'll be an adult soon enough and you won't have to think about it anymore."

Thursday, January 1st

Mibs says: Did you find your gloves?

Luke says: Mom says Uncle Zeke says he thinks he has them.

Mibs says: Well, can you stop by tomorrow and grab 'em?

Luke says: Yep. And I can leave Meggie for the day. She's been alone a lot lately.

Mibs says: You could bring her here. I mean, what's the difference between now and March?

Luke says: I still have to see how she does with Miner and Sammie. I should do that when I'll be around.

Mibs says: I suppose.

Luke says: Mom says Willow enjoyed holding Ian. Aunt Marianne told Mom that Willow joked about you maybe giving him up, so she could have him."

Mibs says: Not on your life.

Luke says: I think that's the gist she got from Aunt Marianne. Mom also says she gave Willow an earful about marriage.

Mibs says: Marriage? Willow? She seems pretty set against it.

Luke says: She is. Mom thinks that Chad wants to go the marriage route and Willow is fighting it.

Mibs says: Willow isn't going to do it if she doesn't want to do.

Mibs says: Hey, got a question for you.

Luke says: Shoot.

Mibs says: Well, today when I went up to get Ellie for breakfast, she hid something from me.

Luke says: Hid something? Like what?

Mibs says: I don't know. If I knew what I'd have told you.

Luke says: Did you ask her about it?

Mibs says: No. I thought maybe a kid needs a little privacy even if it doesn't make sense.

Luke says: Well, if she had a history of it, I'd disagree with you there, but Ellie's usually open if you ask. Maybe she's working on a project and isn't pleased with it. You know how she is if things aren't working out right.

Mibs says: Maybe. Just after this whole thing with Laird, I think I'm a bit jumpy.

Luke says: I can understand that.

Mibs says: I should tell you. I dread Monday.

Luke says: Why?

Mibs says: I think it's going to be telling whether Laird has really come out of his bad attitude or if it's just a calm before the storm.

Luke says: I'm sure it's fine.

Mibs says: I should go to bed. The kids
went to bed early. Even Vannie complained about being tired. I bet they're all up at sunrise.

Luke says: Ok. Mom said that she'll be there Tuesday at eight o'clock, so you can get into town in time for the opening.

Mibs says: Oh, good. Thanks.

Luke says: Get something amazing.

Mibs says: That's easy for you to say. You're not the one without her best friend to advise you.

Luke says: Did you hear from Tina?

Mibs says: Yeah. She's doing pretty well I guess. She's taking over the finding of a place for the reception, where I go to taste test the cakes, and she's ordering the invitations as soon as we have a place for the reception — "the venue." I need a list.

Luke says: Mom's got that.

Luke says: Wait, is there a Cinderella Bridal in Yorktown?

Mibs says: Yeah.

Luke says: Why don't you drive up there Monday night. Your mom can go with you to the store to see and maybe Tina can show up for a couple of hours.

Mibs says: Drive eight hours?

Luke says: You'll be glad you did once you've got the memories. I'll come stay with the kids until Mom gets here on Tuesday.

Mibs says: You are so tempting me.

Luke says: Come on. Do it. Think of how much fun it'll be.

Mibs says: And the gas!

Luke says: Take my truck… or even rent a car.

Mibs says: I can't rent a car! I'm not twenty-five.

Luke says: You can too. Yeah, it costs more, but trust me. You can.

Mibs says: Are you really trying this hard to get rid of me?

Luke says: It's that obvious, huh?

Mibs says: Fine. I'll go. But under one condition.

Luke says: What's that?

Mibs says: You find me a sitter for Thursday or Friday so we can do the big returns. I've got bags of stuff that has to go back!

Luke says: Deal. See you tomorrow. You go to bed.

Mibs says: Ok. Night.

Luke says: Love you.

Mibs says: What a coincidence! I was just about to inform you of the same thing.

Chapter 10

ALL ABOUT A DRESS...

Tuesday, January 6th

Aggie shivered in line as she waited her turn to go into the massive warehouse of dresses. Her mom, parked in a handicapped space only twenty feet away, sat comfortably ensconced in Aggie's rental car, reading a book. The idea nearly drove her crazy, but now wasn't the time to think about it. In fact, all she had time to consider was how to keep her teeth from breaking from the chattering cold like a cartoon character.

"Here he comes!" someone from the front called. Aggie glanced at the car as she punched the button for her mother's phone. Martha nodded from the passenger's seat and managed to meet Aggie in line before Aggie reached the door.

"Perfect timing, Mom."

"Hey, you can't just let her cut in line!"

"She can't sit in the cold. Notice the handicapped placard? They're not both trying on dresses." The man waved them through and warned the protester behind them that he'd refuse service if they started any trouble.

"Where's Tina? What if she doesn't make it in?"

"I believe she's in there already. When she found out I was coming, she said she'd camp out early this morning so she could stockpile dresses as they brought out new stuff."

True to her word, Tina waited just outside the dressing room, engulfed in white. "I've pretty much bribed one of the employees. She has a stack back there for you, but you've gotta be fast."

"What'd you get?"

Tina grinned. "If it had any kind of sleeve or strap, was your size, and wasn't designed for aquatic females of the ocean, it's there. Let's go."

Nothing had prepared her for how ridiculously exhausting it would be—not to mention fun—to try on dress after dress. One was too poofy, the next too straight. The fabric looked wrong on this one and the cut weird on the next. A tiny pile grew next to Martha as potential options, but in her heart, Aggie knew she wouldn't pick any of them.

A commotion outside the dressing area sent a half-dressed Aggie rushing to her mother's side. "What's wrong?"

"This girl tried to jerk that one out of my hands!"

"You can't wear it! It's too small for you!" the young woman hissed. "It's exactly the one I've been looking for!"

"Let her have it, Mom. I was just deciding against it while I put this one on."

"How can people be so rude?" Martha sighed as she relinquished the dress to the gloating girl before them.

Tina stepped close to Martha, almost protectively. "You got the dress, now go. It's pathetic to attack an older woman over a dress."

"It's ok, Tina. Actually, you can send those others to the floor again. I like this one better than any of those, so we'll start a new pile."

Back in the dressing room, Aggie stared at the dress. The spaghetti straps bothered her. She'd always avoided the look, but it was flattering. Then again, it did have a wrap with it. That gave her an idea and she called for Tina. "What if we had Libby take the wrap and cut it into kind of wider gathered straps that would cover my shoulders?"

"That'd work... maybe."

"Well, let's keep this in the pile for now. I think we should hang them in here. I don't want Mom hospitalized over a dress. The headlines wouldn't be good for the store's business for one thing."

After three more dresses arrived, the spaghetti straps were sent back to the floor and Tina arrived with even more dresses. "They just brought out four huge racks. I'll be back."

Fifteen minutes later, Aggie stood in her dress. She couldn't hook the back together, but it made no difference. It fit; she could feel it even while still unfastened. The sleeves weren't awkward like most she'd seen and the fabric was the heavy satin that she'd grown to love in the past—she glanced at her phone—five hours. Her heart sank. Had she really been there for five hours? Her mother was probably exhausted. They needed to go.

"Can you go find my friend please?" she begged a passing attendant. I need this fastened and then I think we'll be ready to go after that. This is the one; I can tell."

"Here, let me fasten you and then you can find her. People are getting ugly out there. If I go out now, I'll be called to referee. I'm not good at that."

Once hooked into place, the bodice fit as if made for her. The skirt was too long, but it wouldn't be a reconstruction to shorten it. The simple a-line skirt would simply need to be cut off and re-hemmed. She stepped from the room and saw her mother glance up at her, weariness evident. From the corner of her eye, she saw Tina stop mid-stride and then turn and hand a stack of gowns to an assistant.

"That's the one, Aggie," Martha and Tina said in unison.

"It's only two hundred dollars. That's a thousand dollars off!"

"The bottom is dirty," Tina said critically, "but then you're short and it'd have to be cut off anyway."

"It's mine."

"Then let's get you out of it and get it paid for," Martha said. "I want coffee."

"Mom!"

"Decaf, of course! Goodness!"

Over the first quiet meal she had enjoyed in an indeterminate amount of time, Aggie and Tina tried to catch up on life in Brant's Corners. "School is really going well, actually. We're getting close to caught up, but the kids are pretty sick of it."

"You have a good plan. I wouldn't worry about it."

"Yeah, well, I've been a bit obsessive about catching up. They're making good progress. Oh, you should have read Laird's paper on that Lemony Snickett book."

"You said it was epic."

"Well," Aggie admitted, "I was pretty ticked off about it. That first one was only one sentence. Luke said he put the kid straight, though." A new thought occurred to her. "I wonder if Luke being hard on him about not showing disrespect to me is what set him off. He's been angsty. Rebellious but sly about it."

"What did Luke have to do with it?"

Aggie cut another piece of meat before she answered, savoring the flavors that she couldn't afford to try to learn to cook. Ten rib eye steaks would feed them for a week—or at least a few days. "I read the second one and it felt like he was mocking me. I didn't want to ignore that, but I also didn't want him to feel attacked if he just meant to be clever instead of disrespectful, you know?" She didn't wait for Tina's response. "I told him to show Luke and whatever grade Luke gave it stood."

"Well, I see why you did it," Tina stated after thinking for a moment, "but do you think perhaps he took it as you being too weak to handle an insolent boy and it gave him a sense of power over you?"

"Oh. Hmm…"

"What grade did Luke give him?"

"An A for the second paper, but he said the F I gave Laird for the first had to go on the books."

"Good for him!" As the patrons at neighboring tables glanced their way, Tina added more quietly. "Laird should get docked for that. He knew what you meant."

"That's what Luke said."

"I think you should apologize to Laird."

"What?" Aggie hadn't expected that.

"Think about it. You sprung another authority on him out of the blue. You passed the buck. You washed your hands—"

"I got the idea three clichéd metaphors ago. Don't you think, since he clearly doesn't respect me now, an apology is going to make it sound like I am even weaker than ever?"

"It takes a strong person to apologize, Aggie. Don't apologize for why you did it—just for the solution."

"Maybe. I'll think about it."

"And pray about it, I expect. So," she continued very obviously changing the subject for Aggie's sake, "let's talk cakes. I've got to get you to a bakery and soon. What kind of cake do you want?"

"I want traditional white with raspberry filling and cream cheese frosting. You had to ask?"

Tina slid her iPad across the table. "Good. Then I'll make an appointment here."

The reviews for the bakery were stellar—particularly on the cake choice Aggie had made. "You're not going to argue that it's boring and uninspired?"

"If you had said plain chocolate, I would have dropped dead of a heart attack—bad joke. You have always insisted that the only kind of cake that should ever be served at a wedding is white with raspberry filling and cream cheese frosting."

"Did you have a style in mind?"

Her mind went to their childhood discussions of cakes. Towers of cakes and fountains all connected by bridges choked her memories, and her nose wrinkled before she could stop it. "No. All I can think of is Allie's giant thing, remember?"

"Yeah. We thought it was perfection personified. Ugh."

Her fingers flew through the bakery's gallery images, showing a few, but after half a dozen, Aggie took the tablet and began scrolling through pictures. Each time she found one she liked, she started to pass it to Tina and then hesitated. After several unsuccessful minutes, while the last few bites of her steak became inedible and cold, she shook her head and set it on the table.

"I don't like any of them. I don't care if it's square or round. No heart shape though. I like them stacked and three tiers look nice, but so do two. I actually seem to like two better. I don't care what design is on it, but no color. All white. We'll figure out the top later. Maybe they can do something with sugar or something."

"Or something," Tina agreed with a wink. "What about orange blossoms? Weren't those popular once?"

"Yeah, but have you ever seen them? They could be ugly!"

"What kind of flowers do you want for your bouquet and such?"

"Red roses. I know," she sighed. "That's cliché too, but it's what I want."

"What about adding some dark pink or red lilies? Just for visual interest."

"Visual interest. You know that it'll probably get left on top of Luke's truck and someone will run over it after we leave."

"You're going to throw it and I'm going to catch it before falling into William's arms, remember?" The embarrassment that Aggie would have felt in saying something like that was glaringly absent from Tina's face. "He called me."

"I expected he would."

"Every day."

Aggie's eyes widened and a grin appeared. "Oh, really?"

"This is about you. Not me and William. Or William and me. Or William and I—no me. Definitely me."

"You're nervous—self-conscious. Since when does Tina Warden ever get self-conscious?"

"Since now. Now what is Luke wearing?"

"Black tux." Aggie knew what was coming before Tina opened her mouth.

"Not white?"

"I was enamored with Allie's wedding, ok?"

"We both were. My sense of style caught up quicker than yours did."

"Wedding bands?"

"Plain white gold to match the ring, of course."

"You're sure about the plain." Tina had an abhorrence for plain wedding bands.

"I know what you're thinking. 'It makes it look like the guy is willing to fork over good money to get the girl and then he shows his real colors when he buys the cheapest band out there.'"

"And don't you forget it. We both know Luke isn't cheap, but not everyone else does. He got you a nice ring. Why not have a nice band to match? You only get one once!"

"But," Aggie protested, "is this about showing the world—people I probably don't know or care about—how great Luke is, or is it about having the ring set I really want?"

"Great. Want me to find a jeweler for you?"

"Yeah. One in Rockland close to wherever I might have bought presents that have to go back."

"I'll have a list for you by the time you get home." Tina took a drink and then said. "Willow mailed my dress."

"How does it look?"

"Fits perfectly and I don't look stupid. How do I not look stupid in that dress? You know how much I hated Music Man!"

140

"I just like to keep you hopping."

"Music."

"I don't know. Know a cellist and an oboist?"

"Oboist?"

"Whatever you call an oboe player."

Tina shook her head. "Knowing you, it's probably oboist. What about something with a higher range for contrast? Flute? Violin?"

"Violin. Whatever. Maybe there's some kind of up and coming ensemble that needs a gig—do they call them gigs for ensembles instead of bands—and they would be affordable. High school musical prodigies or something?"

"Harp?"

Aggie shook her head. "No harp. Too big and too—fussy."

"But a cello is small."

"Oh, leave me alone."

"Ok. No harp. Lyre?"

Though she tried to resist, she failed. Aggie snickered and rolled her eyes. "I really need to go."

"Can't you stay one more night? We could finish up wedding plans."

"Only you could finish wedding plans in one night." An inscrutable expression on Tina's face made Aggie frown. "What?"

"You're different than this morning—more relaxed. I just noticed it. Aggie's back."

"Well, Aunt Aggie has four hours to possess her again."

"You won't make it back before they're in bed. Stay plain old Aggie until morning. You'll sleep better."

"Are you kidding? I sleep with one ear open, and half the time, with several bodies surrounding me." She grinned at Tina, knowing her next words would make her friend shudder. "Ian managed to climb out of his crib, crawl upstairs, and wake me up, so he could sleep with me the other night."

"You're joking, right? You're just trying to totally freak me out."

"Nope. I lowered his crib. I'll have permanent damage to my spine, but he can't get out anymore."

"For now. That kid will be the death of me and I'm not even there," Tina groaned.

"Admit it, you love him."

"Of course I do. I just can't let him know it or he'll walk all over

141

me in his adorable size four shoes."

"How do you know his size?" The extent of Tina's memory and knowledge of fashion for all ages astounded her. "I needed to know while shopping and couldn't get an answer at home. I bought a three and of course, they're too small."

"Um, you put them on him how many times a day? The number is right there on a circle in the heel. It's kind of hard to miss..."

The server brought their check and Aggie sighed as Tina snatched it first. "For once I can afford to pay, and you still beat me to it."

"Tradition. Now, what about accessories?"

"What?"

"Necklaces, earrings, hair 'pretties'... what do you want for those?"

"I don't know!" Aggie gathered her purse and removed her coat from the back of the chair. "I don't care what you guys wear, but it might be good for me to pick mine. Your tastes are a little more..."

"I'm not going to choose tennis bracelets and ropes of diamonds, silly."

Tina signed the receipt before they hurried out of the restaurant and into the frigid air. "I smell snow."

"I'd better go," Aggie said, tempted to stay, but knowing she shouldn't.

"Text me when you get home."

"Ok. While you're at it, think about what we can do for food. I don't think limiting them to cake and punch will be sufficient."

"And we need a place or you won't have anything to put on the invitations that you need to order last week," Tina reminded her pointedly.

"You know what? You know what we can afford. Find the place and book it. I don't care."

"Oh, I found a photographer I think. She's getting back to me tomorrow about the date. She had a cancellation and then got an email saying they'd changed their mind about changing their mind."

"Well, that's one thing she wouldn't have to worry about with me. I'm *not* changing my mind."

"Good. I think William is slightly terrified that you'll kick Luke to the curb and agree to his prior proposal for Kenzie's sake."

Aggie reached her rental car and unlocked the door. "Kenzie

142

will have to settle for Luke. As for me, it's not settling at all."

Luke waited at the bottom of the steps as she opened the car door. "Find anything?"

"Yep." Aggie popped the trunk before she shut the door and then locked it. It was a strange sensation to lock a vehicle again, but it seemed necessary with someone else's property. She dragged the large garment bag from the trunk and slammed it shut. "I can't get used to this thing. I've been slamming everything too hard."

"The van doors weigh more."

"Yeah. Something."

"Do I get to see?"

Aggie shrugged. "Do you want to?"

"I don't know. Obviously I do," Luke said, opening the front door, "but a surprise is nice too."

Inside, she unzipped the bottom and showed the skirt. "There. How's that?"

"Doesn't tell me much—it's just a lot of white satin."

Slowly she unzipped the bag farther, teasing him with more and more white. The bottom of the bodice overlapped the skirt just enough to give the illusion of a two piece dress, and along that edge, a narrow vine of embroidery and crystals trailed delicately. There, Luke's hand covered hers. "Thanks."

"You've seen enough?"

"Can't spoil the entire surprise. It's beautiful, Mibs."

"It could be gaudy with angel wings placed—inappropriately or something equally revolting."

"Then," he teased as he zipped the rest of the bag and hung it in the closet, "it's best that I don't see it before I have to."

Though she was tired, Aggie settled into the couch, grabbed a pillow, and started talking. She told about the dozens of dresses she'd tried on, some of the hideous ones Tina had described, and the dinner they'd shared. She described wedding cake, tuxedos, flowers, and frowned when she said she didn't know what they were doing for invitations. "We mentioned that we had to find a place for the reception so we could order invites, but I don't even know where I'm going to order."

"Tina probably does. She seems to have a good pulse on what's happening."

Something in his tone concerned her. "Do you think I'm putting too much on her?"

"Not at all. It probably keeps her from going crazy while her father is laid up."

"Whew. I suddenly saw you upset that she was doing—well, almost everything—and almost got sick. I don't have time to leisurely plan a wedding. I have kids to raise."

"Well, and we're doing it kind of quickly so that also makes a difference."

"Tina's dad thinks I'm pregnant."

Luke choked. "He what?"

"That's what she said. He said no couple marries that fast unless she's pregnant, and there you have it."

"That's going to be one overcooked baby then."

"What baby?" Exhaustion was beginning to meddle with her ability to follow ambiguity.

"Even if you get pregnant immediately, it'll be a good three months late!"

"Funny. My mom is afraid I will get pregnant immediately. Tina, on the other hand, is hopeful."

"Hopeful?"

"She's convinced that I'm trying to outdo Allie, therefore I'll have to have triplets the first year. That way she can move back in without a trace of guilt."

"I have wondered if twins are likely for you, but triplets? Can't she just move in because she wants to help? Does it have to be a crisis pregnancy first?"

Their laughter should have awakened the children, but not a peep reached their ears. "You should go home. You're tired."

Though Luke nodded, in evident agreement, he didn't budge. "Does Tina have a place she wants Chad and me to rent our tuxes?"

"Probably. Do you want me to get the number?"

"Have her email me everything—down to the stock number in the store if necessary—so I get the right one. Does she have idea for gifts? Don't I need gifts for the guys?"

"Do you want her to get them for you, send you links, or make suggestions?"

"How about make suggestions and send links and I'll let her know if I need her to finalize or not," he suggested.

"Great. Now where can we do the reception?"

"The community center in Brunswick is nice. Why not there? It's not exciting, but it has good lighting and it's on the outskirts, so it's really close."

"I'll tell Tina." She swallowed hard. "Oh, and I told her the kind of cake I want."

"Good. One more thing done."

"You're not even curious?"

"What are your flowers?"

The question seemed odd, but Aggie answered, "Red roses and maybe lilies for 'visual interest.'" Her air quotes were weak but effective in defining whose idea visual interest was.

"Is the cake red velvet?"

"No."

Luke kicked her foot gently and said, "Then we're good. I'm not a red velvet fan."

"Oh, it would be pretty though. What's wrong with it? I've never had it."

"It has a quarter cup of food coloring. Can you imagine Cari after a piece of that?"

"We'll not be doing that," she agreed. "Mine has red in it— raspberry filling."

"Sounds delicious."

"Oh, and she is disgusted because her dress looks good on her."

"Well, I am relieved. I dreaded the idea that she might actually like liking it. It is much better that she should be miserable about a good choice."

"She hates Music Man."

"And this matters because…"

"Shipoopi?"

"Oh, you didn't."

At first, she didn't notice the teasing in his voice and wondered if he truly hated them. "Well, it's too late. They're mostly done."

"Chad is never going to let me live this down."

145

Mibs says: I know you can't be home yet, but I didn't thank you for taking care of everything for me. I also didn't tell you about my conversation about Laird. Tina thinks I should apologize for dumping the problem on you—to Laird that is. Apologize to Laird. What do you think? Anyway, goodnight and thanks.

Chapter 11

REVOLT

Monday, January 12th

The school area was empty—again. It was the third time that morning that she'd gone to do something—switch a laundry load, chase down a wayward twin, or change Ian's diaper—and returned to find the children missing. She mentally calculated the time and decided that once every twenty-eight minutes was once every twenty-eight days too often. "Get back in here!"

Tavish crept from the cubbyhole under the stairs and had the decency to look chastened. "I was studying!"

"Your assignment?" She knew better. Tavish was obsessed with punch card computers and was probably reading about them instead of the Green Mountain Boys.

"Well..."

"That's what I thought. Where's Ellie?"

"Probably upstairs working on your—book list."

Whatever it was, it wasn't going to be a book list and they both knew it. She pointed to the basement and marched up the stairs in pursuit of her missing scholars. Ellie seemed to be stuffing something under her bed as Aggie entered the room, but Aggie focused on the infraction at hand. "You're supposed to be at the table at your desk and identifying prepositional phrases."

"That's so boring! You just look for *of* or *with* and strike through the words that follow it."

"I don't care if it's boring, go do it. And if you think *of* and *with* are the only two prepositions, I see a very red workbook in your future. Where's Vannie?"

"I don't know."

Vannie wasn't in her room, but Laird was in his. "Downstairs, buddy. We're not done correcting your work."

"Just mark it all wrong."

"Go, and furthermore, we're going to have a talk after school."

"Whatever."

It took three attempts at silently counting to three before Aggie trusted herself to respond. "I'm going to try that again and this time you're going to respond like the Laird I know and love instead of this impostor in his room." She waited for him to meet her gaze and added, "Now go and we *will* have that talk after school."

She saw resistance in him. It was only a matter of seconds before he came back with some kind of snarky comment, but thankfully, he yielded and nodded. "Ok."

It wasn't the response he once would have given, but she considered it a concession to the illusion of respect anyway. "I'll be down in a minute. I need to find Vannie and Kenzie."

"Try the basement for Kenzie. She's probably down with Cari and Lorna. Where's Ian?"

For a split second, it felt like she had her "son" back, but then he closed himself off again as she said, "He's napping. Couldn't keep his eyes open."

"Convenient."

"What?"

"I said," Laird repeated as he dragged himself from the bed, "that it's convenient of Ian to sleep while we're doing school."

She found Vannie lost in a book in the library. "Is your work done?" The girl pretended not to hear, or so it seemed to Aggie. She stepped closer and removed the book from Vannie's hand. "Did you hear me?"

"N—yes. I was just finishing the paragraph."

Aggie scanned the cover. "I'm pretty sure I didn't have *Anne of the Island* on your reading list for this week."

"But it's literature isn't it? I mean, it was written ages ago and people are still reading it."

"That's not exactly a good criterion for good literature, but it doesn't matter how good the book is, your assignment was to finish your algebra."

148

Something behind Aggie changed the acquiescence she'd seen on Vannie's face into resistance. "No." Vannie grabbed the book and marched to the door. "I'm not going to spend hours trying to understand those stupid problems. I'm tired."

"Wha—" she began, but the girl was gone. As she turned, Aggie saw Laird's sleeve disappear into the living room. Her temper flared higher than it had in ages and she found herself singing beneath her breath, "—ching as to war. With the cross of Jesus, going on before. Christ the royal Master..."

Her hand reached for her phone, but she hesitated. If Tina was right, calling in reinforcements had only weakened her position the last time. Children spilled from the basement, some racing outdoors and Tavish to his cubby. Her astonishment couldn't have been greater. One pair of shoes at the top of the stairs mocked her more than anything. Somehow Laird was behind this.

Dozens of ideas and questions tangled themselves in her mind until she was certain she'd never extricate herself. Aggie's heart pounded in her chest and her forehead grew moist with perspiration. She had to act quickly. Every moment she delayed was a moment of victory in their eyes. This wasn't normal behavior for Allie's children. Cari, sure. Rarely Kenzie might resist, and Ian had already proven that he'd be a nightmare if she didn't watch and train closely, but otherwise, with the exception of poor attitudes at times while doing it, if she said something, they obeyed.

Her first inclination was to call William and have the students "arrested" for truancy. With her luck, they'd simply end up in school which, at the moment, sounded like a reward for both her and them. Not something she wanted to risk. If they went back, and now it seemed as though they must, it would be because she decided it—not the kids. The last thing she needed was them to get the idea that following house rules was optional.

Laird. She had to start with Laird. They were all following him in this; that was certain. With a prayer on her lips and dread in her heart, she climbed the stairs and knocked on his door. A lack of response at all prompted her to open the door. She found him at his desk, assembling a Lego set as though he'd heard nothing.

"I need to talk to you."

"I'm not doing grammar. We've done enough today."

"I'm not here to talk to you about today's schoolwork."

That got his attention. He glanced sideways at her before asking, "Then what do you want?"

"To apologize."

This earned her a turned head and shock on his face. "For what?"

Aggie seated herself on his bed, leaning her arms on her legs, and tried to maintain eye contact. "I had no business dumping your paper into Luke's lap. It was wrong to change up your school authority like that and it was wrong to put him in that position. I thought it was right—why I did it made sense to me, but I see that doing it was wrong. I'm sorry."

"Why?"

"Why am I sorry? Because I—"

"No, why did you do it. You've never shoved our problems on anyone else before."

That proved it. He did lose respect for her over that. He'd seen it as shirking her responsibility instead of trying to be just. "Laird, I wasn't trying to shove anything on anyone. I see it looks like that and that's what it ended up being, but it wasn't my intent. I was angry. Your first paper seemed to be a slap in the face to my authority as your teacher and a parent. Then I thought maybe I was overreacting, so I tried to have someone distant from the situation look at it— someone who cares about both of us and who might see it with the eyes of an adult and yet one who wasn't affronted. I didn't tell him anything about what happened. I left that for you."

"Oh." He was struggling. The muscles in Laird's face twitched with his attempts to control them and his lip seemed to quiver. Even his voice cracked with that one simple mono-syllabic word.

"I see how it looked to you and I put you in a bad position." She crept forward, hunkered down on her heels and looked up at him. "You know how Grandma Millie is, right? You know how we have to keep her from getting too tired or too upset."

"Yeah?"

"Well, when she'd get upset she knew she had to calm down, so she'd table things and have Grandpa deal with them when he got home. I forgot that this isn't normal—that I have no reason to do that. I forgot that I can be angry but talk about it and see if I'm right before I let it take hold of me like that." To her disgust and dismay, tears choked her and flooded her eyes. "I don't know how to do this,

150

Laird. You know that. I've been a 'mother' for nine months. Most people get that much to prepare for one child. I have eight. I'm going to blow it."

"Yeah."

"Well, you don't have to agree quite that quickly," she said, attempting a weak joke. "Look, I don't want to use this as an emotional whip, but I'm going to say it this time because I think it's really important for you to think about before this thing you have in your heart grows too big to conquer easily. You are Allie Stuart's son. She taught you to love your family, to respect your elders, and to obey those in authority. She taught you to love and serve the Lord Jesus. If you can't obey for me, you really should do it for her."

He didn't respond. She tried to encourage him to look at her— to see what his pain was doing to all of them, but Laird stared at a small plastic piece on the desk as if it was a lifeline to whatever he wanted to hold onto. After a minute, she stood, squeezed his shoulder, and started to leave the room.

At the door, a sniffle made her pause, but following instinct, she kept going. A sound reached her as she turned to take the first steps down the stairs, and she turned in time to feel him slam her into the wall in his rush. "I'm sorry, Aunt Aggie. I'm so sorry."

"Tina was right," Aggie told Luke over the phone that evening. "He lost respect for me when I dumped it on you like that. I almost called for help, but then I remembered the apology idea and tried that first. I'm glad I did."

"You could have called for help, Aggie. I could have prayed if nothing else."

"But see," she protested, "Tina was right. Calling for help just makes things worse. It got better when I handled it on my own."

"I don't think that's what she meant. I think she was trying to say that you can't just turn it over to someone else and remove yourself from the picture. You've asked for help before, and they know it. But you did what needed to be done."

"Oh."

"You ok?"

"I'm feeling a bit overwhelmed, and you should know that I might be calling the school tomorrow."

"Why?"

This was it. If she spoke it, she knew she'd feel like she must make the call. "I'm considering enrolling them. They'd only be a week or two behind at best."

"Are you sure you want to do that?"

She wasn't sure of anything of the kind, but Aggie did feel as if it was necessary. If the children were going to resist doing the work, it'd be better for them to be where they already had respect. She could work on it later. "I wasn't sure... that's why I brought it up. I might just enroll Vannie and Laird, but maybe it's best if I just enroll them all."

"That'll make any kind of honeymoon impossible then. We can't find people who can drive kids back and forth to school. I was hoping you'd consider letting Tavish and Ellie go to Willow's. She doesn't have a car, but she is familiar with learning at home."

The idea of two weeks alone with Luke had kept her going through the past weeks. The idea of missing it because she had to drive the kids to school discouraged her. Then again, was it right to keep them out just so she could have a honeymoon?

"Mibs? You there?"

"I'm here. Is it wrong to want to keep them out so I don't have to miss it?"

"I think you should keep them out because it's best for your entire family."

"Really?"

"I think whatever you do, making this decision while you're upset is probably not the best idea."

She started to agree when William's cruiser pulled into the drive. "Hey, Luke. William is here. I am not panicking. I am not going to run up and accuse Kenzie of calling 9-1-1 again, but if you'd like to pray that she hasn't, I won't complain. Meanwhile, I'd better go. I'll get on the messenger in a bit to see if you're still up."

She had the door open and phone in her pocket before William made it to the steps. "Come in and tell me no one called."

"Called? I haven't called in days."

"Then dispatch didn't send you out here?"

Understanding lit William's face as he shrugged out of his

jacket. "No, no. I just came by to see how your trip went."

"What trip?"

"To Yorktown. I thought you'd gone up there to see your folks and—"

Laughing, Aggie offered him a cup of coffee and led him to the kitchen as she made it. "I see; what you really want to ask, and won't, is how Tina is?"

"Well…"

"Considering her obsession with my wedding, she's bored stiff, and considering she knows the sizes of my kids' shoes and what clothing needs they have, she misses us a bunch." It had been her intention not to tell the rest of her observations, but the absolute torture William appeared to endure as he tried to ask about anything else was too much for her. "She also asked a dozen questions about you, sprinkled among our wedding plans and while dodging girls who would rip a dress from your hands rather than ask if you were finished."

"Her dad?" He apparently had found his voice.

"He's doing ok. Honestly, from what I can tell, she would leave tomorrow if it wouldn't make him feel abandoned. He doesn't 'need' her there, but if he wants her, she stays."

"I guess she does have an obligation…"

Aggie passed the cup of piping hot coffee to William and turned to make herself a cup. "I love this thing. Luke couldn't have bought me a more perfect gift."

"Does she have any idea when she'll be back?"

"Hey, why don't you ask her that? Don't you think she'd like to hear that you miss her?"

"I never said—"

"Oh, come on, William. You come in, ask about my trip, want to know about her dad, when she'll be back… you miss her. That's a good thing."

"I think miss might be strong, but I did hope she might be home soon."

"Um, dear William. She is home. Yorktown is her home. She was just here because she wanted to help me."

"Well, I think she considers here home. She had mentioned getting an apartment when you and Luke got married."

Aggie knew that Tina had looked at a few places, but she had

153

no idea that her friend had shared this information. "I think you need to make a trip up there. Say hi. Take her out to dinner."

"Seems a bit... serious."

"Well, then don't. Let her wonder if she should bother coming back at all. Let her father introduce her to interns and every other unmarried man under forty in his company until one of them shows her the attention she deserves."

"I'll think about it, but..."

"Or," Aggie added with playfulness she hadn't felt in ages, "Or you could go over and make up to Murphy instead. She wouldn't mind."

William glanced at his watch and set his cup on the counter. "I've got to get going. Megan was supposed to be working, but she's got that flu going around."

"And it's a convenient excuse to get away before I convince you that Tina's worth a trip north."

"Oh, I know she's worth it, but..."

"G'night, William. Go work out your troubles. I think I hear kids out of bed."

Laird overheard Aggie talking in the living room and crept down the first few stairs to see if he could see who else was there, but she was obviously talking on her cell to someone—probably Luke. The first clear words he heard were, "...considering enrolling them."

Her next words, emphasizing that he and Vannie would certainly go, unnerved him. *I've got to talk to the others,* he thought. *We might not like having to do school all day here, but it's better than when we had to be gone all day with homework when we got home, and it wasn't too bad before Christmas.* His feet hurried up the stairs, and at the top, he heard a car in the drive. He passed Vannie's room and went straight for the window at the end of the hall. The sheriff's car. What could that mean?

He hurried to Vannie's room and let himself in the door. "Vannie!" he hissed.

"What? I'm trying to sleep here, and you're going to get us into more trouble."

"Aunt Aggie was talking to Luke—well, I think it was Luke— and she was talking about enrolling us in school again."

She sat up, pulling her robe around her shoulders. "What? How do you know that?"

"I heard her say it. Oh, and William—Deputy Markenson—is down there. What if she called him about us?"

"If you got us in trouble with your stupid idea—"

"You liked it well enough when it got you out of algebra," Laird growled.

Curled in the corner of the daybed, Vannie shook her head. "I thought I would, but I was miserable all day. I don't know anything that happened in my book after I refused to do my math."

"I know what you mean. I think we need to apologize and just do our work. We'd have to do it at school anyway—and homework besides." He stood at the end of the bed, his arms crossed over his chest, but this time they were crossed to keep him warm rather than in the defiance he'd felt for so long. "I can't believe I got that upset over a dumb book."

"It wasn't the book, Laird. It's everything else. I was looking up grief on Google. In teens and pre-teens it often comes out as anger and rebellion. In wives, it sometimes manifests in a makeover or decorating or buying things her husband wouldn't have liked. Aunt Aggie is kind of doing that in reverse. She's trying to be Mommy when it's not her. Aunt Aggie is carefree and spontaneous and Mommy was—"

"A bit uptight about things."

"Yeah, but she loved us," Vannie seemed compelled to add.

"Who said she didn't? She was the best mom in the world."

"And Aunt Aggie is the best aunt. We could at least show her the courtesy of acting like we know it."

Laird dropped his arms. "Agreed." He turned to leave, but at the door, her voice stopped him.

"Laird?"

"Hmm?"

"It's ok to miss them."

"I know."

She stopped him once more. "It's also ok to like our life here too. It's ok to enjoy spending time with Luke and be grateful that he's going to be our uncle."

155

"I know," Laird said again. But this time he added, "It just doesn't *feel* ok."

Mibs says: Guess what William wanted?

Luke says: To beg you to reconsider and marry him after all.

Mibs says: You're not getting rid of me that easily. Nope, but he sure is missing Tina...

Luke says: Well, that's obvious.

Mibs says: Yeah, but it wasn't obvious to him until tonight.

Luke says: Oh?

Mibs says: Yep.

Mibs says: More good news.

Luke says: Oh?

Mibs says: I'm not enrolling the kids.

Luke says: I didn't think you would.

Mibs says: Then you were wrong. I was ninety-eight percent decided until about five minutes ago.

Luke says: What changed your mind?

Mibs says: Laird.

Luke says: What about him?

Mibs says: He came downstairs a little while ago. That's what took so long for me to get on. He apologized.

Luke says: I thought you said you apologized and he apologized too.

Mibs says: Yes, but he wanted to confess I guess. You know — get it off his chest.

Luke says: Did he explain himself?

Mibs says: From what I got out of him, he is missing his parents, feeling guilty about liking to spend time with you, and part of him likes how I'm not as persnickety about things as Allie was and then he said he resents that too.

Luke says: Complex thinking for a kid.

Mibs says: He'd been talking with Vannie before he came down. He said he just wanted to feel miserable.

Luke says: I remember that feeling.

Mibs says: What did your mom do?

Luke says: She put me to work and spoke truth constantly to help drown out the lies I filled my mind with.

Mibs says: Why do you think you did that? I can only stand to think of never seeing Allie again by remembering all the things she'd want me to do and trying to do them.

Luke says: And you're killing yourself in the process.

Mibs says: But Allie gave me the responsibility.

Luke says: To raise them. She didn't give you the responsibility of molding yourself into her image.

Mibs says: But consistency. Don't you think they need it?

Luke says: They need you to be the person GOD chose for you to be, Mibs. Anything else is shortchanging them. God didn't create you in Allie's image but in His own. He knitted you in your mother's womb to be Aggie.

Mibs says: I'll have to think about that.

Luke says: I proposed to and plan to marry Aggie Milliken. I would be very disappointed to wake up in five years' time to discover that she has given herself an Allie makeover — inside and out.

Mibs says: And what if I fail?

Luke says: Fail in what? Being Aggie? Not possible.

Mibs says: No, what if I fail in being just Aggie?

Luke says: Then I'll get to know Allie better, won't I?

Mibs says: I'm glad you told me.

Luke says: Told you what?

Mibs says: That you didn't want me to lose who I am. I might not have even considered whether it was good or not.

Luke says: I have to be honest even if it's not what you want to hear.

Mibs says: Even if I don't like it, I do need and want to hear it.

Luke says: I should go to bed. Inspector is coming early in the morning and then I can call Amber and have her get it back on the market. She says she thinks she's got a couple of interested parties.

Mibs says: Is it really all done?

Luke says: And better than ever. Thanks to the insurance paying for the damage, I was able to add the built-ins and now it'll likely sell for more. That might make up for the loss and if it goes in to escrow quickly enough, I'll be able to buy a few I've had to keep on hold.

Mibs says: I'll see you later then?

Luke says: Might not be until after dinner, but I'll stop by. I want to talk to Laird.

Mibs says: Just be careful.

Luke says: Now that I understand him, I think we'll be good.

Mibs says: Night, Luke. Sometimes it amazes me to think that a year ago I didn't know you. I hardly knew you six months ago. Now you're such a huge part of who I am as well.

Luke says: Thank the Lord for women who can articulate what I don't know how to say. Love you.

Mibs says: Night. Love you too.

Chapter 12

BLESSINGS TO BURDENS

Thursday, January 15th

The table was beautifully set—a bouquet of gerbera daisies in a clear glass bowl in the center. Cheerful cloth napkins were folded on each plate. It looked fit for a fine restaurant, but the room was full of chattering females. Aggie stood in the midst of them, trying to keep Corinne separate from Cassie and Olivia separate from Melanie. Libby introduced the women with the pride she always expressed in each of her children and astonishingly enough, Aggie heard that same pride in the woman's voice as she introduced the girls to her.

The tallest, Corinne, smiled and started to hold out her hand before engulfing Aggie in an awkward hug. "I thought you'd be pretty, but I kind of expected it to be in the 'inside shining on the outside' way. I didn't think you'd be pretty too!"

"Is that a compliment or an insult to Luke?" The moment she spoke, Aggie wondered what had gotten into her. Before she could amend her question or apologize, Corinne laughed.

"I think I might like you. She's loyal to him—protective. I like that."

With an exaggerated roll of her eyes, Olivia nudged Aggie. "If you treat Luke like royalty, she'll love you forever. However, Corinne is worse than a mama bear if she thinks he isn't getting his deserved accolades."

Mel and Cassie nodded. "Stay out of her way if Corinne is riled over someone mistreating her Luke."

"Girls, you'll convince Aggie that I raised a pack of half-crazed

159

hyenas!"

"But Mom, you did!" Cassie said, pulling Aggie to a spot next to her at the table. "I'll sit here and you sit there by Mom's chair. That'll keep you a little insulated from the rest."

The banter would have been amusing had Aggie known anyone and had she not been quite so nervous. Luke had been excited about the lunch for days, but her initial excitement had slowly given way to nervousness. Now she found herself tongue-tied and eager to go home.

"What is your favorite thing about Luke?"

Aggie's throat went dry. What kinds of questions were these? Was she there to get to know the sisters or to be inducted into the Sullivan Sorority, complete with hazing and rush week? "I think," she began, unsure how she'd finish, "it would be impossible to narrow him down to ten favorite things much less one."

"Corinne, really. Aggie isn't accustomed to your sense of humor. If I didn't know you, I'd think you were trying to make her feel unwelcome."

There was an edge to Libby's tone that Aggie recognized. She'd heard it when Luke's mother admonished him or one of the children. It meant that they'd gone too far. Corinne turned to Aggie, an apology on her lips, but it seemed to Aggie that it didn't meet her eyes. "I'm sorry. I forget that you don't know as much about us as we know about you. Mom talks about you all the time and even Luke does, but I bet he doesn't say much about us."

It seemed necessary to put herself out there, so Aggie shook her head. "Actually, he does speak of you all—often. Melanie who married her Ryan without benefit of the whole dating scene. He's very proud of that. I like that he recognizes that it was best for you without seeming to condemn anyone else for a different decision. She also transplanted garden plants that Cassie started in pots."

She turned to Olivia. "I learned that you were named for your mother and that Libby's name wasn't Elizabeth because of you. You have two daughters and you weren't mentioned in the grand gardening scheme, so I think perhaps you didn't like to get dirty."

"She got that right," Corinne snickered.

"Well, considering you were the great planner, it doesn't sound like you cared much for the grunt work either. You have a son Rodney who is the dearest little boy, and you or your mother taught

160

him to sign songs during church—I imagine to keep him occupied. I think you have another boy and a girl, but I might have that mixed with someone else."

"And what about me, Aggie. Is my job as seed sower all you know about me?"

"You are single, the director of a nursing home, and you wanted to be a vet, but you couldn't handle the tougher side of it. Your green thumb is unparalleled and you will adore my Ellie."

"Is that your opinion or Luke's?" Corinne asked.

"I suppose both of ours. As he told me, I realized that she sounded like the kind of girl that would appreciate my little Ellie."

"How do you like being a 'mother' of eight?"

"If you haven't realized it yet," Libby interjected, "Corinne is our frustrated lawyer. She was born for interrogation but seems to have left her tact at home."

"Was that an offensive question, Aggie? I didn't mean for it to be."

"The question isn't offensive. People ask me that all the time and not always so politely."

"See? How do people usually ask?"

Aggie had lost all hope of enjoying the afternoon. Luke's doting Corinne, the sister who seemed to feel as though she owned the right to be his favorite sister, appeared to be determined to leave no doubt of her disapproval. It took a moment to gather her courage, but while she chewed a bite of salad, she debated exactly how honest to be. "Well, I am accustomed to questions asking if I know what causes 'it.' Do I have a TV? If they learn that they are my sister's children, the first question is usually asking if she died in childbirth. The world seems to consider her fertility their business and often asks me very explicit questions about her private life—things I'd never know and wouldn't want to. Those bother me the most when they ask in front of children who then have confused questions of their own. The most common from the children is why people dislike children." Corinne and Cassie both seemed ready to ask a question or make a comment, but Aggie continued in a rush. "If people ask about me personally, it is usually with an air of pity and the assumption that my life must be hell on earth. I am a martyr sacrificed for the sake of my sister's children. No man will marry me, or if he will, it will be out of pure pity for my plot. Galahad, it seems, is not dead. I am told

161

that I have jewels in my crown and that 'this too shall pass,' although that one is usually followed by a pat to my arm and a melancholy, 'but of course that'll be a couple of decades from now, won't it?'"

With her outburst finished, Aggie excused herself to the bathroom. Leaning against the door, she pulled her phone from her skirt pocket and punched Luke's number. "I just blew it with your sisters."

"Not possible."

"But I did. Corinne hates me."

"That's crazy," he argued, "she's been dying for a chance to really get to know you."

"Well, she's spent the entire time I've been here grilling me. Your mom has called her on it at least twice that I can remember. I just kind of lost it and told her exactly what I think of people's questions about my status as a twenty-three year old mother of eight."

Luke's laughter annoyed Aggie, but it also gave her a hint of hope. "I think you've just ensured that she loves you. Corinne respects someone who doesn't whine and doesn't take any guff either. I bet most of what seems antagonistic is really just her weird sense of humor. I told you about that."

"Yeah, but you didn't say what it was! I was expecting whoopee cushions or dry British jokes that even Brits don't get."

"Trust me. It'll be fine." Luke seemed to sense her reticence, because he asked, "Would you like me to call her and tell her to back off?"

"No. That'll put her off even more. I want to go home."

That silence—the one that had become comforting to her—now drove her crazy again as she waited for his reply. He eventually said, "Give it ten more minutes. If you still want to come home then, call me and I'll call mom and tell her you need to come home. I'll find a legitimate reason."

"I'm sorry." Tears choked her as she fought to hide them.

"Hey, hey, Mibs. It's ok. I should have done something with everyone there."

"On a brighter note, I think Cassie likes me—or would if we had a chance to talk without interruption."

"Good. Invite her out for coffee." Seconds later, he added, "Maybe you should invite them one at a time. It might be a way to get to know them without it feeling like they're all coming at you at once."

"I'll try."

"Go put some cold water on your face. I know you and your eyes are puffy and red. You won't want them to notice."

The words unsettled her even further. "I thought this was going to be fun. It's horrible."

"I can come if you like. Mrs. Dyke—"

"I'll go, but you know I'll be calling in about ten minutes."

Aggie stepped from the bathroom two minutes later and nearly ran over Corinne. "Oh!"

"I heard."

That possibility hadn't had a chance to register yet. "Oh." Illogically, Aggie pondered how ineloquent she must sound with her variations on a single two-letter word.

"I'm sorry. I really wanted this to be a special day and my nervousness ruined it."

"Your nervousness—"

Tears splashed onto Corinne's cheeks. "Of course! I was meeting Luke's Aggie."

"And I'm supposed to understand what that means?"

"My brother has never shown much attention to women—not special attention anyway. He picked you. We're all a little intimidated you know."

"Intimidated by a kid with a bunch of kids? Are you kidding me?" *Really, Aggie,* she rebuked herself. *Are you really incapable of using anything but the same words over and over?*

"Intimidated that we're meeting the woman that Luke thinks is pretty much perfection on legs? Yeah. We kind of idolize our brother—in the old fashioned sense. If he thinks he's the luckiest guy in the world to have you, then you're a lot more special than you seem to realize."

Cassie hurried down the hall, a phone in her hand. "I thought maybe it was your sitter, but it says it's Luke." She winked at Aggie. "Good girl; stick up for yourself. Don't let us intimidate you."

The call was a text message. Corinne read it, blushed, and then passed it to Aggie. "See?"

BE NICE AND DON'T EVER MAKE MY MIBS CRY AGAIN.

Aggie giggled. She whipped out her phone and her fingers flew

163

over the keyboard. She showed it to Corinne just before punching the send button. ALL IS WELL.

"If you were home, you'd start singing It Is Well with My Soul, wouldn't you?"

Her eyes widened. "How —"

"I told you. Luke, for as little as he talks, has said a lot about you. Well, he and Mom have."

Saturday, January 17th

Bedtime couldn't come quickly enough for Luke. He chased the little ones around the house until he was ready to drop with exhaustion and then sent them up to Aggie for baths. All settled again, he snuggled on the couch with them, reading stories and doing his best to ensure they would fall asleep in no time.

Vannie and Laird were having Ping-Pong wars in the basement. Aggie dragged herself down the steps, giving Luke half a smile as she passed, and then called down into the basement. "Ok, there are two bathrooms open now. Have at it."

"Dibs on Aunt Aggie's," Vannie called, running up the steps at a speed Luke couldn't fathom in his present state of exhaustion. "Can I take a bath?"

"Fine, but when the water gets cool, no adding more hot. Shower and get out then."

"Thanks!"

Laird shook his head as he reached the top of the basement steps. "What is with girls and sitting around in dirty water? You'd think that'd be a guy way to get clean." Three steps up the staircase, he turned. "Oh, I keep forgetting to tell you. My church pants are all too short. I look ridiculous according to Vannie."

"Thanks. I'm not going shopping now, so looking ridiculous tomorrow it is."

"Won't kill me."

She collapsed next to Luke twenty minutes later. "Big change in Laird — sort of."

"What do you mean?"

"He's back to normal now, which is huge compared to what he was for a week or two there."

There was no argument with that. Laird had teased, played, and ignored things that he usually ignored for the past week and it had felt good to see normalcy settle into Aggie's family again. "Hey, Cassie said you guys had a good time."

"We did. I think I hurt Corinne's feelings by asking Cassie first, though. I didn't even think about that. You said Cassie over the phone and I fixated on that."

"That's ok. It's good for Corinne. So, what'd you guys talk about?"

"You. I know all your tricks, your virtues, and your faults now. You cannot get away with hiding anything from me anymore."

"I think Cassie likes you. She sent a text message after she left Espresso Yourself."

"Well," Aggie pushed, "what was it?"

"'She's a keeper.'"

She smiled up at him. "I agree—Cassie is definitely a keeper."

Luke pulled her close, one arm around her, and nearly sighed with satisfaction when her head nestled into his shoulder. "This is pretty much perfection."

"I was thinking the same thing.

"Two months."

"Two eternities," she argued.

"I like how you think. Now, I've been thinking."

"Uh-oh. Whenever Dad says that, Mom cringes. Should I cringe?"

"I don't think so. I was just thinking that it's probably time for me to make a permanent move to the Church. I mean, I'm back and forth all the time already that I really almost have no home. I kind of feel like a foster kid, but in the church."

"That'd be nice."

"Yeah, we could maybe have people over for a game night or maybe a snowman building contest. Didn't you say that looked fun at that party the kids went to?"

"Those kids go to the church." Aggie sounded half-strangled.

"What's wrong?"

"Wrong?"

He peeked around her head, trying to read the expression on her face. "You sound strange."

"The idea is a little... daunting."

Luke chewed on that idea for a while. He realized when she began squirming that Aggie was waiting for some kind of response. "I have a hard time seeing you as daunted by anything."

"That party in December? That about killed me. I feel like I'm still recovering."

"Well, then maybe we should see what kinds of things the church has planned for the next few weeks. It'd just be a nice way to get to know your friends."

"Friends? Luke, I hardly know anyone there. The Vaughns, William. I kind of know the Merchamps, but not much. I know half the names I think."

"It can't be that big of a church. Brant's Corners is tiny and I know quite a few people go to Brunswick to the Assembly."

"No," she agreed, "but I have that much to do each week. Church gets out and I've got to get everyone rounded up. That takes forever in itself. Then I have to get them in the van and home to feed them, so the little ones can get a nap before they are so overtired that they can't sleep and make us miserable for the rest of the day. Then, if it's a week I've promised we'll go that night, I have to manage to get everyone fed and dressed again so we can get cleaned up and out the door on time."

"There has to be a way—"

She sat up, visibly frustrated. "Well, you're welcome to find one, but if the kids don't sleep and it shifts everything off, you can deal with it. I can't handle it. I finally got them on a consistent schedule that works for all of us, and I am not about to mess with it."

"Hey, hey. C'mere." He pulled her back to him, murmuring comforting and reassuring words as he did. "I'm not trying to destroy your schedule. I just thought it seemed like the perfect time to get to know the people you worship with."

"Do you have any idea how exhausting and overwhelming that sounds to me?"

"No." His answer seemed blunt—almost harsh. "We can't make the church an idol, but we can't make it an inconvenience either."

"Well, right now, I just try to make it."

"All the more reason for me to join you now. We've got to make it together."

Aggie says: You there?

Tina says: Yeah. Been waiting, hoping you'd have time to get on.

Aggie says: I want to scream.

Tina says: Why?

Aggie says: Luke wants us to get more involved with the church here.

Tina says: That sounds right up your alley. Why scream-worthy?

Aggie says: Because I can't take it right now. Really? More on my plate? Hospitality? Chatting before and after church? Going to things?

Tina says: Did you tell him?

Aggie says: Yep. He seems to think with him there all will be well.

Tina says: Well, until it isn't, maybe you should assume he knows what he's talking about.

Aggie says: I want to assume he's an idiot and feed him whatever drugs you feed lunatics.

Tina says: I think that was horribly politically incorrect. I think it's probably mentally disturbed or cognitively twisted or something.

Aggie says: I think we're both going to get citations from the PC police.

Tina says: Speaking of police…

Aggie says: He came didn't he?

Tina says: How'd you know? He said he didn't tell anyone.

Aggie says: Yeah, but I told him to go. He misses you.

Tina says: I couldn't believe it when I got a call. He said, "I'm at the Shell station on the corner of Brighton and Lincoln. Where do I go from here?"

Aggie says: He might as well have declared himself like someone from a—historical novel. I can't think of an author or title or anything. I'm so excited he came!

Tina says: You're excited—I thought I was until he met Dad.

Aggie says: Does your dad like him?

Tina says: He offered to give me full control over my trust fund if I'd just marry William.

Aggie says: What did William say to that?

Tina says: I didn't tell him. I didn't even tell him I bought a house.

Aggie says: You did what?

Tina says: I bought a house. You've seen it.

Aggie says: I've seen a house that you bought. You're kidding me, right? Why would you buy a house?

Tina says: Because you're going to be married by the time I get back there—or close enough to it—and I'm not living there with you guys, but I want to be around. So, I bought a house.

Aggie says: You! You're the offer on Cygnet, aren't you? How come Luke didn't tell me?

Tina says: He doesn't know yet. I'm doing it through the landholdings department so that he doesn't know. I want him to give me a good price that he's comfortable with, not just break even to be nice to me.

Aggie says: You could have given him a full-price cash offer.

Tina says: And lose Dad's respect forever? I don't think so.

Aggie says: You'll be in walking distance!

Tina says: Yep, and Dad is talking about maybe putting an office in Brunswick for me to oversee—practice for my future as CEO I suppose. I don't think I'll ever get through to him that I have zero intention of stepping into his shoes.

Aggie says: I guess you can't blame him. He's proud of you and his business. Why shouldn't he want a merger.

Tina says: Enough about me. We've got wedding plans to make. Are you adding any of Luke's sisters to the line up?

Aggie says: You know I can't. We're having so few guests that two apiece is probably overkill. I'll just have you and Vannie as planned.

Tina says: And it's just Chad and William for Luke? He doesn't want to add Laird or something?

Aggie says: He almost went with Zeke and Chad, but Zeke can apparently marry us. Since he can do that, we'll stay with William. Laird is relieved that he doesn't have to stand up there.

Tina says: How is Laird these days?

Aggie says: Back to his normal old self. I can't tell you how great that is.

Tina says: Oh, good. William said he thought he saw something in Laird the last time they talked.

Aggie says: Yeah, that's been a couple of weeks—back when I was ready to have him haul them off as truants. We're good now. Things really seem to have settled down again.

Tina says: That's good. He's good with kids. I guess it comes from being a pseudo-father when he was little.

Aggie says: Oh, man. Is it animal cruelty if I spray dogs with a hose in the middle of a winter night?

Tina says: I think it likely, why?

Aggie says: Then I'm spraying William or Megan.

Tina says: Why?

Aggie says: Dogs are howling thanks to a speeding siren flying past.

Tina says: Aren't you glad cats don't howl?

Aggie says: I'm glad that cats hate people and like to be left alone. That kitten was cute, but cute grows up.

Tina says: She's a good kitty. She likes me.

Aggie says: And leaves hair all over your bed.

Tina says: Which I clean off quite regularly.

Aggie says: Then you come visit and clean up the cat's mess. Oh, and she likes to torment the dogs. She walks the perimeter, jumps to the post, swishes her tail…

Tina says: Keeps 'em in their place.

Aggie says: And tries to do the same with us.

Tina says: Hey, she doesn't chew shoes or run away!

Aggie says: Well, the latter would be a blessing, but I'll give you the shoes. Then again, she did shred the comforter on your bed and dogs don't need litter boxes.

Tina says: Cats are not demanding

Aggie says: Or comforting. Laird has taken to going out to the dogs to chat out his grief. I think they are better than a therapist for that.

Tina says: Ellie does that with Marmalade. She goes in my room when she thinks I'm busy elsewhere and tells that cat everything she wants to tell her mother. It's kind of heartbreaking and charming all wrapped up in one Ellie ball. I think she does it with the dogs too. I've wondered if maybe she uses them to talk to Doug.

Aggie says: Do you think that's healthy?

Tina says: It's what kids do, right? Remember how we used to write stories about dogs who could understand and give kids advice?

Aggie says: Yeah. That's true.

Aggie says: Hey, Tina. I'm beat. I need to talk about several things, but I keep nodding off over here. I'll have to talk to you about stuff tomorrow.

Tina says: Sounds good to me.

Aggie says: Nighters!

Tina says: *poofs*

Chapter 13

WHERE? OH, WHERE...

Monday, January 19th

Ellie dug through her backpack, searching for her library card, but found nothing. With a line growing behind her, she slid her books aside and whispered, "I'll be back in a minute. I forgot. I put it in the pouch on my bike."

"You'll have to go back to the end of the line."

She smiled. "Thank you. May I leave my books here?"

The cantankerous-looking librarian softened. "Sure. I'll just put them under the counter so no one starts putting them away."

"Hurry up! We're going to be late if we don't leave soon!" Vannie hissed. Smiling at the librarian, Vannie pushed her three books across the counter. "I'll take these, please."

"Would you like me to put hers on your card?"

Ellie was already out the door. Vannie shook her head. "No, thank you. Aunt Aggie prefers we keep ours on our own cards so she can keep track of who has read what. It's easier for her."

"Smart aunt."

Vannie waited at the side of the counter for Laird's turn. Ellie still hadn't returned. When Laird stepped up to pass the librarian his books, Vannie whispered, "You'd better get Ellie's. She's still not back. I think she left her card at home. She can just write her books down for Aunt Aggie herself."

Book run accomplished, Vannie and Laird hurried outside to see where Ellie was. The girl, her bicycle, her backpack, everything—gone. "What—"

"Call Aunt Aggie. I'll ride around the block. She's probably playing a joke on us or something."

"Ellie doesn't play jokes. Where is she!" Vannie whipped out the cell phone they took when they rode places away from home, and dialed Aggie. "Aunt Aggie, Ellie's gone." Tears formed as she listened to the voice on the other end tell her to calm down and explain what happened. "She's just gone. She didn't have her library card in her backpack." Tears choked her, making much of what she said unintelligible. "—the packy thingie on her bike and she went to get it but she didn't get it or maybe she did I don't know, but she never came back in the library, and *now she's gone!*"

Vannie stared at the phone, confused. Out of breath, Laird jogged up to her, panting. "I ran around the block, but I didn't see her and no one that I talked to saw a girl on a bike. What's wrong?"

"Aunt Aggie is coming."

"Um, isn't that good?"

"I guess." Vannie stared at the phone even more intently. "Should I call 9-1-1?"

"What for?"

"She's *gone,* Laird! The bike is gone, no one has seen her. People don't just evaporate!"

"I think you should let Aunt Aggie decide. I'll go see if anyone at the hardware store saw anything. They've got that big window that overlooks most of this side of the street."

Before she could respond, Laird tore across the street, jerked open the door to the store, and disappeared inside. A woman stepped out of her car parked in front of the library and called, "Are you looking for the girl with the dark braids?"

As jittery as Vannie felt, she didn't step closer, but she nodded. "My little sister."

"She drove off with a man in a blue pickup not a minute before you and the boy came out."

"Blue pickup? Did you see what the man looked like?"

"He was about average, brown hair… I didn't think anything of it. She came to him when he called and jumped in the truck without hesitation. He got out, got the bicycle, and tossed it in the back of the truck."

Before the woman could answer, Laird dashed out the door and across the street. "She's with Luke. Mr. Vaughn is in the hardware store. He said Luke waved at him when he picked up Ellie."

172

The woman waved and climbed back into her vehicle, apparently waiting for someone. Vannie pointed to her. "That's what she said. Well, she didn't say Luke, but she said a guy in a truck like Luke's that sounds like him."

"Why did Luke pick her up like that?"

Shaking her head, Vannie flipped open the phone to call Aggie, but their van turned onto the street before she could do it. Suddenly, she realized what must have happened. "I bet he took her to get her drawing framed. She probably just forgot to tell us. I bet we were supposed to take longer in the library or ride to the park or something until they got back."

"Why not just take us with him?"

"No room. He doesn't have a car—just the truck."

Laird looked skeptical. "That doesn't make sense. Aunt Tina would have taken her. Why would she ask Luke? It's partly his present!"

The van brakes screeched as Aggie slammed on them. The engine was still running when she jumped from the van and ran to where they stood. "You didn't find her?"

"Not exactly, but we think Luke took her somewhere. Maybe it's some kind of wedding surprise or something."

"Luke? What?"

"A couple of people said they saw her get into Luke's truck. Luke got out, put her bike in the back, and drove off with her. We think it's probably some kind of surprise and Ellie forgot to mention that she was supposed to wait for him."

Already, Aggie had her phone open, the number sending. She glanced around them, unwilling to meet the children's eyes as she waited impatiently for him to answer. "Luke, I need you to call me immediately. This is an emergency. Call."

Her eyes hardly left the phone while she waited for him to pull over or finish whatever was keeping him from answering. Laird and Vannie exchanged confused and somewhat worried glances. "Aunt—"

"Get your bikes in the van. Let's get home. No, we'll stay here, but… yes, put them in the van anyway."

"Are—"

"Just do it, Vannie!" Aggie's eyes closed slowly and she swallowed hard. "I'm sorry. That was wrong."

Vannie didn't answer but threw her arms around Aggie instead. Laird, however, made the highly helpful comment of, "That's ok, Aunt Aggie. Everyone gets snappy when they're scared."

"Laird!"

"What! They do."

The cell phone rang before Aggie could interject any kind of response. "Luke? Do you have Ellie with you? I don't care what surprise is ruined; I need you to be absolutely truthful with me. I'm about to call William."

The answer was evident before Aggie said another word. Vannie had read often in books of people "going white" upon receiving bad news, but until she saw the pallor of her aunt's face as Luke obviously told her he did not have Ellie with him, Vannie had imagined it was merely a literary device. Now she knew it was real. Too real.

Tears welled in Aggie's eyes, and she fought to gain control of herself. She stared at Vannie for several seconds before whispering. "The bikes. Get the bikes." Her fixation on bicycles made no sense to Vannie, but she hurried to help Laird anyway.

As they closed the van doors, Laird and Vannie watched as Aggie punched just three numbers into her phone. "Why isn't it on speed dial?"

"After she thought Ian called a million times with the house speed dial, do you think she'd risk it on there? It's just three numbers. Should we go over there or stay here?"

Vannie slid her eyes sideways to see the expression on her brother's face. When had he started thinking like a man? It was evident from his stance, his eyes, even the way his fingers twitched, that he was anxious to do something to fix the situation. "Let's go. She can send us back if — no, she probably had us take the bikes so we wouldn't hear the conversation."

The hesitation ended as Aggie shoved her phone in her pocket, her shoulders shaking. The two young Stuarts rushed to see what she'd heard and try to offer some encouragement. It didn't quite seem possible that it could be anything too serious. "Aunt Aggie?"

"It'll be ok. They'll find her. They will." Aggie sounded as though she was trying to convince herself rather than them.

Laird listened for a moment, and then steered both of them toward the van. "It's cold out here. We can wait in the van until Luke

174

and Deputy Markenson get here. They'll take care of it. You know they will. Why do you think God brought both of them to us?"

Aggie's voice choked as she said, "Laird? When did you get so wise?"

"Ok, let's go over this one more time. How long was it after Ellie left the library until you got outside?"

"I told you! Just long enough for the librarian to do both our books and the lady between us—five minutes? Maybe? I don't think it even took that long." Vannie sounded angry, but the cause was evident when she added, "Why are you wasting time sitting here asking us the same questions over and over instead of out there finding Ellie?"

"This is how it works, Vannie. Just let William do his job."

William seemed unfazed. He continued with the same questions he'd already asked twice as if there had been no interruption. "Ok, and you are sure that she didn't mention going anywhere with Luke today?"

"No! Ask Luke!"

"Stop, Vannie. Stop."

The air seemed to crackle with tension as the girl glared at Aggie and then sighed. "I'm sorry."

William turned to join Megan in questioning Luke, but something on the girl's face stopped him. He laid a hand on Vannie's head and whispered. "I know it's frustrating, but trust me. It works or we wouldn't do it."

"Luke didn't take her. He would have told you if he did."

"I know."

The truth of his words hit him as he crossed the road to Luke's truck and Megan's side. Luke didn't have the girl and they'd have to waste precious time interviewing him because people thought they saw what they couldn't have seen. He just prayed Luke had an alibi.

"What do we know?" he asked Megan as he reached the side of Luke's truck—the very one in which witnesses swore he picked up Ellie from the Library not much more than an hour ago.

"Not much. He was at a house in Brunswick from about nine

until Aggie called. No one was with him, but he says there are a few people who should have seen his truck there until he left to come here."

"Ok, you take those people, I'll finish with him."

Megan hesitated—waiting to see something in him before she left. "I'll call you when I have something."

He waited for Megan's car to pull away from the curb before he looked Luke in the eyes and said, "You tell me now exactly what you know about this."

Luke didn't hesitate. "Nothing. I've been racking my brains to think of anything that might explain it. I've got nothing."

"It'll kill Aggie."

As if summoned by the sound of her name, Aggie raced toward them, shoving her phone in William's hands. "Tina's dad says that Ellie is under twelve, so we should call the FBI. Should I?"

William's jaw worked as he read the text. Before he could answer, Luke took the phone from him and passed it back to Aggie. "I think that puts William in an awkward position. Call."

She didn't hesitate. Turning away, Aggie punched in the numbers that Tina had provided. Luke gave William an apologetic look. "I know it's probably early, but it fits the criteria and it'll give her something to do. They can decide if it warrants it. Has anyone gone to talk to Geraldine yet?"

"The grandmother?"

Luke nodded. "I doubt she took Ellie home, but maybe there's a maid or a gardener or some kind of house help around. I understand they're quite wealthy."

"And what would this house help tell us?"

"Where to find them?"

"You think she has Ellie?" William's voice grew tense as he slipped back into interrogator mode.

"You have another suspect?"

"Luke, what did Megan tell you?"

"That Ellie was gone. She asked where I've been all day, what Ellie had talked about recently, if I knew any reason the girl would run away. That kind of thing. Why?"

"Did she tell you," William asked quietly, "what witnesses saw?"

"No. There were witnesses? That's good, right?"

William kept a tight rein on his expression as he said. "Well, it's good for us, but it's not quite as good for you."

"Me, why?"

"Luke, two independent witnesses from opposite sides of the street saw you drive up in your truck, speak to Ellie, and while she climbed in your truck, you got out and put her bicycle in the back."

"I—what? How—that's not possible. My truck was never gone from the house in Brunswick. I was out there unloading stuff when they called. I've been unloading for the last hour. Before that, I was ripping stuff out of the basement so I could bring in the flooring. No one could have taken my truck. I would have noticed."

"You didn't hear me," William insisted. "They saw *you* get out of *your* truck. You."

The sheriff pulled up before Luke could respond. While William caught Sheriff Forbes up on the information they had, Luke ran to Aggie, wrapping his arms around her. "I just heard," he whispered somewhere in the vicinity of her ear.

"Heard what."

"That she left in a truck that looked like mine." He steeled himself for any kind of hesitation or rejection. It would only be natural, even if she knew deep down he couldn't do such a thing.

"It has to be preplanned, right? Someone who knows where she lives, what we drive—the works."

"Getting a truck like mine isn't easy. Why not get a white van? There are hundreds of vans like yours in this area."

"The guy looks enough like you that he thought'd be easier to do it that way maybe?" Her voice broke. "My little girl is alone with a strange man who has been stalking her or us or both. Luke!"

"I didn't know until a minute ago. I thought it was the grandmother."

"I wish it was. At least the GIL wouldn't hurt her." Fresh tears overtook her. "She's with a strange man!"

"Don't think about that now. Not now. Think about—what's he doing?"

Aggie turned to look where Luke pointed and shook her head. "Looks like he's going through your truck." Her face blanched. "When was the last time Ellie was in your truck?"

"Has she ever been in the truck?" A new idea occurred to him. "I'll be right back."

177

Vannie and Laird stood huddled next to the van, both visibly shaken, Vannie crying. "Shh, it'll be ok, sweetheart. We'll find her. We will. I need you to think about something. Think very carefully. Did Ellie have on gloves or mittens when she left the library?"

"No. She couldn't find them today so she went without them."

Luke's heart leapt. "You're sure."

"Totally."

"Go tell William. Make sure you tell him exactly what I asked and what you said. Don't leave anything out. Don't add any commentary. Just tell him."

While the kids went to talk to William, Luke returned to Aggie. "Ellie wasn't wearing anything on her hands."

"Oh! That's right!" A smile flashed at him, the first one he'd seen all day and likely the last he'd see until Ellie was home safe. "She couldn't find them, and I didn't let her take Tavish's."

William's eyes met his from across the street, and he nodded. Confirmation that Luke's hunch was correct. If Ellie had been in his truck, they'd find fingerprints, but since she hadn't, he'd be cleared. His relief was cut short when the sheriff emerged holding a knitted hat by a pair of tweezers.

"What's that?"

Luke sighed. "That's Ellie's hat—the one Mom made her for Christmas."

"Why is it in your truck? She hasn't been able to find it—oh. She left it at Corinne's, didn't she?"

"Yep."

She shrugged. "At least this way, you have witnesses. I can't believe they're doing this! No one could believe you could—"

"They do it routinely, Aggie. They'll question you too. Get your alibi. They'll do it because most kidnappings involve immediate family or the mom's boyfriend."

"Well, this doesn't involve either." She gripped his jacket, leaning her forehead on his chest. "I wish it did! I wish it was just the GIL being her usual nasty self. I'd kiss her, right now. I swear I would."

178

The room buzzed with conversation, hushed but tense. People milled in and out of the room, and the children huddled in the library, as if using it like a barrier from the reality outside the door. Aggie sat on the couch, Luke on one side of her, Tina on the other, answering question after question, while deputies examined every inch of the property and her home.

"And why were the children at the library during school hours?"

The weary expression on Aggie's face seemed to bring out the protective side of Luke. "As she has said several times, the children were done with their work for the day, so they went to the library to get the next books on their reading lists."

"I asked Ms. Milliken."

Aggie's eyes rose to meet those of the agent questioning her. "What was my answer last time?"

"Um, ma'am, I need you to answer the question."

"Ellie got her work done first today. She even finished the book that she didn't have to finish until Friday and did the book report for it. My lesson plans are in the desk in the library, along with her turned in assignments, if you'd like to verify that statement. She isn't allowed to go to the library by herself, so she had to wait until Vannie got done. Laird finished first and decided to go too. At one-thirty, Vannie finished and put her things away. They got their books and started to go outside, but Ellie couldn't find her gloves. They looked everywhere. It's pretty cold out there, so I suggested she stay home. She pleaded." Aggie choked, unable to continue.

"Oh, Mibs." Luke's eyes met the questioning ones of Agent Sheridan. "Ellie doesn't ask for much. If you say no, it's no and she moves along. She really wanted to go."

Nodding, Aggie forced herself to continue. "Tavish offered his, but Ellie has been getting careless with things lately, so I decided not to let her borrow them. I told her she'd have to go without gloves. I knew she'd be able to ride one handed and alternate stuffing one hand in her pocket." Her hands covered her face as she wailed, "Why didn't I just let her take the stupid gloves? She's just a kid. All kids lose stuff!"

"With gloves, she couldn't leave fingerprints. Maybe it's best that she didn't have them. Now, if she's been somewhere and they find that "somewhere" they can prove she was there."

Luke's reasoning sounded desperate to Aggie, but the Agent nodded. "Unless the abductor thinks to put gloves on her himself, yes that would be correct." Another agent whispered something into Sheridan's ear, which made him sit up. "Ok, I see that you have a significant amount of money, Ms. Milliken."

"Well, it's not really mine. It's just in my name. Life insurance, 401K, stuff like that. It was my sister's and her husband's."

"It's enough that money just topped the motive options. We're going to get you set up to record incoming calls in case of a ransom demand."

"Ransom? Who would know about the money? It's not like we're listed in some who's who list."

Luke disagreed with her. "But Geraldine isn't exactly discreet. She's proud of her position and money, and she thinks you're an idiot. All she'd have to do is make some comment at that place where her husband is living and some custodian or even family member of a resident could decide it's easy money."

"We'll need the name of that residential home and any other place you think this woman might frequent."

Another agent, one of the ones searching Ellie and Kenzie's room upstairs, came downstairs carrying a picture. "Is there a reason this is hidden under her bed?"

Aggie stared at the lines, circles, and shadows that created highlights—all combining into a remarkably good sketch of her and Luke. Somehow, she'd combined them into a natural pose as if in a photograph—but no such photo existed. "That's what she's been hiding. I was worried over nothing."

"It's supposed to be a wedding gift," Laird said.

Her brain buzzed until Aggie felt as if she had a beehive in her head. While the agents talked, the deputies searched, and Murphy came in and out while she got drinks for the children, reassured them, took them to the bathroom or to get a toy, Luke answered questions and rubbed her back. None of it made sense to her.

Ian screamed. Without thinking, Aggie stood to retrieve her son mid question from the agent. The room spun wildly as if the house was on a large merry-go-round. She clutched at the air for something to stabilize her, but crashed to the ground, striking her back on the coffee table. She didn't stir.

Only a tiny glow of light from the hallway illuminated the otherwise black house. Aggie's eyes tried to adjust, but she closed them again, fighting to remember why a deep sense of dread hovered over her. As she shifted to be more comfortable, a hand rested on her head, lightly stroking her hair. "Shh. Rest."

The voice was familiar. Comforting. Opening her eyes once more, she focused on where she was—the knees— She blinked. Knees? Luke. She was using him for a pillow. Her eyes widened. Luke didn't wear tan pants except to church. It wasn't Sunday. Was it? No, she'd graded schoolwork that morning. Then Ellie—

She bolted upright, her eyes meeting William's. "I'm glad you got a little sleep. You'll need it."

"Where's Luke?"

"Upstairs with the kids. They're having trouble settling down."

She flushed as she realized how close she'd been to another man. He stood, stretching. "You've been out for quite a bit. My legs were getting numb."

"How did I end up with my head in your lap?"

He chuckled. "You should have seen Luke's face over that one. One minute you were asleep on that pillow and the next you just sat up and flopped down with your head on my leg. Every time I tried to move, you got restless, so we let you sleep."

"Awkward."

"You're telling me. I just endured two and a half hours of glare from Luke."

It killed her to ask, but she had to know. "Any updates? Any word at all?"

"None. Sorry."

"Is it on the news?"

"Yes. The Amber Alert, of course."

She nodded and flipped open her phone. "Did Dad call?"

"Yes. He said not to mention it to your mother yet. He kept the news off."

Torn between hearing her father's voice and knowing he couldn't hide the conversation well, Aggie's eyes shifted between cell phone and laptop. "Can you get me a cup of coffee? It's gonna be a long night." She stuffed her phone in her pocket and flipped open her computer.

"Aggie, you need to try to get some more sleep. There's nothing you can do for her if you're worn out."

"I need to talk to my father. If you won't get me coffee, I'll get it myself."

"I'll get it, I'll get it."

It seemed to take forever for the laptop to boot, the internet to connect, and her messenger program to sign in. The box popped up with an offline message the moment she connected.

Milliken says: Ding me as soon as you can. Anxious for news.

Milliken says: Aggie?

Aggie says: Dad. I'm here. What have you heard?

Milliken says: Just that Ellie was taken by a man in a blue truck who is average height with brown hair.

Aggie says: The people who saw him thought it was Luke.

Milliken says: Impossible.

Aggie says: Luke's truck is clean of fingerprints. Ellie's hat was in there, but she wasn't wearing it today. She left it at his sister's house a week ago. He was just bringing it back.

Milliken says: I thought Geraldine until I heard the description.

Aggie says: So did Luke. He just assumed. I think I didn't want to think about it. I was sure she was with him for some kind of surprise until he said he didn't have her.

Milliken says: I can bring Mom if you need us. I'd rather not overtax her.

Aggie says: I need both of you, but I'm going to need you even more if the worst happens. I can't handle looking for Ellie, taking care of the kids, and worrying about Mom.

Aggie says: How long before you tell her?

Milliken says: Tomorrow night. I can keep her off the news and field calls that long, but then she'll start to get suspicious. I don't want to risk someone telling her before I can.

Aggie says: That sounds wise.

Milliken says: I know what you're thinking, Aggie, and you're

---

wrong.

Aggie says: What am I thinking?

Milliken says: Allie wouldn't have lost a kid. If Allie were here, this couldn't have happened. Allie was the perfect mom. I am a failure. I should have these kids taken away from me.

Milliken says: Oh, and EPIC FAIL!

Aggie says: LOL. I needed that last one.

Milliken says: And it's all a lie. It could happen to anyone.

Aggie says: Not if I don't let a nine-year-old ride off to the library.

Milliken says: You sent her to the library alone?

Aggie says: No! Vannie and Laird went with her. She went back outside for her library card.

Milliken says: Then you were a responsible parent who had a normal childhood thing turn into a tragedy. Just like moms who have eight year olds playing in the back yard—fenced—and go check on them five minutes later and the kid is gone. It happens.

Aggie says: Why does it always happen to me?

Milliken says: You have more opportunities for it, Aggs. It's just life.

Aggie says: Daddy?

Milliken says: Yeah?

Aggie says: I have news vans camped out on our street. I can't see Mrs. Dyke's house for the traffic out there.

Milliken says: It's ok. Let them do their job. You do yours. You pray, you take care of those other kids, you sing, you pray some more, and God'll take care of the rest.

Aggie says: He didn't take care of Ellie.

Milliken says: I'm calling Luke. You go hug that man. Listen to him. Let him carry this.

Aggie says: It's not his burden.

Milliken says: Don't be a fool. Of course it is. He is as married to you as you can be without actually being married. Now go get that hug. Pretend part of it is from me.

Milliken says: Love you.

Aggie says: Love you. I'm sorry.

Milliken says: You've no need to be. Go. Scat.

Before Aggie could stand, Luke's feet came crashing down the stairs and she found herself crushed in his arms. "Let's pray, Mibs."

Chapter 14

DEAD END

Tuesday, January 20ᵗʰ

Huddled reporters stood outside the split-rail fence that separated Aggie's house from the street. Men holding large video cameras swept them across the property, down the street, and Aggie had even seen them around the side of the house from the highway. According to Tina, most of the newscasts were positive, but a few more sensationalist stations harped on the excessive number of children and if it was possible to give them all the level of care and supervision they needed.

Inside, William seated himself across from Aggie and Luke, ready to share some of the information that they'd learned in hopes it would trigger some kind of memory or idea. "It's been about thirty hours. The first twenty-four hours are so crucial—" Aggie's face fell, but William shook his head. "No, really. We do have some information that is going to help."

"But no ransom demand. After twenty-four hours and no demand, what are the chances?"

"Chances of what, Aggie."

"Don't," Luke rasped. "Don't. Just let them do their jobs and leave it in God's hands, Mibs."

"I can't do that! I have to prepare myself. I want to know. At what point in a stranger abduction is too long to expect a ransom call?"

"Now is too long for a ransom, most likely."

Her eyelids closed and lay still for several seconds until at last, she forced them open again. She sat up just a little straighter, grabbed

Luke's hand for support, tried to take a deep breath, and asked, "Is it twenty-four or forty-eight hours that means finding her alive is not likely anymore?"

"Somewhere in there, but Aggie the majority of kidnapping victims are returned safely. We'll find this guy. We'll bring her home. It's my job. I won't let you or that little girl down."

"Oh, William. You can't promise that. I love that you tried, but you can't. Don't—"

"What other information do you have for us, William? What'd you learn today that you can share?"

Luke's diversion worked. Aggie's face rearranged itself from despair to hope. "Did you learn anything?"

"We did a little digging on Mrs. Stuart. First, did you know the restraining order expired the ninth?"

Aggie's eyes grew wide. "Really? I forgot all about it."

"I'd take care of that tomorrow if I were you. You do not want her to show up here. It could be even worse than you can imagine with the cameras out there."

"Ok, I'll go into Rockland in the morning. What else?"

William paced the room, recounting his visit with Douglas Stuart. Aggie watched as the veins on the man's neck pulsated with his apparent fury. While he told of the man's confusion, Aggie's heart squeezed to hear he spent most of the interview asking where his wife and son were. A new lump filled her throat as she learned that his wife hadn't been to see him since Thanksgiving.

"How can she do that? It's her husband! He saved her from poverty and this is how she repays him?"

"I don't know. We didn't find her at home. No one answered the door and there were no signs of anyone there."

"Maybe she'll be there tomorrow."

"Maybe. We've got a cruiser driving by every couple of hours. If she shows up, we're going to question her." The determination in his voice was fierce.

Before anyone could speak, Vannie clattered down the stairs, tears running down her face. "I think you should come up. Tavish is really upset and he won't talk to anyone."

Aggie left the men in the living room and dragged herself upstairs. As she passed the bathroom mirror, her eyes met Laird's while he was brushing his teeth. The pain and confusion in them

186

nearly broke her heart. The other face in the mirror—hers she supposed—looked like a stranger. Dark circles rimmed her eyes and disheveled hair gave her the appearance of one of the homeless people on the streets of Rockland. Her arm jerked toward Tavish's and Ian's room as Vannie dragged her along the hallway.

In one corner of his bed, Tavish lay curled on his side in a tight ball. His body shook with sobs, but his eyes and face were dry. When she touched him, he whimpered, drawing back as if afraid of a beating. "Tavish?"

There was no reply. Snow fell outside the window, a cruel beauty to contrast with the tormented hell they all felt they endured. She watched flake after flake fall, creating that wonderful blanket of silence that hushes the world after snowfall. For one brief moment, it seemed as if the Lord had added a little soundproofing in order for them to hear Ellie's cries for help.

Aggie wept. Little arms wrapped around her and her nephew—her son—who had seemed such a little man just the previous week, now crawled into her lap like a small child. "It's all my fault. I should have gone. She's not coming back. I just know she's not coming back and it's all my fault."

"Shh, it's not your fault," Aggie sobbed. "No one could have prevented this. I think if it wasn't yesterday, it would have been today or tomorrow. Maybe it should have been last week, but she had a cold and was inside. For some reason, this had to happen."

"But she's gone!"

A voice, Laird's, from the doorway called to her. "Aunt Aggie?"

"Hmm?"

Tavish sat up abruptly and shook his head, but Laird continued. "He was listening on the stairs."

"Laird!"

"She needed to know. Sometimes you have to choose between doing what will hurt someone now or what will hurt them for a long time."

Fresh sobs wracked Tavish's body, but this time, hot tears fell as well. "Daddy used to say that."

"Well, now I see why. It's true."

Aggie chose to ignore the brewing argument and focus on the overheard conversation. "What did you hear, Tavish?"

"You said that after twenty-four hours..."

Every song she'd ever sung to comfort herself seemed just out of grasp. Every verse that had ever admonished and rebuked her crashed down on her head. She was drowning in her own condemnation and didn't know how to swim to the top to be free.

"Did you stay? Did you hear what William said?"

"No."

"He said that the majority of children who go missing are returned alive—safe. We have to trust that Ellie will return. We have to."

"What if she doesn't?"

Her eyes closed once more as if to block out the idea. She swallowed, took a deep breath, and swallowed again. "Tavish, I can't think about that right now. Right now, I need to focus on what I can do to keep the rest of you safe and to help bring her home. If the Lord shows us that she's not coming back, well, we'll deal with that then."

"She's my sister!"

Aggie's spine grew rigid. She sat up, squared her shoulders, and gripped the boy's face by his chin. "Look at me, young man. Yes, she is your sister; you may even be closer to her than the rest of us, but you are not alone in your pain. Vannie was a mini mommy to both of you. She's Laird's first baby sister. She's the others' older sister and they love her dearly. She's my niece—my wonderful big sister's daughter—" Her voice cracked, fresh tears falling down her face. "She's my daughter now—just as if I'd given birth and raised her. She's Luke's beloved little Ellie. Don't you dare act as if your pain is somehow superior to ours. You get under those covers. Turn out that light. And you pray. Pray for that little girl. Pray that God would give the police wisdom. Pray that whoever has her will repent and bring her back to us."

"I—"

Her next words cut him off almost before he started. "And then you pray that if the Lord already has her home in his arms, if your parents are already rejoicing to see one of their children again, you pray we can find a way to accept it without losing our faith. Do you understand me, young man?"

"Yes, Aunt Aggie."

"Go to sleep."

She stormed from the room, anxious not to lose anymore of her control. As she passed the other children staring shocked in the hallway, she waved them to their rooms. "Get in your beds. You all pray too. Go to sleep."

Tina stood at the head of the stairs. "Aggie, I really think that was a bit harsh—"

"Please go tuck them in, Tina. I've got something to do."

She descended the stairs, pausing on each step to gather a little more courage and trying to smooth her hair. It was futile, and she knew it. At the closet, she shoved her feet into her boots, grabbed her coat, and pulled a stocking cap over her head. Luke and William called out for her, but she opened the door and stepped outside.

Halfway down the driveway, the men finally caught her, but Aggie ignored them. Luke grabbed her arm and begged her to come inside, but her voice was reinforced with steel as she said, "Don't, Luke. Come and support me or go back, but don't ask me not to do this."

"You can't say anything related to the investigation, Aggie. It'll compromise—"

"I don't intend to, William. If you hear me start to say something, squeeze my arm or something."

Reporters scrambled from their news vans, peppering her with questions before she could get close enough to be heard. She walked up to the edge of the fence and waited until they'd all assembled. The din was incredible for such a small group in a world hushed with the thickening snow beneath their feet. Not one question did she answer. Not one reporter was acknowledged. At last the group quieted to an occasional murmur between reporter and his or her camera man.

"I have a statement."

Questions erupted again. "Has there been a ransom demand?"

"Is it true that your fiancée is a suspect?"

"Do you think she's still alive?"

That question earned the woman who asked a growl of protest from the men on each side of her. Desperate to say her piece and get back into the warm house, she held up her hand and shouted, "I'm making a statement and leaving. You can either have that or nothing. The next person who interrupts me ends this."

She waited until she knew they were listening, every camera and microphone trained on her. "Yesterday at approximately two-thirty, my niece was abducted in front of the Brant's Corners library.

Eyewitnesses saw a man who looks like my fiancée and who was driving a similar truck pull over, speak to her, and retrieve her bicycle while she willingly got into his truck. The police have satisfied themselves that this man was not the man next to me. This means, we're looking for someone else. Who or why, we don't know. What I do know is that I want my niece back. I want Ellie home. I beg whoever has my child to bring her back to us. If you have a tip that leads to the arrest of the man or people who took her, I ask you to call the Rockland County Sheriff's department or the FBI and tell them. I am offering a fifty thousand dollar reward to the first person who provides a tip that is substantiated and leads to the arrest of the criminals who are terrorizing my child. Thank you."

She turned and walked back to the house, ignoring the calls, pleas, and questions. William's shocked grunt and Luke's squeeze of support were both expected. Her actions, however, weren't, and she knew it. Inside the house, she shed her boots and coat. The hat she clipped onto a "clothesline" hung over the washer and dryer in the laundry room. While the men stood in the doorway exchanging confused glances, she pulled towel after towel out of the dryer, folding them carefully, each wrinkle smoothed before the next fold. Never had her towels been handled as gently.

"Leaning... leaning..." she choked, but forced herself to continue. *"...secure from all alarms. Leaning... leaning, leaning on the Everlasting Arms."* Another towel snapped as she shook it before folding. *"What have I to dread, what have I to fear..."* Her hand reached into the dryer and pulled out a pair of colorful argyle leggings—Ellie's favorites.

William watched as Luke pulled Aggie into his arms and held her while she wept and then he shuffled down the hall and into the kitchen. He poured another cup of coffee, stared at it, and dumped it. The sobs grew louder, stronger, deeper. Each one twisted his heart until he thought it would explode with the pain. Where was the girl? Why her?

"You ok?"

Tina. She was amazing. She'd arrived in record time and installed herself back in her former room. She was a fireball with the press, fielding the never-ending phone calls, and researching ideas almost nonstop. "I'm ok. How about you?"

She jerked her head in an emphatic negative. "I was better

190

before Aggie lost it again."

"Did you sleep last night?"

Again the shake, no. "Not much."

"Come on." He laced her fingers through his—how small her hand was—and led her to the living room. "Got a favorite section?"

"That one, why?"

He gave her a quick once over and nodded at her shoes. "Take 'em off. Your jacket too. I'll be right back." While she untied her shoes, William pulled the comforter and pillow from her bed and carried it back to the living room.

"Why here?"

"You'll never fall asleep alone in that dark room. I'll start a fire, and you'll lay down and try to relax. Got an iPod or something?"

"In my purse."

Determined that she'd fall asleep quickly, he retrieved the purse and handed it to her. Within minutes, a fire crackled in the fireplace, the lights were all but off, and Tina was tucked into the couch, William by her side on the floor. His hand rubbed her shoulder, but he didn't talk. Instead, he watched the fire as she listened to whatever played on her playlist. It took less than five minutes for her to sink into a sound sleep.

With Tina settled, he went to grab her other pillow and another blanket from her bed. The floor looked too uncomfortable, so he took the other section of couch and tried to relax. Tomorrow. They'd find Ellie tomorrow. They'd find Geraldine tomorrow. She'd be the one responsible. Somehow, William just knew it.

Wednesday, January 21st

Sunlight streamed through her window, but Aggie pulled the covers over her head. A sudden need for the bathroom sent her flying in there, emerging quickly. She glanced out the window, the line of news vehicles still camped out front, but in different orders. Had any of them gone home? Surely, they had.

The red eyes of the clock told her it was almost six o'clock. Lately, Ian had been sleeping until nearly seven. If she hurried, she could get a shower. Her teeth felt fuzzy. A shower, tooth brushing, and flossing. Wow. No wonder she'd felt as if she let herself go lately. Aggie couldn't remember the last time she'd done any of those things.

Her closet held an array of new clothes—some she'd not even worn yet. She snatched a brown corduroy skirt from a hanger and grabbed a green cowl-necked sweater. The sight of argyle leggings reminded her of Ellie's and she grabbed them. It had seemed like something she'd never wear when she'd opened them, but now for Ellie, she would. Yes, she would.

Hot water pounded her body, better than any massage she could imagine. She wanted to stay there forever where the noise, the heat, the steam could all drown out the pain in her heart for as long as she stood there. Her mouth opened to sing, but the words wouldn't come. "Give me back my comfort, Lord!" her heart cried out within her.

Her low flat boots covered the leggings, giving the outfit a much more polished appearance than she'd expected. The reflection in the mirror did not reflect her heart. Where her clothes were cheerful and comfortable, Aggie felt broken and irritated. She looked like a young woman just out of college but felt older than her mother.

Tina and William were asleep on the couches—their personalities shining in their body positions. Tina was sprawled awkwardly, one leg hanging over the back of the couch and a hand lying on the floor. It looked truly painful. William, on the other hand, was almost rigid, his arms crossed over his chest as if at his own memorial service sans the casket.

From the kitchen window, Aggie saw that Luke hadn't left. She checked the guest room, but it was empty. After a glance around the first floor and a peek into the basement, she jogged back upstairs to see if he'd gone to check on Ian or help one of the others. She found him sleeping on Tavish's bed, Ian curled up against his chest with the boy's tiny hand wrapped around Luke's thumb.

Instinctively, she looked for Tavish on Ellie's bed, but the boy wasn't there. Panic began to set in as she flung each door open, examined each bed, and then raced to the next. She ran upstairs, stared hard at her own bed, almost willing Tavish to be there, and then thundered back down again. Luke met her, Ian rubbing his eyes with his pudgy fists at the landing. "What—"

"Tavish is gone."

"I know; he slept in Ellie's bed. He said he wanted to feel closer to her."

She shook her head wildly. "He's not there, Luke. He's not there! He's not in my room; he's not downstairs or in the basement."

Ian reached for her, but Aggie didn't notice. She was on the run again, hurrying outside, without her coat, shimmying up the tree house ladder. By the time she was back down and rounded the corner of the house, William and Tina were outside with coats on, calling for him. William grabbed her arm as she rushed past. "Where have you looked? Exactly, Aggie. Where?"

"Um…" Her mind seemed foggy. She stammered, searching for a coherent thought.

William's hands cupped her face and forced her to meet his gaze. "Slow down. Breathe. Did you look in his room?"

"Yes."

"What about Ellie's room?"

"Yes. I looked in every bedroom—mine included. I was looking for Luke before I knew he was missing. I looked in the guest room, all over the downstairs, and in the basement."

Her friend's hands dropped as he rested them on his hips in his usual "I'm the lawman and I'm thinking right now" stance. His head dropped as if his shoes were of vital import to finding Tavish and then snapped up again. "The closet under the stairs. Did you—"

She never knew if he'd finished asking or not. She ran into the house, slipping on ice on the porch steps, but it hardly slowed her race to the closet. Aggie flung open the door, but Luke caught her in time to keep her from shaking the boy awake. "Shh… let him sleep."

"But he—"

Luke pulled her away from the door, closing it gently, and led her down the hall to the laundry room. Once inside, he shut the door and pulled her into his arms. "Cry it out, Aggie."

"I'm too angry to cry," she argued. Despite her protest, Aggie rested her head under his chin and then sighed as a few rogue tears made a liar out of her. "I'm now relieved I don't have time for things like mascara."

"And why is that?"

"I hear the laughter that you're trying to stifle. You're failing." She sounded confused as she muttered, "What was I—oh, right. Mascara. Can you picture me with black streaks down my face right about now?"

193

"You'd just look like one of those French clowns with the long black tears." Her pain prompted another attempt at encouragement. "It's going to be ok. It is. God knows what He's doing even when we don't understand it."

"God may know what He's doing, but that doesn't mean I happen to agree with Him."

"I thought you were going to say you didn't *have* to agree. I was going to argue," Luke said, attempting a smile.

She closed her eyes and ignored the prick in her spirit that told her she had the wrong attitude. "I have to go to Rockland. The restraining order."

"Do you want me to take you?" Luke sounded anxious.

"Would you? I'd rather not have to do this, but William—"

Luke stepped back, turning the knob behind him. "I'll shower and be ready in a few minutes. She stared at the empty doorway for several seconds as she wondered how she would have gotten through this without her friends, without Luke. His face appeared in her vision seemingly out of nowhere. "Oh, I forgot to tell you."

Dread began to fill her heart. "What?"

"You look wonderful. I love you in that green."

Aggie stared at the empty doorway for the second time in less than a minute. "He's lost it. We're all going crazy."

A man carried three suitcases and an overnight bag past William as he stood in the foyer of Geraldine Stuart's imposing home. "Do you remember the flight number?"

"Six thirty-seven. Continental." She placed her purse on a small table and pulled out a wallet. From inside, she passed him her passport, printouts of internet tickets, and a receipt from a hotel in Willemstad.

"Willemstad?"

"Curacao. Beautiful Dutch island in the Caribbean. All the beauty of Dutch architecture in a tropical paradise and below the hurricane belt."

"You sound like a travel agent."

"I've heard those words a few dozen times over the years."

Geraldine laced her fingers together and faced William, her eyes cold. "Now, will you please tell me why you are here? I have not violated that restraining order."

"I came to ask where you've been. We've tried to contact you for the last few days, but no one has answered the door."

"I usually give George and Pilar a vacation while I'm out of the country." She held out her hand for her passport and paperwork. "However, that does not answer my question, *Deputy* Markenson."

William, not inclined to answer and give the woman fuel for her easily roused rage, reached for the door handle. "I think you should know that your husband misses you. He's very confused, scared, and lonely."

"What business is that of yours?"

"None whatsoever. Good afternoon, Mrs. Stuart."

"But—"

He pulled the door shut behind him and ignored her irate demands for information as Geraldine Stuart stormed after him. Once inside his cruiser, he started the engine and slowly eased it away from her house until he was sure she wouldn't get in its path. She was just the kind of woman who would allow herself to be injured to prove some sick point or another.

Frustrated, William sped toward Brant's Corners. The road past Fairbury was slick with ice, forcing him to slow down while a truck salted the roads. His fingers tapped the steering wheel impatiently while his mind whirled miles ahead of his tires. She'd been gone. She wasn't even in the country.

He punched a number on his phone and waited impatiently for the station to answer. "Markenson here. Got a question. Can you check Geraldine Stuart's financials for the past few years? See if she goes to Curacao every winter? I just talked to her. Saw her passport, but it only goes back a couple of years. She's been out of the country."

Assured of the information as soon as it came in, William disconnected the call and began watching the clock, comparing it with the speedometer. Twenty-five miles per hour on a two-lane curvy highway was slow enough to ensure he'd be insane if he ever reached the turn off to Brant's Corners. Thankfully, at the turnout half way there, the truck pulled in and turned back toward Fairbury, and William whizzed down the road.

The station was still abuzz. What few news vans weren't camped out at Aggie's place seemed anxious to hound the Sheriff and his deputies. Megan's voice greeted him before he could shut the door behind him. "Got a call from Judge Vernelli about Aggie and her stalker-in-law."

"Good one. What'd he want?"

"Agreement that the order should still stand and for all of them."

William frowned. "There was doubt?"

"She let it lapse."

There was no arguing with that. It did look bad. "What'd you say?"

"I reminded him that she hadn't had the kids for a full year yet and without seeing the woman or having trouble with her thanks to the restraining order, it was probably the last thing on her mind what with educating them, planning a wedding, and feeding everyone. I also pointed out that with Ellie being missing, things could get very ugly with the woman and we don't have the resources to search for a kid and fend off a dragon."

"You've got spunk; I'll give you that," William said, shaking his head.

"Hey, it worked. She should be served before nightfall."

"Good." William glanced at the stack of papers on his desk. "Financials?"

"Yep. She goes every winter just like you asked."

Dejected, he sat down and began reading. Just as everyone else had surmised, every year's expenses seemed a carbon copy of the previous year's. There was something horribly predictable about it until he realized that the same could be said of his. "Remind me to tell Tina I need more spontaneity," he muttered to himself.

"What?"

William's head jerked up. "Did you say something?"

"No, you did. Something about spontaneous."

"Oh, nothing. I just noticed that everything seems terribly predictable here—nothing spontaneous about this trip. She goes every year. She does the same things in every month of—" He flipped the papers back, circling hotel dates on each year's pages.

"What is it?"

"She went in January this year."

"So."

"So, she usually goes in early to mid-February. Look!"

Megan obliged by getting up to see his stunning discovery, but she seemed skeptical. "Ok, the woman doesn't think she'll feel much like a vacation the week of the first anniversary of her son's death. Can you blame her?"

He dropped the sheets, frustrated. "I can't shake the feeling that she's involved. It makes no sense, everything points to something else, but..."

"I know. It was my first thought. I can't shake it either, but I think that's why. It's logical and as the first thought, it's had more time to grow."

"I suppose." William stared at the papers in front of him. "Do the Stuarts own a plane?"

"What! What would it matter? The guy who took Ellie was a man—not an elderly woman!"

"True. She could have hired him..."

"You're reaching, Markenson. Why don't you comb through the pile of tips we got today. The phone has been ringing off the hook, so John's forwarding tips to the FBI and calls to us."

"Any 9-1-1 calls?"

Megan shook her head as she grabbed her jacket from its peg. "Nope. Ian's been a good baby. I'm going to get pizza. Want some?"

"Yeah. Get me a salad too, will you? I need something green."

The door banged shut, but William hardly noticed. His mind was already on the tips. Setting aside the financial records, he pulled out the folder of tips they'd received. Most were obviously worthless. People who saw a blue truck in a parking lot, in front of a house, or driving down the freeway—all too old, young, light, or dark to be the one that took Ellie. One woman was convinced that Ellie was living next door—had been for six weeks.

William found it nearly impossible to concentrate on them. He checked item after item off the lists, with only one in twenty being the remotest possibility. Those he left alone. They'd get around to those tips eventually. The idea of an airplane interjected itself into nearly every tip until he thought he'd go crazy. It was a ridiculous idea. She'd still have to show and have her passport stamped, even from a small private plane. A smaller airport, however...

Frustrated, he jerked open his notebook and flipped to the page

197

with the phone number of Geraldine's hotel. He'd ask if they'd seen her every day. It wasn't a solid alibi, but flying back and forth to Rockland in a day would mean she likely wouldn't have been seen. He needed that assurance in order to concentrate on something that might actually help.

Getting a manager at the hotel was more difficult than he'd imagined. At last, a woman with a cultured tone of voice came on the line and asked if she could be of assistance. That she spoke English was a relief after Geraldine's stressing of Dutch in her tour-guide description. "I need information about a guest of yours—she checked out early this morning—Geraldine Stuart?"

The woman seemed hesitant to divulge any information, but upon learning that he was using it to establish her whereabouts in connection to the kidnapping of a child, the hotel manager became eager to help. While she researched hotel charges for room service, and other amenities, he listened to her question several employees about having seen her on each of the days. From his end, it seemed as if she made herself as memorable as ever.

"Well, thank you for your help." It hadn't been helpful at doing anything but clearing the woman, but that wasn't the manager's fault. "I suppose you'll see her next February, unless she decides that January is her new favorite time of the year."

The woman in Curacao chattered about Geraldine Stuart's plans, and William's eyes grew wide, his pen scratching information as quickly as he could get it onto the paper. "Thank you again. You've been a great help."

Megan stepped into the station in time to see him drop the phone in its cradle and stab the paper on his desk with his pen. "Gotcha."

"Got what?"

"Geraldine Stuart had her trip scheduled for February eighth through the twentieth. She rescheduled this on the ninth."

"Of this month? Why is that date familiar?"

William grinned. "That is the date that the restraining order expired."

Aggie says: Are you there?

Milliken says: Yes.

Aggie says: Mom?

Milliken says: No, it's Dad. Mom's sleeping. I had to give her a sedative. She's a bit overwrought.

Milliken says: Any news?

Aggie says: Maybe. William is sure it's Geraldine Stuart.

Milliken says: But you said the guy looked like Luke.

Aggie says: Something about hiring someone... he's plowing through financials looking for any regular withdrawals in the past year—particularly since the restraining order.

Milliken says: Well, as much as I'd like it to be her at this point, it seems a bit far-fetched.

Aggie says: He seems to have some kind of support, but he's not telling me what.

Aggie says: Dad, the kids are falling apart. Tavish is scaring me, Vannie takes it all very personally, and the little girls are convinced that the TV crew will be taking them next. Cari even blames herself.

Milliken says: Cari blames herself?

Aggie says: Yep. She says if she wasn't so "bad" that Ellie would be here. I know, it makes no sense, but to her it does.

Milliken says: That's endearing in a sad little way.

Aggie says: Kenzie informed her that everything isn't about her. According to Laird, she (Kenzie) was quoting him.

Milliken: We need to come, don't we.

Aggie says: If we don't find her tomorrow or the next day, yes.

Aggie says: I'm sorry, Dad. I'd say come now, but Mom...

Milliken says: We'll be on our way first thing in the morning.

Aggie says: You don't think the kids will think that means she's not coming back, do you?

Milliken says: We'll cross that bridge when I get there.

Aggie says: I'm sorry. I can't help but think this was preventable, but with the Luke look-a-like and the same truck... I think it would have happened no matter what we did. Same thing, different place.

Milliken says: That's probably true. Keep praying, Aggie. It'll be ok.

Aggie says: It doesn't feel like it. I should go. I think Tavish is

crying again. Night.
Milliken says: Night.

Chapter 15

TIPS oF THE TRADE

Thursday, January 22ⁿᵈ

After several days of no school, no structure, and minimal supervision, the children were more than a little restless. Aggie's nerves, stretched to the point of snapping, seemed to dictate the tone of the house—something she was not particularly happy to realize. The latest victim of her impatience, Kenzie, crumpled into Libby's arms, wailing that Aunt Aggie hated her now, making Aggie feel like the world's most unfit aunt-mother.

Whatever Libby said made all the difference. Kenzie raced to her, threw her arms around Aggie, kissed her cheek, and skipped downstairs to play with Luke and the younger children. If only her heart could be as easily soothed.

At the kitchen window, she stared out at the back yard, wondering where her world had gone. What happened to playful children building snowmen or having snowball fights? Where were the kids who couldn't stand to be away from those dogs— She stared at the dog kennel. What was wrong with Sammie? She wasn't moving. Miner circled her, sat, and circled her again.

Aggie grabbed her jacket and stumbled across the back yard to the kennel. "Sammie! What's the matter?"

Miner's whimpers tore at Aggie's heart. "What's wrong with her, boy?"

The dog dashed to her side, raced back to Sammie, nudged his sister, and then bounded to Aggie again. The back door opened, causing Sammie to raise her head expectantly. When Tina stepped onto the porch and called to see what was wrong, the dog dropped her head to her paws again with a huff.

"It's Sammie. She's—something." Aggie returned to the house, dejected. "I think she knows Ellie is missing or something."

"Sounds crazy," Tina said, "but considering how much time Ellie spends with her, it's probably normal. Dogs can sense trouble, right? Some kind of instinct thing?"

She stood at the island, thinking. Should she take the dog to the vet? Could a vet do anything? Probably not. Sammie would be fine when Ellie came back, and if not, well, she didn't have time to think about a dog at a time like this.

Tina's phone rang. She gave Aggie a reassuring smile before stepping into the corner to answer questions. "That's right... mmm hmm..."

Her eyes slid toward the clock—again. It would be an hour before her parents could arrive. Maybe she could just take a drive somewhere. It would help to clear her head if nothing else. One look at Tina gave her the answer she sought.

"Thanks." Aggie mouthed the word and reached for the keys in the bowl on the hall table. She hurried to tell Luke she was leaving.

In the basement, Luke pushed Ian and Lorna on swings while Cari and Kenzie chased each other up and down the slide. "I'm going to go for a drive."

"Do you want me to come with you?"

She shook her head. "I need to be alone for a bit or I'll go crazy."

"I don't think alone is a good idea right now, Mibs. There's someone out there—"

"Talking about it in front of 'little pitchers' isn't exactly the best idea."

His face looked confused, but suddenly, understanding dawned. "You're right." He thought for a moment, his jaw working and his hands catching the chains a little more firmly than necessary as he pulled the swing slings back a little farther. "Considering the possibilities of the motives of the perpetrator's apparent shenanigans, solitude seems unwise at present."

Aggie giggled. "That was brilliant. Um..." Her brain felt positively dizzy as she tried to match his over-the-little-ones'-head vocabulary choices. "Considering the alternative is acute mental distress, I—" she shrugged. "Um... disagree with your assessment of risk."

Luke seemed to be working double-time to formulate a reply when Kenzie said cheerily, "Uncle Luke, Aunt Aggie says she doesn't agree that there's much risk." The child watched as Aggie and Luke exchanged stunned glances and added, "I don't think you should use words that you don't understand. That's what Aunt Tina always says."

"Regardless of what Tina says, I'm doing it and Luke understands why and will support my decision."

"Mibs—"

Without a word, Aggie gave him half a smile and dragged herself up the stairs. At the top of the stairs she called down, "Mom and Dad will be here in about an hour. I should be back by then."

"You've got your phone, right?"

She called back to him before the door shut behind her, "Yep. Call if they get here before I do."

She didn't wait to hear more. Grabbing her coat, she carried it with her out the door and to Tina's car. As usual, she cranked the engine too hard, not having heard it turnover. Silent cars weren't part of her experience, and each time she drove Tina's car, she proved it. She waved at Tina, who stood at the window, and rolled down the driveway, dodging reporters who rushed at the car.

Once on the highway, she just drove. Her mind wanted to sing, but her voice choked with every attempt. Aggie punched the CD button, but at the blare of Metallica through the speakers, she hit it again. Tina's eclectic tastes were rarely Aggie's preferred options.

She tried praying. Her mind couldn't formulate the words. She couldn't sing, she couldn't cry. Her heart was heavier than it had ever been. Even losing Allie and Doug hadn't caused such unbelievable pain. Twice, black spots seemed to float in front of her eyes, blinding her for a second or two. Terrified, she pulled over onto the side of the road, shut the car off, and closed her eyes. The black spots were still there—even behind shut eyelids.

Where it came from, she didn't know, but Aggie exploded in a primal scream that nearly deafened her as it bounced against glass and metal, filling the car. The tears that eluded her earlier now overtook her. Her chest squeezed, her hands tingled from gripping the steering wheel, and the black spots floated through her vision until the last tear fell. Then, as if the Apostle Paul's scales, they dropped from view, leaving both her eyes and mind clearer than she'd felt since she'd answered Vannie's panicked call two—no it was three—days earlier.

The clock taunted her. Her parents would arrive soon. She should return home. Aggie started the engine, put the car in gear, and made a U-turn, heading back toward Brant's Corners. The sheriff's station outside Brunswick beckoned to her. She pulled into the gravel parking lot and hurried out of Tina's car and into the station.

"William?" The empty room confused her. His cruiser and corvette were outside, but although the door was open, no one was inside the station.

The door opened behind her before she could call out again. "Ti—Aggie!" He stepped inside, rubbing his arms to warm them.

"Oh, William. I thought maybe you weren't here."

"Just taking out the trash. I was coming to your place as soon as Ginny got in to man the phones. We have an interesting development."

Hope leapt within her. "What?"

"Geraldine hasn't been home since I spoke with her yesterday. The server cannot serve your restraining order. He's been trying for nearly twenty-four hours now. We've called, Rockland police have done drive-bys—nothing."

Aggie chewed her lip, trying to think of where the woman could be. "Do you think it means something?"

"Why would she be gone from home for two weeks and then leave again, without word, within hours of her return?" He squeezed the back of his chair in frustration. "She's involved in this. I know it. I just can't prove it yet."

"Ok, that's good though, right? If she really does have Ellie, then that's good. We can work with that. For all her weirdness, Ellie is at least safe. She's not being assaulted—" Her choked sobs belied her confidence. "I'm sorry. I—"

William's arms wrapped around her and gave her a big squeeze. "It's ok, Aggie. You're right. *If* I'm right, and I'm sure I am, but I can't promise it, then she's safe in that regard. Do you have any idea where she'd take her?"

Wiping her tears away did little to staunch the fresh flow. Aggie shook her head and frowned. "But what about the man? Two different people saw the man and the truck."

"It makes sense, Aggie. If she's out of the country, she has a perfect alibi. She buys the right truck, hires someone, and then skedaddles out of the country. I bet the plan was to take her that day all along. She's gone when Ellie is taken but arrives the next day? It's too coincidental. There are no coincidences in crime. Ellie isn't with a stranger for too long…"

William's explanation faded into the kind of watery garbled nonsense of movies. Her mind tried to hear what he said, but failed. Her forehead must have wrinkled in concentration, because he shook her shoulder gently. "Aggie?"

"Wha—"

"Did you eat this morning? Sleep last night?"

"Neither. Mom and Dad are coming. I should get home, but is there something I should do? Can do? How sure are you?" As if her mind had the fog wiped from it, the questions flew faster than William could answer. "Should I mention the possibility of Geraldine, or is it too early? It'd really be good for Mom, but I don't want her to crash harder if we're wrong."

"Don't tell her until we find Mrs. Stuart. I'm sure I can read her well enough to give encouragement at least."

"So what are you doing to find her? I mean, it's almost like you've got two missing persons now." Aggie knew she sounded accusatory, but she didn't care. She wanted Ellie found and preferably yesterday.

"I have a fresh stack of tips—"

The phone rang. William answered it, frowned, and then pumped his fist in the air. "Gimme the address again? Washington. Willis & Foster—children's department. I'm on my way."

William grabbed his coat and hat. "Got her. You can call your mom. She was seen with Ellie at that department store downtown. The clerk heard the little girl say, 'Aunt Aggie wouldn't approve, Grandmother. It's indecent. Maybe we should just go get my clothes from home.'" He opened the door as he spoke, gesturing for her to follow, and then locked it behind him.

Half in a daze, Aggie stared at him, blocking his access to the steps. "Really? Someone saw her with Geraldine? That's good, right? What about the man?"

"They only mentioned a little girl calling someone grandmother and mentioning an Aunt Aggie. The clerk said she seemed a bit irritated about the clothing choice."

"Wait, she's not afraid. That's good! Right?"

"It's very good," William agreed as Aggie whipped open her cell phone and called Luke.

"Is Mom there? Ok, well when they get there, tell Dad that Ellie has been seen with Geraldine. He can decide what to tell Mom. Tell the kids to pray for Grandma. I'm going to drive around and see if I can think of places she'd take Ellie."

"Aggie no!" Two men's voices echoed in stereo in each of her ears, but she bounced once more, effectively ignoring them.

"I'm going to look! Now it's not crazy. Now we have a chance. I can't stand it! I've got to try." With a quick hug for William, she rushed to the car and climbed inside.

While William zoomed toward Rockland, Aggie wasn't far behind. Slowly, his cruiser pulled away until she no longer saw it. The police would be combing the entire downtown area. They'd probably check the Stuart home too. Where would Geraldine take the girl?

At Willow's driveway, Aggie pulled off the road and dialed William. "Where is Douglas Stuart? I want to see if he's seen Ellie lately."

"I've already been there. Even if she has, she won't be now."

"I need to do *something*, William. Where is it?"

Seconds later, with the address programmed into Tina's GPS unit, Aggie zipped along the highway toward the Loop.

Cheers erupted in the Milliken-Stuart-soon-to-include-Sullivan home. Tavish hugged everyone within reach and then scurried into his favorite nook to wait for his sister to arrive home. The little girls raced around the room singing, "Ellie's coming hoo-oome, Ellie's coming hoo-oome" and Laird made high fives with Luke. Ian took advantage of their diverted attention and dismantled a shelf of games in the library, creating a mess that everyone would rue when they saw it. Only Vannie was quiet—too quiet.

While the others talked about welcome home banners and

enchiladas for dinner, Vannie crept upstairs and closeted herself in her room. Her grandparents arrived with much shouting and shrieking, but she didn't move. Eventually, Luke's gentle knock sounded on the door.

"Vannie?"

"Yeah..."

"Are you ok?" Luke crossed the room and sat on her bed, watching the pained expressions cross her face. "Didn't you hear? Ellie is with your grandmother."

"I hate her." The venom in the girl's voice couldn't be mistaken.

"Vannie, don't. Don't let yourself become bitter."

"She's evil! She took my sister! What am I supposed to do, be happy?"

"Happy that she was never in any real danger, yes. Happy that your grandmother is so very lost, of course not."

"She's always done this," the girl whispered. "She decides she wants something a certain way, swoops in, and takes over. It's like she runs everything. No one stops her. We've been scared to death about Ellie, but she thinks it's no big deal to come in and take her just because she wants a visit or something."

"Luke, have you seen—" Ron Milliken's voice at the door startled both of them. "There you are, Vannie! I didn't see you when I came in." He glanced at Luke. "Should I go—"

With a squeeze of her hand, Luke stood and crossed the room. "No, you're good. Why don't you talk to Vannie? I think she could use a grandparent's perspective on what has happened."

"I—" Vannie stared after Luke, angry and confused. Why had he run out like that? He was usually ready to try to talk with her on any subject.

Her grandfather sat at the foot of her bed and opened his arms. "Come sit with me, Vannie-girl?"

"You won't make me forgive her."

"Who?"

"Grandmother Stuart."

"Aaah, you're angry with her. I can understand that."

She smiled at him. Grandpa Milliken always understood. "Luke doesn't understand."

"Of course he does. The little girl who will be his daughter, for all intents and purposes, was snatched by Geraldine Stuart and he

207

was prime suspect for long enough for the news to get wind of it. He'll never live it down—even when a judge finds someone else guilty."

"But he just told me to forgive her—not be bitter."

"I can see why he'd say that. It doesn't hurt anyone but you, sweetheart. Anger, bitterness, unforgiveness—those only hurt you."

"I remember you telling me when I was Cari's age that anger could kill another person—inside. Now you're telling me it only hurts me."

Her grandfather smoothed her crazy curls as he tried to comfort her. "You remind me of that little girl right now."

"Which one, little Vannie or Cari?"

"Both... you were a lot like Cari at her age."

Vannie's head shot up and stared at her grandfather, shocked. "I was not!"

"You certainly were—still are a little. When I came in the first words you said to me were, 'You won't make me forgive her.' What would Cari have said?"

Her groan escaped before she could recognize and resist it. "Cari would say can't make me, but it's the same thing."

"When I said it'll only hurt you, I meant it won't hurt Geraldine Stuart. Aggie isn't going to let you within five miles of that woman. You can't hurt her back by being angry or bitter or refusing to forgive her..."

"Forgiving hurts when people don't recognize that they need it."

"This is true," he agreed. "Not forgiving hurts more, though."

"She always gets forgiven," Vannie complained. "She's horrible and we all are told to love and forgive her because she's Daddy's mother. Well, she was a bad mother to Daddy too. I just wish I could pretend she didn't exist."

"Well, after this," Ron Milliken whispered into her ear, "I think that's the only thing you can do. Pray for her—sure—but she's out of your life for good now. She kidnapped a child. That's a crime, Vannie. An old woman is going to jail, possibly for the rest of her life. She's going to jail because she's lonely and has an unhealthy love for her family." He stared down into the young girl's eyes. "If you feel anything for her, learn pity."

Vannie jumped up and rubbed the angry tears from her eyes. "I need to apologize to Luke and say hi to Grandma Millie." She grabbed his hand. "I can do that at least. Maybe later I'll be ready to forgive. I'm not there yet. I'm still angry."

"I'm going to need to see the security tape from that area for the time Ms. Farina said they were here."

William was all business. The young woman who identified Ellie was certain beyond any doubt and apologetic—much too apologetic. "I just can't believe it didn't click when they were here."

"Did she pay with cash or a credit card?"

"Car—no, maybe cash. I don't know. I had two customers waiting for help and the woman was rude. It flustered me."

They stood around the store security center, waiting for the technician to find the appropriate section of video. The salesclerk fought to think of any helpful information, but as hard as she was trying, he didn't credit most of what she said with any validity. Several calls came through, each one with the same message. "We can't find any evidence of either one of them anywhere."

"Ok, here it is."

William watched the screen closely. Geraldine seemed to know where the security camera was, but she used her left hand to fiddle with her hair to hide her face—the hand that wore her unique wedding ring. Ellie looked fine and healthy. There seemed to be no agitation in the child at all. "Well, she's not afraid, she looks happy and normal. This is good," he muttered. "I need a copy of that tape please." The next scene showed Geraldine handing over cash and receiving a large store bag in exchange. "And it was cash."

Minutes later, William forced himself out the door and onto the street. Aggie was going to the residential home. He'd start there. It seemed the most reasonable action.

His phone rang non-stop as he drove through the streets, onto the loop, and then through the quieter areas of Rockland to the home. The FBI wanted all information he'd gleaned. Aggie wondered if it was violating the restraining order to see Douglas. The next call was from Megan, telling him that a woman matching Geraldine's description was seen alone in a grocery store approximately ten blocks from Willis & Foster.

"I'm turning back. I'll go to the home if I don't get anything from the store. Can you call ahead and have them get any video from the parking lot or the store?"

Megan assured him she would before disconnecting. William did something he rarely had the chance to do and flipped on his lights, making a sharp U-turn on a yellow light. "We're getting close, Mrs. Stuart. I knew it was you."

The residential home looked nothing like any residential home Aggie had ever seen. Located in the older upscale area of Rockland, it wasn't very far from the house she'd sold back to the Stuarts after Allie and Doug died. The place was enormous but certainly not large enough to house more than a dozen people—if that many.

"At least Mr. Stuart is getting good care in a nice place in the absence of his wife," she muttered as she rang the doorbell and waited for the intercom to answer.

To her surprise, the door opened, and a young man wearing slacks, dress shirt, and tie stood there. "May I help you?"

Aggie suddenly felt very out of her element. "Well, I hope so. I understand Douglas Stuart is a resident here."

"I'm sure you'll understand when I tell you that we do not give out personal information like that. Do you have an appointment?"

"No."

He studied her suspiciously for a moment and then asked, "Are you on his list of approved visitors?"

"I doubt it. He is my children's grandfather—I'm their aunt. My sister—"

"Are you Aggie Milliken?"

Her heart sank. Geraldine had probably told horror stories about her. "Yes."

"Come in, please. I'll take you to Mr. Stuart's room. He's having a bad day today, but maybe a familiar face will help." Her hesitation must have been obvious, because the young man beckoned her encouragingly. "The sheriff's department called and told us you were coming—and why. I'm very sorry."

210

He led her up a grand staircase to a wide hallway. The house felt nothing like the nursing homes she'd sang in as a child at Christmas and Easter. The furnishings, décor, and even the air seemed to wear an engraved announcement that read, "Expensive."

The young man knocked on a door at the corner of the house and then led her into a small sitting room. "I'll get Mr. Stuart. He's always happy to have visitors, but it's usually just people visiting others here stopping in for a minute out of courtesy."

Aggie allowed her eyes to roam the room as she stood just inside the door. Her hands nearly shook with nervousness. Mr. Stuart had always been pleasant to her, but would he be now? Would he blame her for being shut away in this place?

Two pictures sat on the mantel, one on each side of a vase of fresh cut flowers. On the right, a slightly younger and even more imposing Geraldine stared back at her—nearly mocking her with the merest hint of a smile. On the other, the previous year's Christmas picture with Allie, Doug, and the children.

"Allie?" Mr. Stuart's voice startled her, making her drop her purse.

"Mr. Stuart! You look... well."

"Don't call me Mr. Stuart. Geraldine isn't here. You can call me Douglas when she's not around."

"Ok... Douglas," Aggie said. "Do you remember me? I'm Allie's sister."

"Allie's sister? The little girl at the wedding with bucked teeth? I don't think so, Allie. I'm not easily fooled."

The young man helped Mr. Stuart into a comfortable-looking wingback chair and promised to send up something to drink. Just as he left, he caught Aggie's eye. "I'll be back in about ten minutes. I'm afraid that's all the time Mr. Stuart has. We keep a strict routine here..."

"Thank you."

Aggie waited until the young man left and then turned her attention back on Douglas. "Did you have a nice Christmas, Mr.—Douglas?"

The faraway look in the man's eyes disappeared as if on command. With perfect clarity of mind, he shook his head. "They try here, of course, but it isn't home. I don't know when Geraldine will be finished with her project and come to visit again. Sometimes it's

211

nice to have the reprieve but—"

A gentle knock sounded on the door and a plump woman, dressed too nicely to be a maid or a nurse stepped in with a very small tray holding two mugs and a covered bowl. "Hot chocolate?"

"That was fast!"

The woman smiled but didn't respond. Instead, she lifted the lid of the bowl and offered Aggie the spoon. "Marshmallows?"

"I'm fine, thank you."

"I know you don't want them, do you, Mr. Stuart?"

"What?" The man stared blankly at his cup as if unsure what he was to do with it. "I—" He frowned and glanced at the two women in his room. "What are you doing in here? I am tired of strangers wandering through my quarters. It's bad enough that I'm trapped in this strange place; you'd think I'd at least be left alone." His face grew stony as he threatened, "My wife won't tolerate me being disturbed. You should leave. She'll be here any minute and will not like to find you here."

Without taking a single sip of her hot chocolate, Aggie gave the man a brief hug and hurried out of the room. Across the house, down the stairs, and out the door she flew, anxious to get away from such a disturbing scene. He was going downhill rapidly! The young man chased after her, catching her just as she reached Tina's car. "Are you all right?"

"He's just so different than even six months ago. I never saw a hint of any kind of dementia then, and now he is in and out of lucidity within seconds."

"He started going downhill just after Thanksgiving. Once his wife quit visiting, he couldn't hold onto reality." He opened her door for her as Aggie punched the unlock button on the key fob. "Will you be back?"

She shook her head. "He doesn't know me. I doubt it'd help."

"Consistency helps more than anything. He can still make friends, and at times when his memory is clear, he'll appreciate knowing you've been there."

Though tempted, she shook her head again. "I have a restraining order against his wife. I don't know if that allows me to see him or not. If he ever needs anything though…" Aggie dug into her purse for her ever-present stack of sticky notes and a pen. Scribbling her name and phone number on the top note, she peeled it off and handed it to him. "Just call. We'll find a way to help. Meanwhile, I'll ask my lawyer about visits."

The man folded the note and tucked it in his shirt pocket. "I hope you find the child, Ms. Milliken."

She nodded. "We will. Now that we know Geraldine has her, we'll find them. At least Ellie is safe—reasonably anyway."

"If they do show up, everyone knows to call immediately. We'll lock the gates behind them."

She eased herself into the car, inserted the key, and rolled down the window before pulling the door shut. "Thank you." Her eyes took in the house and grounds once more. "Mr. Stuart always seemed like a kind man. I'm very glad he is in such a nice place."

The car turned over, and for once, with the windows lowered, Aggie heard it. She gave the man a slight wave and put the car in gear, pulling through the rest of the wide circular drive and back onto the street. A glance in her rearview mirror caused her to shudder when she realized that such a beautiful place was the ultimate in grandiose prisons for Douglas Stuart—a place to be locked away and out of the way until he died.

The streets were familiar enough—likely the result of her getting lost so often in her first days at Allie's house as ad-hock mother—that Aggie found herself following them back to the street where her sister had lived. She passed the house where Cari and Lorna picked the tulips and tried to rip the "rocks" off the bottoms and wondered if the woman had replaced them yet.

As she neared the house, her throat constricted to see the driveway, the garage with its door halfway down—the opener must still be sticking—and the car that sat parked inside. The temptation to park and stare at it for a few minutes was strong, but the gates were shut and it would look suspicious for a car to be idling in the entrance to the drive.

With one last glance at the window that had once been "her" room, she turned the car around and headed back down the street. She'd only made it about three houses down when her eyes widened and her foot stomped on the brake. Aggie didn't even bother to make another U-turn. She threw the car in reverse and punched the gas, backing down the street at a speed she usually would never have attempted. She peered through the gates once more, staring intently into the garage. The silver car inside looked like the back end of a

Mercedes — exactly the kind she'd seen drive away from her house all too often.

Fumbling for her phone, Aggie took a deep breath, slid it open, and called William, whispering, "I think I found them."

"What?" His voice sounded a little garbled.

"I said," she repeated, assuming he hadn't understood her, "I think I found them. I'm at Allie's old house — it's near the residential home, so I drove by. I think I see Geraldine's car in the garage. The door is half open and I've just got a perfect angle for it."

"Why are you whispering?"

She snickered at the ridiculousness of the idea. "I don't know. I'm making sure she can't hear me?" She swallowed her excitement and asked, "What do I do?"

"Back out and park down the street where she can't see you. If she leaves, call me again. I'm only a couple of miles away. I'm calling the Rockland police now. This is almost over, Aggie."

The scene felt ripped from a movie. Police cars and black, unmarked vehicles raced as swiftly as safety allowed down the residential streets of one of Rockland's oldest neighborhoods. Children stopped on their scooters and bicycles, pointing. Drapes were brushed aside while curious neighbors craned their necks to see what was happening outside their doors. Younger people with less pride stepped outside and strolled down the street for a better look. Cell phones buzzed with tweets and texts.

Aggie waited for just one car. The rest could do their thing, but until she saw William, she had no intention of moving. The last thing she needed was to invalidate her own restraining order, and it seemed like she'd been told that would happen if she got too close. It wasn't worth the risk.

While she waited, she sent Luke a text message, called her father, and then called Tina and asked that she let Tavish know his sister would probably come home soon. Either way, she was fine. William said he'd seen her and she was fine.

Her fingers drummed the armrest. She dragged her purse from the floor and fished around the back seat for a plastic grocery bag.

Miraculously, Tina's car had one. Chauffeuring her children had destroyed the woman's pristine interior. Systematically, she plowed through her receipts, tossing most, and filing one or two in the checkbook she rarely used. It was at least good for that.

Gum wrappers, mint wrappers, empty tic-tack boxes, and a torn diaper she'd meant to use at night with duct tape ended up in the bag. She pulled hair from her brush, both fascinated and revolted at the kaleidoscope of colors in it. "I remember the days when I wouldn't have dreamed of using a brush someone else had touched," she muttered as she dropped the hairball into the bag.

One clean purse later, she started in on the door pockets, console, and floorboards. Who knew how long it had been since the last cleanout—since Christmas if the wrapping paper under the passenger seat was to be believed. As she worked, she sang. "…be it by water or by fire. O, make me clean, O make me clean! Wash me, Thou, without within…"[3]

"Aaak!" A tap on the window startled her. Aggie made an exaggerated frown as she opened the door. "You scared me."

"I've never heard that hymn."

"It's a bit obscure, but I learned it one year and every now and then…" She shook her head. "Off subject. How's Ellie? Do they have her yet? Can I take her home?" Her neck craned around him as she tried to see something.

"They're inside. I asked them to let me bring Ellie out myself. I need to serve that restraining order for you too before they haul her off."

A sick feeling filled her gut. "Oh! I didn't think about that. Will she go to jail?"

"Definitely."

"Can I post bail for her without violating anything?"

William shook his head. "Her lawyer will take care of it. Stay out of it, Aggie. She knows it's wrong. Don't let your—"

"I really think she's gone a little insane since Doug died. Perhaps if they put her in the same home with Mr. Stuart…"

William's phone made a funny sound—much like the entrance sounds in small stores. "Ok, I'll be right in."

He opened the door for her and pointed to the front of the car. "Stay there. Let her come to you. We do not want anyone to be able to say you stepped too close."

215

His words irritated her. Why was she, the other victim in all this, being held hostage by rules intended to protect her? Other "mothers" were able to run to greet their returned children, but she'd be shackled to the stupid vehicle by the invisible chain of the law.

The sheer volume of law enforcement at the house astounded her. News vans slowly converged on the neighborhood, all hovering around the gates for a story. Thus far, no one had noticed her there alone, and hopefully they wouldn't.

At the sight of William leading Ellie down the driveway, the crews began shouting questions, but he kept an arm around her and continued toward the gate. Relieved tears flooding her eyes, Aggie tried to watch his expression, but he was too far away to see clearly. Then a reporter turned to see what had captured his interest.

A shout of, "There she is" panicked Aggie. As half the reporters rushed toward her, William pointed and called, "Get in the car!"

She didn't hesitate. The door barely pulled shut when the first microphone was thrust at her. Never had Aggie appreciated the safety of glass and steel more.

Ellie's confused face wrung Aggie's heart. They were so close, and yet it seemed an age before William ordered the reporters and cameramen to back away, and he pushed Ellie inside the car. "Go! Don't stop until you get home—even to hug her," he added as he saw her reach for the girl.

For a moment, she almost complied. However, the scared confusion on Ellie's sweet face was enough to ignore him. She crawled between the seats to the back and wrapped her arms around the bewildered child. "Are you ok?"

"I'm fine, Aunt Aggie. What's wrong and why are all these people here? The police are in there."

"We've been looking for you for days. The news is just excited that you're ok. We're all excited that you're safe."

Ellie wiggled from her arms and stared at her. "Why? The restraining order is over. Grandmother said—"

"It was, but William gave her the new one now."

"But why did you say I could come with her if—"

"I said what?" Aggie's eyes slid to see if the reporters heard her. From the way they leaned closer, it seemed as though they did.

"Remember? When Josh came to get me while she was flying back from Curacao?" The child smiled. "I thought it was Luke."

216

Quickly, Aggie reached for the horn and blared it. William turned, his face darkening at the sight of the car still there. He jogged back to the vehicle and pulled the door open. "What are —"

"Get in."

Once William was squished in with Ellie between them, Aggie pointed to Ellie. "Tell William what you just told me."

"About Josh?"

"Aggie, we'll question her after we've processed Geraldine. Take her home."

"Processed? What's wrong with Grandmother?"

William's eyes widened. "What's wrong with her?" Frowning, he added, "It'll be ok, just go home, and tell me about it all later."

Without another word, William jumped from the vehicle and pounded the door before threading his way through the crowd and back to the house. Aggie stared after him. "Well, ok then."

"Are you taking me to see Grandfather?"

"What about your grandpa?"

"I was supposed to go see him, but he wasn't feeling well yesterday, so we had to wait until today. Grandmother bought me new clothes —"

"I just came from his home. He's doing well." As she spoke, Aggie crawled into the driver's seat and started the car. The reporters stepped aside as she edged her way into the street. Several vehicles followed, but most stayed to wait for an announcement by the police. And of course, they wanted to get footage of the kidnapper's trek to the police station.

"I don't understand why you couldn't just take me. Why did I have to come with Grandmother?"

"I don't think you have the full story yet, Ellie."

Once out of the neighborhood and onto the city streets, Aggie concentrated on not plowing through the cars in her way as she drove to the loop. Twice Ellie asked a question, but Aggie's non-committal, "I'll explain when we get home," silenced them both.

Once they turned off the loop and onto the highway that led to Fairbury, one last question twisted Aggie's heart. "Is Tavish with Grandfather yet?"

"With Mr. Stuart? No, he's at home, worried about you."

"Why? He's supposed to come with Josh to Grandfather's today."

217

Aggie says: Did you make it home ok?

Milliken says: Twenty minutes ago. Mom is sleeping already.

Aggie says: Was it too much for her? Such a long trip for nothing.

Milliken says: I wouldn't say nothing.

Aggie says: You know what I mean. Anyway, thanks for coming. I wish I'd have known we'd find her.

Milliken says: I think by that point, we needed to see that she was ok ourselves. Does Ellie understand yet what happened?

Aggie says: She thinks it was a mix up in communication. She prayed tonight that Grandmother Stuart wouldn't have the same memory problems as Grandfather Stuart.

Milliken says: Ellie thinks Geraldine forgot to get the permission she said she got?

Aggie says: Something like that. They're still looking for Josh. Apparently Geraldine refuses to give any information about him.

Milliken says: Well, the police will take care of it.

Aggie says: I suppose. Anyway, I am tired and I know you are. I'll talk to you tomorrow. I think I'll finally get real sleep tonight.

Milliken says: Night, Aggie. We love you. Have fun planning wedding stuff tomorrow instead of child retrieval strategies.

Aggie says: I have to go get a cashier's check and take it to a sales associate at Willis & Foster.

Milliken says: Now that will feel good.

Aggie says: It sure will. I almost asked William to do it for me, but I think Ellie will feel most normal if I don't hover. I want to hover.

Milliken says: Will you try to explain what really happened?"

Aggie says: I don't think so. It seems like it's best just to continue with life. She isn't really bothered by the experience; she thought it was all pre-arranged, and insisting she understand the reality at this point isn't going to help anything.

Milliken says: I think that's probably wise. She'll figure it out soon enough if it comes up.

Milliken says: I'm tired. I think I'll take your advice and go to bed.

Aggie says: Night, Dad. Love you. ☺

Milliken says: Night girl-o-mine.

CAN'T CATCH A BREAK

Monday, January 26th

"She is not evil! She's our grandmother! What is your problem?"

"She kidnapped you. That's the problem. You act like it's a normal thing for some strange man to pretend to be someone you know and take you away like that. I was scared, Ellie! Why didn't you come in and at least say something like, 'Luke is going to take me to see Grandmother?' At least that way, I could have stopped it."

"But I wouldn't want you to stop it. Don't you want to see Grandfather before he dies too?"

"She wasn't going to take you there, Ellie. Don't you see? It was just a lie to get you to come with her without fussing." Vannie's disgust showed in every piercing word.

"She was too! I even saw the letter that Aunt Aggie sent saying it was ok and the letter from Grandfather saying that he wanted to see each of his grandchildren before he died."

The argument raged as the two girls played with the dogs, throwing sticks across the yard. In the house, oblivious to the war outside, Aggie assembled enchiladas, humming and singing occasionally as she worked. "...of the soul, blessed kingdom of light. Free, from all care, and where fall...mmmmm."

"It's good to be home where Aggie sings and hymns fill the house."

Nothing thrilled Aggie more than to feel as though life was normal again. She smiled at Tina as she spooned another bit of enchilada sauce over the next one. "It's just amazing how a couple of weeks ago I felt like a big failure and today I feel like I can conquer the world."

"How about conquering a wedding instead?"

"What's next?"

"Reception. Oh, and your dad informed me that they're paying for at least the reception hall and the caterer. Apparently they've been saving for it for years."

"Yeah... I forgot about that, but they have."

Luke burst into the house, stomping snow off his feet and shaking his jacket out over the laundry sink. The two women listened to every movement and knew, even without seeing, when he started down the hall for the kitchen. "Have I got good news all around!"

"Have you?"

"Yes! Thank you for asking, Tina. First, the house is officially in escrow and it's going to be a short one. I'll be putting a couple of offers in this week. It's a cash offer, so no waiting on financing etc."

"That's cool," Aggie said while hiding a smile.

"Sure is. I'm going to love it."

"And second—wait, what?" He stared at Tina, confused.

"The house. I'm going to love it. Can I start putting things in now?"

"You—" He stared at Aggie for some kind of confirmation, "She—"

"Bought the house. Yes."

"You knew this?" Luke seemed stuck in stunned mode and incapable of moving forward.

"I found out the day I bought my dress. Tina told me then."

"Why didn't you tell me you wanted it? I could have given you a good deal and still made a nice profit."

"You did. You gave me the deal you really wanted and I was perfectly happy with it," Tina assured him. This way I can tell my father about the twelve thousand you knocked off the price and that I did it without you knowing it was me. He'll be tickled pink that I got one over on you—in his mind anyway—and it'll give him something to brag about. I consider it essential to his recovery."

After several long moments of his head swinging back and forth in search of something from the girls, Luke shook his head and asked, "Is this what it's going to be like?"

"What?"

"Marriage to Aggie. Never knowing what you two will come up with next?"

Tina laughed while patting his arm on her way out to check on the children. "As long as I'm her friend, pretty much."

"Wait, don't go. The other thing—I figured out a reception hall. Close, inexpensive, gorgeous, and perfect."

"Where's that?"

"That private school that meets in the old schoolhouse. That whole place has been completely restored. It's amazing in there—just beautiful. There's also that huge deck outside so the kids would have a place to go out without getting all dirty if it's muddy that day."

"Is it available?"

Luke flicked Tina's phone across the island toward her. "Only one way to find out, coordinator lady."

Excited, Tina snatched up her phone and hurried to grab her coat. Aggie went back to rolling enchiladas, her mind already decorating her mental image of the schoolhouse. "Is it painted wood inside or stained?"

"What?"

"The schoolhouse."

"I think it's all wood. The walls are painted though. It's very bright and airy."

"It has those really nice windows, doesn't it? I wonder if they would let us take down the curtains and put up tulle..."

"Tulle?"

"Well, I don't know it, of course, but I'm picturing the curtains in there to be pretty old-fashioned—kind of like ruffled country things."

"True. Hmm..."

"Can you text Tina and ask her to ask about it—never mind. We can do that when we go look."

"From the way she's dancing like a crazy woman, I think that's going to be right about now."

The room was large—surprisingly immense. The director of the school showed them where the original teacher's quarters had once been behind a wall. "When we renovated, we tore that wall out. It wasn't even a full wall to the ceiling. They'd just built it like a permanent screen. So, we didn't think it was too inauthentic."

"What's the maximum capacity?" It was perfect in Aggie's mind.

"A hundred forty-eight with tables. More just sitting in rows. They built with an eye to the future. It was one of the later schoolhouses. It was technically one room designed for expansion when the area grew, but it didn't. Brunswick grew instead."

"What decorating leeway would we have?" As she spoke, Aggie's eyes traveled to the curtains and then back to Tina.

"Nothing permanent or disfiguring, but as long as everything is back in place and undamaged by Monday…" The woman glanced around her. "What did you have in mind?"

It sounded lovely, but Aggie wanted the curtains changed — or at least removed. Tina stepped in. "Curtains. Can we remove them? We'd envisioned hanging tulle instead, but we'd be fine if we could just remove them."

"That shouldn't be a problem. They are just pocket rod style. Go ahead. Anything else?"

While Aggie tried to imagine where the cake would go and what kind of table set up she'd have, Tina discussed particulars. "Let Luke know that I'm on my way," she called as plans were finalized. "If he likes it, you guys can sign the contract."

Ten minutes later, the contract was signed and Aggie and Luke stood in front, grinning. "I feel like celebrating."

He slid open his phone and typed out a text for Tina. WE NEED A COUPLE OF HOURS. MIND STAYING ON DUTY A LITTLE WHILE LONGER? "There. How's that?"

Aggie peeked at it and grinned. "Send it."

In less than fifteen seconds, a message came back. DON'T COME HOME BEFORE TEN. PRETEND YOU'RE TEENAGERS AND BE LATE FOR CURFEW. DARE YA.

"Where do you want to go?"

"Show me your new houses and then feed me."

"We can't go in, but we can try to take a peek through the windows. I've got a flashlight in the truck."

The first house was brick and beautiful externally, but the interior was lost in the mid-seventies and half-demolished. "What happened in there?"

"People started demo-reno but obviously didn't have the skills to go any farther."

"They just knocked out part of the drywall? Why?"

Luke showed the top of the wall near the ceiling. "They were looking to see if it's load bearing. My guess is they thought it was and quit there. It's not. That wall is coming down." He led her around the corner, dodging a half-dead shrub, to the next bedroom. "This is a four bedroom, but it's going to become three with a large master and a master bath."

"How do you see this stuff? To me it looks like a scary nightmare. That carpeting looks like it was vomited there by leftovers from the reject vault."

"Let's go see the other one. It's just a few streets over."

The next house was almost the antithesis of the last. The outside looked horrible. Peeling paint, no landscaping at all, and a sagging roof made her nervous to get close, but peering into the old Victorian styled home made her excited. "Wow. Look at that dining room. Are those pocket doors?"

"The inside is almost perfect. There'll be a bit of interior stuff upstairs when I rip off the roof, but—"

"Rip off the roof? The whole thing?"

"Yep. I'm taking it down to the rafters and maybe replacing those."

"Wow."

"Laird is excited about it. He's convinced that we'll find some kind of historical something in the attic and the house will be worth millions."

"For a laid back kid," Aggie said as they walked back to the car, "he sure has an imagination on him."

"Not to change the subject—"

"Yeah, I'm hungry too."

"Where do you want to eat?"

"Surprise me."

Their table at Marcello's in Fairbury overlooked the ice rink—

something that added to a romantic ambiance neither was accustomed to and therefore resisted. Aggie half-choked on her salad, tears flooding her eyes. Luke's hand reached across their little table and covered hers. "You ok?"

"Not really, no."

"Feels awkward, doesn't it?"

"If I told you..."

Luke squeezed her hand. "Tell me."

"I feel like I'm out with William again. It feels all fake and horrible."

There were worse things she could have said, of course, but he couldn't imagine not preferring even something worse to any reference to her date with the deputy. Luke swallowed hard and thought quickly. If only his lips followed the speed of his brain, awkward moments like this might be a much rarer occurrence. "Close your eyes and tell me what is fake about it?"

"Candles," she said instantly. "We don't use candles at home. If Ian didn't knock them over and burn the house down, Cari or Lorna would."

"If you could, would you like candles at home sometimes? Maybe on the coffee table or even on the mantel?"

"The mantel would be pretty. They'd be nice on the coffee table after the kids go to bed and we have dessert alone."

Alone sounded good. Luke could feel eyes on them and knew that someone, if not many someones, had realized everything at the table by the window wasn't peachy. "You could also have them in your room. The mantel in there would be pretty with candlelight on it."

"I don't think I'm used to candles, but I like them."

"Let's go get some on the way home."

She stared at him as if he'd lost his mind. "Are you kidding?"

"No. This feels fake because it's unfamiliar rather than unreal. Let's make it familiar and then we'll enjoy ourselves next time."

"Ok..."

"What else?"

Though she appeared uncomfortable, Aggie seemed to try to enter into the spirit of his exercise. "The music. We never have music playing in the house."

"That's because we have you."

She flushed. "I'm not exactly Wagner."

"Is that what this is?"

She shook her head. "No, I think this is Glenn Miller."

"Doesn't sound like Miller." This felt better. She seemed relaxed now and nothing seemed forced.

Aggie swallowed and took a sip of water. "No, I mean he wrote it. "Moonlight Serenade." Dad loves this song. It's just a different arrangement."

"It's pretty." He skewered a shrimp with his fork and as he chewed, tried to think of what to do to regain that brief moment of normalcy. "Look, someone's skating."

"She's good."

By the time the skater warmed up and began jumping and spinning, Aggie was visibly excited. "You know, we should bring the kids. They'd love this."

"Saturday?"

"No, I think sometime before Friday night—while everyone is in school. It'll be P.E. and we'll have most of it to ourselves, I bet."

"I can come Wednesday if you go then."

A grin showed a piece of lettuce stuck to one tooth, but Luke said nothing when he heard her say, "Then we'll have to come Wednesday."

The awkwardness was back almost instantly, but this time, Luke knew the source. "I know what's wrong."

"You do? Enlighten me. I'm lost."

"We're trying to avoid talking about the kids."

"We are?" She shook her head. "No, we just decided to bring them skating on Wednesday."

"Yes, and the minute that was decided, we both clammed up as if we felt guilty."

Her protest died on her lips before the second syllable escaped. "You're right. That seems weird."

"We're acting like we are on a 'get to know you' date rather than an engaged couple who are out to enjoy a nice quiet meal."

"So when you're out with your fiancée, it's ok to plan a party for your twins—a party that will have to happen within days of returning from your honeymoon?"

Luke speared another shrimp and passed it across the table. "Taste it, and yes it is. What were you thinking?"

"I don't know anymore. Right now I'm too busy enjoying just being here."

Wednesday, January 28th

The ice looked like a safety advertisement. Nine bodies were decked out in helmets, elbow pads, and kneepads. Luke alone risked life and limb without protective head and joint gear. The girls wore snow pants under their skirts and looked positively ridiculous in Aggie's opinion, but they all insisted. She, on the other hand, wore two layers of thermals covered by her thickest knit tights under her warmest skirt. "I should have considered all ramifications of my decision to stick to skirts for the girls' sake," she complained as the third down on the ice managed to ensure her backside was officially frozen."

Luke helped her up again and waited for her to steady herself before taking her hand and leading her around the rink. "I think it was a wise thing to do."

Aggie pointed to the walkers the twins and Kenzie were using to help steady them as they skittered across the ice like a dog on a slippery floor. "*That* was a wise thing to do. Brilliant."

"Mom suggested I stop at the thrift store and they had exactly three."

Tina whizzed by with Ian in the stroller. "Now that's what I like to see!"

"What?"

"You two acting like two people in love!" she screamed. The children tittered.

"We obviously are much too staid for her tastes."

A wicked gleam filled his eye, making her laugh. "You know how to look absolutely diabolical which, considering I know you're probably thinking of something like calling William to come get her mind on her own romance, is pretty funny."

"Oh, that's a good idea! Think I should?"

"I think if he wasn't working, he'd be here. I have no doubt she already asked him."

"We could try…"

The answer that formed on her lips never had a chance to

226

materialize. Kenzie whizzed past them, going faster than Aggie had thought possible while pushing a walker, and hit a rough patch on the ice. The walker toppled. Kenzie screamed, and Aggie joined her as the little girl flew over the walker and landed a few feet away.

"Are you ok?" Aggie tried to help the child to her feet, but Kenzie jerked her arm away, holding it close to her body, tears streaming down her face.

"No!"

Luke lifted Kenzie and skated to the other side of the ice. The child screamed with every bump and jostle. "It's swelling, Aggie. I don't know if it's just bruised, sprained, or if it's broken."

"Get her skates off. I'll take her to the clinic. They have one here, right?"

"Down the street to that corner and turn left. Two blocks up on the right."

Aggie's fingers felt like sticks as she tried to untie her skates and tie on her boots. She grabbed her purse and waited impatiently for Luke to get his shoes on to carry the weeping Kenzie to the van. The two and a half block trip felt like a trek across the country. Kenzie screamed and wailed at every slight bump or turn.

Once at the clinic, the child refused to try to walk, holding her arm and kicking if Aggie got near her. A nurse came to see who was in the unloading area and tried unsuccessfully to urge the child out of her seat. "We can't help you if you don't come, sweetie."

"I can't! It hurts!"

Patience exhausted, Aggie stepped up into the van and hung herself over the back of the seat in front of Kenzie. "You will get out of that seat, Kenzie. Do you want to do it with my help or without? That's the only choice you get. You can do it yourself or I will help. Five seconds to decide or I decide for you."

"I don't want to get out! It's going to hurt more!"

"Two seconds left."

"No!!!!!!!!!!!!!"

With a glance at the nurse that clearly said, "Get ready for this," Aggie situated herself behind Kenzie and hooked her arms under the girl's. The child kicked and fought, obviously making her own pain worse, until Aggie froze and said, "Stop kicking. Now."

That magic word, "Stop," seemed to snap some sense into the child. Her screams subsided into pain-filled tears and she allowed herself to be led from the van. Another nurse appeared with a wheelchair, obviously trying to appease the little drama queen, but Aggie shook her head. "Her legs are fine. I think she needs the exercise."

Aggie had no idea if it was the right thing to do or not, but she felt like if she didn't make sure Kenzie obeyed on something small, the girl might turn the coming visit into a nightmare of monumental proportions. Once inside, a volunteer with clacking teeth and a hearing aid that clearly needed a new battery thrust the usual mountain of paperwork into her hands. They were shuttled into a small cubicle and left while Aggie filled out the forms.

"I'm sorry."

The voice was so quiet, Aggie almost missed it. "I forgive you. It's hard not to get upset when you're scared."

"I don't think I like ice skating."

As she suppressed a giggle, a young doctor stepped into the room. "Kenzie?"

"Yes."

With great effort, Aggie managed to stifle a snicker. The hero-worship Kenzie had once reserved for William seemed to have instantaneously transferred to the man now asking her to move her arm. "Can you lift it up?"

Pigtails whipped Kenzie's face as she shook her head. "Hurts."

"Can you put it down?"

She tried, but pulled it close to her chest again. "Nuh uh."

"I think we need x-rays."

"Do they hurt?"

"Not too bad. The x-rays themselves don't hurt, but you might have to hold your arm out for a second. We'll see what Jan says. She might be able to get you lying down. We'll bring in the machine and see."

He turned to Aggie and pointed to the door. "May I speak to you for a moment?"

"Of course. I'll be right outside, Kenzie."

The doctor signaled the nurse who had helped them in and she disappeared down the hall. "We just have a few questions that aren't on the form. Um, what happened again?"

"We were at the ice rink and she was skating with a walker."

"A walker?"

228

"Yes. Luke—he's my fiancée—bought walkers for the twins and Kenzie at a thrift store so they'd have a bit of stability until they got used to the ice."

"Twins? You have other children?"

Frustrated, Aggie pointed to the paperwork. "If someone would take that, it'd explain a lot. I have eight kids, Dr.—" she stared at his nametag. "—Singh. All of them nieces and nephews."

"Will her parents—"

"Who are dead, no. They won't be coming. I'm their guardian. Again, this is in the paperwork that no one has come to get yet. Perhaps you'd like to call the clinic in Brant's Corners. Dr. Schuler is familiar with my kids. Someone seems to try to give me premature gray hairs at least once a month. It's an improvement," she added as she saw him begin to protest that she must be exaggerating. "It used to be weekly." Another sigh escaped before she was aware it had formed. "I can't seem to catch a break."

"Looks like she did."

She managed a weak smile and nodded. "I think I could do without breaks."

"And they are out of school because..."

"P.E. for today—ice skating. We homeschool."

The man nodded but didn't seem satisfied. He scribbled notes on his clipboard and then tucked his pen in his pocket. "If you don't mind my asking, how old are you?"

"Twenty-three, and yes I am too young for all this responsibility, but no I won't resent them for it later."

"I wasn't going to—"

Aggie sighed, pinching her nose to help clear her mind. "I'm sorry. If you only knew how often someone says something about my situation..." A woman wheeling a large cart neared. "Is that the machine?"

Dr. Singh nodded. "Yes. I'll get that paperwork from you and see if I can forestall a few more questions."

The other nurse, Rose, appeared again. "I think her family is in the waiting room. There's um—a lot of them. We don't have room..."

"I'll send them home. Tina or Luke can come back to get us," she said as she waved at Kenzie. "Be right back."

229

Aggie says: Mom?

Milliken says: Hello! Isn't today the ice skating day? How'd it go?

Aggie says: Great. Wonderful. Perfect. Kenzie even got a new wardrobe accessory.

Milliken says: I sense a touch of sarcasm.

Aggie says: A cast.

Milliken says: No! Really?

Aggie says: Yep. They called it a "greenstick." It's kind of like the bone is bent but not fully broken off.

Milliken says: How long?

Aggie says: As long as everything heals normally, she'll get it off the week of the wedding.

Milliken says: Like you'll have time for that. Oh, ugh. I'm sorry. At least it's winter!

Aggie says: What does that have to do with anything?

Milliken says: No bugs to crawl in it. That's the worst part about casts.

Aggie says: I think I'm going to be sick.

Milliken says: Well, it's true. How did she do? Did she get pink? Does she like it?

Aggie says: No, she got green because it is Dr. Singh's favorite color. She did horribly at first—threw a terrible tantrum—but she came around when push came to shove or some other equally hackneyed cliché that I can't think of at the moment.

Aggie says: Oh, but never fear. Ian has taken up the tantrum baton. Out of the blue, our little almost sixteen-month-old tyke has decided that he will be an over-achiever and become an absolute terror.

Milliken says: That sweet cherub? Not possible.

Aggie says: I have aged in the last twelve hours. I know I must have gray hairs somewhere.

Milliken says: They hide until you're convinced that they aren't ever going to appear and then they jump out one night while you're sleeping.

Aggie says: Well, isn't that just dandy?

Milliken says: Well, he'll probably be fine tomorrow or the next day. Things have been a little off kilter there for the past few weeks. He's probably reacting to that.

Aggie says: Speaking of off kilter, remember how Sammie was lethargic and refused to move? She's bouncing like crazy. That dog is so excited that Ellie is home it's almost scary.

Milliken says: Aw, poor dog. Isn't it amazing how they sense these things?

Aggie says: Well, I'm just glad she's better. I got tired of letting her sleep in the mudroom. Once she was in, she was fine, but then of course, we had to let in Miner and well... We're only down five shoes from three pairs.

Milliken says: Oh, boy. When do puppies stop chewing?

Aggie says: Luke says sometime before they die.

Milliken says: Ugh. Well, I'll remember to have Dad add dog chews to your care packages.

Aggie says: Thanks. I always forget them... and they always seem to bury them. I thought that was a myth, the burying thing.

Milliken says: Apparently not.

Aggie says: Anyway, I've got to go to bed, but I thought I'd let you know about the latest drama at the Stuart-Milliken abode.

Milliken says: You know we love you. You're doing great.

Aggie says: Okkkkkkkk. Whatever.

Milliken says: Hey, how go the wedding plans?

Aggie says: I'll give you particulars tomorrow, but if we don't get a caterer figured out this week, I think we're going to make the reception a jeans and t-shirt potluck. Tina did order invites today.

Milliken says: Good. When do they arrive?

Aggie says: Get this. They'll be done on Friday. It pays to have someone with connections. We're already addressing envelopes. She brought them home with her.

Milliken says: That was smart!

Milliken says: Ok, that's enough. Get some sleep.

Aggie says: Love you, Mom. Hug Dad for me.

Millken says: Will do. Goodnight.

Aggie says: Nighters.

Chapter 17

PLANS & PROBLEMS

Saturday, January 31ˢᵗ

The bowl of soup flew across the kitchen. "No!"

Aggie blinked as soup sprayed her cabinets and the bowl shattered on impact with the granite. "Ian!"

"No!"

Feet raced into the kitchen and Vannie stopped frozen in place, stunned by the carnage—or appearance thereof. "What happened?"

"He is either not hungry or he has figured out that I'm a mediocre cook at best."

A sippy cup flew from the highchair as if to wash it all down. "Ian!"

"Down!"

Vannie started to unlatch the highchair, but Aggie stopped her. "Wait."

"Huh?"

"Just watch him. I'll be right back."

Just out of sight and earshot, Aggie dialed Libby's number. "Ian is freaking out. He threw his soup and his sippy cup across the kitchen and now he's demanding to get down. Am I crazy to think that letting him down now will just let him think—something. I don't even know what he'd think, but it seems like it's crazy to let him down now…"

"You're right. He's too little to help clean it, so he can sit there until you're done."

"Earlier he pulled every school book off the shelves in the basement and shredded two. He also threw a fit when I changed him. I think I have a bruise on my chin where he kicked me."

"Sounds like he's asserting his independence a little early. Just keep making it fail."

"Making what fail?"

"Whatever he does to get his way that you don't like or is dangerous, don't let him have his way. It teaches him that ugly behavior gets him what he wants." Libby's voice was soothing, but her next words nearly made Aggie cry. "You're going to have to keep him with you at all times for a while."

"At all times?"

"Do you remember how you described those first weeks with Cari and Lorna?"

"No. I have chosen to forget those days," she protested.

"Very funny. They wouldn't have been as crazy if you had simply kept them near you, so you could stop things before they got started."

"That house was huge! This house is much smaller and it's huge! How am I supposed to keep them close? They disappear if I blink."

"Then don't blink." Libby's voice softened. "Look, it's not easy at first, but you won't regret it. The trouble Cari and Lorna still get into probably means they should be with you as well."

"How do I go to the bathroom? I can't take them in there with me!"

"It always amazes me that moms latch onto the two minutes a day that they must be alone as a reason not to take charge of the other several hundred minutes."

"That doesn't solve the bathroom thing." Aggie held onto the idea tenaciously.

"Have one of the others keep them corralled or something."

"That was much too easy. Don't you think you need to think about it for a few weeks?"

"Aggie, you don't have to do it. You asked for help. You asked me what I would do. I told you."

"I know," she admitted. "I just didn't think you were going to tell me how to smother myself with the kid."

"It works the other way around, Aggie. You smother the kid with you until you rub off on him."

Once the call disconnected, Aggie stood in the hall, trying to pray and failing miserably. A wail from Ian jerked her from her trance and she pushed away from the wall, striding toward the kitchen with renewed purpose and a quick p-mail begging God to pray for her since she failed at prayerful concentration. "Coming, Vannie!"

"I tried, but he got madder and madder when I wouldn't let him out."

"Go get your science done. I know you're avoiding it."

"I don't want to do the experiment."

"Skip that until tomorrow. The kitchen won't be clean before then anyway."

That sent the girl away with a bounce in her step, leaving Aggie feeling more overwhelmed than ever. "Well, bud. You are going to sit there until I get this mess cleaned up."

"Down!"

"Nope. Sit there."

The child strained, trying to force the tray off the chair, but Aggie refused to notice or react. It seemed wrong somehow to ignore a tantrum, but taking him out to deal with it got him his way. She was doomed no matter what she did.

All through the kitchen cleanup, Ian screamed, kicked, and protested in every way his vast knowledge of sixteen months could devise, but Aggie pretended she couldn't hear him. Pieces of bowl seemed to appear out of nowhere as she dumped one after another into the paper bag. The soup, on the other hand, was the worst. It dripped from the strangest places and always where she'd just cleaned.

As she mopped the floor for the second time, something niggled at Aggie. Something wasn't right. Her eyes scanned the room looking for the problem and rested on Ian snoozing with his head on the tray. Success — for now.

Luke burst through the door. The empty main level sent him flying down the basement steps, but Laird shook his head. "She's upstairs."

He hardly paused. Five very confused looking children watched as he spun in place and took the stairs two at a time on his way upstairs. He found the twins napping and the other bedrooms empty. He pulled Cari's blanket over her shoulder before dashing back into the hall and up the stairs to Aggie's room. "Aggie?"

"Shh!"

He stuck his head in the door and grinned at the sight of her. Crooking his finger, he beckoned her. With a glance back to ensure that Ian was still sleeping on her bed, Aggie stepped out of the room and shut the door behind her. "What?" she whispered.

Arms around her waist, he swung her in a half arc, laughing at the stunned expression on her face. "I sold the Victorian."

"You just bought it!"

"I know. Amber called me today. A man contacted her about finding a house just like it. When she told him we were in escrow on one and I'd probably have it done by May at the latest, he asked for particulars. He wants me to finish the basement with a few specific things, but he's putting an offer in contingent on the agreed changes."

"Wow!"

"I know! I'm amazed, but this is perfect. She had the interior pictures to show him; he knows what it looked like, and I emailed pictures of my plans. He loves it."

"How does it affect your profit?"

"Best offer I've ever gotten. Obviously something could go wrong, but with the dates and the things in the contract, he'll lose his deposit if he backs out before the agreed completion date." He pointed to her room. "What's Ian doing in there?"

"He crawled out of the crib again."

"What? How!"

"I am calling him Hou-Ian-i. The kid is an escape artist. I watched him grab the rail and hoist his hips over like he was a professional vaulter or something." Aggie sighed. "Your mom is right. I can't let him out of my sight until I can trust him out of my sight. I'm guessing we'll be joined at the hip until I'm eighty."

"Or until he's eight," Luke muttered. "I think that's how old I was before Mom truly trusted me to obey in her absence as much or more as in her presence." He cracked the door open to check on the tyke. "He looks so innocent asleep."

"It's one of those things God did to ensure survival of the

species—make 'em cute while they sleep so auntie-mommies don't murder them like some animals that eat their young."

Luke pointed to the table she'd set up by the fireplace. "What are you doing?"

"Choosing decorations, flowers, and food. Well, narrowing. I was getting it down to final two options for you to decide."

"Let's see what you have." At her panicked expression, he assured her that he would whisper.

Silk flowers in various shades of red and pink were lined up along one end of the table. She pointed to the roses and whispered, "Those are a given, but then I have to have things to go with them. I kind of like the lilies and the tulips. There's something about the long smooth lines that kind of remind me of my dress."

Luke pulled several flowers from the table and passed them to her. "I think any, but those look good. I don't like those with the red."

"Well, they'll come in any color I think..."

He glanced at the motley bouquet in her hand and pulled back the orange tiger lilies. "If those came in other colors—that shape I mean—then it'd work too. You'll pick something great."

As if his words gave her confidence, Aggie pulled the tiger lily, calla lily, and a red rose from the table. Then, in an apparent afterthought, she grabbed the tulip as well and whispered, "I'll tell Tina that if these are significantly cheaper to use them instead of one of the others. Now..." she dug through a pile of pictures and pulled up a document on her laptop. "Ok, we have these..." Aggie chose three photos from the stack and deleted several on the document before turning it to him. "Or those. Which do we want for vases? I don't even know if we're using vases, but Tina insists we choose them in case."

"Here at home or at the schoolhouse?"

The question seemed to befuddle her. "What?"

"Are the flowers for decorating the house for the wedding or the schoolhouse for the reception?"

"I don't know. How'd you think of that?"

Luke shrugged. "Just wondered..."

She was already calling Tina. When three tries to ask resulted in a stage whisper to wake the dead, Aggie stepped from the room. Luke grinned as he heard her say, "Oh, Luke came by with great news and now we're working on wedding stuff."

Wedding stuff. He and his fiancée were working on "wedding stuff." How something could be equally tedious and delightful, Luke could not comprehend, but it was. He stared at fabric samples, photos of chairs, tables, and if the dozen or two documents in Aggie's laptop tray was any indication, she had even more decisions to make in a very short amount of time. A stack of invitations waited for postage and addresses next to a list of partially scratched out names. He set the half-addressed one on top aside and began working on the next on the list. Mrs. Doris Gantry of Westbury was invited to the reception.

"What are you doing?"

Her whisper startled him. "I didn't know what else I could do, so I thought I'd address a few invites. This stack is just for the reception, right?"

She nodded. "The wedding and reception list is under that."

"Just making sure I'm doing it correctly."

Aggie removed the pen from his hand and led him to the laptop. "We have more pressing needs." She opened a document with computer generated design ideas for the schoolhouse. "Tina went all out with some program her father suggested. Do we want round tables..." She clicked on the picture of how the room would look. "Or oblong/rectangular?"

The questions seemed to come in such rapid succession that Luke's brain seemed to congeal into a pile of goo. When the menu options were placed before him, he shook his head. "Ask Mom. I want to say barbeque because it sounds delicious right now, but my brain is telling me there's a reason to reject that. I just can't figure out what that reason is."

"It's messy," she admitted. "I agree though. It sounds good."

"What's for dinner?"

Her eyes grew wide. "I forgot. Everything is frozen. I guess pizza again." Aggie's head dropped into her hands in defeat. "I'm sick of pizza."

"Where's Tina?"

"Rockland. She could bring home chicken nuggets or something, I guess. We could have the oven pre-heated."

Luke didn't feel any more enthusiastic about the suggestion than Aggie sounded. "I'll go to Willie's. Bet I can get back before it's

238

cold if I bring some towels and an ice chest."

"You really do want barbeque don't you?"

"Hi!"

The couple turned to the bed where Ian sat looking much too alert for a baby who had just awakened from a three-hour nap. The child scrambled for the edge, but Aggie was faster. "Hold on, buddy. I bet you need a diaper first—whew! Oh, yeah."

Once fresh, she brought Ian to Luke and handed him over to his soon-to-be "uncle daddy." "At what age do we do the potty training thing? This gets more disgusting every day."

"I don't know," Luke admitted, "but I know Mom and Corinne both complain that boys take longer and start later."

"Oh, great."

Ian clapped his hands. "Yay! Gate!"

Tuesday, February 3ʳᵈ

"But why? The books are overdue," Vannie wailed. "We forgot about them with everything that happened."

"I'll take them tomorrow and pay the fine then."

"I don't understand why Laird and I can't go now."

"Because," Aggie insisted, "I said so, and that's going to have to be good enough." Before Vannie could launch a new protest, Tavish walked past carrying his snowshoes. "What are you doing with those?" Aggie asked.

"I was going to go out back and use them, why?"

"Stay in the yard."

Tavish stared at her in disbelief. "There's no room in the yard. At Christmas you said I could walk in the field behind the back fence."

"Well, today I'm saying to stay in the yard. You can go all around the perimeter. It'll be clear of footprints too—better shoeing that way."

"I—"

"Give it up, Tavish. She's determined to keep us prisoner today."

"Vannie…"

"I'm going to go find something to sew."

239

"Good idea. Tina brought home some cool fabric from when she was looking in Rockland. It's in the laundry room in the dryer. I prewashed it for you."

"Thanks."

The girl didn't sound thankful; she sounded angry, but before Aggie could say anything, the phone rang and Vannie dashed to answer it. Seconds later she called out, "Mrs. Dyke wants Kenzie to come over. She baked snickerdoodles for her."

"I think that jumble of pronouns means that Mrs. Dyke made cookies for Kenzie."

"Yes."

Aggie dove for Ian before he could escape into the kitchen. "I'll take Ian over and get them."

"She wants Kenzie to come. I think she wants to sign the cast."

"Well, Kenzie isn't going—well, she can come with us. Kenzie!"

The first days with her cast had found Kenzie favoring her arm. She had held it close and was unwilling to move much unless forced. It hadn't lasted long. Twice she'd caught the girl using it in foam sword battles as a shield and now she barreled up the stairs and forced her way through the door with the same sword still clutched in her other hand. "What?"

"Mrs. Dyke made you cookies and you're flinging your arm around again."

"That's what the cast's for! To protect it."

"Well, you help the cast a little more by not using it to block strikes by swords. Let's go get those cookies."

"That's ok, Aunt Aggie. I can go. Vannie, will you zip me up in my jacket?"

Kenzie had no trouble getting her good arm in her jacket, but the other wouldn't fit in the sleeve, so they'd taken to zipping her into it with her arm ensconced inside. Once ready, she pulled her stocking cap on crookedly and dashed for the door. "Be right back!"

"Wait for me," Aggie called.

The child froze, staring at her in shock. "Why?"

"Because I'm going with you."

"Why?"

"Because I want to." Aggie bundled Ian into his jacket as she spoke. "I think his jacket is getting too small already!"

"I'm confused."

"You and me both, Kenzie. Aunt Aggie has lost it."

Before Aggie could respond, Vannie stormed out of the room and down the hall, presumably to the laundry room for the fabric they'd discussed. She hesitated. Should they go now while they were dressed and then deal with Vannie's attitude when they returned, or should she halt the process?

"Let's go." She'd talk to Vannie in a minute. There was no reason to make Mrs. Dyke wait.

Luke's truck pulled into the driveway just as they were about to cross the street. Kenzie gave a one-armed wave and Ian bounced excitedly. "Uke!"

"I like how he says that. It sounds like uncle and Luke all combined into one. Uke."

Aggie had to agree. It was endearing. "I wonder that he's never tried to call any of us da-da or ma-ma like a lot of babies do. I mean, they're the first sounds babies usually learn."

"But no one says mommy or daddy to him."

"True."

"I think he should call you mommy. He doesn't remember our mommy."

"I think it might hurt some of the others though. They still remember your parents—as they should—and they want to preserve that. It makes sense."

"But it doesn't for Ian. He should get to have a mommy too."

Thankfully, Mrs. Dyke's appearance on the porch with a Christmas tin removed the need for Aggie to answer. It wasn't a comfortable subject for her. She agreed with Kenzie at times, but the closer it grew to the anniversary of her sister's death, the stronger Aggie's desire to reserve parental titles for Doug and Allie.

"I couldn't believe it when I saw all three of you! How's that little man?"

"Driving me crazy and loving every minute of it," Aggie admitted.

"He wouldn't be a boy if he didn't—on both accounts." Mrs. Dyke handed the tin of cookies to Kenzie. "I put them in that one 'specially for you."

Kenzie grinned at the ice skating children depicted on the lid. "I bet *they* won't break *their* arms!"

"I have a pen. Can I sign it?" Their neighbor glanced up at her.

241

"Can you come in for a few minutes?"

She'd neglected their neighbor since the beginning of school, and it showed in how eager she was to spend a few minutes with Kenzie. "Let's go! Luke can keep an eye on the girls if they wake up."

"They will. Murphy is home."

Aggie stared at her, confused. "What?"

"You always say that Murphy 's Law will make something bad happen. She's home, so it's going to happen."

Mrs. Dyke erupted in laughter that likely carried to the other houses. "Out of the mouths of babes…"

"You've got to do something. She's going crazy. She made Ian bundle up and go with her, so she could escort Kenzie to Mrs. Dyke's. I mean, come on!"

It sounded crazy to him after seeing the children dash back and forth all summer, but Aggie wasn't given to unreasonable behavior. "I'll see what is up, but if Aggie says no to the library and the neighbor's house, then it's no. It's that simple."

"But she's being ridiculous. She'll listen to you."

Luke's expression seemed to temper Vannie a little, but Laird passed without seeing the look on his face and said, "She's paranoid that Grandmother will arrange a kidnapping from the jail or mental hospital or wherever she is."

"Laird…"

The boy turned, his eyes wide. "What? It's true!"

"You're not going to do this, guys. If Aggie says you have to stay home, you stay and without giving her grief about it. If she says you can't go across the street, don't go."

"But you're going to be her husband. Can't you make her—"

"I don't care what I can 'make' or not make her do. I'm not doing it. If Aggie says we eat oatmeal for breakfast, lunch, and dinner for a month, then I'm behind her. Got that? You guys can't divide us."

"Do you think this makes sense?"

The change in Vannie's tone was evident. She'd gone from demanding to curious. For several long seconds he pondered whether he should admit to disagreement or not and finally decided that honesty combined with support was better than avoidance. "Actually, without knowing why, I can't be sure but on the surface, no. I don't see the point, but that doesn't matter. She said it and I'll back her up. I will always back her up even if I think she's wrong unless I know it's going to cause real harm. Even then, you're not going to be part of that change. Got it?"

"Just like Mom and Dad," Laird mumbled as he continued into the library. Awkward sounds of tentative guitar strums reached their ears moments later.

"I don't understand. I don't see how it's good for anyone to let fear take over her common sense. I understand why you want to support her, but I don't understand why it isn't unhealthy for her to do it."

Aggie, Kenzie, and Ian stepped into the house and began shedding their jackets. Seconds later, Lorna marched down the stairs singing, "I'll fly away oh, *gory...*"

The child would have been oblivious to the amusement she created had Aggie and Luke managed not to catch one another's eyes. She snickered; he choked. Kenzie glanced back and forth between them, obviously trying to understand what amused everyone. The realization dawned seconds later. "Oh, glory, Lorna. Oh, *glory!* Gory is like blood and guts and stuff—you know, like the movies we can't see."

"What's glory?"

"It's like cool—but spiritual coolness, not the regular kind."

"Oh. um..." the child thought. "I'll fly away oh cool—ie. I'll fly away..."

Luke's choked chortle became unrestrained laughter as Aggie tried not to laugh and succeeded only in dissolving in near-silent hyena chuckles. Ellie danced downstairs and stopped at the bottom, staring at the group. "What did I miss?"

Laird called out from the library, "Lorna is modernizing Aunt Aggie's hymns. Just ignore them."

"Ok." She beckoned her sister to follow. "Vannie, can you come help me with something?"

"I'm going to make a skirt. Maybe later."

"I'll help you," Aggie offered.

Ellie looked panicked and backed up the stairs. "I—I'll be fine.

Thanks."

As Ellie hurried away, Aggie turned to Luke. "I don't understand. She's different lately—even before Geraldine's little stunt, but now it's worse. She's always holed up in her room and if I come near her, she acts like she wants me to go away."

"Want me to talk to her?"

Ian dove for his toys and Aggie dragged the basket near the couches, collapsing on one as he began pulling them out. "I don't know. What do you think?"

Seeing the trouble in her eyes, Luke started for the stairs, but then heard Laird call him from the library. He stepped inside, pulling the doors closed behind him. "Something wrong?"

"I think you shouldn't worry about Ellie."

"Why would you say that?"

"I know Aunt Aggie is bothered, but there's nothing wrong— really. I think if she—well both of you—thought about it, you'd remember. Since you don't, I'm not going to say anything, but I know you'll agree."

"You thought I would agree with you about Aggie and going to town."

Laird shook his head. "No, I thought you *should* agree. I already knew you wouldn't do it. Aunt Aggie comes first—even if she's wrong. I get that."

That "even if she's wrong" was nearly Luke's undoing, but he managed to keep a straight face. "And what would Vannie say about Ellie?"

"Same thing. We all would. Just trust us. She's fine. She doesn't even get that what Grandmother did was wrong. She thinks it's a big misunderstanding. I've heard her pray that Josh won't get into trouble for helping Grandmother." The disgust in the boy's voice told Luke Laird's opinion of the idea.

"How long do you think we should give her before we talk to her?"

"Another week or two. I'm not sure. She might be do—fine tomorrow for all I know." He winced at his near gaffe. "Just trust me. She's fine." The boy blinked and then said, "Actually, if you think about it, I think you know. You've known since the FBI and sheriff searched her room."

With sudden understanding, Luke nodded and started to leave.

He hesitated at the door and added, "I think your D-string is a little flat."

"Thanks."

Toys were already strewn from one end of the living room to the other, but Aggie seemed willing to ignore it as long as Ian stayed in eyesight. "I think we should let Ellie alone for a few more days. It sounds like this is more of a surprise than a secret or a problem."

The skeptical look in Aggie's eyes bothered him. At some point, she'd have to learn to trust him on these things. Maybe if she knew that he supported her... "By the way, we need to talk when we can get a moment of privacy."

"Tina's gone until after dinner. We could talk then."

"I've got the keys to the house for her anyway."

"Is escrow closed?"

He shook his head. "Not for a few more days it seems. I just thought she might like them and I actually remembered today."

Aggie scooted closer, her eyes darting around the room to see who might be listening, and murmured, "I've been thinking about the fourteenth."

"Yes..."

"I think I should take the kids to the cemetery. I found these grave urns that can be driven into the ground on a stake. They're air and watertight. I thought they could write notes or draw pictures or something. Next year, maybe they could see what they left this year and so on. What do you think?"

"It sounds like a good idea. I wouldn't plan to stay long, but I'd be prepared to."

"Do you think it's too much for kids? I can't forget the morbid introspection that Geraldine demanded of the kids that first day. It was terrible."

"As long as you're willing to give them time to decide they want to participate, without insisting that they do, I think everything will work out well."

During their conversation, a new idea occurred to him—one he'd have to take up with Tina. If he had his dates straight in his mind, it might just be the perfect way to distract the family after such a trip. Mid-thoughts, Tina burst in through the door, carrying several bags in her hands. At the sight of Luke, she stopped. "I had a question for you. Now I've forgotten it."

245

"I have keys for you."

"That's my question! Thanks." As if that settled everything, she jogged up the stairs calling Vannie's name.

"Well, guess that explains it, whatever it is," Aggie muttered dryly.

Mibs says: We were supposed to talk tonight, but that never happened.

Luke says: Pesky kids have the audacity to want to spend time with us or something.

Mibs says: What did they want?

Luke says: They wanted me to convince you to let them go to the library. I actually suspect they will ask me in the future and hope I don't ask what you said.

Mibs says: You have got to be kidding me.

Luke says: Nope. Not a bit, why?

Mibs says: I just didn't think they'd pull that yet. I thought they'd at least have the decency to wait until we're married.

Luke says: Well, I let them have it. Informed them that I would back you up 100% even if I didn't agree with you.

Mibs says: That helps.

Mibs says: Wait, does that mean you disagree with me?

Luke says: I don't know if I do or not. What was the reasoning for not allowing them to return the books? You'll have a few more dollars in fines now.

Mibs says: Josh is still out there, Luke. I can't risk them out like that until I know he's caught.

Luke says: Do you really think he'd risk coming around to finish a job he isn't going to get paid for now? That man is long gone.

Mibs says: I don't know...

Luke says: What about Kenzie and the cookies?

Mibs says: She's only six and she has a bum arm. She can't get away as easily...

Luke says: Well, I'm going to back you up, but I'll admit that I do think you're wrong. It's understandable, but I disagree.

Mibs says: Once they catch him, I can stand it again, but...

Luke says: And if they never do?

Mibs says: Oh, I can't stand that thought.

Luke says: Are you going to find it impossible to relax for two weeks? Should I cancel honeymoon plans?

Mibs says: Why should you do that? I'm looking forward to those two weeks.

Luke says: You won't be worrying about some strange man lurking outside Willow's farm or at Mom's or Uncle Zeke's?

Mibs says: No, actually, I think they'll be safer. He won't know to look there. Geraldine wouldn't know.

Luke says: Whew. I was getting nervous.

Mibs says: You really do think I'm a bit nuts, don't you?

Luke says: I think you should talk to William and ask his opinion on things.

Mibs says: I can do that.

Mibs says: That seems weird.

Luke says: What does?

Mibs says: Asking William's opinion when you've already given yours. Why should his carry more weight?"

Luke says: Maybe because it is his job to know these things?

Mibs says: Well, if you're going to put it in logical terms like that.

Luke says: I'm not going to pretend that I didn't like that you wanted to put my opinions ahead of William's. I'm not completely ego-free.

Mibs says: Tina just came up with a list a mile long of things for me to answer.

Mibs says: Wait, she is having trouble with catering ideas and wants to know what you think about cold cuts, rolls, potato salad—picnic fare.

Luke says: Sounds good to me.

Mibs says: Ok, then. I'll talk to you later.

Luke says: Night. Love you.

Mibs says: Those are the coolest seven letters ever. Or, should I say the gloriest?

Luke says: Say goodnight, Gracie.

Mibs says: Goodnight, Gracie.

Chapter 18

ANNIVERSARIES

Saturday, February 14th

Two weeks of misery culminated in a very dark and gloomy Valentine's Day. It seemed like the weather had remembered the day and chosen to grieve with Aggie and her little clan of Stuarts. They drove into the cemetery after a long, tedious morning of eating breakfast, dressing, and frantic searches for that special picture or note. She drove alone, neither Tina nor Luke there to lend the support she desperately craved.

To be truthful, she felt a little sorry for herself. That was almost as bad as the memories that threatened to choke her. The twins didn't seem to remember the cemetery at all. Kenzie shrunk from it, begging Aggie to be allowed to stay alone in the van. That wasn't going to happen. It simply wasn't an option.

When they neared the little area that the Stuarts had been buried in for the past hundred years, Kenzie began to relax. "Grandmother isn't here. I thought she would be. She made me sing."

"No, it's just us today."

"Why didn't Luke come?" Laird seemed as bothered by the absence of the man she intended to marry as she was.

"I think he thought we wanted a little privacy."

"Did you?"

She shook her head. Aggie wanted nothing more than his arm around her and a chance to weep with physical as well as emotional support. Her thoughts from the previous year were absolutely true. Valentine's Day was ruined forever.

"He should have come," Vannie managed to force the words from somewhere.

"I should have asked. He was being thoughtful and I wanted him to read my mind. I hate it when I do stupid girlie stuff like that."

"But—"

"No, Vannie. We're not going to blame people for a lousy day. This is just a horrible day and I'm not going to pretend it's anything else."

Aggie pulled the stake and urn from a tote bag and asked Tavish for the hammer as she stuffed the bag in her pocket. She cleared the snow from in front of the double headstone and drove the stake into the ground. The force required to make it work was nearly cathartic in its intensity. Once firmly driven into the ground, Aggie added the urn to the stake and unscrewed the lid. "You can put your notes and pictures in here if you like."

A few small notes and a couple of colored pictures were added to the urn before Aggie found the strength to pull hers from her pocket. Vannie touched her sleeve. "Can I read it?"

Though awkward, Aggie nodded. "If you like."

A few sentences into the letter, Vannie stopped. "Can I read it to the others?"

Aggie didn't think she'd get through a reading of it, but she nodded anyway. "It's up to you."

Without hesitation, Vannie gathered the others around her and said, "Listen to Aunt Aggie's note. I think you should hear it."

Doug and Allie,

It's been a year — the most horrifying, agonizing, stretching and growing year of my life. It has also been the best. I hate that you're not here to talk to. I hate that your children don't see you. It kills me that your son will only know you as a picture and I get the privilege of being his mommy.

I also feel guilty because I love my life now. I have purpose and you gave that to me. Your death gave me a different kind of life. Because of it, I met the man I'm going to marry. I wouldn't have otherwise.

I know Allie felt guilty about "burdening" me with this responsibility so young. I am glad there's no guilt in heaven or she'd still feel guilty. That's just how she is. Well, it'd be unnecessary anyway. It's been hard. I won't pretend it hasn't. I don't know what I'm doing and the kids know it. Thankfully, you guys did a good job and they haven't really taken advantage of that.

I just wanted to say thanks. Thanks for trusting me with your children. I don't think I've completely failed you yet.

I'd give almost anything to have you back, though.

Miss you,

Aggie

By the time she finished, Vannie wept openly. Laird fought back tears, but he too caved after a time. Tavish and Ellie clung to each other for a minute or two, crying. Then, as if they had left the past where it lay, they tried to distract Cari and Lorna from bothering the others. Kenzie soon followed, uninterested in unburdening her little heart just yet.

Aggie clung to Ian, the full weight of all that was gone hitting her fresh. The baby squirmed and protested, but she kept herself wrapped around his little body, wondering how to keep a mother fresh in a baby's mind. He'd hardly known Allie. Certainly, there was no chance of memory. Still, she should try to do it. Shouldn't she? Again, she wished for Luke or Tina's comforting presence.

A snowball whizzed past her head, missing Ian by a breath. "Wha—"

Ten eyes widened in horror as she turned to stare at them. From the look on Cari's face, Aggie had a fairly good idea of the culprit. Lorna, in an obvious attempt to protect her slightly younger sister from yet another foray into Trouble 101, grabbed a handful of snow and packed a small snowball herself. With every ounce of strength the girl possessed, she threw it at Laird, hitting him squarely in the back.

"Wha—" He grinned, jogged several yards away, and packed his own.

Aggie watched in stunned fascination as her children began a snowball war right there in the cemetery. She and Ian stood on what appeared to be no man's land. *Surreal — this is surreal,* she thought to herself. *My children are playing on the anniversary of their parents' death, in a cemetery, and disturbing the ground in the process. What next, a snowman? Snow angels?* That thought prompted a snicker. How appropriate. Snow angels in the cemetery. It would tie into the erroneous idea that people become angels when they die.

Ian squirmed to get down and ran for Laird. Another snowball

251

flew past much too closely for her comfort. Without thinking, Aggie darted around the headstone and dropped to her knees. The stupidity of that action was obvious in seconds as her tights became wet and cold.

The incongruity of her position hit her as she imagined seeing it from an outsider's perspective. To her left, Laird and Vannie balled more snowballs in a short amount of time than she had thought possible. Ian "helped" by throwing half of them a foot or so. Most didn't even break. To her right, both sets of twins and Kenzie worked hard to build quite an arsenal — making it nearly twice the volume of their unofficial "opponents." And there she was, peeking over the top of the grave. It belonged in a wacky Norman Rockwell painting. She'd call it "Battle with Grief."

War erupted when Laird fired on Fort Younger. Though they had fewer snowballs and a "helper" to destroy things as fast as they made them, Vannie and Laird had size, speed, strength, and accuracy on their side. Cari and Lorna couldn't throw past the headstone. Kenzie couldn't throw much at all with her broken arm putting her off-balance.

Perhaps the strangest part of all was the hush. There were no screams, squeals, or exaggerated groans on impact. Even Ian was quiet in his attempt to demolish their pile of weapons. Cari didn't make a sound as one snowball exploded on her hat. Tavish's trademarked primal yell was noticeably absent. A glance over her shoulder showed an elderly woman watching.

Without thinking, she stood. "Time to go—" All balls redirected and bombarded her. Her coat was almost white with the residue of snowballs that had pelted her. "Note to self: Wool doesn't allow snow to slide off," she muttered.

The group marched to the van, still much too quiet for Aggie's comfort. It seemed unnatural for her crazy brood to be almost completely silent. With the children settled in their seats, she hoisted herself up into the driver's seat and stared at the roses on the dashboard. "Laird, I forgot the roses. Can you go put them on top for me?" Her voice cracked. "Thanks."

The occupants of the Stuartmobile watched Laird trudge back along the slippery, half-shoveled walk. It was a strange sight. The cemetery was almost pristine in its snowy brilliance. Footprints followed what should be paths, and there was an occasional footprint or two on a plot with flowers lying there, but most of it was a smooth blanket of white. Well, except for the area around Allie and Doug's grave. It was rumpled, dirty, and yes, it looked like children had held a snowball fight over the grave. Laird reached the headstone, laid the cellophane wrapped red roses on it, and stood back.

Kenzie's question spoke for all when she asked, "Why isn't he coming back?"

Laird picked up the roses again and pulled the wrapping from them. He unwound the rubber band holding the stems together and then laid them on the stone once more. His gloved hand covered the stems for just a moment. Aggie's breath caught. It was beautiful. "I wish I'd brought the camera," she whispered.

Vannie pointed to her pocket. "Your phone!"

It was far away but better than nothing. She snapped the picture just as Ellie said, "I'll sketch it from the picture, Aunt Aggie. I can do it."

"I'd love that."

What Laird was saying—or if he was praying—Aggie didn't know, but the lump welled larger in her throat as he turned. With the movement, a single rose rolled from the top of the stone and lay against the rumpled snow. It seemed to her that it was a perfect picture of her life... beauty amid the chaos that was her family.

"That wasn't too bad," Aggie whispered as she put the van in gear and began to back out of her parking space. *Maybe we should change to their birthdays though,* she thought to herself. *There's no snow in May or September.*

"Nine hot chocolates—whipped cream on all," Aggie asked, her eyes on the van full of children behind her.

"Nine?"

She sighed. "Yes." Aggie slid her card across the counter. "I need to pay quickly please. I'll send in two kids to carry them out."

"Two kids for nine chocolates..."

"They're thirsty," she snapped. "The card? I have kids alone in the car."

The moment she had her receipt, Aggie dashed out the door

and into the van. "Whew. There was almost no one ahead of me, but ugh."

"Um, can we go in and get them now?" Laird's hand was already on the door.

"Go for it."

The numbers on the van clock changed, one after another after another, but Vannie and Laird still did not return. Aggie was ready to go in after them when she finally saw the door open. Once inside, Vannie apologized. "I'm sorry. The guy in there wouldn't stop asking questions. I wanted to throw the hot chocolate at him, but Laird made me leave."

"I believe that assault with a liquid weapon is still considered assault, Vannie."

"Very funny."

For one brief moment, Aggie was tempted to go in and give the baristas a piece of her mind. Burning tears at the back of her eyes warned her that she'd never get through her lecture without falling apart. Her fingers turned the key in the ignition and she backed from the parking place. "Let's go. When yours gets cool enough to drink without burning you, give Cari, Lorna, and Ian theirs."

"I want mine now!" Cari protested.

"Well, you can have it when it's cool and not before. Or, if you prefer, I can pour it out."

Tears flowed then. "That's not faiw!" the child wailed as she demanded her drink.

Great, Aggie thought, *she's back to the baby talk. What next?* Even as the thought occurred, Aggie realized it was like inviting disaster, and she was right. Lorna bawled in commiseration with her sister's cocoa-less plight. Kenzie stared out the window, a look of determination—for what Aggie couldn't imagine—on the girl's face.

"Should I try to cool it?" Vannie asked.

"No. She can wait." Aggie grabbed her cup from the holder and took a quick swig. Her mouth burned. "Aaaak! Oh man! Aargh!"

Her cries of pain terrified Ian who began screeching at the top of his unreasonably strong lungs. Ellie tried to calm Lorna and Cari, but failed. Though quite out of character, she took the rejection personally and began crying herself. Tavish's attempts to soothe her also culminated in his own tears. By the time Aggie made it onto the loop, she was the only one not weeping in earnest.

Her own tears hovered—a storm ready to break. She just wanted to make it home first, but by halfway to Fairbury, Aggie knew there wasn't much time before she couldn't see the road for her crying. The van slid slightly as she turned into the rest stop and pulled into two parking spaces with a jerk.

Her hands hung over the steering wheel while her head rested on them. Shoulders shaking, she sobbed out the pain of loss and weariness. Her heart constricted when she thought of Luke and Tina. Throat aching from her pain and despair, she mentally railed at God for having such thoughtless and selfish friends and then at herself for thinking something so utterly ridiculous.

They stayed in that parking lot, cars coming and going in the usual manner of desperate stops for a drink or a bathroom on a long trip, until their grief slowly dissipated as they grappled with their loss. At last, Aggie dug a pack of tissues from her purse, kept one, and passed the package back to the others. "I should have come prepared."

"Can we go home now?" Kenzie asked. "I don't like being sad. Home is happy—most of the time."

"We sure can. We'll watch a movie or something. Maybe we'll put on pajamas and eat junk food all day. Sounds like a great way to spend a horrible Valentine's Day to me."

Ellie's voice barely reached her ears, but the words etched themselves onto her heart as the girl said, "Since we can't have our own mommy, I'm glad we have you."

"Well, I'm glad I have all of you too. Let's go."

Sniffles still echoed in the van from time to time, but the rest of the trip home seemed to calm everyone. A few times, Aggie found herself half-humming, half-singing Proverbs 3:5, and soon the van was filled with singing. Over and over, they sang the words of trusting in the Lord for direction; at times, their voices blended and "harmonized" in ways that would make the Von Trapp family reach for ear plugs.

Luke stood on the steps, his hands stuffed in his jacket pockets, watching. Aggie hardly had the van turned off before her door opened and he pulled her from the seat. "Are you ok?"

"Better now, I think," she whispered.

"I've been going crazy wondering if I should have insisted that either Tina or I go with you whether you wanted us or not. We could have stayed in the van."

"Wanted? Of course I wanted you guys." She swallowed hard. "It was horrible and funny and horrible all over again."

"Funny?" He leaned back to see her expression as if it would confirm her utter mental collapse.

"Well, there was the bit about the snowball fight..."

"You've got to be kidding me."

"Would I kid about a snowball fight over their parents' grave?"

"Aunt Aggie, can we change?"

She tore her eyes from Luke and saw her little clan of red-eyed, sniffling children and shooed them toward the house. "Definitely. Change and wash your faces." To Luke she asked, "What have you been doing today?"

"Something I hope you won't hate me for..."

"Hate you? Why?"

"Well... just remember that it was supposed to help keep your mind off things, ok?"

"If you got us another dog, or another cat, or some other animal..."

"No animals. I promise." Luke hesitated. "Well, actually..."

"Luke!"

"Come inside."

The mysteriousness of his actions seemed bizarre, but there was no option. She must go. Once she stepped inside the door, her jaw dropped. "But Tina's birthday isn't until tomorrow."

"We thought today would be a good—"

"Wait—" Aggie interrupted. "It's your birthday too?"

"Yep. Tomorrow."

"How did I not know when your birthday is?"

"I'm so happy! A party!" Lorna seemed beside herself with excitement. "It doesn't have to be a bad day anymore."

"Go change. People will be arriving soon."

"I don't need—" She stopped mid-sentence. Her cold wet legs told her she did need to change, and soon. "I'll be down in a few."

The excited chatter of the children warmed her heart as Aggie hurried past their floor and up to her room. Not for the first time that day, much less ever, Aggie thanked the Lord for her little sanctuary at the top of the house. A fire in the grate warmed more than her room. "Lord, he's too good to me."

She stepped into the bathroom and stared into the mirror, looking for something but unsure of what. The face looking back at her didn't seem familiar at all. It was harsh, empty, cold. The hair tie was the first to go. With her hair down and less severe looking, she felt more normal. How strange when just months earlier it was her usual style. How had Luke ever seen her as anything but a snippy looking... something? Aggie couldn't even think of the word.

Several handfuls of water later, Aggie's eyes seemed less red and puffy. Her closet, thanks to Tina's obsession with shopping lately, was full of options she'd never had a chance to wear. "She's buying for my honeymoon!"

"Of course I am! You can't go wearing the stuff you've worn for over a year!"

"Happy birthday!"

"Luke is worried."

Aggie pointed to the clothes. "I'm overwhelmed. Pick." Without hesitation, Tina pulled an outfit from the rod and shooed her into the bathroom.

"I really should run down and tell him you're ok."

"Wait!" Aggie stared at the clothes in her hands. "How do we know these clothes will work for the honeymoon? I don't know where we're going!"

"What?"

"I don't know where we're going. This could be all wrong. Maybe I shouldn't—"

"Put 'em on. No matter where you're going, that outfit screams Aggie. Meanwhile, I'm going to go find out where you're going."

"What if— aaaand she's gone, isn't she?" Aggie waited a few seconds and peeked out the door. "Yep, sure is."

The outfit was perfect and her hair definitely looked better, but still she seemed a little pale. A bag of cosmetics, reserved to ensure wedding pictures looked top-notch, taunted her from her vanity drawer, but she shut it quickly. She'd just end up with streaky mascara and blotchy cheeks if she did.

Tina burst through the door. "Oh, this is exciting. Most of your clothes will work, but we're going to have to get you some jeans or something."

"What?"

"He got you a cabin in Colorado."

"Skiing?" she whimpered.

"Nope. Just a nice cabin with lots of snow, but close enough to a town to give you something to do if you get bored."

"Do not laugh," Aggie ordered, seconds before she snickered.

"Hypocrite."

"That's me."

Tina pointed to the mantel. "I think you were supposed to look up there. I'm going. Someone else wants to come in."

"Wait. Jeans. Don't. I told Vannie—"

"For two weeks out of the years you live with her, you can have jeans if you need them. Even Allie would have let her put them on to go skiing or whatever."

"Maybe under a skirt... Allie was pretty picky about stuff like that."

"Ask Luke what he thinks. I think he'll be unlikely to want to go exploring if he's worried about how warm you are."

"Laura Ingalls—"

"Wore about six petticoats, skirts to the ground, and itchy wool flannel underwear."

"Point taken."

Tina grinned. "Good. Oh, and I put my birthday present on the table. I thought you'd want to know so that you didn't go nuts looking for what isn't there."

"How do you do that? You always know exactly what I got you and where I've hidden it!"

A knock interrupted them, and Luke's head peeked in through the door. "Tina, William is down there being smothered by children and disappointed that someone else isn't doing that smothering..."

"Then he'll have to be disappointed because he's exactly the kind of man who would lose interest if I did too much smothering too soon."

Laughing, Aggie shook her head. "It scares me not only how much she knows about most men but how accurate she is."

"Don't you know it," Tina said as she left the room.

Luke kicked the door open all the way before he stepped any further in the room. "Sorry about the honeymoon. I didn't realize I hadn't told you."

"We've been busy. I didn't realize I didn't know until it dawned on me why Tina was buying me all these new outfits."

"Is that one?"

She smoothed the skirt and went to grab her favorite flats. "Yep."

"I approve."

"If that's meant to be a compliment, then I thank you—for one of us anyway."

"For one of you?" Luke shook his head in confusion. "I'm lost."

"Well, either thank you from Tina because you think she has good taste in clothing, or thank you from me because you think I look nice in the clothing. Works either way."

"How about both?"

"Speaking of clothing," Aggie said as she went to hang her wet things over the shower curtain, "Tina suggested getting me a couple of pairs of jeans for Colorado."

"Ok... any reason you should or shouldn't?"

"I told Vannie that I wouldn't wear pants as long as they were in our house. That if I was going to require them to stick to Allie's rules, then I'd do it with them. Remember?"

"Ok then, no jeans. Not a problem."

"Think I'll be warm enough on a hike?"

"I'll get Mom to take care of it. How's that? She always wore skirts when we went out in winter and I don't remember her getting cold." He pointed to the mantel. "Off topic, but it is Valentine's Day, so I thought..."

Already feeling terrible that they were celebrating his birthday and she had no idea of any kind of gift, the little box on the mantel just made her feel worse. "I wish I'd known—"

"C'mon, Mibs. I've had that for three weeks now and it's driving me nuts."

"I don't even have a card for you for Valentine's Day," she admitted. "I just didn't—"

"Are you going to open it or not?"

Aggie tore the paper from the package and laid it on the mantel. She lifted the lid and smiled at the little pendant that hung from a leather string. "Marbles. You found my marbles!"

"Funny. The smaller ones are clay mibs and the middle is agate—blue lace."

"Where—"

"Mom found a gal on the internet who makes all kinds of

jewelry. She arranged it for me."

"It matches my outfit."

"Another reason I approve of the outfit then."

Aggie hooked the necklace and presented herself for inspection. "What do you think? How long before Ian tries to eat them?"

"It's going to end up hidden in your sweater, isn't it?" The exaggerated sigh was nearly as funny as the forced ruefulness Luke tried to manufacture on his face.

"Looks like it'll be like my messenger name — mibs are only for your eyes."

"I'll take that. Let's go."

Libby says: I'm home!

Aggie says: Yay! Ok, we've got a few things I need to bug you about.

Libby says: Bug away. I would say "bug off" for amusement's sake, but that makes it sound like I want you to go away.

Aggie says: Thanks for your help with my necklace, by the way. It's perfect.

Libby says: I tried to talk him into matching earrings, but he didn't like any of the marbles. They didn't match well enough and he insisted that there is only one Aggie so we couldn't go that route.

Aggie says: Silly man.

Libby says: So, I am suspecting that you want birthday gift ideas.

Aggie says: Exactly!

Libby says: I expected this and have come prepared. Be impressed.

Aggie says: Most impressed, of course.

Libby says: First idea. Take him to that place in the mall where they do portraits in an hour. Get engagement pictures done so he has one for his wallet. The only picture he has of you is folded oddly and crammed in that thing. It's not even the most flattering picture, but don't tell him I said that.

Aggie says: I'm afraid to ask.

Libby says: Your birthday. Let's just say that it's good that restaurants usually have no flies.

Aggie says: Ok, that's the leader. What are the others?

Libby says: Gift certificate to some place in the city — kind of a forced

260

date for you guys after you get back.

Aggie says: Ok, that works too. Next?

Libby says: An official Milliken-Stuart-Sullivan family Bible.

Aggie says: Oh, like for writing marriage, births etc. Good idea. I think I'll save that for wedding and do the other two. One for birthday, one for my missed Valentine's Day.

Libby says: Well, you don't have to do both.

Aggie says: No, but now I have an excuse to.

Aggie says: You know what amazes me?

Libby says: Nope. Sure don't.

Aggie says: He loves me. Isn't that just the most amazing thing!

Libby says: You're going to laugh.

Aggie says: Why?

Libby says: Last night when we were wrapping your gift, my Luke said the same thing. "She loves me, mom! Isn't that just the most amazing thing?"

Aggie says: You know, when I took on these kids, I did it with the firm conviction that no man was going to look twice at a twenty-two year old with eight kids… or a twenty-six year old… or a thirty-nine year old…

Libby says: And yet within months you had two men asking you to marry them.

Aggie says: Yeah, but pity proposals don't count in my book.

Aggie says: I wasn't really upset about it either — the not marrying part, not the proposal from William. That one ticked me off.

Libby says: Rightfully so.

Aggie says: I just took it as God's direction for my life. Now I'm trying to imagine life without Luke and I can't.

Libby says: I think that's how it always works, but in your case, it's magnified a bit.

Aggie says: Probably.

Aggie says: Did Luke mention the Colorado issue?

Libby says: Yes. I've got you covered — so to speak.

Aggie says: Oh, thank you. I think it'd be best for Vannie anyway.

Libby says: Luke agreed.

Aggie says: Did he? He didn't say. I mean, he didn't act like it bothered him either way, but I wondered if he thought it was another silly promise.

Libby says: Not at all.

Aggie says: Oh my!

Libby says: What?

Aggie says: I wonder what the groundskeeper at the cemetery is going to think when the snow melts and he finds a hammer lying around the graves.

Libby says: A hammer?

Aggie says: Yeah. I brought one for the urn—to drive in the stake. I think we forgot it after the snowball fight.

Libby says: Well, he'll have something to tell the wife and kids that night, eh?

Aggie says: Can you imagine the things he might wonder? Especially depending on where Tavish dropped it. It could be far enough not to be on Stuart "ploterty."

Libby says: Oh, that was bad. You should go to bed. You're getting punchy.

Aggie says: Did you see William and Tina?

Libby says: Yes. I thought I was going to die laughing when he pulled out that whoopee cushion. He looked so confused.

Aggie says: Contrast that with the way he looks at her when he thinks no one is looking.

Libby says: I told Luke that if he ever figures out what the rest of us have, he's going to fall hard and fast.

Aggie says: Let's hope he doesn't realize he's done that until it's too late. He won't handle not being in control very well.

Libby says: It'll be good for him.

Aggie says: There's the first knock of the night. I expect more. Gotta go.

Libby says: I'll be praying for you.

Aggie says: Thanks. Night.

Chapter 19

SHOWERS OF SOMETHING

Saturday, February 21st

In her red sweater and black skirt, Aggie felt quite out of place. Normally, she wouldn't have noticed, but upon entering the church fellowship hall, it was impossible not to see that everyone else, including Vannie and Tina, were all wearing blue. "Did I miss a memo about dress code?"

"Nope. We wanted you to stand out just like the bride does on her wedding day," Myra Vaughn assured her.

Tina's smirk behind Myra nearly choked Aggie, but she managed to keep composed long enough to hang her purse with her coat and follow the group to the long table full of food. A plate was thrust into her hand—by whom she couldn't say. "I take it we're hungry?"

"Yes! We all wanted to be here before you, so we came half an hour early."

"And I'm ten minutes late. Dead battery."

"Hey, it was worth it. Your expression!" Tina giggled and elbowed Mrs. Dyke. "Wasn't it hilarious?"

"I'll get you for that. I'm probably going to lose some game because of it."

As they reached the end of the line, Tina whispered, "They all wrote the recipes for the dish they brought and put them in the album there. One lady suggested everyone copy their recipe a couple dozen times so that everyone else could take one if they liked the dish. She was hoping to convince Tilly Vernon to reconsider her peanut butter tuna bake as a potluck offering."

"It's always the first thing gone…"

Tina giggled. "I found out the secret of that. It appears that the ladies all put a large helping on their plate and scoop into the trash immediately. They take turns distracting her. Our gal with the brilliant idea seems a bit tired of the charade."

"Well, it does seem dishonest…"

As a woman passed, Tina stopped her. "Oh, Tilly! Thank you for bringing the punch. I can't believe I forgot something so basic!"

The woman beamed. "I was happy to. I've always wanted to try this recipe."

Aggie nearly choked at Tina's half-suppressed look of horror that she could only hope no one but she recognized. "Oh, what kind is it?"

"It has raspberry sherbet, raspberries, lemon-lime soda, coconut milk…" Tilly fumbled. "Well, there was something else. Also, I had to make the coconut milk myself. The stuff in the container didn't have any coconut flavor at all! That was what took so long. I didn't have time to make my casserole, but Tina said we'd have enough food without it."

"Tina is a master at stuff like that." In her peripheral vision, Aggie watched as Tina crept to the punch table, ready to knock the bowl off if necessary, and take a sip. "Well, if Tina's expression is any indication, your work was well worth it."

Beaming, Tilly hurried to hear from Tina herself just how lip-smacking good the drink really was. Aggie's eyes scanned the room, trying to see who all had come. Several ladies from Allie's church were there, and according to Vannie, the ladies who had been prepared to take the children if she had declined were among them. Luke's aunts and sisters waved energetically from one corner, beckoning her to join them.

She hurried to Libby's side and said, "Save me a seat. I'll sit with you all once I'm done eating, but I should try to visit with Allie's friends for a few minutes at least. I can't believe that Tina invited them and that they came!"

Tina called the room to order the minute the last fork dropped on its plate. "We have a few games to play. I know everyone says they hate them, but if they were really horrible, I don't think they'd still be a part of showers or have websites devoted to ensuring their continued use! And, play we shall!"

264

Two teams were formed to design toilet paper wedding gowns on Aggie and Tina. With Libby on Tina's team, it was no surprise to Aggie when a full petticoat was constructed before they ever attempted to layer a skirt onto her dress. Aggie's, by comparison, looked like a ghost's bride — and a tatty one at that. "Nice crinoline there, Libby!"

"You're just jealous," Tina teased.

"No, I was thinking I could use it and take back the one we bought!"

"I tried to get blue toilet paper, but I couldn't find any — even online. You just can't get it anywhere anymore. So, instead of 'blue' this game had to be 'new' because I do not want old or borrowed toilet paper anything."

"Hogwash," Aggie protested. "If I run out, you'd be thrilled to get borrowed toilet paper from Murphy or Mrs. Dyke."

"I might be," the antebellum-looking tissue bride agreed, "but they certainly wouldn't want it returned. I say the TP is given, not loaned and therefore received, not borrowed."

"And she wonders why her father wanted her to be a lawyer!"

Vannie was in charge of the next game. For her game, the ladies were instructed to "loan" an accessory to Aggie. Aggie didn't quite understand the point of the game. Sure, she'd look totally ridiculous with two hats, four bracelets, several purses, and the list kept growing... but to what purpose?

"I see that Aggie is just as confused as you all were about this one. It was Vannie's idea and at first, I thought it was just a way to make her look silly. Now," Tina added with a mischievous look in her eye, "I am all for doing my part to make Aggie look silly, but she usually doesn't need my help."

"You are so dead. Watch yourself... someone taught me all sorts of tricks like short-sheeting beds and such."

"Ah, and now I am warned. Glad to know it. Anyway, look at our lovely bride. Doesn't she look charming?"

With the way the cameras were clicking, Aggie had a feeling that charming was not the word she'd use. "I feel like I must be a runway star with all those camera flashes."

"See! Just beautiful. Vannie, get the mirror."

It truly was a horrifying sight. Aggie looked worse than any of the twins' attempts to "dress up" in her clothes and shoes. "I think that second pair of shoes was overkill, but the rest..."

"Ever the diplomat. She looks ridiculous, doesn't she?"

The room agreed, their laughter bubbling over now that they seemed to have been given permission. "I feel ridiculous."

"Now, Vannie's idea was that the accessories were like advice. It works to wear a few things at a time, but all at once is too much. We've all written down our ideas for how to help you have the best marriage you can, but I think Vannie's 'advice' is best. Don't try to 'wear' them all at once or you might end up looking pretty ridiculous."

Several of the younger girls helped Vannie remove the excess things and return them to their owners. "That was brilliant, Vannie. What gave you that idea?"

"Mommy said that the stupidest—and you know how Mommy hated that word—thing she ever did was to try to follow all the advice she got at once. She was talking about with me when I was a baby, but I thought it might fit here. Mommy said she felt like she was wearing everyone's mantles and they were stifling her."

Aggie hugged her niece, whispering, "Thank you. That was definitely the best advice of the day."

"And here's the basket of other pieces of advice. I'm sure you'll appreciate 'borrowing' the ideas one or two at a time."

The next game was a modern take on an "old" TV show. "We're going to play the 'Newlywed Game!'" Tina called.

All eyes turned toward the door, but it didn't open. However, a TV was pulled out from the cabinet and Tina turned it on, ready with Luke's pre-recorded answers. "Ok, we have ten questions. The one to get the most right wins. If there is a tie breaker necessary, Luke said I could call and he'd let us do it over speaker phone."

The first question seemed easy. *What day of the week did Luke say he first saw Aggie?* Without hesitation, Aggie scribbled Friday and put her index card in her lap as instructed. The second question was called just as she realized she wrote the wrong answer. "Wait, can I change it?"

"Nope."

"Meanie."

"Yep. Next question. What did Luke say would be his nickname for Aggie if he couldn't call her 'Mibs?'"

The question seemed impossible. He could call her a million

266

things. Why not just Aggie? He didn't seem like a dear or darling kind of guy. A new idea occurred to her and she wrote her answer — Aggie-Sully-Mommie. It had to be.

Strange questions about why his favorite dessert was his favorite and what number would never be on his speed dial flew out. The women didn't hesitate in their answers, which made Aggie very suspicious. Rigging the game in order to make her the winner seemed to be a very inhospitable thing for Tina to do.

"Ok, let's hit play and see what the answers were! First question." The video played and the room heard Tina ask, "Ok, Luke. What day of the week did you first see Aggie?" She hit pause. "Ladies, show me your answers."

Reluctantly, Aggie showed her answer, and then scratched it out and wrote Sunday. "I forgot he saw me at the house in Rockland." Her eyes scanned the room. "How did you guys all get that right?"

"We're good," Mrs. Gantry called out gleefully.

Without hesitation, Luke said, "I think Aggie would say Friday, but the truth is on Sunday."

"Ok, second question." Tina punched play. "What nickname would you give Aggie if you couldn't call her Mibs?" the TV Tina asked. This time, Tina allowed the DVD to play without interruption.

Luke seemed to take his usual time to think and ponder, causing chuckles from those who knew him. "I think I'd probably be a lot like my mom and call her 'my Aggie.' It's not very original, but it seemed instinctive. I know what she'll answer though."

The DVD paused again while Tina called, "Show those answers!"

Again, every woman in the room had "My Aggie" on their cards except for Aggie. She waited for Tina to hit play again and snickered as Luke said, "She'll probably say Aggie-Millie-Mommie — or better yet, Aggie-Sully-Mommie."

"Impressive!" someone called out.

Libby seemed incapable of letting that one pass without comment. "My Luke knows his Aggie."

"Ok, on to the next!"

Answer after answer followed. Aggie got three correct — all three ones Luke predicted she'd get, which confused her. It took until the cards were collected and Tina played the rest of the DVD to understand what they'd done.

"Um, sorry, Mibs. We kind of rigged this with questions we were sure you wouldn't get and gave the other ladies the answers beforehand, so there'd be a tie. The tiebreaker is yours. You ask the question and Tina will call me. We'll do it until someone gets it right, but Mom is disqualified. She knows both of us too well."

Vannie brought out a large gift basket full of everything a woman could want to pamper herself. "Good luck, ladies."

Trying to think of a question that the women could answer correctly, even though several did not know her at all, was not easy. At last, she grinned and said, "What will Luke say that I said — and man that already sounds convoluted — is my one regret about our getting married."

Answers were scribbled much slower this time. Some women stared at the floor or the ceiling as if asking for guidance from those directions — something that amused Aggie greatly. Others pursed their lips or bit the end of their pens. A few stared at her as if the answer would appear on her forehead, but Aggie just smiled and played with her engagement ring. A giggle from Vannie told her that the girl had figured it out. She put her finger to her lips. "Shh."

Slowly, one answer at a time, the cards were placed on everyone's laps. "Ok, let's call," Tina announced. He picked up on the first ring. "How'd she do?"

"You're on speaker, Luke. She did great. Got every one right that you said she would."

"That's my Aggie."

"Very funny."

"Did you go millie or sully."

"Sully."

"Yes!"

The room erupted in laughter. Tina had to settle everyone down again before she could ask Aggie's question. "Ok, Aggie's question was, 'What will Luke say that she said is her one regret in you guys getting married?'"

"Hm..." The silence from the other end was occasionally punctuated by the clear sounds of Ian trying to get the phone. "Well, Ian thinks he has the answer. My first thought was that the wedding wasn't soon enough, but I think my second one is better; it encompasses that. I guess I'm going to say that she says I'll say that it is that I didn't ask her sooner."

The grin on Aggie's face gave it away before she said, "And I bet you're going to say that you would have asked sooner if I had been more forthcoming with my feelings, no?"

"No... wasn't going to say it but I did think it."

"That's what I thought. Hmph."

"Say goodbye, Luke. This is a ladies' function after all," Tina chided. All the ladies called out congratulations and goodbyes before Tina disconnected the call, but Aggie's mind was already on the prize.

"Ok, did anyone get that answer?"

Three ladies did, but two pointed to Iris Landry. "She was first, though."

Vannie nodded, as she carried the basket to Iris. "She was first out of everyone."

"Time for presents! Now, Aggie," Tina began, "obviously the theme of the party is 'Old, New, Borrowed, or Blue.' So, your gifts are supposed to fit that theme, but I told the ladies not to kill themselves. Some had traditional gifts they always give to brides. Also, if they couldn't find anything that fit the theme, I told them to go with whatever they liked since it'd likely be new or old. Of course, I also encouraged everyone not to feel obligated to bring a gift. This is a shower of love."

Never had Aggie enjoyed opening gifts more. The ladies joked, teased, and the lengths to which they tried to avoid the "new" option of the theme were sometimes hilarious. One woman admitted to buying a book for another woman and selling it to the second woman for a penny less so it could be considered "used." As Aggie pulled candles, CDs, notecards, and similar things from their wrappings, she realized how much work Tina went to in order to spare them triplicates of things they already owned.

A few pieces of lingerie appeared, causing Aggie to blush furiously, something the rest of the ladies all seemed to find inordinately amusing. Libby seemed to wince as Aggie picked up one box and read the card attached. "It's from my new mother! I can't—oh no. Not really..."

"Well, I wanted to be... encouraging. I thought it might be a nice thing to get from a mother, especially since your mother wasn't doing well enough to come last minute."

Poor Libby couldn't have said anything worse. Tears filled Aggie's eyes as she pulled the ribbons from the package. Her mind filled with questions of what her own mother would have brought. Sure, they'd mail it or bring it to the wedding, but not to have her mother there that day, already hurt. To be reminded of it was a second blow.

Nestled in lovely pink tissue was the prettiest pair of matching bra and panties that Aggie had ever seen. Her hand traced the lace, marveling that it felt soft instead of scratchy. There was uncertainty on Libby's face, making Aggie feel terrible. She hurried across the room and hugged Luke's mother. "Thank you. It means a lot to me."

As Aggie passed the last gift to her right, she looked out over the group and sighed. The feeling of contentment was unreal. These people, even those she didn't know, had come together to give her a special day. The effort in gift giving alone seemed incredible to her.

"Can I just say, and I know it's probably tacky to do it, that I appreciate every single gift. Even if each one had been a toaster or a waffle iron or a regular iron—"

"That I'm pretty sure Aggie doesn't know how to use," Tina interjected.

"It would have been amazing that you took the time to find them and bless me with them. However, I just really appreciate how much work you guys went to in order to give me a variety of things that I don't already own. That little vase from your own windowsill?" Aggie smiled at Theresa Torres. "It's perfect. I'll always think of you when I put the—ahem—flowers in it that the little ones bring me."

"Oh, dear. She's getting sappy. I think it's time we send her home so Luke can enjoy the benefits, and we don't have to be embarrassed."

Milliken says: Hey sweetie, how was it?
Aggie says: Not the same without you
Milliken says: I'm sorry.
Aggie says: Don't be sorry. I just missed you.
Milliken says: The doctor has me on some strong antibiotics and

promises (after I threatened him with sure death otherwise) that I'll be fine by the wedding.

Aggie says: That's good. I think if you couldn't come, we'd just have to move it to earlier that day and do it at your house.

Milliken says: Oh, don't be silly. Now, what'd you get?

Aggie says: It was fabulous. Everything is perfect for us. I think there were only a couple of things that weren't something we really liked, but even those were useable.

Milliken says: Like what?

Aggie says: Mrs. Dyke gave us her favorite afghan. It's probably the ugliest one I've ever seen, but it's hers and we'll use it.

Milliken says: I was a little afraid Tina would make it a "personal" shower.

Aggie says: There were a few personal items but not many. I think maybe five? Six?

Milliken says: That's good. At the church, it probably means they were nice and tasteful?

Aggie says: Definitely. I was probably most embarrassed by Libby's.

Milliken says: Libby's? Really?

Aggie says: Gorgeous bra and panties. Totally tasteful, but Vannie commented about how she loved pretty underwear, but what was the point? No one sees them anyway. Then she "got it" and we were both embarrassed.

Milliken says: It's good for her to see a healthy attitude, not only from you, but from his mother. I'm glad she did it, and I suspect it was deliberate.

Aggie says: Now that you mention it, you're probably right.

Aggie says: Anyway, I told Vannie that pretty things make you feel pretty even if you're the only one who knows you're wearing them, so we're going shopping for a nice set for her to wear on Sundays.

Milliken says: That's a good idea. It'll also help her keep perspective on things. Otherwise, she might get silly notions about them.

Aggie says: Yep.

Milliken says: And, how did Luke like everything?

Aggie says: He helped me find homes for it all tonight—except the half-dozen boxes I put away first.

Milliken says: Two weeks.

Aggie says: Can you believe it?

Milliken says: Are you ready?

Aggie says: Yes and no. I mean, I could be thrilled if tomorrow was the day, but then when I think about the dozen things Tina asks me every day and how we don't even have a license yet—yikes!

Milliken says: Well, it'll be here before you know it.

Milliken says: How is Kenzie's arm?

Aggie says: Fine. The doctor trips are killing me though. It itches, she wants to scratch, she doesn't like to protect it in the bath, but I insist, and so on and so on… It's a nightmare.

Milliken says: No more ice skating, eh?

Aggie says: You got that right.

Milliken says: That was a joke. She needs to go out as soon as she can.

Aggie says: No way.

Milliken says: I recommend you reconsider that. You'll teach her to be fearful and a coward. Those things are worse than a broken bone now and then.

Aggie says: We'll see. I can't think about that now.

Milliken says: I'm getting the "glower" from your father. He says I have to close the laptop or you'll suck me in by talking to him. He knows me too well. Well, goodnight. See you soon.

Aggie says: Ok, then. Goodnight.

Chapter 20

JITTERS & SPATS

Wednesday, February 25th

After days of waking up feeling like she'd been run over by a train, Aggie jumped out of bed completely refreshed. Panicked, she glanced at the clock, terrified that it would read ten o'clock or something, but it was only six-thirty. Just to be safe, she stuffed her feet in her slippers and hurried down the steps to the second floor. The children were, as the poem says, "nestled all snug in their beds," although she didn't expect any kind of sugarplums in their heads. It was probably more like assignments and chore lists.

She started downstairs but then remembered her bed. Perhaps she might get it made before the first child woke up. Wouldn't that be a novelty? The sheets looked extra rumpled, prompting her to try smoothing the top sheet in place. It was asking for trouble, but Aggie couldn't resist the idea of changing them. She whipped the old ones off and had fresh ones in place in minutes.

The room looked great. She scooped up the sheets and a few pieces of dirty clothing that needed to be washed and hurried downstairs. Not a sound on the second floor indicated that anyone had left the world of slumber for consciousness. She stuffed the sheets as well as a few towels in the washer, dumped soap in, shut the lid and cranked the dial. Hands in the air, she cheered breathily. "Yes! Score! I did it!"

The kitchen clock said it was six forty-five. How was that possible? The kids would love it if she made pancakes. Should she do it? With pancakes, they'd need eggs for balance, but those were fast. Vannie could do them if time got away from her. Griddles oiled and heating, she began mixing ingredients, one eye on the clock at all times. If everyone arrived before the first one was done, she'd put it in the fridge and they could have pancakes for dinner.

As usual, her first pancake was inedible. It seemed like there was an unwritten rule of pancake cookery. Her father had never been able to make a good first one either—Aggie's one consolation as she dumped it in the garbage.

Ten pancakes were stacked in a warm oven by the time she heard Ian's chipper, "Hi, Tav'!" over the baby monitor.

With a quick glance to ensure nothing would burn while she was gone, Aggie rushed upstairs and greeted her little man. "Good morning, sunshine. Let's go get dressed downstairs so Tavish doesn't have to wait for us."

"What's for breakfast?"

"Pancakes and eggs."

"Oh, be right there. Can we have orange juice?"

"If you make it."

Tavish grinned. "Nice!"

Ian hadn't soaked through his diaper for the first time in weeks. He giggled as the dryer bounced him while she changed and dressed him and tossed his sleeper in the washer. Tina's idea of using it for a changing table was brilliant. A quick wipe over the pad and she was ready to go.

"Ok, guy. Let's see how many pancakes we can get done before Tavish comes in."

Content to suck his thumb and snuggle against her, Ian grew heavy quickly. The first pancake was sizzling on the griddle when Tavish burst into the kitchen. "Everyone is up. Thought you should know. Where's the pitcher?"

"Where would you look if I wasn't in here?"

The boy grinned. If he ever learned to look for things instead of asking for them, she'd consider herself a parenting success. "...to the feast, come for the table now is spread... famishing...thou shall be richly fed..."[4]

"Aunt Aggie?"

"Hmm?"

"I hope my wife sings like you do."

"I thought wives were gross and men shouldn't bother with them," she reminded him.

274

"Not wives like you. I could stand a wife like you."

"Gee, thanks."

"Or, maybe Ellie and me could be like the Lambs—only like in inventions or research or something. She could sing. You should teach her to sing when she's working."

Ellie stepped into the room. "Who could sing?"

"You. You should learn to sing while you work like Aunt Aggie. We could have a house when we're older and invent things and you could sing."

Sometimes, Aggie was astounded at the disparity in maturity between Tavish and Ellie. The girl smiled indulgently at her brother while reaching for Ian. "Do you want some juice? Tavish is making juice. Maybe we should sing about mixing juice for him."

"Bottle of wine, fruit of the vine—"

Aggie interrupted him before he could continue. "Don't even think about finishing that, Tavish. I think I know the next line."

Without Ian wearing her out, Aggie was able to fry pancakes much swifter. As she waited for the bubbles to pop on the cakes, she began breaking eggs in a bowl. "Where's the whisk? I just had it."

A twang came from the direction of the highchair. "Sorry, I let Ian play with it."

"That's ok. I can use a fork."

All through preparation, children filed into the kitchen looking reasonably well groomed and chipper. She slid plates across the island nearly as quickly as they arrived, and the noise in the room rose to what she hoped was a "dull roar." It seemed like a mini-version of a school lunchroom, but something about it worked.

"What are we doing today?" Vannie asked.

"We have to get everything ready for you guys to take your work with you while I'm gone, so the rest of this week and next are for getting things ready."

Laird stood with fork raised and shouted, "Let's roll!"

School hadn't run this smoothly since they'd started. She managed to get Kenzie, Tavish, and Ellie current on their core subjects—even taking into consideration the month lost to sickness.

Vannie and Laird were each still over a week behind, but considering how many months they had left, she felt confident that they'd catch up in April or May.

The children worked quietly and diligently, and the little ones played until naptime without a hitch. Once the little children were down for naps, she hurried to clean the kitchen and get dinner into the oven. "Three meals without having to be reminded of time or defrost; it's a record!"

As she opened a can of tomato juice to pour over the stew, the phone rang. She dove for it, hoping it wouldn't wake the kids. "Hello?"

"Hey, Aggie."

"William! Tina's not here, remember? She went to visit her dad for the day."

"No, I'm calling for you. Just thought you should know, we caught Josh. He's in custody in Illinois. Someone saw the picture that they had of Luke and 'recognized' Josh as someone living in their motel."

"You got him?"

"It's completely over. From what the FBI guys say, he's spilling everything."

Relief washed over her. She put the lid on the stew and shoved it in the oven while listening as William explained what would happen next. Once he finished, she asked the question the kids would love to hear most. "What you're saying is that the kids are safe to leave. They can ride up and down the street or to the library or to your house without anyone out there looking for them specifically."

"Well, they could have before. The chances of him coming back after her getting caught were pretty much non-existent. He's not going to bother if he didn't get paid and he can't get paid with her in jail—so to speak."

"Oh."

"Oh, and just so you know; it looks like he might have been blackmailed into doing it. We're not sure about that, but he has no reason to say so, and he might have supporting evidence."

"This is really over." Aggie gripped the counter. "Over."

"You ok? Is Luke there?"

"No, he's working on that new house of his. They're trying to

276

get the roof on before we leave."

"Want me to come over? Send Murphy?"

"I'm good. I think I'm going to make cookies. Feel free to stop by for some."

"Snickerdoodles?"

She grinned. William loved his snickerdoodles. "If you are coming, definitely."

"I'll be there sometime after four."

"I'll save a few to bake then so you can have 'em hot. I am grateful that Luke talked me into that double oven thing."

Aggie pulled out mixing bowls, measuring spoons and cups, and the ingredients she could remember. As she worked, she prayed. Resolved, she left her work and hurried downstairs.

"Who is aching to go for a ride? I could use some things from the store."

Laird stared at her. "What?"

"Do you want to run an errand? Vannie? Tavish? Ellie? Anyone?"

"But we're not done with school yet."

"How much do you have left?"

"Not much, but—" Laird stopped abruptly. "Are you feeling ok? Should I call Luke?"

Vannie spoke up before Aggie could answer. "Something happened, didn't it?" Her eyes widened. "They caught him!"

"Yep! You guys are free to be kids again. Your wacky over-protective aunt is appeased. Now, get out of here and go buy stuff."

"What! You didn't tell us what to buy."

"I don't care. I just need a few things. I'll know what they are when you get home with them."

She turned and hurried up the stairs, grinning as she overheard Tavish say, "I think she's losing it. Some people become Bridezillas; she becomes sugarbride or something."

Luke was gone. He'd only had a few minutes to spend with her, not arriving until well after the children were in bed. Aggie reflected on how he laughed at William making her promise to teach Tina how to make perfect snickerdoodles and over Tavish's decision that a wife might not be the end of the world as she dragged herself upstairs to go to bed. It was a good night.

No, it was a good day — perfect really. Nothing could have been better. The house is clean, the kids had good meals, a criminal is behind bars, and my family is safe. William is falling in love with my friend; Luke took the time to come see me. All is right with the world.

In her room, she grabbed a pair of pajamas and hurried to change. As she reached for the toothbrush in the cup on her sink, Aggie froze. Hair, disheveled and looking like she'd slept in it greeted her in the mirror. Her eyes traveled south to see her favorite pajama shirt spattered with catsup from the mishap with the bottle at lunch. "Grumpy sleeps here is right," she muttered.

She didn't want to do it, but Aggie couldn't resist. A peek at her legs told her what her mind had already accused. She'd never gotten dressed, never brushed her hair... "Oh, ick! I didn't brush my teeth!"

Her phone sat on her nightstand, blinking furiously from unanswered texts and voicemails. Tina had called five times and sent at least twenty-five texts. There were two calls from her mother, three from Luke, and one from Libby. William's voice came on and she frowned. Why hadn't he told her he'd tried the cell phone?

"Lord," she whispered as she crawled beneath the sheets and snapped off the light, "did my perfect day have to end with proof that I can't even dress myself? So much for finally getting my act together." Seconds before she drifted off to sleep, Aggie added, "But thanks for the good parts. It was mostly perfect. Oh, and thanks for Luke showing up after the kids were in bed. He probably didn't realize I've been dressed for bed all day..."

Friday, February 27ᵗʰ

There was a line at the county clerk's office — something Aggie hadn't expected. "I thought marriage was almost dead. It kind of surprises me that there are so many people here."

Luke shrugged. "I suspect when people figure out that they can do a wedding for the fun of it without the commitment of a marriage, numbers will drop drastically."

"Oh, that's true. I'd never thought about that."

"Well, and this state doesn't recognize domestic partnerships or common law marriages, so for most health insurance and tax purposes, people will keep getting married until that changes."

The discussion was depressing. Suddenly, she felt panicked. "Luke, don't do this if—"

"What? Don't do what?"

"Marry me. Don't do it if you have any doubts. I will fight for my marriage once it exists."

"Good. That's one of the reasons I'm marrying you." His grin was a little too lopsided for her comfort.

"I'm serious, Luke. Have you heard how many people are talking about their second, third, fifth marriage? I get one shot."

"Well, how about we agree that if we want to be done with this marriage, one of us will have the decency to die right about then."

"Deal."

At the clerk's desk, they presented drivers' licenses, birth certificates, and swore that their information was correct. It took less than ten minutes to walk out the door once they'd been called. "That was anticlimactic."

Luke grinned. "I doubt signing it will be."

"I'll look forward to it. Well, what do we do now? We've got hours before your mom needs us home and no errands from Tina—yet."

"I was thinking…"

"Oh, I like it when he thinks," Aggie giggled. "Do tell."

Luke led her to the parking lot, explaining his mission. "We have four different people taking care of our kids, right?"

The way Luke said "our kids" without hesitation sent strange flip-flops through her heart. "Right."

"Well, I say we do a little shopping for thank-you gifts."

"Oh! That's a great idea. Let's start with your mom. I've always wanted to really shop for her. Things were so busy at Christmas that I had to go with the first idea I had that I liked."

"She loves that robe, Aggie. I see her in it nearly every day."

Aggie's face fell. "You're going to miss that; she will too."

"Aw, Mibs. It's the way God planned things. Mom knows that. And, it'll just be an excuse for her to be a doting grandmother all the more."

"You know, when she gets to where she might need help—

that's years away I know—she could have the guest room. We could shrink the laundry room. We won't need two washers and dryers anymore by then."

Luke's arms nearly crushed her as he stopped mid row, only feet away from the truck, and hugged her fiercely. "I can't tell you how much it means that you love my mama."

"I've never heard you call her mama."

He opened the door and waited for her to get her legs inside as he said, "I can't remember the last time I did—probably when she first met you. I was upset about something I think. She said something about it later."

"Let's go buy her a gift, eh?" Aggie frowned.

"Let's go."

They started at the mall, but little interested them. As they passed a gourmet cooking store on their way out, Luke paused. "You know, Mom's mixer is dying. I've jury-rigged it so many times that I don't know if it'll come back from the dead next time or not."

"Mixer?"

"Sure. Let's try Target."

There were three mixers on the appliance aisle that Luke liked. Luke read the boxes of each carefully. Aggie stared in sticker shock at each one, uncertain of how she'd afford to spend a thousand dollars or more in gifts. The wedding alone was killing the budget. She'd tried to economize in a hundred ways to make up for it, but guilt still plagued her. The money was meant for the children's upkeep, not for elaborate parties.

"I think we want this one."

She sagged in slight relief. At least it was the two-hundred fifty dollar jobbie. "If you think she'll like it. It comes in red and white."

"I'd better stick with white, although if I was buying for you, I'd definitely want red."

"I want to say something like 'is that because I'm a hot mama,' but that just sounds all wrong."

"I'll answer that one any time after four o'clock next Saturday."

Desperate to change the subject, Aggie nudged Luke with the cart and said, "Who's next?"

"Willow? Tackle the hardest one now?"

Before she could answer, Luke's phone rang. He listened for several seconds, a grin splitting his face and his eyes lighting with delight. "That is great. Thanks for calling. I'm so excited!"

"What?" Aggie asked as he slipped his phone back in his pocket.

"Guess who Corinne saw go into a bridal store just a little while ago?"

"Who?" Realization dawned before he could answer. "No, Willow?"

"Yep. Corinne called Mom who called Aunt Marianne to confirm. They were keeping it quiet until after the wedding. Chad wanted to make sure we had 'our day' without splitting attention."

"That is both exciting and really cool that they thought of you like that!"

They paid for the mixer and stowed it behind Luke's seat, but he seemed preoccupied with the news. After a full minute sitting and waiting to leave, Aggie nudged him. "I know you're excited, but can we get this shopping done before Tina sends us on sixty errands herself?"

"Oh, sorry. I was just thinking... what if we used this as an excuse to leave the reception a tad early? We could make an announcement and turn it over to them as their engagement party. It'd be a great way for Willow to get to know everyone. People who don't know Chad could leave, of course, but the rest..."

"And we get to go earlier? I'm all for it." She winked and nudged him. "However, this isn't reducing our gift list."

For several minutes, they talked about the reception, Chad, Willow, and of course, Willow's gift. Even after a dozen ideas were tossed into the pool, nothing seemed right for Willow. "Would Chad know?"

"If we ask Chad, he knows he's getting something. That's awkward, but..." Luke seemed lost in thought. "That does give me an idea. Chad made her that dulcimer for Christmas. I wonder if we could find a stand for it."

Aggie whipped out her phone and began searching music stores and calling. "Ok, there's one two blocks off Washington on Crescent. He says they have a variety. Sounds like they deal in folk instruments."

All the way there, she scolded herself for selfishness. The cost of paying someone for watching her children for two weeks would have run more than a thousand dollars. This was no different, and yet it felt different somehow. "How expensive are stands? I should have asked." What if it was more?

"Shouldn't be too bad — under a hundred I'm sure."

"I don't suppose there'd be enough sheet music to balance the costs…"

"Why balance them? It's perfect for her. That's all that matters."

"Well, that'd be at least a hundred fifty dollar disparity. Don't you think we'd want to find a way to bridge that a bit more?"

He turned onto Crescent a little while later, having seemingly ignored her question and said, "I guess I don't understand. If the perfect gift for Mom was a five dollar potted plant, and the perfect gift for Willow was a five hundred dollar cow, why wouldn't we buy the perfect one for each one without worrying about what we spent?"

"And you don't think in that case your mom would feel a bit—" she searched for the right word and then settled. "Disrespected at such a gross discrepancy? I mean, I know the thought is what counts and I know that money doesn't demonstrate how we feel about someone, but I'd be afraid of it looking glaringly preferential."

"I think if it was the 'perfect' gift for Mom, she wouldn't think a thing of it. It's just kind of what we do in our family. It never occurred to me that you'd spend more just because you did on someone else."

"Well, I wasn't thinking of adding a cash difference, but sheet music or gift cards?"

"I don't think Willow would understand that, Mibs. She's kind of different. I think she'd tell you straight that she thought you'd gone overboard. There is a quantity idea in the other direction too. Would Mom maybe feel slighted because she got one gift and Willow got several?"

"Well—" It took more inner strength to shut her mouth and not say the things she wanted to say than Aggie realized she had left. It felt as if Luke were mocking her — showing his superior opinion by being sarcastic. She didn't like it.

"If you think it'll be ok… With her being new in the family, I wouldn't want her to feel slighted or overwhelmed."

"I think overwhelmed is more likely than slighted."

It took almost no time at all to purchase the stand. The moment they stepped in the door, Aggie saw exactly what she wanted and felt settled immediately. "There. That. Isn't it gorgeous? Will it match?"

"It'll compliment the dulcimer perfectly." Luke grinned at the man coming to greet them. "This might be your easiest sale of the day." He pointed to the stand. "We'll take it. Do you have a box?"

Two gifts down left them with one for Iris and one for Chad. Luke's mind flew in a dozen directions, but nothing for either person fit. "What about..."

"What?"

Aggie picked at her skirt. "Well, what if we did kind of a family gift for Iris' family. Something they'd really enjoy for a long time like a membership to the zoo or the aquarium, or Storyland or something."

"That's a great idea!" Luke grinned. "What's it gonna be?"

"Hey, I came up with the idea!"

"Well, I wouldn't want Storyland myself, but that's because it'd be a nightmare with our age ranges. It'd work perfect for them unless Iris hated it or something."

"There's that train to Chicago... I wonder how expensive tickets are for that."

"Definitely more than Mom's mixer..."

Somewhere deep in the most rational part of her heart, Aggie knew it was just a joke, but it felt like a dig. She wanted to confront him, but it seemed silly and petty. This was Luke. He wouldn't rub salt into a wound. Then again, he didn't know there was one. Somehow, knowing that she was the one with the issue and that he was oblivious just made everything seem that much worse.

"Well then, what'll it be? I came up with the idea."

"Yes, and it's a perfect one," he reassured her.

It felt patronizing. With every passing second, the panic of expense, the stress of last minute preparations, the uncertainty of etiquette, and the teasing seemed to culminate into a whirlwind of emotions she didn't want to address. "Storyland." Oh, how she hoped he wouldn't ask why she chose it. Aggie suspected that it had something to do with knowing he wouldn't want it for them.

"Let's get it and on the way we can try to figure out Chad. Before that call, I'd have said something to give his apartment a more homey feel, but now..."

"Sparse?"

"You aren't kidding."

"What are you going to do with all your stuff?"

"Anything not personal, I'm leaving at the duplex. I'll rent it out fully furnished. They can pack anything they don't want or need in my storage shed."

"Good idea."

He reached for her hand. "Just a week from tomorrow and I'll walk out of it for good."

"I have a feeling it's going to be a very long week." *And a long day,* she added to herself.

Traffic was crazy busy. "It must be getting close to lunch. Have an idea what you want to eat?" Luke asked.

"You're going to laugh at me."

"I doubt it. What?"

"I want one of those gourmet hot dogs from that place near Storyland."

"Gourmet dogs it is. I haven't had one of those in ages."

"I wonder if Willow has ever been to a place like Storyland or the Aquarium. Maybe…"

"I know the Aquarium freaked her out. I don't think she'd understand the point of Storyland, but she might enjoy the symphony or maybe the Zoo…"

"Maybe something for outside — to make her work easier."

"Wait, this is supposed to be for Chad. We got Willow's."

Frustration bubbled over before Aggie could stop herself. "Well, if they're getting married, what's the difference?"

"Are you ok? Did I—"

"No. Ok, I don't really know Chad. What does he like? Does he have a good camera?"

"I think so. Willow used it at the house that day…"

"Of course she did. Then what about—"

"Aggie, you seem upset. They're just gifts. We'll figure out something. I can call Aunt Marianne."

"Well," she snapped, "everything I come up with isn't right; they may just be gifts, but obviously they have to work too."

Without a word, Luke pulled into a supermarket parking lot, parked far away from the rest of the cars, and shut off the engine. "Something is wrong."

"Really? I hadn't noticed."

284

"And now you're sarcastic." His voice seemed cooler.

"I'm sarcastic? Who is Mr. Superior in the gift department?"

"What are you talking about?"

In a near perfect imitation, something she didn't know she could do, Aggie recited, "'Would Mom maybe feel slighted because she got one gift and Willow got several?'"

"I don't understand."

"That's just the point. You don't understand. I've got this crazy thing going here. We're talking two-hundred fifty dollars for one gift, seventy-nine for another. Who knows what Storyland will be for a family season pass, and then we still have Chad."

"Who I just figured out. We'll get him a fishing license."

"Seriously? What's that, fifteen bucks?"

"Sure—or thirty. Something like that."

She closed her eyes, willing herself not to storm out of the truck. It would look even more ridiculous than she felt already. "Ok. Let's just get it. I'm hungry."

"You're angry."

"That doesn't seem to matter; let's just go."

When he didn't answer, angry tears attacked her, making a very bad situation worse. She glanced at him as he pushed a packet of tissues across the seat and saw that he was praying. A new wave of fury washed over her and with it, sobs. It was ridiculous. What on earth was wrong with her?

"Oh, Mibs." Luke unsnapped his seatbelt, jerked the armrest out of the way and slid across the seat, pulling her to him. "What's wrong?"

"I don't know. I keep getting angry over all kinds of things that don't make sense. I know it, and it just makes me angrier."

"What did I say?"

"You think I'm stupid for being concerned about the price differences, but it's really stressing me out."

"I don't think you're stupid at all. I was trying to reassure you that I don't think anyone would care even if they did notice. Why spend a thousand dollars on gifts just because one was two-hundred fifty?"

"And your mom's, no less. No favoritism there, right?"

"Would it take the stress off," he asked, blatantly ignoring the dig she'd tried to inflict, "if I paid for everything and gave them from

285

me?"

"So that I look like an ungrateful jerk? That makes so much more sense. Gee, thanks."

His patience seemed worn thin. He re-buckled his seatbelt and started the truck. Aggie watched amazed as he pulled into traffic and drove without a word to Storyland. "I'll be back in a minute."

Left alone in the truck, Aggie seethed. What did he think he was doing? "Lord, I'm about to throttle him!"

When he returned, he passed the envelope to her. "An annual pass was only fifty dollars more than a season pass, so I went for it. It brought it closer to your target price."

"Luke..."

"Hot dogs."

Her mind spun. What did hot dogs have to do with anything? It made no—lunch. It did too make sense. It wasn't the silent treatment, but it felt like it. He was mad now. Great. Just what they needed.

"What kind of hot dog do you want?"

"Huh?"

"What kind—"

"I heard you," Aggie said. "I meant why do you ask?"

"Because we're almost there and I want to know what to order."

"They don't have a drive-thru..."

"No, but I want to be prepared."

"Ok..." She took a deep breath and said, "I want the Polish dog with sauerkraut and pickles."

As he pulled into the only empty parking space, Luke said, "I'll be right back."

Left alone in the truck again, Aggie's anger level rose exponentially. She stepped outside and glanced at the ignition. Keys were still in it. Once retrieved, she locked it and hurried inside. Luke was already ordering so she waited in line to order a drink.

It was almost worth the morning's irritation to see the stunned look on his face. "You shouldn't have left the truck. Someone might steal—"

"I locked it." Oh, this was going to be good.

"Aggie, the keys are in there!"

"Well, they were. I took them out. Apparently this immature little pipsqueak can do something right." She jingled the keys and stuffed them in her pocket before stepping up to the register. "I'd like

286

a large Coke—extra ice."

"It might not hurt to help you cool off," he muttered.

"I thought it'd work for that, but I planned to cool you off."

The girl behind the counter snickered and filled a cup. "That'll be one seventy-nine, please."

She dug out the bills and passed them across the counter. "I'll take mine over at that table, Luke."

"Do you think that's a good idea?"

She rolled her eyes at the girl behind the counter. "Apparently I'm an idiot now too."

"Mibs…"

With every effort to appear cool and collected, Aggie walked to the table she'd indicated and seated herself. *Who am I kidding? I just stormed over here like Cari when she doesn't get her way,* she thought. *Then again, he is being such a jerk about it all…*

"Is that one mine?" Aggie reached for the one with a big S on it.

"Yes."

She wanted to gloat over his sulking, but there was a problem. He wasn't. He might be angry; she couldn't tell. Without any other idea of what to do about their situation, she focused on what she could control—her enjoyment of the hot dog. Unfortunately, it was almost tasteless. It almost seemed as if her taste buds were powered down when her anger levels rose.

"I'm mad at you."

"So I gather."

"And we're just going to ignore this because my silliness is not worth addressing, right?"

"No, I'm not going to argue with you in public."

Aggie glowered at him. "How utterly mature of you."

He didn't answer, but his eyes met hers and the pain in them managed to prick the tiniest hole in the armor she'd donned. It might have caused a crack that would eventually break if he had not added, "And what is the safe response to that?"

"Take me home."

He stared at her, shocked. "What?"

She rose, dumped her food and cup into the nearby garbage can, and waited by her chair for him to acknowledge her "request." "I said, take me home."

"I'm not finished."

287

Her cell phone rang. Glaring at Tina's name flashing on the screen, she answered it with a curt, "Hello."

"Still in line there?"

"No. Coming home."

"What's wrong?"

Aggie forced herself not to sniffle. "I am finished for the day."

"There's more to it. Let me talk to Luke."

"No."

"Aggie, I'm serious. Either hand the phone to him or I'm hanging up and calling him."

Infused with a new level of fury, Aggie shoved the phone at Luke. "Tina wants to talk to you. I'll be in the truck."

He stood and followed her, dumping his trash as they left the restaurant. "She is angry with me, yes."

Listening to one side of the conversation was annoying. What was Tina saying? Why did Luke look so calm? He should be furious that she made him miss half his meal.

"I'm not sure. I think I don't understand something. She wants to pick a fight, but I'm not going to play that game."

"Really, Luke? Really?" Aggie was on a roll. "This is just what makes me furious! You think you've got the corner on the market of whatever it is you've got—the only word I can think of is supercilious, which just sounds ridiculous."

"Maybe because it is."

Something Tina said caught his attention. He listened, eyes on her, but his mind fully engaged in whatever he heard. "Ok, I'll try." He passed the phone back to her and said, "She wants you again."

"How generous of her." Aggie was tempted to turn it off and deal with the consequences later, but she knew Tina would just call Luke's phone and he'd be on her side. "What?"

"Stop it. You are behaving like Cari. What's the matter with you?"

"Of course," she began as she unlocked her door and let herself into the truck. For just a moment, Aggie was tempted to lock the doors and not let Luke inside, but of course, that'd just prove Tina's assertions that she was being childish, "this is all my fault. I am stupid and unreasonable."

He muttered something—she could have sworn it was something about "half-truths"—and held his hand out for the keys.

"I told Tina I'd bring you home."

"Fine. You'll do what she asks, but not what I do. Gee. That makes me feel good." Aggie dumped the keys in his hand, her stomach churning with the misery of the morning. What should have been a great time out together was nothing but a miserable experience.

"I'm not going to argue it," he said as he started the truck.

"You said not in public, but you meant not at all."

"No, I meant not in public, but now I am adding that I'm not going to argue. I don't know what's wrong, but arguing about it while driving is a great way to get us killed. Not going to do that."

"Fine with me."

Several minutes later, she stared at the phone in her hand, wondering if she'd ever said goodbye. A sinking feeling hit the pit of her stomach as she realized not only had she not said goodbye, but Tina had likely heard their exchange. "Great."

"Hmm?"

"Nothing."

Aggie says: Mom?

Milliken says: Yes?

Aggie says: I'm really upset.

Milliken says: About what?

Aggie says: Luke and I had an argument.

Milliken says: It doesn't sound resolved.

Aggie says: It's not.

Milliken says: Then why are you talking to me instead of to Luke?

Aggie says: I don't want to talk to Luke.

Milliken says: Why?

Aggie says: He's being all superior about this. He won't dignify my frustration with an argument.

Milliken says: I thought you said you had one.

Aggie says: Well, we would have if he wouldn't have ignored me!

Milliken says: Did you read that?

Aggie says: Read what?

Milliken says: What you just wrote. You want an argument? That's

289

what you just said.

Aggie says: I want him to talk about a few things that are bothering me.

Aggie says: He just totally ignored the fact that I am bothered by this whole gift idea.

Milliken says: Don't talk to me about it until you and he are ok. I'm not getting in the middle of your arguments and before you say anything else, I bet you anything Libby would say the same thing — to both of you.

Aggie says: Ok. Talk to you later.

Milliken says: Aggie, don't shut me out because you don't like what I said.

Aggie says: You just told me not to talk to you about it, Mom. What am I supposed to do?

Milliken says: Is that all you want to talk about? You don't have any fun stories to share about the children or want to tell me that you got a license or that a crazy gift arrived from someone that makes no sense…

Aggie says: I have the license, although today makes me wonder what I'm getting into. The kids are fine and Ian says Lunkle Luke now. Thankfully, we have no obnoxious gifts from people, but I've got three that I hope work for others.

Aggie says: I've gotta go, Mom. I love you. Sorry.

Chapter 21

MURPHY STRIKES AGIAIN

Saturday, February 28ᵗʰ

"...lead me on, let me stand," a sniffle broke the flow of the words. "I am tired, I am weak, I am worn."[5]

The song had been little comfort, but Aggie had sung it all day in snatches. The children, clearly unsettled at her uncharacteristic silence, avoided her whenever possible. Never had she felt so alone; it seemed almost unbearable.

A suitcase—the very one she'd lived out of at Allie's for all those weeks—lay open on the bed as she chose what clothes to bring the next week. Tears splashed on her cheeks as she put in the leggings, thermals, petticoats, and heavy skirts that Libby had purchased and chosen from Aggie's closet. The sight of one skirt sent her digging through the shelves for a sweater she rarely wore.

Clothes were spread throughout the enormous closet, but it was still really half-empty. Not for long. A new pang struck her heart. There was something wonderful and terrifying about knowing that she was at odds with the man she was going to marry, but there was no doubt that they *would* marry.

Slowly, she moved all her shirts and skirts to one side of the closet. She stacked her clothes on the shelves to the right, leaving the entire left for Luke. It looked both forlorn and expectant. Her hand slid across the empty rod where his jeans would hang. Maybe she should forget it—let it go. They usually got along well enough that this might just be the time to overlook an offense.

"Mibs?"

She turned, dreading to see the look on his face. Would he be

291

hurt? Angry? That same cold arrogance that had infuriated her the previous day? "Hmm?"

"Can we talk?"

Outside, children called dibs on favorite seats and van doors shut. "What is going on?"

"Tina is taking them for a drive. I thought maybe you'd want to... talk." He nodded at the rod her hand still held. "Making room for me?"

"Yes. You should bring things over that you won't be needing next week. My closet won't look lonely anymore."

He stepped closer. "You've been crying."

As if the magic words to open a dam, new tears spilled onto her cheeks. "Maybe..."

All the softening her heart had done hardened again as she passed him and placed the sweater into the suitcase. He reached for her, but she ignored him. "I still do not understand what happened, but I apologize for hurting you."

"How very magnanimous of you."

"Mibs, please."

"What do you want from me? You want to know what is wrong? I'll tell you!"

The cold self-control was back. "Please do."

"That! That's one thing that's wrong. I'm hurt; I'm angry. I want to scream with the frustration of it all, and you stand there with your self-righteous smug expression and act like you're all holy. I can hear it now, 'Yes, well, we had a disagreement, but I died to myself and forgave her. I let her rail at me because it is what a godly man must do.'"

"I'm sorry if I don't know how to 'fight' in your expected manner. I don't yell. I don't *want* to become a yeller. I am terrified of what I would become if I did. But yes, I'd love to die to myself if it'd solve this problem. I just don't know what the problem is and it doesn't work to try to die to myself if I kill you in the process. That's just not very efficient. Why don't you explain to me why we're arguing, and we can work from there."

"You made me feel petty and stupid. You wouldn't talk about it. You treated me like a child who wasn't worth discussing it with." She frowned. "Yeah, I know I'm supposed to say I felt this and I felt that and leave you out of it, but I can't think that clearly."

"I didn't mean—" Luke sank to the corner of her bed and played with the zipper pull on her suitcase. "I guess it doesn't matter what I meant to do. I did that. I'm sorry."

"You meant to be superior, Luke. I could see it in your eyes and in the way Tina reacted to you. You liked being the calm one who was too godly to stoop to an argument."

Several minutes passed. Aggie packed item after item, but Luke seemed unwilling to address her accusation. "Mibs," he began at last, "you're right. I thought you were upset over nothing, so I decided to take the 'high road.' It was wrong."

"I want to stay mad at you."

"But I want you to forgive me."

"Next time I say I want to talk about something, can we talk?"

"But you never said you wanted to talk. You told me to take you home when I wouldn't argue in public."

Aggie closed her eyes. "Regardless of how we each see this particular situation, would you agree to talk next time?"

"Deal. Wanna talk now?"

She shook her head. "Nope. Wanna tell me what we got Chad?"

"Found out that he doesn't have a GPS in the truck. Got him one."

"Perfect." Aggie glanced at Luke and grinned. "Can I have a hug? I really need one."

Wednesday, March 3rd

"Get up! It's almost eight!" Aggie shouted in each door for the third time that morning. "Next time I come around, I'm taking blankets and bringing cold water."

It didn't work. She carried her spray bottle with her, jerking off covers and spritzing each one but Ian, who seemed to find the entire proceeding hysterical. His gleeful screeches were likely more responsible for Tavish's appearance than her attempts. "That's the last time I get caught up in wedding prep and forget bedtime!"

"We had fun. We watched the entire second season of the Waltons!" Ellie exclaimed. "It's almost like watching our house." As Tavish passed, the girl called, "Good morning, Tavish!"

"It just doesn't work for morning."

293

"Granola bars for breakfast. Just get dressed and comb your hair. Kenzie, wear short sleeves."

"But I want—"

"It wasn't a suggestion," Aggie growled. "Wear. Short. Sleeves."

The girl sighed. "Fine." A glance at Aggie's face prompted her to amend her response. "Yes, Aunt Aggie."

With Tina fighting the caterers about soup in Rockland and Luke supervising the final touches on his roof, Aggie's trip to the doctor was solo. Solo trips to places that were not child-friendly on days when the children were sleep-deprived was asking for trouble, but Aggie dressed Ian with as much cheerfulness as she could muster and hurried downstairs.

One look in the pantry, and Aggie yelled, "Who ate the granola bars? I did *not* give anyone permission to eat the granola bars!"

"Yes you did."

Aggie turned and glared at Laird. "Don't start with me."

"But you did! We asked last night while you and Aunt Tina were making those vases and you said yes."

A sick feeling washed over her as she realized he was probably telling the truth. "What else did I agree to?"

"No school for today, ice cream after Kenzie's cast is off, and pizza for dinner."

With each item, the sickness grew. She had agreed to everything. "You took total advantage."

"Sure. Wouldn't you?"

It wasn't the time to address doing what was right regardless of whether you had permission to do wrong or not. "Ok, we'll stop for bars on the way." She glanced at the clock. Eight-twenty. Not enough time to play around. Kids filed downstairs and she pointed directly to their coats. "We've got to go."

Their appointment was at nine o'clock. By the time she stopped for gas, granola bars, and made it past a spun out car on the highway, they shuffled into the clinic at five after. "Sorry…"

"Dr. Wisenberg is just finishing with a walk-in. There's an empty room but—" The assistant glanced over the heads around the counter. "There isn't really room for everyone in there."

Aggie nodded. "Ok, Vannie through Tavish stay in the waiting room. The rest of you, follow Miss… Angie."

"There's really not—"

"Look, I don't want to have to admit this, but you do not want these three out there without me. You just don't."

"Most people find it helpful to arrange child care and don't find it necessary to keep siblings out of school for a simple cast removal."

"And most people aren't the single, homeschooling mothers of eight. Lead the way," Aggie insisted.

Dr. Weisman arrived quickly. "Good morning, Kenzie! How is the arm today? Still pain-free? Itchy?"

Kenzie nodded. "Both."

"Good, then let's take that thing off."

The doctor showed the little mini saw, how it worked, and what Kenzie was to do if she wanted him to stop for any reason. Three seconds into the process, she squeezed his arm. Once confident that he really would stop if she asked, Kenzie watched the process, fascinated.

"That was cool!"

"Well," Aggie interjected, "don't get any ideas about breaking something else. One broken bone per decade is my limit."

"I'm sorry, Aggie, but I'm afraid that with your family, I expect you'll have more than one per decade."

"Don't," she said with as much severity as she could muster, "destroy my delusions. They are essential to my sanity."

As they stepped from the room, Laird's eager expression reminded her of something. "Oh, by the way. Where would you suggest that I find ice cream at nine-thirty in the morning?"

A delivery van arrived near four o'clock, bringing chairs for the ceremony. It looked odd to have four dozen white wooden chairs stacked up on the porch in midwinter, but there was nowhere else to put them. Not five seconds after she signed the receipt, a horrible crash came from the kitchen.

Kenzie flew out the door and into Aggie's arms. "You know how you said if there's an accident and I tell the truth that I won't get spanked? Well, I had an accident. I slipped on the mat in the kitchen and didn't want to hurt my arm, so I grabbed the cloth on the island

and all the vases are all over the floor."

The alarm on Aggie's face must have made Kenzie panic because she began reassuring her aunt at warp speed. "I was wearing shoes, so I didn't cut myself and Ian is upstairs with Laird now so he can't get hurt and the twins are in the basement so they can't get hurt and I did tell the truth so I'm reminding you in case you forgot that it was an accident and I'm telling the truth."

"Your arm is ok."

"Yes."

She closed her eyes. "Take off your shoes at the bottom of the stairs and leave them there. No one comes downstairs until I say so." The girl turned to go, but Aggie thought of something else. "Wait. Where's Tina?"

"She's cleaning up the vases."

As Aggie suspected, the bottoms of Kenzie's shoes sparkled with imbedded glass. She'd probably crunched over it on her way to come confess. "Oh, thank you, Lord that she was even wearing shoes."

Inside, Aggie called out to Tina. "How bad is it?"

"Were there any décor ideas that you didn't consider because you thought it'd be overkill? They won't be now…"

"Is my dress ok?"

"Perfectly clean and hanging in your room."

Aggie grabbed the mudroom broom and began sweeping the path across all floors to the door. "Shoes?"

"On the floor, in their box, beneath the dress."

"Suitcases?"

"Luke has everything you're taking except your carryon."

Certain that her essentials were covered, Aggie went to retrieve the vacuum cleaner for the area rugs. As she worked to ensure every sliver was removed from her carpeting, Aggie sang. "…work while the dew is sparkling. Work 'mid springing flowers…"[6]

Luke's arms wrapped around her waist and he murmured, "I'll never get tired of this."

For once, his surprise arrival didn't startle her. She snapped off the machine as she said, "I don't think I will either."

"Getting ready for guests?"

"Cleaning up a nightmare of glass."

"Cari?"

296

"Kenzie," she countered. "She also reminded me that it was an accident and she told the truth, so I can't spank her."

"Well, that's good to know. You put your feet up and tell me what we need to do tomorrow. I'll finish."

"Like you could hear me with that thing going. I think I have it all. I just kept making sure. Can you imagine Ian pushing a little truck across a chunk or sliver of glass? Eeek!"

Tina joined them when Luke finished with her laptop. "Ok, we've got work to do folks — starting with table decorations. We have one salvaged original vase decorated. That's not going to cut it for twenty-five tables."

Before Aggie could make any suggestions, and before Luke could consider what could be done, Tina fired off half a dozen more items. "We also need to pick up the truck by three o'clock on Friday, but that's also when we get the school; we can start decorating then. Who is watching the kids Friday night? Oh, and do you have your suit yet?"

"Um, which question or topic do we answer or address first?"

"All of them and preferably yesterday."

"Well, yesterday's gone, so now is good," Aggie sighed.

"Oh, and that reminds me, are we making the upstairs off limits? That would save a huge amount of cleaning…"

"Sure."

"Good. Your dad can put up the baby gate after you guys start down the steps."

"Gotcha. Gate. Done."

Tina glanced at her screen. "The photographer's assistant is coming to Luke's house while he gets ready and she'll be here at noon for you. You guys are sure you don't want pre-ceremony pictures with each other, right? You only have tomorrow and the next day to change your minds."

"No," Luke said quickly. "Aggie would, but I want the surprise moment."

"He's such a sap."

Luke grinned. "Guilty as charged. You will learn, my dear Mibs, that the Sullivan-Tesdall families are terribly sappy."

"We still have to figure out décor…"

Silence descended over them as they all pondered the problem. "Same idea," Luke said at last. We do the same thing with fresh flowers in vases, but instead of glass, we do metal pails—like lunch pails. We'll tie it into the building just a little. Maybe add apple candleholders on each side or something. Little squatty candles in the apples so that the flames don't burn the flowers."

"Great idea!" Tina's fingers flew over her keyboard. "I think I'll see if the craft store in Brunswick has them before I go all the way to Rockland. What else?"

Children seemed to converge on them before they could make any further progress. "Are we going to go get pizza now?"

Aggie glanced at the clock in shock. "It's barely five—"

"Yes," Tina said, jumping up. "Get in the van. It's time to go!"

Luke and Aggie stared at one another and then at Tina. "What—"

"The earlier they eat, the earlier they feel like it's bedtime," she hissed. "Last one in the van is a rotten something or another!"

Friday, March 6th

Chaos. Mayhem. Pandemonium. Despite the desperate need for quiet for Martha Milliken, the house seemed to pulsate with craziness. While Aggie's mother lay in the guest room with earplugs and Luke's industrial fan pointed toward the ceiling in the hallway to make white noise, the rest of their families were working on something—anything. Luke's sisters were at the schoolhouse, taking orders from Tina on what to put where and how. The men were moving tables as fast as Tina could direct them, and Libby kept the children corralled downstairs as much as possible.

Aggie skittered from place to place, nearly worn to a frazzle with frustration and one crisis after another. Her phone buzzed. "What? I mean, sorry. Hello? Tina?"

"The guys have moved all the big stuff into place. The bakery is going to be here soon with the cake, but they assured us they don't need help moving, so I'm sending them your way. Luke has the rental truck."

"Ok. Does that mean that I need to make sure the kids are out of the way for the furniture?"

"Right."

"Operation piñata."

"You go, girl."

The phone clicked off before Aggie could respond. Great. She stuck her head downstairs. "Libby?"

"Yes?"

"Piñata time." Her almost mother-in-law's response was impossible to understand over the children's excited screams. Aggie waited for the din to die down before she added, "I'll send down the hot dogs and fries as soon as they're done."

The moment lights turned into the driveway, Aggie dashed to the basement door and called for Vannie. "Can you come help with this? I've got guys coming in!"

The girl hurried up the steps and grinned. "This is so exciting! I think Kenzie is going to break it on her turn too!"

"Well, that's cool. Just don't let her break her arm again."

"That's not likely. Oh, they're taking out the couches!" Vannie cried excitedly. "It's going to be beautiful in here. Aunt Tina said the tulle curtains look amazing."

"How —"

"I called to ask."

Aggie set down the tongs and looked at her niece. "Oh, Vannie. Oh, I — just wait there. Get your jacket. Get in Libby's car."

"I can't do —"

Aggie ignored the girl's protests and ran down the basement steps. "Libby, I need you. Laird, watch the kids."

"Okkk…"

Libby turned to follow her back up the stairs. "What's wrong?"

"Vannie. We've completely left her out of the fun. She's a bridesmaid, so she should be there helping and enjoying this thing. I just spaced it."

"You're right. I'll be right back. Laird can handle them until I get home."

Before Aggie could return to the kitchen, men started asking questions. "Yes, everything that isn't built-in goes. Bye bye. Gone. Kaput. Outta there!"

Hotdogs were getting cold, but she didn't care anymore. She piled them on one big platter, added the pot of beans, and carried it all downstairs, terrified she'd trip and dump it on whomever was at the bottom. "I'll be back with plates and utensils. There are water bottles in the fridge. Drink that."

"Did you see all the candy in there? It was huge!" Cari announced. "Kenzie did it, too! She's good."

When she hurried to retrieve paper plates and plastic spoons, Aggie saw the men take the table but leave the chairs. "Don't forget the chairs!"

"Won't we need them?"

Aggie shook her head. "We rented plenty. If we have room for more, we'll have Tina bring some back from the schoolhouse."

While the men moved things, Aggie cleaned the kitchen. They were all going to a Mexican restaurant around eight while Murphy and Mrs. Dyke watched the children. As late as they might be there, she didn't need to come home to more house cleaning. She'd been at it all day!

An hour later, Luke stepped into the kitchen. "Ok, what can I do?"

"Did you set up the chairs?"

"No, that's next?"

"Yeah. You set them up and I'll start decorating as soon as I mop this floor."

"You look beat."

Aggie glanced up at him. "Not really. Just trying to remember everything and I know I'm succeeding in forgetting even more." Her eyes widened. "Where's my phone?" She patted her pockets and then dove for the house phone's handset. Ignoring Luke's alarmed face, Aggie dialed Tina. "Hey, do we have music?" A sigh of relief escaped. "I suddenly couldn't remember. Cellist and keyboard in the kitchen. That's right. I remember now. Whose kids were they?"

She hung up and grinned at Luke. "Music. Check!"

Luke took the mop from her and sent her to decorate. "I'll finish this and then put up chairs behind you. It'll be easier for you to work if you don't have to fight the chairs."

The children were asleep. The house—silent. Aggie and Luke found themselves seated across from each other at the island playing paper hockey with plastic knives as sticks. The clock struck a quarter 'til midnight. Luke grinned. "Fifteen minutes and it's our wedding day."

"I thought you were going to say you had to leave, so I wouldn't see you."

"Are you kidding? This is the first chance I've had to be alone with you all day!"

Feeling quite flirtatious, Aggie shook her head. "What, two weeks of no one but me isn't enough?"

"Never."

Her knife batted the wad of paper around on her side for several seconds before she sent it flying across the countertop. "Are you nervous?"

"About what? Tomorrow or two weeks?"

"About all of it?" Illogically, her lower lip trembled.

"Mibs? You ok?"

"Yeah... I think."

Luke didn't hesitate. In seconds, he engulfed Aggie in his arms, murmuring reassurances and prayers for comfort and confidence. "If you have any doubts—" his voice cracked as he tried to say the last thing he'd ever want to speak.

"No! No doubts—just a few fears and a lot of worries."

"Do you trust me?"

She nodded.

"Do you trust Jesus?"

Smiling, Aggie whispered, "Yes, of course."

"Then it'll be ok. He'll never fail you, even when I do."

"If—"

"Unfortunately it isn't if, Mibs. It's when."

The clock struck midnight. Aggie's face brightened. "Today is my wedding day! Last year—right now—I was probably stumbling downstairs, tripping over toys and laundry and today my house looks like it was decorated for a bridal magazine."

"Not a magazine—just you. It's decorated for you."

"For us."

Though he'd been given permission at their engagement party, Luke hadn't risked another brotherly kiss on her forehead or cheek, but after just a moment's hesitation, he kissed the palm of her hand, closed it, and murmured, "Hold it there for a few more hours. Goodnight, my Mibs."

"Night."

Mibs says: I wanted to say something while you weren't around to make me too shy to say it.

Mibs says: I love you. I know you know that, but I don't think you really realize just how much I really do love you. How's that for a lot of real-ity?

Mibs says: So, I want to tell you while I know you can't get on and make me self-conscious. I love you. I love how you think of my children as yours. I love how you put us before you even when it is uncomfortable for you or a financial blow.

Mibs says: Sigh. This is hard. I love how you smile at me. The way those smiles make my stomach flop is the most wonderful feeling.

Mibs says: The way you reach for me and then hesitate, making sure you are being honorable in your actions.

Mibs says: I love the tone of your voice when you say you love me.

Mibs says: I love knowing that you mean it when you say it.

Mibs says: And how you protect me, even from my children and from myself.

Mibs says: I love your delight in your sisters, your nieces, and your nephews. I love how you cherish your mother and how that spills over into cherishing me. I've never doubted how you'd treat me. It shows every day in how you treat them.

Mibs says: And I love how you call me "Mibs." I love the way you say it, the tone of your voice, the little smirk around your lips...

Mibs says: Whew. This is killing me. I love that you find me attractive. You don't say much, but I see it in how you respond to me. It amazes how much I see that you desire only me.

Mibs says: But most of all, I think I love the way you love the Lord even more than you love me. I couldn't ask for anything more.

Mibs says: I love that I get to be the one you call wife.

Mibs says: Goodnight.

HERE WE COME

Chapter 22

Saturday, March 7th

Never had Aggie been more covered while wearing only her underwear. The photographer snapped a dozen pictures, promising that she would not upload them to the website, and hurried downstairs after Tina. Left alone, Aggie stared at her fingers, trying to remember when they'd been painted the delicate pink that now sparkled at her in the light. The room smelled strange — like a florist's shop and beauty parlor combined into one unique business.

Her eyes rose and gazed into the mirror. Was it really her in the reflection? It wasn't just the cosmetics that she rarely wore or the hairstyle that she loved but had taken much too long to repeat on any kind of regular basis. No, something else was different. *She* was different. Maybe that's what becoming a wife meant.

Fingers slid across the vanity for her phone. She hesitated and then typed a quick message. ARE YOU GETTING EXCITED?

The reply came much swifter than she expected. GETTING? I'M ALREADY THERE. Another followed seconds later — Luke was much swifter as a texter than as a conversationalist or messenger. I LOVED YOUR MESSAGES LAST NIGHT. I WROTE A SET FOR YOU TOO.

Happiness welled in her heart. It had been the right decision. As difficult as it was, telling him was probably the best gift she could give someone like Luke. Her fingers flew over the keys. JUST A FEW MORE MINUTES — LESS THAN FIFTEEN!

He replied with just three simple letters. CYE

Aggie flew to her laptop, flipping it open as the photographer stepped back in the room. "Tina is on her way back up, but you've got to see what I caught."

Frustrated at the delay in reading the note, Aggie tried to give real attention to the picture the photographer, Vickie, tried to show her and was rewarded. "Oh, it's perfect! I can't wait for her to see that."

"You'd think she was the bride, wouldn't you?"

"He loves her. He just doesn't know it yet."

Vickie disagreed. "I think he does now."

Tina burst into the room, "Ok, I think everything is nearly ready. Ian is settled in with Libby, the little girls have their baskets full of petals, and Vannie is coming up right away. I promised her some pale lipstick and a slight gloss, so don't panic."

The email popped up and Aggie turned away from the others, lying on her stomach across her bed, reading. Her feet kicked the air absently, as each line filled her mind and heart. Once finished, she scrolled up and read again.

To: aggie.mommy@leterbox.com
From: luke.sullivan@letterbox.com
Subject: My Dear Mibs

I just read your "how do I love thee, let me count the ways" messages and was inspired? compelled? anxious? to open my heart in a similar fashion.
I love your smile. It reaches from somewhere within you and radiates until it touches everyone in sight. I think it is what first touched my heart.
I love your grit. No, it doesn't sound very romantic, but it is a beautiful thing to see you pick up, time after time, and keep going when I know you want to quit—even if just for a while.
I love how much you enjoy life. You make it an adventure and take everyone you know along for the ride. I will never be able to merely exist. That is marvelous.
I love that you accept all of me. I'm slow to say what I think and feel, and you never make me feel awkward about that. I don't have your education,

but never have you made me feel intellectually inadequate.

I love that already you think of me as "your" Luke. I can almost hear you at ninety, rocking away in your chair, toothless and silly saying, "My Luke..."

Most of all, though, I love how your love of the Lord shows through every song that overflows your spirit in praise to Him. Your smile may have first touched my heart, but your songs first drew me to you.

We have a lifetime together starting in just a few hours. I am sure it will be as beautiful as you are.

I do love you dearly,
Luke

"I need Kleenex!"

Tina threw the box onto the bed and ordered, "Do not cry, Agathena Grace Milliken! Do. Not. Cry. We don't have time for reconstruction on your face!"

"But it's so beautiful."

"Close it."

Aggie glared at the women who dared order such a thing, but Tina's hand snapped the lid shut before she could stop it. "I can't believe—"

"We can't afford it. You can read it again later. I always knew that man was a sap."

A giggle escaped. "Isn't it great?"

"Get her in that dress before we have a mess on our hands."

Vannie arrived just in time to help protect the skirt from getting wrinkled. While they zipped and hooked her up, the photographer stepped outside the door and beckoned someone. Martha stepped in the room seconds later.

"Oh, Aggie!"

"Mom! Should you be up here?"

"Try to keep me out!"

Mother and daughter clung to each other, both trying ineffectually not to cry. Desperate to salvage Aggie's face, Tina thrust tissues into their hands. "Please try to keep from wiping off her

305

foundation!"

"You should have used waterproof and smudge proof mascara!"

Tina snorted. "I did! I'm worried about the rest of you!"

A knock at the door signaled the beginning of the rest of her life. "Aggie? Are you ready?" Ron stepped into the room. "It's time…"

The next moments passed in a blur that her memory could never seem to separate into discernible and distinct moments. She remembered a prayer — that familiar time of communion with her father and her Father. The gate that was supposed to take just a moment to attach behind them refused to stay in place, nearly causing her to fall several times. Had people heard their giggles?

Music drifted to them, changing from one song to the next — what songs were they? Aggie couldn't remember the names. Illogically, she thanked the Lord for enough room on the stairs for her father to walk beside her. The wide stairs that seemed such a waste of space during her first days in the house were now cherished memories in just the flash of a second.

She refused to look at Luke's face at first — certain that she would weep. Her eyes sought her mother, Libby, Zeke. Lips — they must be her father's — touched her cheek. A trail of dampness slid down her face. Were they her tears or his?

Hands covered hers and Zeke stepped up to face them at the base of the stairs. Aggie's eyes lifted and met Luke's. Love. In Luke's eyes, she saw the love that he'd written of in his letter.

Anticipation. That was the only purpose to processionals of bridesmaids and flower girls — anticipation. It was designed to ensure that a groom was half-crazy by the time his bride appeared. It was designed to befuddle him so much that if he had any doubts, he forgot them. Luke had no doubts, but the anticipation was killing him.

The tips of her shoes preceded a simple satin hemline. Of that much, Luke was confident. Any other design elements were likely beyond his description. He didn't care. Her waist appeared and had

306

he strained, he could have seen her face, but he was determined to wait for the full picture now. A veil... of course she'd wear a veil. It was enough for him to want to let out a primal yell, jerk it from her head, and drag her from the house declaring she was his by right of conquest.

That thought brought a smile to his lips. Did she see it? She didn't. She looked everywhere but at him. Why? Her father tossed back the veil and kissed her cheek, leaving tears behind. Would he feel the same way when Vannie married? He had five daughters— five! Were there more daughters in store? Would he have to hand them over to men like him someday? He'd never be able to do it. No man was good enough for his little girls. He wasn't good enough for his Aggie.

He stepped up beside her and took her hands, wrapping his around the small, trembling fingers that held her bouquet. His Aggie. Luke met her eyes and saw all the love she'd written of on the messenger just hours earlier. She was truly *his* Aggie.

Uncle Zeke's voice jerked Luke from his reverie. "Friends and family, thank you for coming. Luke and Aggie have asked you not only to share in the joy of this celebration, but to be witnesses of the vows they make together today."

He pulled her just a little closer, marveling that it was really happening. Their wedding. His bride. What was Uncle Zeke saying?

"...the hard times come, you can bear witness to these vows. You can take them aside—and they ask today that you will—and remind them that they vowed for better or worse. They vow today to glorify the Lord together in this marriage and only death will tear them apart.

"Luke promises to love and cherish Aggie as Christ does the church."

Those words hit Luke in the heart and lodged there like a weight. Such a solemn promise and trust. He must not fail her— especially when hard times came. His eyes rose and roamed the room, meeting the gaze of many of their guests, pleading silently and earnestly for them to hold him accountable. His mother, sisters, brothers-in-law, Chad, Uncle Christopher and Chris... What was that? What had he missed?

"...submit to him as unto the Lord. That is a terrifying promise for a woman. My wife tells me that childbirth with a breech baby was

307

a million times easier, but Aggie makes that vow today. It won't be easy, but with your prayers and his servant heart, it can be done."

Servant heart. He couldn't forget that. He must be a servant to lead his family. Luke's eyes met Laird's. The boy nodded solemnly. Tavish grinned and the little girls almost exploded from repressed excitement. Vannie's heart shone through the love in her eyes. He wasn't her father—he never could be. He was, however, now her uncle. He'd show her what to look for in a man with whom she could trust her heart. He'd show her by being that man to Aggie.

Aggie—her eyes were on him, smiling with full trust and pure love for him. His breath caught as Zeke said, "Luke?"

"Yes?"

"Do you take Aggie to be your wife?" The rest of the words blurred in his mind. Wife. One short little word made her his wife. It seemed too easy, and yet, what a terrible charge it was! Terrible—magnificent.

"Yes."

"Aggie?"

Look at her—that face. How can I never have noticed how beautiful she is?

"Yes?"

"Do you take Luke to be your husband?"

"Yes. I most certainly do."

She said yes—again! It wasn't possible, was it? What did Uncle Zeke say this time? Why couldn't he concentrate on the ceremony? He'd forget it all—he'd missed it all.

"…and wife. You may kiss your bride."

Luke's mind jerked to present as Aggie's eyes widened and she fidgeted. When had her bouquet disappeared? He could finally kiss her and her hands were reaching—for something. What was it?

Two bouquets appeared, shielding their faces from the crowd. His lips sought hers and after what had seemed an impossible wait, they refused to part. The kiss was much longer than he'd planned. He hadn't wanted to make a scene, however behind the relative privacy of those bouquets, Luke couldn't bring himself to let her go. But at last, he stepped back again—grinning.

"I'd like—" Uncle Zeke's partially repressed chuckles interrupted his announcement, "to introduce Luke and Aggie Sullivan. Perhaps now they'd like a moment of privacy…"

"Hey," Aggie quipped, laughing. "I waited a long time for my first kiss!"

Without a moment of hesitation, he wrapped arms around her waist and murmured, "Well, you won't wait that long for the second."

Lips on her forehead. Was it time to wake for school? Aggie opened her eyes and saw Luke smiling down at her just seconds before he kissed her gently. She jerked, panicked, and then fully awake, remembered. She was his wife. "Hi."

"We're here."

"Where? Oh, Colorado?" Her eyes glanced around the plane and saw people pulling their baggage from the overhead compartments. "How did I sleep through all that?"

"You were tired."

It was cold, the wind whipping around them, fighting to break through their jackets, but they made it into the car, out of the city, and to their destination without a single mishap. The cabin was larger than she'd expected—almost a small house. A fire in the fireplace told her they had good hosts, and a hot meal told her that Luke had been thorough in their preparations.

"I didn't see you call anyone."

"I had a text ready to go. Just had to hit send when we turned off the highway."

The impulse to kiss him was strong, but she resisted. Then, laughing, Aggie threw her arms around him, kissing him without a second thought. "I can do that now!"

"And you should. Often. Now get out of that coat so we can eat."

After dinner, as she awaited her turn for the bathroom, Aggie flipped open her laptop and sent a quick message to her family.

Aggie says: We're here. Just wanted you to know we're here and

---

we're safe.

Tina says: We're all in the living room and I'm reading this to them.

Aggie says: Thanks for everything.

Tina says: Your mom says to tell you to relax and have fun and stay off the phone and the computer.

Tina says: Your dad says to tell you to stay warm. I will not repeat the eye waggle he gave, but be sure, your mother has whacked him with the pillow.

Aggie says: I want to say I miss you, but I don't yet. Tell the kids I love them and that I know they'll have a lot of fun the next two weeks.

Tina says: They all say they love you. I think Ian is very confused without you.

Tina says: Your mother is now irritated at me for telling you that.

Aggie says: I think Luke is done in the bathroom. My turn.

Aggie says: Just so everyone knows, I'm very happy. God is good to us.

Aggie says: Nighters

Tina says: *Poofs* from all the Stuart-Milliken-Warden-Markensons!

Luke read the conversation while Aggie brushed her teeth, calling to her with a hint of amazement in his voice, "We have a good life already, don't we?"

"Yep."

"Ready for the future?"

Aggie leaned around the doorframe, toothbrush scrubbing away, and gave him a silly expression. "Are you trying to weasel out of it already?"

"Nope. I told you; I'm in for keeps."

"Then ready or not..."

Luke grinned. "Here we come!"

Aggie's Accidental Snickerdoodles

Ingredients:

1/2 cup butter at room temperature
3/4 cup sugar (for a sweeter cookie — William — use 1 cup)
1 egg
1/2 cup sour cream
1 teaspoon vanilla extract
½ tsp almond extract
1/2 teaspoon baking soda
1/2 teaspoon baking powder
1 teaspoon cream of tartar
1 ½ teaspoons cinnamon
1/4 teaspoon salt
2 cups flour (do not accidentally use self-rising!)

Cinnamon & Sugar Mixture:

1 tsp cinnamon
1/8 cup sugar

Directions:

Preheat the oven to 375 degrees.

Line baking sheet with parchment paper.

Cream the butter and sugar until smooth and fluffy. If you have a stand mixer, you can just put them in, turn it on low and leave it alone while you mix the dry ingredients. Add egg, sour cream, almond, and vanilla. Continue mixing.

In another bowl, stir together the baking soda, baking powder, cream of tartar, cinnamon, salt, and flour. Slowly combine bowls

311

mixing well. The mixture will be sticky. Don't panic.

In a small bowl, combine sugar and cinnamon, stirring thoroughly. Form balls (1-2"). You'll need a bit of flour on your hands OR pop the dough in the fridge for 20 minutes or so. Coat each ball in the cinnamon-sugar mixture. Place on cookie sheet an inch or so apart.

Bake for 10 minutes or until are golden on the bottom.

12 Women. 12 Months. 1 Happily-Ever-After

Adric Garrison has a lot to offer the right woman but he hasn't found her. Soon after his move to Fairbury, his brother-in-law offers a unique opportunity — January through December he will meet one new woman a month to determine interest and compatibility. Is it the chance of a lifetime or a man's worst nightmare?

313

[1] *There's a Fountain Free (Free Waters),* Words by Mary B Slade (1876)
[2] *All Things Are Ready,* Charles H. Gabriel (1895)
[3] *A Clean Heart,* Words by Walter C. Smith (unknown)
[4] *All Things Are Ready,* Charles H. Gabriel (1895)
[5] *Take My Hand, Precious Lord,* Thomas A. Dorsey (1932)
[6] *Work, for the Night Is Coming,* Anna L. Coghill (1854)